OUR DUTY

OUR DUTY

GERRI HILGER

KAT BIGGIE PRESS

Columbia, SC

Our Duty is published by Kat Biggie Press.
www.katbiggiepress.com

Cover design by Michelle Fairbanks, Fresh Design
Book design by Alexa Bigwarfe, Write|Publish|Sell

ISBN-13: 978-1-948604130
Library of Congress Control Number: 2018956514
First Edition: October 2018

10 9 8 7 6 5 4 3 2 1

Dedication

Pauline (Garrity) and John Wetta---my parents who kept the home fires burning during WW II
Agnes (Beat) Pauley---dear friend, gracious lady and WWII Air Corps Flight Nurse
Veterans of WWII and all wars since--- in gratitude for their sacrifices to protect our freedom

I hate war as only a soldier who has lived it can, only as one who has seen its brutality, its futility and its stupidity. . .
Every gun that is made, every warship launched, every rocket fired signifies, in the final sense, a theft from those who hunger and are not fed, those who are cold and are not clothed.

~ Dwight D. Eisenhower

CHAPTER 1

"LORDY, IT'S HOT! I didn't think I'd ever get finished trying to make patients a little comfortable," Polly sighed while shedding clothes. She joined several young women in swimsuits lying on the roof of the student nurses' dorm. "At least there's a breeze up here. How long have you all been escaping the heat like this?"

Dismissing the question, a long-legged blonde, yawned, "We had about given up on you." She opened her eyes and gasped, "Pauline Garrity, where's your swimsuit?" Six pairs of eyes popped open, and some girls sat up, gawking open-mouthed.

"Lord, Mildred, shut up. No one would have noticed if you didn't have such a big mouth."

"Well, what are you doing? We know you have an hour-glass figure, but we don't want to see all of it," said Stella Zedrich.

"Then just close your eyes, Miss Priss!" Polly retorted.

"Boy someone's in a nasty mood," Mildred observed.

"Oh, I'm just so hot! It was unmerciful on the wards, and every one of my patients wanted alcohol rubs to cool off," Polly explained as she spread her towel. "Really, I don't know how they survive lying in those beds. Even the luxury of fans only moves hot air!"

"You should've just told 'em you were off duty at 3:00," Stella advised, closing her eyes.

Polly looked at her in disbelief, ready to spew her frustration when Mildred shook her head and said, "Well that explains your mood, but not the birthday suit."

"I don't have a swimsuit, and my underpants are worn so ragged; they're a hell of lot uglier than my birthday suit." Polly lay down placing her bra across her kinky pubic hair.

"There; I'm decent. It's not like we don't see people naked all the time!"

"Polly, you're a hoot!" Eileen Hay, one of Polly's best friends laughed with the others.

"But, they aren't naked for no good reason!" Stella huffed.

"Oh shut up, please, and let me rest." Polly's voice drifted as she relaxed in the warm rays.

Soon, a low droning rose from the west. "Here they come, right on schedule," Mildred lazily observed.

"Here comes who?" Stella sat straight up.

"The fly boys. New pilots on training maneuvers from the air base across town. They always fly over about the same time and tell us hi." Mildred stood and stretched.

"Sister Gregory will kill us. We gotta go!" Stella grabbed her towel and headed for the door to lower floors.

"Go on and miss the fun, Miss Priss!" Eileen called as the worry-wart disappeared. "Lord her name sure fits! Who invited goody two shoes up here anyway?" Reaching over, she snatched the bra barely covering Polly's privates.

Polly squealed, jumped up and tried to grab the bra. Eileen scurried out of reach then stole the towel Polly had been lying on.

"You bitch, give me that towel," Polly yelled as she grabbed for her friend. "I'll be damned if I'll share any shoe stamps if you don't give it to me."

Laughing, Eileen jumped out of reach.

"Ladies, you're making a spectacle and gonna miss the men!" Mildred sang as she waved to the PT 17s skirting the Wichita skyline.

"Oh shit!" Polly gasped. Then in defiant surrender to Eileen she grinned, bent her rear to the sky, and shook it like a peacock displaying his glory. Even above the roar of engines, the girls could hear shrill whistles while the planes' wings tilted.

As the aircraft disappeared, Mildred interrupted the others' laughter with, "Thank God Miss Priss left, Polly, or she'd report you for sure!"

"For what? Doing my patriotic duty? I was just entertainin' the troops a little. Giving 'em something sweet to think about when they're in a God-forsaken jungle or fox hole." Polly stood at attention and saluted her friends, which fueled more cackling.

She picked up her clothes and snapped the end of her towel at Eileen, who squealed. "Stella will probably report me anyway," Polly muttered as she began to dress.

"What for?" Mildred asked. "She was up here sunbathing, so she's not innocent."

"But, Miss Stella Zedrich saw the Carsons give me some shoe stamps as thanks for my help with their new baby. Stella was delighted to remind me, 'Accepting gifts from patients is against rules.' "

Eileen glanced up from pulling on her shorts. "Is that why you were so upset that you almost knocked Mrs. Alexander and her baby out of her wheelchair as you stormed into the hospital earlier this afternoon?"

"Yeah, Miss Zedrich's such a prude; she's probably telling old Gorgon about the stamps right now."

Mildred quipped, "You better watch calling Sister Gregory such names. She'd eat you alive if she heard."

Eileen added, laughing, "She sure will. GRRRRR!! However, I can't wait to tell Aggie about the fun she missed on the roof this afternoon. Where is she anyway?"

As they walked toward the door, Polly answered "I think there was an emergency surgery Gorgon wanted her to observe." Looking directly at Eileen, she added, "And you don't need to be a blabber mouth Eileen, The more people who hear about this the better chance of Gorgon learning about it too. Then there'd be hell for all of us to pay, and no more sun bathing even if we live!"

CHAPTER 2

A COUPLE OF DAYS AFTER her patriotic exhibition, Polly, dressed in white surgical scrubs, stomped from the operating room. She threw a handful of instruments into the enamel sink and gripped the sides. Her shoulders shook as she tried to stifle angry sobs. She fought for control as she heard someone enter.

"Polly, are you crying?"

She looked over her shoulder as another young nurse pulled off her mask. "Don't let that pompous ass Jackson get to you." Agnes Beat wrapped her arms around her friend but was met with a marble statue. "Polly, try to relax."

Pushing away, Polly said, "Aggie, you're right. I think I'll call him Dr. Jackass from now on. Bet he thought it was real funny when I contaminated myself and had to leave." She mimicked the surgeon, "What the hell! Don't you know the difference between a retractor and a clamp?" Then she flung her hands in the air as if throwing instruments at the wall.

"Don't think about that. I don't know if Jackson thought your frustration was funny, but his and Sister Gregory's eyebrows almost hit the ceiling when we heard those instruments banging. D'ja chip the sink?" Aggie tried to lighten the air, as she pretended to examine the enamel.

"Why couldn't he just ask for a different instrument if I made a mistake?" Polly ranted. "This is my first week on surgical rotation, and I'm scared to death. That prick just makes it worse. Doesn't he know we're *student* nurses?" She brushed at hot tears. "He was lucky that you or McHugh had another full set of instruments ready, or we'd be waiting for the autoclave to sterilize those he threw!"

Running water, Aggie replied, "Mary helped me adjust to surgical rotation and warned me about Jackson's tantrums. She also told me to always prepare at least two surgical trays for him." She handed instruments to Polly to dry. "You're right, though; he's a real ass in surgery but even worse out on the floor—gives me the willies."

"I know exactly what you mean!" Polly gasped. "The first time he put his arm around my shoulder while giving post-op orders, I thought I'd puke! My sister Helen had warned me about him, but I couldn't believe her stories until I saw him in action." She furiously dried and polished instruments. "He is such a lech! I'd like to do a little snip, snip surgery between his legs!"

They immediately squelched giggles, becoming as quiet as soldiers at inspection when the door opened and a nun in surgical attire entered.

"Young ladies, is there any reason people who caused problems in surgery are laughing? Miss Garrity, I do not ever want to hear you throwing instruments and having a temper tantrum like a two-year-old! Do you understand?"

Aggie and Polly's eyes met as Polly's mouth flew open as though jerked by a marionette string. "But, Sister --"

"But what? Are you so impertinent to argue with your superior? You are a student nurse! Will we need to cancel your next weekend pass so you learn your place, Miss Garrity?"

"No, Sister, I apologize. It won't happen again."

Turning to Aggie, the nun continued, "Miss Beat, before finishing your surgical rotation, will you please attempt to teach your friend some proper operating room protocol?"

Aggie's embarrassed, "Yes, ma'am," was swallowed by the sound of a hollow, tinny voice grating through the intercom.

"Sister Gregory—Sister Gregory, are you out of surgery?"

Sister finished pulling off her cover as she jabbed the answer button.

"Sister Gregory here."

"Sister, is Mary McHugh still assisting in surgery?"

"We're finished, and she's cleaning the O.R."

"Can you spare her right away down here in emergency? We just received several patients from a head-on crash."

"I'll send her down." Sister turned to the student nurses. "You two get that O.R. spotless before coming to class, and you'd better not be late." She called into the surgical room, "Miss McHugh, you're needed down in emergency. Bad car accident. It'll be good practice for the gore you'll be seeing in the Army." At those words, Polly jerked a glance toward Sister.

"Well, Miss Garrity, stop dawdling and get out of the way so Mary can wash up and get to emergency and I can get ready to check on our surgery patient before class."

Polly and Aggie were puzzled about leaving the instruments unfinished but moved toward the inner room where they passed a young nurse coming out of O.R.

"Sorry, ladies," she whispered.

Before the door closed completely, Sister Gregory called to Polly, "One more thing, Miss Garrity..." Polly cringed and looked back. "I've heard some very nasty rumors about you up on the roof! I pray to our dear Lord they are just vicious chitchat. Do we need to have a private conversation about morals and the sixth commandment?"

Polly's mouth gaped, and her eyes popped wide open before she gasped, "There's no need, Sister. Whatever you heard must have been nasty gossip!"

"Well, I'd better not hear about any more deleterious behavior from you, Miss Garrity!" The tall, austere nun glanced back as she reached for the door handle. "I will see you ladies in class, and you had better be ready to explain in detail the new research about the heart. Now get that room cleaned!"

Aggie ran steaming water into a small sink in the operating room. She poured in carbolic detergent, tossed Polly a pair of surgical gloves, and whispered, "Put them on, even though they're supposed to be for surgery only. Our hands look and feel like tumble weeds. Patients probably sometimes wonder if we're using sandpaper when we give them back rubs. Sure wish the nuns could find something easier to sterilize our hands and wash instruments." She scrubbed the countertops as Polly ripped soiled sheets from the surgical table.

A minute later, as she was gathering blood-soiled bandages from the floor, Polly hissed, "'I had better not hear about any more deleterious behavior from you!' What in the hell does 'deleterious' mean? Why doesn't that old coot talk like normal people?"

"Shh, Polly, she's probably listening."

As though on cue, Mary McHugh poked her head in. "Sorry to leave you with the mess, but we can't argue with Sister Gregory, or is it Gorgon?" She winked at Polly. "Don't let her get to you, Garrity; you're doing great for your first week. Gotta run. Bye, Aggie."

She started to close the door, but Polly called, "Wait! Thanks, Mary, that means a lot. But, what did Sister mean about the Army. You aren't really joining, are you?"

"Already have. Just hanging around here waiting for orders. We'll talk later."

"Whew! That was close!" Aggie said slumping against the wall.

"Yea, I almost peed my pants when that door opened." Polly giggled then was serious. "Did you know Mary had joined the Army?" Aggie nodded. "Why in the world would she do that? She's so pretty and a great nurse."

"Polly, have you forgotten? There is a war going on. Men are being shot and killed, and Uncle Sam needs good nurses. Mary's brother's in the Air Corps some place in Europe, and she said she felt it was her duty. If he ever got wounded, she hoped there'd be good nurses to help."

"Well, that's just nuts. When Uncle Sam starts drafting nurses, I'm going kicking and screaming."

"You talk so tough." She asked quietly, "Polly, have you really been calling Sister Gregory, Sister Gorgon?"

"No," Polly smirked, "I call her just plain Gorgon."

"Polly, she's a nun. You shouldn't be so disrespectful. What if she hears you!"

"I don't care. If she's a nun, she's supposed to be a good, holy person. Instead, she's horrible and more like a devil. She and Jackass make a great pair." Sarcasm grated her voice as she attacked the black and white tile floor with steaming water from the mop bucket she had just filled. "Can you believe her telling me that I was acting like a child for throwing instruments in the sink after Jackass threw them at the wall! When he did that, I was shaking so hard I couldn't even remember what I was supposed to hand him."

"Polly, you're doing fine. Jackson is young and arrogant, the worst of the surgeons. Maybe tonight I can fill you in on the way he likes some things done."

"Humph!" Polly took the dirty linens into the scrub room, tossed them along with Aggie's and her surgical coverings down a chute, and dumped the scrub water.

As she placed the instruments into a large autoclave, Aggie remembered, "Oh, what happened on the roof? I've heard whispering and now Sister—"

"Not now, Aggie, look at the time! We'll be late for class, and I'll be in more trouble."

"Polly, you gotta tell me," Aggie begged.

"Some other time; we have to go!" Polly dried her hands while making a final inspection of the operating room then flicked off the light. She looked at Aggie, devilment twinkling in her eyes. "By the way, what is the sixth commandment? If I'm going to fry in hell, I'd like to know what for!"

CHAPTER 3

POLLY CLOSED HER BOOK and rubbed her eyes then lay her head on the small wooden desk. "I'm never going to pass state boards next year, Aggie. I can't even remember all the crap for the test tomorrow. The atriums and ventricles and vena cavas just swim in my head in a mess that could never pump blood."

"Don't worry so much, Polly. Lordy, state boards are almost a year away; take one test at a time." Polly lifted her head as Aggie massaged her neck and shoulders.

"Hmmmm, that feels so good. Thanks, Aggie."

Maybe we both need a break. I have a couple of nickels; let's go get a coke."

"Well, I am really thirsty. But, I'm bringing my book. If Gorgon sees us, I don't need her thinking that I'm wasting study time."

"Garrity, you have got to stop calling Sister Gregory 'Gorgon.' One of these days you're gonna slip and do it to her face." Polly hmphed as they neared the canteen. "And, you need to get some confidence and stop worrying so much. We all know that you're one of the best, most caring nurses in our class." Polly opened the door and clinking cups and cheerful chatter broke the quiet of the hall. Aggie continued, "Think about Mrs. Hunt who wanted to hire you as her private nurse. She never had a decent word to say about anyone or anything. And how many new parents have given you shoe stamps in gratitude for all you did?"

"Oh, I just knew how to butter Mrs. Hunt up, and those stamps got me in hot water too."

"How?"

"Old Gorgon has an eagle eye or a snitch. She told me, 'Nurses are not allowed to accept gifts from patients, and you, young lady, are not even a nurse!' I bet I know who her snitch is too."

Lowering her voice, Aggie gasped, "Who would be so awful?"

"I think it's that damned Zedrich!"

"Stella? Why would she?" Waving to a couple of other young women leaving a table, Aggie added, "Besides, I think the government needs to give nurses extra stamps since we're on our feet so much. I think I'll ask Daddy to write our congressman about it."

"You get right on that, Miss Aggie Beat. Like Congress has time to think about nurses—other than maybe drafting us!"

Moving to the counter, Aggie ordered two cokes while pretending not to notice the flirting from the rail-thin waiter. Turning toward Polly, she whispered, "I still can't believe you think Stella told Sister about the stamps."

"Here you go, ladies. Specially cold for the cutest nurses at St. Francis." The soda jerk smiled.

"Thanks, for the cokes, Roy. Seems I heard you tell Cavanaugh and Hay the same thing yesterday; you're such a ladies' man," Polly teased. The girls chuckled as he bowed slightly, spinning his towel toward the counter.

"What can I say? The Lord blessed us all when I was designated 4-F and got a job at this hospital."

Noticing a vacated table, the girls wove through others filled with white uniformed nurses and doctors. "Everyone must've gotten thirsty at the same time," Polly said. "You know, Aggie, the more I think about it, since Zedrich has no bedside skills to impress Gorgon I'm sure she's teacher's tattle tale! What a joke for a nurse. Can't even give a shot without the patients cringing." Then Polly whispered, "She probably reported me to save her own ass if Sister found out she had been sunbathing on the roof."

A young intern rising from an adjacent table bent and whispered into Polly's ear, "Maybe I'll sign up with Uncle Sam so you can feel patriotic and entertain me." He sauntered to the door but glanced back and saluted mischievously.

Polly's eyes exploded as her face flamed. "That son-of-a-bitch!"

"What did he say about being patriotic? Did it have something to do with the whispering about you on the roof?"

"For heaven's sake nothing really happened. Some of us just tried to cool off and get a little tan. It's the only place around here where we could."

"If there's no story, why is there hush-hush talking about you giving the fly boys a treat?"

"If you must know…" Polly bent close and whispered a silly version of her flashing the pilots.

Aggie sputtered coke across the table. "What in the world were you thinking?"

"Oh, I was just doin' my patriotic duty, entertaining the troops a little."

When Aggie lost control and chortled loudly, Polly couldn't help but join in while everyone in the canteen looked their way.

"Garrity, will you please stop being so crazy! You'll be a fantastic nurse, but not if you get kicked out!"

"Oh, Beat, they won't kick me out. What would the nuns do without all the slave labor from us student nurses?At least we aren't freshmen any more. I think I'd puke right in the basin if I had to clean all those bedpans again." Polly wrinkled her nose. "Besides, haven't you heard? We're at war, and nurses are valuable. The minute we graduate we'll be drafted and sent to some hell hole! Gotta live it up now!"

Aggie looked seriously at her friend, "Uncle Sam is not going to draft women, Polly! But, even if you don't get kicked out, Sister Gregory can make life really miserable." The girls saw others coming in, so they waved them over and rose to leave. "Try to behave yourself. Life wouldn't be half the fun if Sister takes away your privileges and you're always working."

They waved to Roy and left the canteen. Aggie stopped when struck with thought. "I have an idea how you can get on Sister's good side. Why don't you start going to 6:30 Mass once in a while with some of us? It might even help you have more confidence with the book stuff."

"Beat, you're so damned holy. How did we ever get to be friends?" Polly gave Aggie a hug. "I guess I'll show up once in a while if you think it'll help keep Gorgon off my back. Besides, I'll need all the help I can get from the Man upstairs when I'm in a field hospital in the South Pacific or Europe." Now it was Aggie's turn to roll her eyes, but Polly continued, "Hey, I just thought of something; maybe Gorgon is a blessing. After her, if we get drafted, we'll be able to survive any sergeant in the Army!"

CHAPTER 4

A COUPLE OF MONTHS LATER, Sister Gregory and Stella Zedrich were leaving a patient's room as Aggie and Polly approached.

"Good morning, Sister," they chimed. "Hi, Stella," Aggie added. Polly looked away.

"Don't good morning me with that ugly stick lip on your mouths. You both look like sinful hussies. Get in that bathroom and clean it off before a patient sees you. I will not have my nurses looking like street walkers!"

"Sorry, Sister."

"This is not your first warning, Miss Garrity. And, Miss Beat, I expect more from the class president."

"Yes, Sister. It won't happen again."

"Not until next time, anyway," Polly sneered as they ducked into the closest restroom to remove the sinful stain. "And it's *lipstick*, not stick lip! How stupid! You'd think she'd want us to look nice for patients?"

"Polly, don't let her ruffle your feathers. In a few months we can wear all the lipstick we want."

Polly rubbed her lips. "Great! Now I look like a baby with spaghetti sauce smeared all over her face. I need some Vaseline." She searched a cabinet as she made room for Aggie in front of the mirror.

"Polly, I heard you're going to a dance at Colwich Saturday night."

"That's the plan, Stan," she mumbled as she rubbed her lips with Vaseline. "Gotta find out how the love story ends."

"What about bed check? You already used this month's late pass. Ole Hattie's actually been checking students' beds to make sure they aren't just camouflaged. If you get caught, you won't get a pass til we graduate!"

"Shsh." Holding a finger to her mouth, Polly jerked the door open. "What are you doing out here, Zedrich?"

"Sister wanted me to remind you both that freshmen have testing today and won't have time to wash and sanitize the bedpans and emesis basins. Make sure you don't forget to do them."

"And just how many have you cleaned?"

"I'm on special IV duty with Sister Gregory."

Aggie intervened, "Well, you'd better get back to Sister and the IVs." She closed the door and whispered, "How long do you think she was out there?"

"I shushed you when I heard her. Can you believe she thinks it's an honor to have special IV duty with Gorgon? She should have had that down pat since we were freshmen. What a dumb broad!"

"Don't worry about her. But back to this weekend, how are you going to keep from being caught?"

"My sis Nonie is coming to Wichita job hunting. Hope it's ok that I told her she could sleep in our room." Aggie nodded and put Vaseline and tissues away as Polly continued. "I knew you had the night off, so I set everything up with Celie to let her in. So, you don't have to worry about me, Mother." She winked.

"Well, someone has to. I would say have fun but you always do."

"We're really gonna whoop it and kick it!" Laughing, she entered a patient's room with a bright, "Good morning, Mrs. McKnight."

That evening in the cafeteria, Polly had a thought. "Hey Aggie, that guy you're always talking about—Cy? Isn't he from around Colwich?"

"No, he's from Pretty Prairie. Why do you ask?"

"Why don't you come to the wedding dance with us?" Polly rolled her eyes with an exaggerated sigh. "Maybe have a chance to squeeze your dreamboat."

"It'll be fun," Celie Carlson chimed in.

"Even if sometimes we have to dance with each other because there's so few guys around?" Mildred Cavanaugh snickered.

"I doubt Cy'll be there, but Mom and Dad could be, and they'd have a hissy fit if they found out I was at the dance."

"You're kidding?" chorused the girls.

"Daddy insists I'm in nursing school," Aggie's voice dropped to a male register, "to work hard and learn all about medicine. Fun can come after graduation." Then she added, "Whose wedding is it?"

"Don't know. But, everybody seems to know everyone in those small towns and all go to the dances to have fun and forget about the war."

"The band was the cat's meow last time we went," said Eileen. "And, there were even some single guys under 50!"

"And talk about booze!" Polly almost sighed.

"Better be careful drinking with those farm boys. Their booze is probably leftover bootleg," Aggie warned.

"Bootleg or not," said Polly, "the last 'short snorts' I had from those country boys were pretty smooth. By the way, isn't Cy one of those farm boys you're suspecting of nasty intentions?"

"Well, he's from Reno County where the men are much more trustworthy and gentlemanly than those in Colwich."

"Yeah, right!" Celie giggled.

"The last dance Hay and I went to, we met some really nice guys. Didn't we, Eileen?" Polly said.

Eileen looked up from adding catsup to her potatoes. "You met Mr. Nice Guy while I was dancing."

Aggie asked, "Why haven't we heard about Mr. Nice Guy before this?" Stealing bleeding potatoes from Eileen's plate, she added, "What'd he do that's so wonderful?"

"I didn't really meet him, and someone has a big mouth." Polly shot darts at Eileen. "I was outside having a drink with some couples when this nice look'n fella came over, asking for extra gas stamps and any old car tires he could borrow. I thought, *Good luck, buster!*"

"What in the world was he going to do? Start a black market business?" Celie asked.

"No, Johnny—that was the guy's name—wanted to drive his brother's wife up to Lincoln where her hubby was graduating from flight training then heading to Europe. Johnny told everyone that all day while working in the field, he kept thinking about Ben (I'm pretty sure that was his brother's name) and his sister-in-law. He was wishing he could get them together before Ben flew overseas."

Comments of, "How romantic!" and "He does sound like a nice, guy!" interrupted until Aggie said, "Shsh, let Polly talk."

"Johnny said his bald tires wouldn't make the trip and he needed more gas stamps. He hadn't even mentioned his plan yet to his sister-in-law until he got the stuff."

"So, what happened?" Eileen asked.

Polly looked at her ditzy friend, "The guys started giving Johnny a couple of stamps from their billfolds, and then they left to look for tires. Dancing didn't seem fun after that, so we hopped the last train back to Wichita. Remember?"

"Oh, that's right," Eileen laughed. "I forgot. All of a sudden, there were mostly just old folks around. You told me about Johnny on the way back in such a dreamy voice." She sighed dramatically.

"I did not!"

"Well, that's the shits!" Cavanaugh complained. "Here you tell us this romantic story, and we don't know the end!"

Polly answered, "Well, I imagine Johnny took his sister-in-law, the way everyone was eager to help!"

"Maybe you do need to go to that dance this weekend, Polly, so we can find out about this real-life love story. Might find out more about this Johnny fella too. He sounds too sweet to be real." Aggie's suggestion surprised the group.

"Why isn't he somewhere fighting like all the other great guys? Does he have one leg? Oh! Is he a Section 8?" Cavanaugh sniggered in a girlish voice while holding her glass of water in an exaggerated feminine attitude,

Everyone gasped, "Cavanaugh!"

Even though Aggie had never met Johnny, she said, "He probably doesn't have any problem—just one of the few farm boys the government left to feed all the fighting men and the entire nation. That's why Cy isn't in the military."

"I sure wish we could get a little of the meat the farmers are raising. I'm so tired of eating potatoes, and they don't do a thing for my girlish figure," Eileen whined.

"Well, Miss Hay, if you worked harder, you wouldn't have to worry about your figure," Polly imitated Sister Gregory, initiating more laughter.

Chapter 5

"STRAIGHTEN UP AND FLY RIGHT," surged from the band while the crowd cavorted to the zany rhythm. As the song ended, laughter and conversation replaced the music. "Boy, I'm hot. How about you? Uh, was it Polly?"

"Yes, Polly Garrity. And yes, it's stifling in here." She glanced at the window openings where the crowd blocked any hope of air.

"Ya wanna go outside? It might be cooler, and maybe we can get a drink." Jim moved toward the open door.

"Sure, but first I need to head out back." Waving at Eileen Hay, Polly added, "I'm going to ask my friend to walk with me."

"You can both join us in the parking lot afterwards. Hi, I'm Jim," he greeted as Eileen came up to them.

"Hi, Jim, sorry to be rude, but I gotta go. Polly will ya come with me?"

Jim laughed as the girls hurried away. The September night air was refreshingly cool compared to inside the low-roofed, old wooden building. "The music is great, but I think I'm gonna pee my pants if I don't get to use the john soon," Eileen said. A faint light from a kerosene lamp beside the privy door cast shadows of three other women waiting.

"Well, you may jist hafta get your fancy dress all messy, sweetheart," a voice slurred. "You two are some of those bitches from St. Francis come to steal our men, aren't ya?"

Eileen cut off Polly's, "Takes one to know one," retort and pushed her into the wooden shack. "Whew! That broad sure stunk up the place!"

The girls found Jim with a group in the parking lot. "Looks like lots of people had the same idea," Polly noted as they approached. Light chiffon and seersucker dresses were romantic in the moonlight. Most of the young men had discarded their jackets and ties. Amid friendly conversation and laughter, the group passed around a bottle or two of liquor.

"Hey everyone, these are some St. Francis girls, Eileen and uh…"

"Polly."

"Sorry, Polly. Anyone got a short snort to share with them?"

"We thought you were bringing the booze tonight," one of the guys joked while passing a bottle of Old Crow.

Polly shivered as the liquor seared her throat and fondled her nerves. Eileen pushed the bottle away.

Several laughed, and one young man said, "Jim, when are you going to learn how to treat a lady?" He handed Polly a bottle of RC Cola. "You're quite a woman to drink that straight, but here's a chaser."

"Thanks." Polly took a big sip of cola and passed it to Eileen as introductions began. The last was the young man who had shared the RC.

"I'm Johnny Wetta."

"Thanks again for the chaser. Did you take your sister-in-law to Lincoln?" Polly smiled.

"Yes. How do you know about that?"

Polly recited the events of the dance several weeks prior. Then, in a secretive voice, "Actually, I'm on a very important mission tonight at risk of being kicked out of nursing school!"

"Oh really, what's your mission?" All within hearing turned their attention to the pretty brunette.

"A bunch of student nurses think your plan to unite your brother and his wife before he had to fly overseas was just about the most romantic thing we've heard in ages. We've been dying to find out if you went."

Groans arose at Polly's words. "Oh wow!" "Some secret mission!" and "Let's get out of here and dance!" blended with the notes of "Strip Polka" that drifted from the hall. Someone called, "You tell her the romantic story, Johnny"

"If you don' mind, I'll leave you with Johnny to complete your war mission. Wanna dance?" Jim asked Eileen. They sauntered toward the music.

Johnny took Polly's hand. "Well, is it dance or talk?"

"Dance first, then talk," Polly answered, and they joined the polkaing crowd.

"You're really great," Johnny complimented as the notes faded and he brought Polly into his arms with a double twirl.

"You're a lot better than my sisters or friends at the dorm," she grinned, easing away but continuing to hold his hand.

"How many sisters do ya have?" Johnny maneuvered her toward some men selling soft drinks from a long cow tank filled with melting ice.

"Five, always fighting like banshees and driving Mom and Daddy and our two brothers nuts. Mom says it's the crazy Irish blood. My sister Nonie is sleeping at the dorm in my bed tonight, so I don't get caught for sneaking out." She took a bottle of ice-cold Royal Crown Cola (RC) dripping with frigid water, and they walked toward the door amid greetings from Johnny's friends.

"That's why this is a dangerous mission?" he wondered.

Just then a young woman stumbled near, throwing her arms around Johnny's neck. "Hi, handsome. You haben't danced wid me yet."

"Maybe later, Gladys." He eased her arms from his neck and took Polly's hand.

"You're rather popular."

But she stuck her tongue out at Gladys who seethed, "Whore," as Johnny moved Polly toward the cool air outside.

She said, "Now tell me all about your trip. Was your sister-in-law just terribly excited when you told her your plan? Was Ben surprised?"

"Can't believe you're so interested."

"Well, remember the only thing we student nurses usually get to talk about are babies, bedpans, and bloody surgeries. And those stories get a little old. A romantic story is so much better than work and war news all the time."

They reached a car in the lot, and Johnny handed her his drink then easily lifted Polly to the hood. She tingled at the touch of his warm, strong hands. "You really wanna hear this?" He looked at the lovely, intent face gazing at him. "When I told Margie that I had enough tires and gas stamps to make the trip, she burst into tears and hugged me like a vice-grip. The next day when I pulled into the drive of her dad's house, she flew out the door with her little satchel like she'd been waiting for hours."

"Did Ben know you were coming?"

"I'd called him a couple of weeks earlier.

CHAPTER 6

"HI BEN, how's my hot shot pilot brother?"

"Hey, Johnny, what a surprise! I'm not officially a pilot yet, but what's up? Something wrong with the folks that you're calling?"

"No everything's fine. Just wondering if you have a date for your graduation?"

"Funny you'd call tonight. The Brass just told us at this morning's briefing we'd graduate on September 25th and fly out later that afternoon." Johnny could just picture his brother shifting his tall body from slouching against the wall to full attention as he realized why his brother might be calling. "You thinking of coming up, Johnny? Maybe bringing Margie?"

"I'd sure like to, but you know how it is this time of year trying to get the wheat planted. Pray for rain the day before, and that I can scrounge up enough gas stamps."

"That'd be swell Johnny. I'll help with the money if you can get here."

"The hell you will. I'll try my damndestthough! It'd be great to see my little brother get his wings, and you and Margie need to get to say goodbye." A brief second of silence, almost made Johnny think he'd lost the connection until Ben's, now somewhat raspy voice, was back. "I'll pray for rain, Johnny. Thanks a hell of lot."

"You saw me getting the gas stamps and tires, so the rest is history," Johnny offered Polly a drink of liquor..

"She took a swig straight, following it with RC. Johnny smiled and did the same before continuing.

"I tried to convince the folks to go too since it had rained, but Dad didn't think the farm would survive with us both gone. Mom patted my arm and choked out, 'I told my boys goodbye once; I can't do it again.'" Polly gently squeezed his hand. "Margie and I got up to Omaha right after Ben finished final briefings and other official Army stuff. We had a few beers and shared laughs before I made myself scarce for the night, so he and Margie could have a little time together. Graduation would be the next morning."

Johnny continued describing the graduation and send-off as he and Polly sat on the roof of his old '35 Plymouth and the evening cooled

"If you ever want to feel proud to be an American, attending a military graduation will do the trick. The new pilots in their crisp uniforms were spit shined like they just walked out of a catalogue. Sousa's music from the Army band was best I ever heard, especially as the guys marched off to the sound of Stars and Stripes Forever."

"Did the pilots leave right away then?"

"No, the guys had time to eat lunch with families before taking off. When we heard the band on the parade grounds again, I gave Ben and Margie a few final minutes alone. Then while the new pilots put on all their flight gear she and I headed to the observation areaset up near the run way."

Polly said, "I'd have been a wreck bawling like a baby if I was Margie."

"She was a real trooper. I know it about killed her, but she was strong for Ben. As the pilots came out to their planes, I think the band played "The Army Goes Rolling Along" extra loud to drown out the sobs of lots of wives and mothers. And, when the planes fired their engines, the roar of all those planes drowned out everything. I was sure glad we had come and felt mighty proud seeing Ben wave goodbye from his cockpit and give us a thumbs-up before rolling down the runway. Margie did grab for my hand then, and I put my arm around her shoulders, but I couldn't look at her."

"I get teary eyed just thinking of it," Polly observed. "You have a right to feel proud."

"Well, I'm proud of Ben and my other brothers but pretty jealous too." In answer to Polly's questioning look, Johnny continued. "Ben's going to do heroic things fighting that maniac's armies in Europe. Joe also signed up for the Army Air Corps and was ready to start classes when his physical came back. He was turned down due to a heart murmur. He came home and joined the Army and is in California for training, so we know he'll be fighting the Japs. That really has Mom worried.

"So, is Joe older or younger than you?" Polly asked.

"He's about four years older, but, my younger brother Leo just left for California too. He's in the Navy. They're all gonna be heroes and all I'm doin' is milking cows and plowing fields."

"You shouldn't feel that way. Someone has to feed the fighting men and all of us, too."

"Yeah, but Leo's so young; he should stay home, but Dad wanted me. Says Leo is book smart but can't tell the difference between a manure spreader and a spring-tooth." This made Polly laugh, breaking the serious tone. "Dad is right, someone has to stay behind, especially since the government is trying to get city women to work on farms with that Women's Land Service."

Polly said, "I heard about that and I'm glad to be in nursing school

Had enough of that hard farm life before the folks lost our's by the end of the dusty, dirty 30's." Then laughed again and finished the last of her cola before adding, "I'm happy that you're staying here."

"Hey, don't you two hear that music?" Jim called, strolling by with a different young lady. "Last dance."

The melancholy strains of "I'll Be Seeing You" floated from the old hall. "How about it?" Johnny jumped from the car hood and offered Polly his hand. As she slipped in front of him, the soft breeze ruffled her light peach dress in an enticing manner. Johnny took her in his arms, admiring her beauty in the early autumn moonlight. "Everyone calls you Polly. Is that your real name?"

"It's really Pauline."

"I'll call you that from now on. You're too pretty for the name of an old parrot."

She smiled as Johnny brushed a loose curl from her face. Her nerves shivered, but Polly played the coquette. "Oh, you think you'll be calling me anything after tonight?" As his lips brushed her forehead, she warned, "We're gonna miss the last dance."

Johnny smiled and they joined the pulse of the bittersweet music. His hand thrilled her lower back and the booze seduced her head to his shoulder. Suddenly, Polly jerked it up as she realized that she hadn't seen the other student nurses for ages.

Then she caught sight of Deloris, another student nurse, in Robert's arms. Their eyes met, and Deloris winked and waved dreamily. Even in the low light, the sparkle of a ring shimmered. "Wow, Congrats!" Polly mouthed, relaxing her head. *Life is already changing for us and it' still months til graduation. And, I can assure the group that I'm almost positive that Johnny Wetta's not a Section 8.*

As the last notes died away, Johnny held Polly until Eileen Hay assailed them. "Wow, weren't they an awesome band? This has been a great night," she chattered. "This is Mildred Cavanaugh," she added, as Mildred edged through the crowd.

"Happy to meet you, ladies; I'm Johnny Wetta."

"Oh, really!" Mildred's enthusiasm met Polly's eyes, which were screaming, Shut up! Deloris and Robert joined them.

The men shook hands. "Looks like you've met my flock," Robert said and winked at Eileen and Mildred.

Polly interrupted, "Congratulations, you guys. This is so exciting!" She turned Deloris' hand to the light.

"Wow!" and "That's gorgeous," squealed Mildred and Eileen.

Johnny thumped his friend's back, "This calls for a drink." They shared sips of whiskey and the remainder of cola.

"Deloris, you are finishing school, aren't you?" Polly asked.

"Of course. After all the shit we survived the past couple of years, I wouldn't quit now."

"What if Sister Gregory finds out?" Eileen gasped. "You'll get kicked out!"

"And who's going to tell?" Mildred threatened.

"No one." Polly wrapped her arm around Eileen.

"Sister Gregory'll be berserk by March wondering who all's engaged," Deloris said. "I've put Robert off for so long; I don't want to chance losing my handsome guy." She plastered him with a kiss.

The ladies cackled, and he asked, "Are you all ready to grace me with your beauty back to Wichita?"

They teased answers, but Johnny suggested, "I could take the girls back if you and Del want to celebrate." Polly's heart skipped as giggling Hay pinched her.

"Let's all celebrate together," Deloris begged. "Who cares if we're a little crowded?"

Robert said, "I'm starved and don't want to go home and cook.

Anyone mind a stop at the all-night chop shop on North Broadway?"

"Great," "I'm hungry too," and "Terrific," mingled with honking horns as they dodged cars.

Polly didn't mind being crowded against Johnny on the way to Wichita and never once thought about the events unfolding at St. Francis student nurses dorm.

CHAPTER 7

BECAUSE POLLY'S adventurous behavior enlivened what could be boring dorm life, there was no shortage of friends who joined in support positions for the covert mission. Celie and Aggie, along with Polly's sister Nonie had key roles in providing cover for Polly. Since the young nurses had never met Nonie, the mission was more risky. Added to this was the dodgy ability to get a phone call in the dorms. Working at the hospital gave better access to phone calls, but Celie's concern in the success of their endeavor grew as the night became later.

"Celie, things finally seem quiet with all our patients tucked in and quiet for now," the head nurse on the medical floor, said. "Mind if I take a break before charting?"

"No, go ahead. I can handle it," Celie told her supervisor and glanced at the clock, which was nearing 9:00.

"I won't be long; then you can relax a little while."

"Mind if I start the charting?" Celie inquired.

"That would be terrific," the head nurse complimented as she grabbed her purse from below the desk at the nurses' station. "I'll be back soon." She waved and headed down the hall toward the elevators. As she started to step in, the phone at the nurses' station rang. She glanced back to see if it was still safe to leave the floor.

Celie waved her on, mouthing, "Nothing important." But as she listened to the voice on the phone, her hands began to tremble as she realized that this little escapade could end both her and Polly's nursing career if caught.

"Hello, my name is Nonie and I need to speak to Miss Celie Carlson about bringing in a patient needing bed rest."

"Hi, Nonie, it's Celie. Your timing is perfect. My supervisor just took her break. Thank goodness. She would have been awfully suspicious with your silly request. Anyway, when she returns, I'll take my break and come down to let you into the student nurses' dorm. Where are you calling from?"

"I'm in the hospital lobby by the main entrance,"

Celie gave instructions about how to get to the safest door to sneak into the dorm. "I'll be down as soon as I can. But, you better hide in the bushes beside the door just in case the night watchman comes by. He'd just love to put some excitement into his boring night by dragging you in to see Sister Gregory."

"From what Polly has told me, I really don't want that to happen," Nonie answered. "I'll be waiting for you."

Nonie followed Celie's directions to the dorm and glanced around to make sure no one would see her struggle to hide among the almost leafless, overgrown spirea. The branches grabbed at her jacket and scratched her face and legs, and as she slunk down into the bushes Nonie thought, That damn Pauline is really gonna owe me for this. How do I let her talk me into this crazy shit? Anticipating a short wait, she squatted down in an uncomfortable position. However, as time dragged on. Nonie's legs and back cramped, so she stood and stretched. Just then, she heard voices and noticed a young couple coming toward the area.

The white doctor's coat designated the occupation of the man who was saying, "...so tired of all these stupid rules and sneaking around.

The nuns may be good teachers and nurses, but they sure need to lighten up a little on you girls and realize the more rules they have, the more trouble they have."

A giggling immature voice answered, "Let's not waste time worrying about them now. Just kiss me, handsome." She threw her arms around his neck as he pulled her into some cedars along the walk. Nonie could see the young woman wrap a leg around the doctor's, hitching herself closer and higher. "Oooh, I wish you could just take me right here," she crooned.

Goodness! This is better than the picture show I just spent money to see. Nonie snickered to herself. She felt her face heat, and she knew she was blushing at the scene in front of her.

Suddenly, a low beam of light swept the air about 25 yards away as the watchman came around the corner of the building. "Oh shit! That must be damned, nosy Elmer," the voice complained. "Now I hafta go in or he'll report me, and --"

"Shsh, move back farther into the cedars. He won't see us. You think you're going in after you..."the man's voice lowered, and Nonie could no longer see them.

Nonie thought, Damn, you sure ruined a sexy scene, Elmer. Oh Lord, don't let him see me. My legs are cramping so bad; I'm afraid that I'm gonna fall over in these bushes. Nonie tried not to breathe as her thoughts ranged from mutilating Polly for talking her into this hairbrained scheme to praying that she wouldn't be caught, which would probably be the end of Polly's nursing career. Elmer haphazardly shone the flashlight around the bushes while humming a melancholy tune. As he approached, Nonie's heart beat so fast, she was afraid the bushes would start shaking, and she nearly fainted when she heard, "Well, well, well, what have we here?"

She was ready to stand up when she realized the flashlight was pointed to the cedars on the opposite side of the walkway. "Come out of there, you two," the watchman ordered. "Trying to hide with a white coat on isn't too smart!"

A young woman's voice whined, "Oh, Elmer, it's just us doin' a little smoochn' before I have to go in."

"Well, what're ya doin back here instead of the main entry you're sposed to be usin'?" the watchman asked as he shone the light into her face. Nonie could now see the young lady with short bobbed, dark hair and that the man in the doctor's coat was quite handsome. She noticed the name Jackson stitched on the pocket. "Oh, excuse me, Doctor. I thought you were one of the sailors our young ladies met at the USO. Some might have questionable intentions, might try to take advantage of our nurses. Can't be too careful protecting them."

"That's fine, Elmer. You can put the flashlight down now."

"Well, Doctor, you know the rules, as well as you, young lady. Student nurses aren't allowed to be friendly with the doctors. Sister Gregory is going to—"

"Damn it, Elmer, Sister Gregory does not own this hospital or the nursing school. In six months Stella will be graduated, and we can date all we want and even get married. Man to man, you wouldn't be protecting this young lady if you mentioned to anyone that you saw her here with me. You'd just get her kicked out of school and prevent her from helping our fighting men," the young doctor ranted.

Stella started, "I'm not—"but Jackson's grasp tightening around her waist warned her.

He pulled out his billfold and said, "No need to upset an apple cart and get Sister Gregory in a stew. We'd all have hell to pay for a week. Right?" He handed Elmer a couple of bills.

"Well, yes, when she gets upset, she can make life…" Then regaining a little of his authority, the watchman turned toward the lady called

Stella and advised, "Miss, you better get yourself on in the front door where you're s'posed to come in. I think you're close to missing curfew." She giggled and kissed the young doctor again before scurrying down the sidewalk toward the front entrance. "Night, Doctor," Elmer said and hummed a livelier tune than earlier as he fingered the bills in his pocket. He smiled at the young doctor who glanced back before walking across the street toward the hospital.

After Elmer strode down the sidewalk and finally disappeared around a corner, Nonie let out a burst of air and stifled a laugh, thinking, Wow, that was close! What a scene! That was worth sitting on the damp ground being punctured by these damned branches. She eased back against the wall of the building and sat with her knees pulled to her chest. *But, darn, it's starting to get cold. I sure hope Celie didn't forget me.* Whether from the adrenaline drop after the wild experience or the long day of job hunting, Nonie suddenly felt exhausted and closed her eyes.

"Nonie, Nonie, wake up," Celie whispered desperately pulling on the leg sticking out from under a bush. "You've got to get upstairs now while the coast is clear."

"Huh? What?" Nonie mumbled, completely disoriented waking up on the ground in the middle of a prickly bush.

"Come on, Nonie. I'm Celie," she pulled her to her feet. "Sorry so late; we had a patient code just as I was going to come down to let you in. Then everything went nuts, and I couldn't get away 'til now. I was so nervous worrying about you," Celie chattered as they sneaked through the door. "I almost panicked when I got down here and couldn't find you. Then I saw your feet and legs sticking out from beneath the bushes. Not a great way to hide, Nonie. You're lucky Elmer didn't come by."

"Believe me, he did," Nonie yawned. "Scared me to death, but I wasn't the only one he scared."

"You sound just like Polly," Celie smiled. "You even look like her, except taller. This should work if you get in fast before Hannah does rounds." Peeking down the dimly lit hall, Celie motioned Nonie to hurry as she scurried to Polly's door, unlocked it, and gave her the key. "Goodnight," she whispered and hurried back to work.

Heavy breathing greeted Nonie as she stepped into the small room. A nightlight shone on the desk where a note lay.

Hi Nonie, welcome. Sleep well. Hope I don't snore too much. Don't worry about making noise; living with your sister, I've learned to sleep through a circus. Aggie.

Nonie glanced at the bed where Aggie was sleeping with her face to the wall. Moonlight was shining on blond hair cascading across the pillow, and Nonie sighed with envy. The Garrity girls all had dark hair with degrees of red reflecting their Irish heritage. When Nonie heard whispering outside the door, she jumped into bed, jacket and shoes still on. Then she remembered the note. Would this Hannah person come in to snoop? Remembering Polly's griping, she threw back the covers and sprang to grab the note before bounding back to the bed. A key turned as she pulled blankets halfway over her head. Slit-eyed, she perceived the glow of Hannah's flashlight as the old lady shuffled into the room. Nonie's heart was racing again.

The small desk light clicked off to a, "Humph—wasteful!" Nonie fingered the crumpled note breathing a prayer of relief. The soft brush of slippers neared the bed, before Hannah roughly pushed on the lump that was Nonie. When she pushed again, Nonie turned flat on her stomach moaning, "Ahhhh! What d'ya want?"

Hannah jerked back and shouted, "Oh me Got!" as the lump started to sit up.

From the doorway someone asked, "What's happening?" Nonie recognized that voice.

"What's going on?" Aggie groaned.

"Nothing, go back ta sleep!" Hannah plodded across the room and slammed the door, muffling angry whispers. "Ya ninny! Ya said ya knew for certain Garrity's bed would be stuffed. Well, I almost had a heart attack when them pillows turned over!"

"Well... well! Are you sure it's Garrity?"

"Of course, I just saw her."

"But, yesterday I heard her say—"

"Oh, shut up! If ya warn't Sister Gregory's niece, I'd report ya. Just go ta bed and stop being such a snitch!" The voices moved down the hall.

"Wow! That was too close," Nonie whispered.

"I can't believe that darn woman—and Stella!" Aggie said from across the room. Then she added, "Sorry I was asleep. I thought maybe you had a change of plans, so I had piled the pillows praying Hannah wouldn't do a thorough check. How long you been here?"

Nonie sat up throwing back the covers. Seeing Nonie still in her jacket, Aggie gasped and Nonie said, "They had some kind of emergency on Celie's ward. She just now let me in. It's almost one o'clock; how late does she have to work?"

"She's on til 7:00."

"How do you girls work all night and learn all that crap I've seen in Polly's books? And, how can you stand this curfew?"

"You sound so much like Polly. Same voice questioning the rules. We only have to work all night some weekends. Weeknights it's just til 10:00, but you're right; it is hard to find time to study." Aggie attempted to stifle a yawn.

"I better let you get back to sleep before crazy Polly gets in and wants to yak, too. Think it's safe if I use the bathroom and brush my teeth now?" Nonie asked as she hung her clothes on the back of a chair near Polly's desk.

"Better wait a few minutes, and be sure to rough up your hair." Aggie snuggled back into her bed. "That snitch Stella might still be sneaking around. Keep your head down, and anyone who comes into the bathroom will think you're Polly. Her robe's on the back of that door." Aggie's voice floated off.

Nonie waited a few minutes, thinking about the eventful night before going down the hall. She was almost finished brushing her teeth when someone came in and tossed toiletries on the metal shelf above a sink.

Nonie spit out the toothpaste and rinsed her mouth. Keeping her head down, she splashed water and lathered her face. The student nurse sneered, "Why are you brushing your teeth and washing your face now, Garrity? You were supposedly sound asleep when Hannah checked."

"Why are you such a busybody?" Nonie mumbled into a towel drying her face. Then she yanked open the bathroom door and almost screamed as she ran right into Polly. Putting her fingers to her lips, she pulled her sister toward her room.

Inside, Polly whispered, "What's the matter with you? I've got to pee."

"You better not get huffy with me, Pauline! I've had a hell-of-a-night. First, I almost froze to death when Celie…" For the next few minutes Nonie unloaded details of her night hiding in the bushes so her older sister could shake a leg. She ended her colorful narrative with, "…and that gal who was with Hannah doing bed check is in the bathroom. She just grilled me about brushing my teeth now if I was asleep earlier. Why was she tagging along with the dorm mother anyway?"

"Probably brown-nosing again!"

"She seems like a real bitch! What an irritating busybody for someone who has a huge skeleton rattling in her closet!"

"What do you mean?" Polly whispered as she undressed.

"She's the one who was with that Dr. Jackson in the bushes."

"Really! Are you sure?"

"Absolutely! She's got that same whiny voice. That Dr. Jackson and Aggie both called her Stella."

"That damned bitch! Why's she trying to get me in trouble again? I used to be nice to her, but ever since we worked together, she's been a real pain in the ass," Polly said. "She better watch out, or I'm gonna have to teach her a lesson."

"That doesn't sound very smart if she's Sister Gregory's niece."

"What? What in the world makes you think Zedrich is Gorgon's niece?" Polly blurted out. Aggie moaned and pulled covers over her head.

"Is Zedrich, Stella?" Nonie moved closer to Polly on the bed and explained what she had heard outside the door. Polly exclaimed, "Well, that explains a lot. I can't wait to tell everyone."

Polly would have jumped onto Aggie to share all the news of the night, but she was afraid of wetting her pants. Her bladder was ready to burst, so she had to shimmy to the bathroom hoping not to dribble on the hall floor as she prayed to avoid Miss Stella Zedrich.

CHAPTER 8

OVER SUPPER LATER IN THE WEEK, the friends encircled Deloris and admired the small forbidden treasure sparkling on her left hand. She had taken the ring from her bra strap. Suddenly a familiar voice asked, "What'cha all up to?"

"What do you want?" Polly sneered as the ring disappeared into Deloris's pocket.

"Goodness, Polly, why are you being so rude?" Celie sat down, and the others found chairs.

"She knows. Don't you, Miss Priss?"

"I have no idea what you're talking about." She glared at Polly then asked the others, "So what're you all looking at?"

They looked from one to the other; then Eileen said, "Well, if you must know, I was doing my nails this afternoon and was sharing this new shade, *Soldiers Downfall.* What d'ya think?" She held her left hand close to Zedrich's face. The nails glowed an outrageously bright red.

"You can't wear that stuff. Why would you waste your time and money?"

"I can dream about life in seven months when I can be as glamorous as I want and Sister Gregory can't do a thing about it."

"If you're working at St. Francis, she'll let you know you look like a hussy," Cavanaugh laughed.

"I can't believe you all are so interested in some dumb nail polish." Stella walked away.

After she moved away, Aggie looked around the table then asked, "Think we fooled her?"

"I'm pretty sure she'd have sneered about the ring if she'd seen it," Polly said. Then turning to the scatter-brain queen, "My gosh, Eileen , you came up with a doozy excuse. How'd you think so fast?"

Eileen smiled as others joined the praise and shrugged before taking a bite of her salad.

"Well, I certainly appreciate it!" Deloris said. "My heart about jumped through my mouth when I heard Zedrich's voice. Guess I was really stupid."

Putting her fork down, Celie said, "I just wish Stella wasn't so snoopy and such a snitch. She was my freshman roommate, remember? She's kinda nice when you get to know her."

"You gotta be kidd'n," Cavanaugh said. "I used to try, even invited her to sunbathe with us, hoping she would be nicer if we included her more. We all know how that turned out." They all nodded or giggled as they recalled that day.

"Guess being mean just runs in the family," Polly said. Questioning eyes waited for an explanation. She looked at Aggie. "Tell them what happened Saturday night."

Most already knew about the bed check. However, they were shocked when Aggie told them she heard Hannah say, "If you weren't Sister Gregory's niece, I'd report you."

"Well, that explains so much," Celie said. "I always wondered why she's still here. She's the worst student I've worked with in all our rotations. I always had to watch that she didn't hurt someone."

"I know what you mean," Eileen said. "More than once I had to cover her mistakes."

They all joined in with tales of working with Stella. Finally, Aggie said, "Well, I kinda feel sorry for her; it's almost as though she's afraid of the patients. You hafta wonder why she stays. Sure can't be for all the fun."

Amid other comments, Polly said, "Well, I have to get to the fun of studying for that test tomorrow. Stella Zedrich may not have any patient skills, but I would give anything to have her brains. She knows everything from the books and acesevery exam and lab experiment."

A few days later, an angry Sister Gregory was returning tests. "If some of you do not put more effort into learning the medical technical language, you will never pass the state boards. Psychiatry may be a newer and somewhat questionable field of medicine, but that is no reason my students can't master the information. If you scored below an 80% on this test, you will be spending extra time with Sister Rosemarie until you master this. Sister has just posted the next rotation schedules with partners assigned." A younger nun walked in and smiled at the students.

Sister Gregory continued, "Students who need to meet with Sister Rosemarie, stay behind so a mandatory tutorial schedule can be established." Her piercing glare squelched any thoughts of skipping out. When, "Excused," was pronounced, a cacophony of chairs scraping the wooden floor filled the room as the students rushed to learn who their next partner was. Five red-faced young ladies remained.

In the hall, Cavanaugh said, "Congratulations, Polly. I knew you could do well if you started believing in yourself."

"Thanks, Mildred. My sister Helen has been helping me too. She remembers most of what Sister likes to test. And, Aggie drills me—even in my sleep! Right, Ag? I'll sure miss working together on our next rotation." They joined the group at the bulletin board.

"You have no idea how much you'll miss her," commented Eileen who had been at the front of the bulletin board and now moved out of the way of others. Polly's and Aggie's puzzled looks were interrupted by an outburst.

"Sister Gregory has lost her mind!" Stella Zedrich almost screamed as she pushed back through the students. When she bumped into Polly, her eyes flashed.

"What's her problem now?" Polly asked, watching Stella stomp down the hall.

Moving to the front of the group, Celie almost whispered, "I think she's right. Sister must have lost her mind! Take a deep breath, Polly, and don't scream." She moved aside so Polly could see the assignments.

Polly's face blanched as her mouth flew open. Attempting to stifle hot tears, "This has to be a mistake. Even Gorgon isn't this mean." Students were now as interested in looking for Polly's name as their own.

"You have to talk to Sister."

"Go see her right away before she gets off duty."

"She must not realize that you two are gasoline and fire." The advice from surrounding students barely pierced the dark cloud saturating Polly's mind.

"I'll talk to her, but it's no mistake. Gorgon really wants me to quit." Words of encouragement echoed in a vacuum of gloom as Aggie, Eileen and Celie guided Polly to the canteen. Over soft drinks, they roused her spirits and convinced her to be honest with Sister Gregory about her nemesis.

Later, outside the closed door marked *Director of Student Nurses,* Polly's elbows poked into her knees as her head drooped in her hands. Her dejected reverie was disturbed by muffled crying and impassioned words from within. "Spoiled… father… ridiculous… my position…" When Polly heard Sister Gregory say her name and follow it with, "learn something… gentle… most skilled," she was amazed. Her frustrated features softened.

Is Gorgan really saying that about me? Lord, what am I gonna do now? Maybe I better go think. As she stood, the office door jerked open and Stella Zedrich exited.

"What are you doing here?" She brushed away angry tears, shoved past Polly, and didn't wait for an answer.

"Well, I, um," Polly stammered.

"Is that you, Miss Garrity?"

"Well, yes, I, I was confused about something, but I don't think I need to bother you."

"I presume you were also going to ask me to change your rotation partner."

"I just wondered if it was a mistake that me and Stella are together, again?"

"Stella and I, Miss Garrity."

What?" Polly was confused.

"Your grammar, Miss Garrity. You said, 'me and Stella.' My students need to speak intelligently. Please use correct grammar."

"Oh." Polly sighed, thinking, *I can't even talk right for this woman.* At the same time, she was inspired to take a different approach. "I wanted to thank you if it isn't a mistake. Stella is so smart, and well, you know how hard things are for me."

Sister's eyebrows rose to her wimple determining Polly's motives. "Miss Garrity, you know very well that you have much better patient skills, so don't be ridiculously humble. We are all aware that you two obstinate young women have conflicts. But, nurses must learn to set aside differences and work with many personalities. Mrs. King will be monitoring to make sure you give the proficient and compassionate care you usually demonstrate and that you help Stella attain some of those skills. If you can't work together, we will decide if there is any reason for either of you to finish your studies after Christmas." Polly's mouth dropped as Sister Gregory's stare pierced her.

"Ok, Sister."

"Now get to your studies or duties or whatever you're supposed to be doing."

Polly felt all five floors of the hospital on her shoulders as she trudged down the hall. She was surprised to find Stella sitting on a bench outside of an adjoining unit.

"What are you doing here?" Polly pushed through the doors. Her new partner trudged along in silence, reluctant to take a pick to the iceberg that had formed between them for over two years.

Polly finally stopped. "I don't know why you hate me so much, Zedrich, but I sure don't plan to get kicked out four months before graduation. We have to talk."

Tears filled Stella's eyes as she turned to Polly and tried to take a stab at the frozen wall. "I… I just…" But, she shook her head instead and marched away, leaving Polly muddled.

CHAPTER 9

THE NEXT AFTERNOON, Polly dried her hands as she prepared for duty and looked at Stella. "We better start talking to each other now, Zedrich, so we don't explode in front of a patient. I'd like to knock that nasty attitude to kingdom come, and if you don't talk to me, I just might."

"I've dreaded surgical floor since starting training. And now, Sister assigns you as my partner, Miss Uppity herself, so perfect all the patients love you!"

"What're you talking about? Me? Miss Uppity? That's rich coming from you, Miss Priss, too good to do any of the nasty jobs!"

"Well, you always walk around with your head up high and think rules don't apply to you, breaking every one you can."

"You gotta be kiddn'! I walk with my head up because when I was a kid, I slumped all the time. My dad would yell, 'Stand up straight. None of my daughters better walk around like a whipped dog.' One day he tied a board across my back, threatening worse if anyone took it off. Mom untied it after Dad was asleep… or passed out. After wearing it during the day for a week, Dad asked, 'Have you learned to stand up straight?' "

"Your dad didn't do that! He'd have to be worse than mine!"

"He sure did, and more than once until I learned to stand up straight. Can't believe you thought I was uppity as dumb as I am."

Suddenly Polly smiled about the backhanded compliment. "Thanks for saying the patients love me; I do enjoy helping them. But I don't feel special at all around you with almost perfect scores on every test."

"Test grades don't help when—"

The door flew open and almost hit Polly as Sister Gregory demanded, "What are you two doing in here gabbing?Mrs. King was ready to give report five minutes ago. We have patients waiting. Let's go, ladies." Stella finished drying her hands, and they followed the clanking rosary beads.

"Miss Garrity, you will take the lead on the first couple of patients since I haven't heard any complaints recently about your skills in giving enemas or starting IVs." Stella's face was ashen as their instructor's words confirmed tasks she dreaded. "Miss Zedrich, you will observe at first and then compassionately administer care." Sister fixed her pale niece with a doubtful glare before introducing the students to the head nurse. Afterwards, the rosary beads clicked rhythmically toward the stairs.

Mrs. King greeted the young nurses warmly and outlined the needs of each patient. Stella looked close to fainting as their new supervisor reviewed surgical-prep for two patients. "You've performed the duties required on this floor for the past couple of years, so you will work with little supervision. However, do not guess about anything. Ask questions if you're the least bit unsure. You have our patients' lives in your hands." Looking at the other nurse at the station, she said, "Sadie, while lights and bells aren't flashing and ringing, I'll take these two around so the patients aren't too confused by new faces."

"Good luck, nurses." The younger woman smiled and raised her hand saying, "Hi." Stella was calm as she met patients until the final room. A disgruntled man who looked like a withered old tree was fumbling with the new call button. The odor that greeted the nurses testified to the cause of his frustrated growling about "damned shit" and "just a helpless baby."

Mrs. King introduced Stella and Polly, assuring the patient that he was not a baby and the young ladies were quite capable to care for him. She left with a smile and a thumbs up.

"See you later," Polly waved. Stella's red face held a dam of tears, and she stifled a gag. "You want to get a basin of soapy water, please?" Polly asked her partner. When Stella returned, Polly had the patient wrapped in a towel; his soiled gown lay on the floor. She motioned Stella to put the basin down and help move the fragile patient to the side so they could remove the sheets. Stella helped but was totally confused as Polly said, "My uncle raised the biggest worms you ever saw, and did they ever catch fish!" Through eye contact she directed Stella in helping with the sponge bath while Mr. Krews laughed and talked about noodling on the Arkansas River.

Stella gathered the reeking linens as Polly combed the patient's hair. She suddenly said, "Mr. Krews, what happened to your cheek? It is swollen like a chipmunk's! We probably need to clean it with hydrogen peroxide." Stella looked up even more confused.

The old man shook his head while keeping his mouth tightly shut. Polly continued, "Maybe if you take a big spit, you might get rid of the swelling." She handed him an emesis basin and shook her finger when he expelled the disgusting black matter. "Now, Mr. Krews, you know you can't have chewing tobacco in here." Offering a glass of water to the elderly patient, Polly handed the repulsive container to Stella who swallowed hard attempting not to gag again.

Mr. Krews was growling, "Damned few pleasures left in life," when Polly said something about searching for his stash. He looked up crestfallen; however, when Polly winked at him with a pretty smile, a sparkle glinted in his cataractic eyes. Stella finished tucking in the fresh sheets and Polly waved cheerily before picking up part of the soiled linens and motioned to Stella to get the rest.

"We didn't look for his tobacco," Stella remembered, turning back toward the room.

"And we aren't going to," Polly answered. "That old guy deserves a little comfort. We'll check his chart later to see if a little chew is going to hurt his recovery."

"What about…?"

But Polly was determined.

"Next stop is Mrs. Jorgenson who is having gall bladder surgery tomorrow. You wanna give the enema, or do I need to demonstrate as Sister suggested?" Polly was unsuccessful in restraining scorn as her partner's face told her the answer. "Oh, alright, but you'll do the next, and I'm not holding your hand."Pushing open the supply room door, they dumped soiled linens down the shoot. As they washed their hands, Polly said, "Help me get things ready." They soon emerged with a metal can filled with liquid, extra towels, and rubber gloves.

"Hi, Mrs. Jorgenson. What beautiful flowers." The patient's miserable expression softened at Polly's greeting. Polly chatted during the unpleasant procedure. "My grandmother raised beautiful zinnias and gladiolas, but she could never grow roses like those." Stella, repulsed and holding her breath, stood close and took Mrs. Jorgenson's hand when Polly's eyes directed. Her face turned bright red and she again squelched gagging when Polly held out to her the enamel bed pan holding the results of the enema. "Please empty this," Polly pleasantly directed. "And bring a couple of fresh washcloths. I think Miss Jorgenson could use one for her face."

Stella left to dispose of the nauseating contents, and when she returned with the washcloths, Polly was chatting with the patient about her children. She had her partner apply a cool fresh washcloth to Mrs.

Jorgenson's face for comfort. When the young nurses finished tending the patient, Stella asked, "How can you do that so casually and all the time talking about your grandmother's roses? You weren't any more disgusted than you were cleaning up Mr. Crews mess."

"Good Lord, Zedrich, I sure don't enjoy cleaning up shit and giving enemas. But, think how lousy and embarrassed the patient is. Talking about unimportant things helps take our minds off the crap."

"How did you know Mr. Crews had tobacco in his cheek?"

"My dad chews; the tobacco aroma hit me even amid the revolting shit vapors. I also noticed the clump in his jaw while changing his gown." Pushing open the door to the prep room, Polly attempted civility. "Thanks for emptying the crap and cleaning the bedpan. Let's just soak this equipment til we're finished then we'll sterilize everything at once."

As the nurses washed their hands again, Polly said, "I'll run some water for these to soak while you fix the solution this time and get the gear." Stella moved like a sleepwalker as she made preparations for her dreaded job. "Ok, your turn. When we go in, look around the room to find something to talk about. Oh, and my turn to empty the crap and clean that basin." Polly tried to be encouraging as they finished prepping.

"Well, I can't talk about rose bushes. I don't have a grandmother who grows flowers so…"

"Well, neither do I. My grandmother hates flowers. In fact, I think she hates most everything. I saw the flowers by the window and just talked to help us both think about anything but the procedure. If it means making up something, use your imagination."

As they neared the patient's room, Polly's frustration became a firecracker when Stella weakly implored, "Can't you please do it? I'll empty the—"

"No, you have to; it's part of being a nurse. Good lord, didn't you give lots of enemas on medical rotation last year?"

"Oh alright!" Stella stomped into the patient's room. "Afternoon, Mrs. Maynard. Gotta give you an enema before surgery."

The firecracker fuse in Polly's brain was almost lit at the abrupt greeting. She pulled the privacy curtain and attempted more sensitivity. "This is Miss Zedrich, and I'm Miss Garrity. I think Mrs. King told you we'd be in." The woman in the bed nodded as tears escaped her closed eyes in rivulets of tears toward the pillow.

"Roll over on your left side,—please," Stella added when her eyes met Polly's, and she was almost singed by a glare shooting fire. "Do you need any help?" Zedrich asked as she pulled the covers back.

Polly arranged the sheet for less exposure and encouraged Mrs. Maynard. "If you bring your right leg up toward your chest a little, this will be easier." She glanced at Stella and nodded toward the tears.

Stella mouthed, "What?" Then she added, "I'll be as gentle as possible and try not to hurt you."

A frustrated sigh escaped from Polly when Stella used the forbidden word. She reached for a handkerchief. "Mrs. Maynard, have you ever had an enema before?" The patient stifled a sob as she shook her head, and Polly wiped the tears. "Do you understand how it is done?"

Mrs. Maynard sniffled, "I think so."

Polly briefly explained the procedure then said, "Why don't you tell me about that pretty young woman in the picture on your stand. Is she…" Polly stopped and sniffed the air deeply then grabbed Stella's hand before she could insert the nozzle.

"Oh my, it looks like we have defective tubing. I'm so sorry, Mrs. Maynard. Just relax a minute; we'll be right back." She covered the patient and grabbed Stella's arm and dragged her from the room.

"What are you doing? Let go of me, Garrity!"

"Get in the prep room!" Polly ordered. Once there, Zedrich jerked around to face her partner as the firecracker exploded. Dropping the medical paraphernalia, Polly thrust Stella against a supply cabinet. One door flew open hitting her in the head.

Attempting to jerk away, Zedrich shouted, "Get your hands off me, bitch! I'm gonna tell Sis—"

Polly slapped her face. As the dazed Stella reached for her cheek, Polly caught the gauze and tape falling from the cabinet and grabbed Stella again. Adrenaline took over as she wrapped the tape twice around Zedrich's mouth and head while fighting her flying hands. Then she grabbed both and wrapped them with more tape and shoved her partner against the wall. Panting, Polly said, "You stupid, ass! Smell the solution!"

Stella coughed and gagged as ammonia fumes from the container stole her breath. Her eyes popped wide, and sparks from both pair of eyes collided. "You could have burnt that poor woman's insides and possibly killed her! Now, I'm going to let you go, and I'm going to watch as you mix the right solution. Then you're going to gently give Mrs. Maynard that enema while talking about how much fun the nurses' dances are or something stupid to help her relax through the procedure."

Zedrich closed her eyes and nodded. As soon as Polly let go and pulled the tape from Stella's hands she started fighting with the tape around her mouth and head. "Oh, stop it! You're getting it tangled and making it worse. Polly reached into the cabinet for a scissors and cut the tape, "Better fix your hair a little." Stella turned to the mirror, but when Polly bent to pick up the scattered supplies, Stella kicked her to the floor.

Before opening the door, Stella kicked her again, "I'm not giving a damned enema. I'm going to Sister Gregory! You are crazy, and I'm not working with you." She swung the door wide and exited.

"Be sure to tell her about your little fling with Dr. Jackson!" The door closed on these final words. Seconds later it opened, and Stella stared at Polly.

"What did you say?"

Turning her back, Polly began mixing solution.

"You don't know anything!"

Polly grinned. "Wanna bet?"

The door shut. "What do you know?"

"Not now! We have a distraught patient."

"You have to tell me what you know," Stella whined.

"We've kept Mrs. Maynard waiting too long already. Come on." Polly leaned against the door and took a deep breath. "I... I'm sorry I got so mean, Zedrich. I just couldn't believe you were so careless. I'll do the procedure, and then we'll talk."

Polly almost fell into Mrs. King as she opened the door. "So, this is where you two disappeared; I went to check on you, and a patient said she heard something crash in here."

"Oh, I dropped some of the enema equipment then got mad and kicked it against the cabinet," Polly lied. Mrs. King looked doubtful but followed her and Stella to Mrs. Maynard's room where Polly apologized for taking so long. Then she entertained the patient with stories about antics in the student nurses' home and ridiculous rules. Stella couldn't avoid joining the conversation with Polly's pointed questions. Mrs. King smiled approvingly before she left.

Soon the procedure was over, and Polly offered, "I'll empty the commode while you make Mrs. Maynard comfortable, Miss Zedrich."When she returned, Stella was saying, "The pinks and corals on this card blend so beautifully. It almost looks like a real sunset."

"Have you read the inside?" Mrs. Maynard asked.

Stella began reading but burst into loud laughter." That's hilarious, and totally unexpected with that dainty front." She handed the card to Polly who also began guffawing with the surprising remarks inside the card.

After making sure their patient was comfortable, they wished her a successful surgery and promised special care afterwards. Mrs. Maynard said, "Thank you both for being so kind. You'll think I'm silly, but I was more afraid of that enema than surgery." Tears rolled down her cheeks again, and this time Stella gave her the handkerchief before they left the room.

It was over an hour and three patients later before the young nurses had a chance to talk in the prep room. While cleaning instruments, Polly complemented, "Nice of you to talk to Mrs. Maynard about her cards, Zedrich. It gave her something to think about after the procedure."

"Thanks. I could hardly talk to her about Dr, Jackson." A quirky smile lit her face. "So, what do you know about us?"

Picking up on the "us," Polly controlled her sarcasm and answered, "Enough."

"You're just guessing, Garrity." Zedrich was irritated at herself for falling for Polly's lucky guess.

Polly put instruments into the autoclave and turned. "Must be nice to date a rich doctor who could pay Elmer off."

"How?" barely escaped Stella's gaping mouth when the door flung open, and Sister Gregory appeared.

"I see you made it through your first shift together." Looking directly at Stella, she asked, "Did you learn anything?"

"Much more than I expected." Stella glanced at Polly.

"Good. And you, Miss Garrity?" Sister asked.

"Yes, Sister."

"Stella, is that a bruise and welt rising on your face?" Both girls blanched.

"Uh, I was a clutz and hit my face when I yanked open the cabinet door."

"Hmph!" Looking dubious, Sister added, "You ladies better move it. You are missing supper." Their eyes followed hers to the clock which noted almost 6:30.

They both said, "Thank you, Sister," and hurried down the hall as Sister Gregory sighed watching them.

The dining room was half empty, and students were cleaning trays as the partners entered. Aggie saw her roommate and waved for Polly to join their table even though most were finished eating. After filling their plates, Stella shook her head to something Polly said and found a seat with another young woman. Polly relished the cool air from an open window near the table before she sat her tray down. She closed her eyes and rolled her shoulders then pulled out a chair.

"You and Zedrich are late," Eileen observed.

"Yes, but they're both still alive," Celie laughed.

"Yeah, we wondered if you two would have a knock down fight about every patient," Mildred Cavanaugh joked.

"Not quite," Polly mumbled.

"So how was your first shift with Stella?" Aggie noted Polly's subdued demeanor.

"It was ok." She broke off a piece of dinner roll and half-heartedly chewed it. "How were all of your rotations?"

Noting Polly's unusual demeanor, the friends glanced at one another. "We already talked about us," Cavanaugh said. "What's the matter, Polly?"

Celie added, "Was Stella that terrible?"

"No, I was terrible. I slapped her."

"What?"

"Shush!" Polly glanced toward Stella.

"Well, she must have deserved it," Cavanaugh declared. "I've wanted to belt her more than once."

Celie noticed tears welling in Polly's eyes and reached for her hand. "You want to talk about it?" Aggie felt her friend's shame.

"Not right now." Looking at Cavanaugh, she said, "Be glad you didn't get the chance." She twirled her fork in her mashed potatoes, took a bite, and wrinkled her nose. After taking a bite of peaches, she said, "If Sister Gregory's right about this rotation determining if I'm fit to be a nurse, today I failed big time." She pushed her plate away. "I need to go study." Her friends exchanged concerned glances. They realized how upset Polly was when she didn't call their supervisor Gorgon.

"Polly, Stella must feel guilty too because she obviously didn't run straight to Sister Gregory. You'd be packing and we'd all wonder what happened to you."

Polly half smiled. "Well, it's lucky I had that juicy scuttlebutt from you." In answer to Hay and Cavanaugh's puzzled looks, she reminded them, "Dating a doctor."

"Ooooh!"\

Glancing at the table where Stella sat, Polly waved slightly as she noticed her partner looking her way.

In an attempt to raise Polly's spirits, Celie said, "I'm sure you two aren't the only ones who've had a cat fight in the past few years. Slapping her isn't so bad; maybe it knocked some sense into her."

"Well if I'd only slapped her, it would be bad enough, but then I tied her up." Polly's friends stared in disbelief.

"Everyone to our room. Polly, you have to tell us the rest," Aggie insisted. "I can't imagine what could have happened, and you still walked into the cafeteria together."

"I need to study," Polly objected.

"We all need to study, but we won't be able to until we know the story about the Great Cat Fight at St. Francis School of Nursing," Cavanaugh joked.

Stella and her friend pushed through the cafeteria door. She glanced at Polly's friends. "All enjoying a laugh about Garrity putting me in my place?" she asked as she passed.

Aggie said, "No, we were actually trying to get her to tell us what happened because she's so upset at herself."

Stella glanced back without her usual haughty attitude but with the bruise more discolored and swollen. Looking directly at Polly, she said, "Forget it, and get ready for tomorrow. We have a big test and then surgical patients to care for."

"Was that a threat?" Eileen whispered after Stella moved down the hall.

Polly shrugged as the entourage followed her up the stairs. Realizing that she could never concentrate enough to study until she confessed, Polly replayed the scene in the prep room explaining how the supply cabinet door flew open banging Stella senseless. "When the tape almost jumped into my hands, I think I went berserk."

Gasps of, "You didn't really!" "How did you do that?" and "Remind me never to make you mad!" mixed with subdued giggles when the girls visualized the scene. Someone said, "You're such a skinny little thing; I didn't know you were so strong!"

"I used to help Dad wrestle down calves and hold 'em so he could castrate them." Polly's serious reply caused Eileen to muffle cackles of laughter with a pillow and caused the others to hold their mouths to keep erupting guffaws from bringing Hannah to the room.

Celie jumped up, "I'm gonna pee my pants," and she ran out of the room.

"Well, I'm glad you all think it's so funny." Polly attempted irritation. "I'm the one who acted like a banshee and could get kicked out after all this hard work."

"Polly, I don't think Stella is going to report you." Aggie

squeezed her shoulders. "She really acted a little remorseful. Besides," Aggie smiled, "we've all been under so much pressure, we needed a good laugh!"

Celie returned and said, "Sister Gregory's making rounds. Everyone grab a book and act like we're studying."

"If we're together, we need to be studying the same thing," Polly instructed. "Aggie, grab your notes, and start asking questions."

Hearing the rattle of beads nearing, everyone scrambled for studious postures. Hannah provided extra time. "Good evening, Sister. I was just coming to check this room. Someone complained that it sounded like a party in here."

"Well, it's quiet now." Sister reached for the door knob.

Polly had passed notes to Eileen and Celie, then opened her pharmacology book to share with Cavanaugh. As Sister opened the door, Aggie asked, "What is the recommended initial treatment of syphilis?"

Eileen cackled, "What?" and attempted to control snorting laughter.

"Why is that such a hilarious question, Miss Hay? You are aware of the current awful epidemic, especially among our soldiers?"

Everyone looked at Eileen in disbelief at her outburst and then at Sister who said, "Well, I'm waiting, Miss Hay."

"It's just pharmacology stuff is so confusing and hard. I was surprised Aggie asked something so easy."

"And what is the answer?" Sister probed. Eileen rattled the answer about penicillin protocol verbatim from the text, and her friends sighed collectively.

"Ladies, you know we discourage study groups. Sometimes, as Miss Hay demonstrated, the stress of exams can cause silly behavior. But, considering you all seem involved, carry on. However, no more outbursts or Hannah will disperse you to your rooms. Right!" She glanced pointedly at Eileen as she closed the door.

No one said a word until the clacking of rosary beads had completely receded. Then the room sounded like someone opened the valve on a huge balloon.

"My god, Hay, what a time to get the giggles!"

"Good lord, Aggie, what a question to ask as Sister walked in!I almost fell off this bed!"

"It was the first note my eyes focused on."

"Wow, Eileen, I'm so happy you knew that answer word for word after the excuse you made up. That was great!"

"Yeah," Eileen replied as she rose to leave. "But I wasn't kidding about the rest being confusing. I gotta go study alone so I can concentrate."

A couple of the others said, "Me, too."

"Well, thanks, guys." Polly became serious. "I feel lots better, but I don't want a word about today leaked from this room. Understand?"

Mildred replied, "Mums the word—until the commencement ceremony issue of The Stethoscope. I can see the headline now, *Survived to Graduate, After Cat Fight Rivaling Battlefield Action.*"

"You wouldn't!" Polly gasped. Mildred winked and gave her a quick hug.

CHAPTER 10

THE FOLLOWING AFTERNOON, as they prepared for duty, Polly asked, "So, Zedrich, I guess you breezed through that test like usual?"

"I'm really not bragging, Polly, but that is what I love about medicine: the research and reactions from combing elements and all the lab stuff." Stella was almost animated. "Obviously, the patient stuff is awful for me."

Mrs. King peeked in. "Hurry, ladies, don't want to miss report again." They followed her to the nurses' station where those going off duty were gathering. Each patient's status was updated. When the charge nurse said that Mrs. Maynard had expired after surgery, Stella and Polly were stunned. Miss Atkinson looked up. "I should tell you two that she mentioned to Nurse Martin that the two student nurses who tended her yesterday afternoon were real angels." She winked and added, "Now don't go gett'n big heads. Some procedures are disconcerting at first, and it helps to hear an occasional compliment."

After report, Polly said, "I can't believe Mrs. Maynard died. I had no idea she was so bad."

"Yea, and thanks again for giving her that enema, or else I'd be afraid that I killed her." Then Stella sighed loudly as she began getting supplies ready. "I know you'll find this hard to believe, Garrity, but I hardly slept at all last night worrying about what I had done. I don't think I can make it through this."

Polly shook her head as though dislodging webs of confusion. "Don't worry, I'll help you, and I promise not to whack you today." Her face flushed. The day went much smoother, and Stella completed the abhorrent procedure while Polly talked about the latest movies and antics of The Three Stooges.

After finishing the day's work, they were cleaning up when Stella commented that she and Dr. Jackson hoped to go to the movies Friday night and might just go see Meet John Doe. "Is it as romantic as you described to Mrs. Westbrook?"

"I have no idea. I was just repeating what I overheard. I sure don't have money for movies, and I don't have a handsome doctor to take me." Polly winked. "Zedrich, aren't you worried someone will recognize you with Jackson?"

"We never go to movies here in Wichita. We go to Newton or Augusta or someplace else. By the way, how did you know about us, especially about Maurice paying Elmer to keep quiet?"

"I have my sources." Polly laughed and added, "I'm starved. Let's go eat and hope for something better than leftover liver and onions smothered in mashed potatoes again." She hurried from the small room and motioned for Stella to follow. As they walked to the cafeteria, Stella tried unsuccessfully to discover how Polly knew that Maurice paid Elmer to keep his mouth shut.

The days of medical floor rotation seemed to fly by for Polly. She loved talking with patients and trying to brighten their days, knowing that she could help alleviate fears and pain. She also enjoyed trying to help her partner and often teased Pricilla to take life less seriously. Teaching her to relax and enjoy the personal side of nursing was her goal. One afternoon, she was embarrassed but proud when she glanced up to see Sister Gregory observing her guiding Stella as they tenderly cared for a critical burn victim. Sister's placid expression and quiet nod were the positive confirmation they both needed.

The day a patient's legs required redressing of abscesses, Polly asked Stella if she thought maybe Mrs. King should come observe. "I just don't feel confident with diabetic sores."

Stella's enthusiastic reply surprised Polly. "Oh, that is something I do know how to do." She adeptly removed the soiled, brownish stained wrappings and cleaned the seeping wounds. Then Stella applied ointment, being extra gentle where dried scabs had pulled away with the bandages. All the while this confident young nurse chattered about the patient's struggle with diabetes. Polly thought, Wonders will never cease, when Stella consoled the patient. "Now don't feel bad about your legs. Sometimes no matter how hard you try to follow your diet and medication, lesions occur." She suddenly stopped talking, and her hands trembled.

"Miss Zedrich, thank you so much for showing me how to take care of those ulcerated legs. Would you like for me to finish with Mrs. Marshall?" Polly asked when she noticed her partner's sudden, peculiar change. Stella rose, averting her face as Polly picked up the conversation with, "You're lucky Miss Zedrich is so skilled in tending diabetic wounds. I'm still learning."

"Miss Garrity, where is Miss Zedrich?" Polly's heart leapt, and she almost dropped the bandage she was winding when Mrs. King spoke.

"Gosh, she was just here. Maybe she went for more bandages."

"Looks like you're in good hands, Mrs. Marshall. Miss Garrity, a word when you finish."

At the nurses' station she said, "This is totally confidential, Polly. Sister Gregory is adamant that Stella is totally involved in all types of treatment during this rotation; that's why you're her partner. Sister told me she knew you wouldn't let her get by with some of the tricks she's pulled to shirk work during other rotations." Polly attempted to squelch a smile as Mrs. King continued, "So tell me why wasn't Stella helping with Mrs. Marshall?"

"Stella cleaned Mrs. Marshall's wounds and did everything when all of a sudden I noticed her hands shaking, so I offered to finish. I only was doing the final bandaging and didn't even know Stella was gone until you spoke."

"I didn't think you would let anyone walk all over you," Mrs. King laughed. "Now you better try to find Miss Zedrich."

Stella was slumped on the floor of the prep room, looking ashen and still hiccupping tears. "Are you sick, Zedrich?" Polly sat down and gave her partner a friendly shove. "Well, you better tell me what's wrong. Don't want me to hit you again, do ya?"

Stella attempted a smile. "Maybe you should; it seemed to get me through this rotation until now."

"Oh, come on, Zedrich; we're almost finished, and you're doing great. You were so fantastic with those diabetic legs that it give me the willies. But, then you disappeared. What happened?"

"Those sores looked just like my mother's did, but no one wanted me to be close when the nurses took care of her legs. Guess they thought I would be afraid of her because of how awful they would look. But, I used to hide in the wardrobe and watch the nurses change her bandages. That's when I decided I wanted to be a doctor and find a cure for diabetes. At first, with Mrs. Marshall, I almost felt like I was taking care of my mother. Then I thought about how much pain Mother was in by the time she died, and..."

"Jeez." Polly sighed. "I didn't know your mom was gone. But, why in the world are you becoming a nurse if you want to be a doctor? You're sure smart enough."

"My father made me. He's a hot-shot physician in Kansas City, so I could get into med school easier than most girls can dream. But, he won't help unless I finish nurses' training first. I'm sure he'd never make a son do this."

Polly started to ask a question, but Stella continued. "Dad said if I've worked with sick people, I'd be more dedicated to searching for cures during long, lonely days in a lab. He doesn't realize that I'd rather be alone most of the time." Glancing at Polly, Stella half smiled. "That's why I'm so uppity and mean."

"Good lord, Zedrich. I can't imagine going through all the past three hellish years and not even want to be a nurse!"

Stella half smiled and her eyes sparkled. "Hey, you wanna know something really funny?"

"Sure."

"I know you all think I'm Sister Gregory's pet. I know you do, so don't try denying it." Polly sheepishly shrugged her shoulders as Stella continued. "Well, she's my aunt, and she has made me do extra work every time she heard about me paying someone to do my duties."

"Really?" Polly gasped, as though surprised. "But, you've also been her little snitch too, haven't you?"

"I'm not proud of that, but I had to try to butter her up. She can be a real bitch." They both laughed as Stella continued, "That's why Daddy made me come here for nurses' training—didn't want instructors in KC to go easy on me. He said Hortense wouldn't let me get by with anything."

"Hortense! No wonder she's so mean. Who would saddle a baby with a name like Hortense?" They were holding their stomachs trying to squelch their guffaws when the door burst open.

"There she is," an obviously puzzled Mrs. King said to Sister Gregory.

The girls were instantaneously silent; as though someone had un-plugged a radio until Sister Gregory demanded, "What is going on here?"

They looked at one another and cackled as they both visualized baby Hortense with the face of Sister Gregory.

"When you two can pull yourselves together, you're excused for today. Oh, amidst your cackling, you might say a prayer for your class-mate, Miss Carlson. She collapsed this afternoon while working with a patient."

"Really!" "What's wrong with her?" "Is she ok?" fast fired from the two student nurses.

"Ladies, we don't know yet. She's probably just exhausted and for-got to drink enough water. Now get to the dining hall so you don't end up fainting also.

The young ladies left, and Sistershook her head. "Stress, happens every year the closer they come to the end." The sound of laughing echoed down the hall.

CHAPTER 11

UNSEASONABLY WARM spring breezes and bursting leaves seemed to reflect the young nurses' growing confidence and anticipation of graduation. Working full shifts and still studying didn't allow time to count the days. Even though illness and death were part of daily life, nothing prepared them when tragedy struck in their midst.

The sound of sniffling mixed with the jangle of rosary beads occasionally hitting wooden pews. Most who had finished this Catholic devotion were in tears. Their faces reflected anger, and unbelief when Sister Gregory announced that their classmate had lost her short battle with death. As prayers ended, most left the chapel with crumpled, damp handkerchiefs in hand.

Exhaustion painted their faces, making Aggie's words seem redundant. "I'm so tired; it hurts to breathe. Even though Sister told us to sleep a few hours before duty, I know I can't. Want some coffee, Polly?"

Polly nodded wearily and dabbed the tears that escaped her swollen, red eyes.

The canteen was filled with somber medical staff; many nodded as the girls headed for the large coffee pots and helped themselves to the heavy white cups and steaming caffeine. One group of nurses motioned for the girls to take their table then wrapped their young cohorts in hugs before leaving.

Polly's exasperation ripped away the shroud of silence. "This is 1943 in the USA, not Africa! How can someone die from appendicitis in a modern hospital? How did she get sepsis so fast? Why couldn't the doctors save Celie?"

Aggie squeezed her hand as they both quietly wept.

Polly put her head on the table and sniffled. "She was so sweet, and even stood up for Zedrich while she was still a rip." She lifted her head and wiped her eyes. "I don't think I can be cheery with the little kids in pediatrics today. I just want to curl up and cry for a week."

"I guess how we act today is the test if we're ready to be real nurses. At least we have time for a shower before we go on duty."

"I'm not sure anything will help me feel better. The faculty could never have designed a more difficult way to teach us to control our emotions with our patients. I couldn't believe Sister Gregory actually suggested we leave chapel and get some rest. Celie's death must have even chinked Sister's stony heart."

"Her's isn't the only one chinked."

"Huh?" Polly looked puzzled.

"That's only the second time you've said Sister's name correctly in months. Maybe you're maturing, Polly."

"Oh, hell, I'm just a zombie and don't know what I'm saying. Let's get a move on so we can look ravishing for the kids and old folks." They waved a couple of waiting nurses to their table then placed their cups on the conveyor belt.

Pushing through the canteen door, Polly was solemn. "I have a couple of darling five-year-old boys who need cheered. Suppose lots of bright stick lip will do the trick?" Polly's devilish grin shone on her tear-streaked face.

CHAPTER 12

POLLY, EILEEN HAY, Stella Zedrich, and a couple of other students were hanging crepe paper from lights and windows around a large room. Someone was setting up a heavy microphone when several young men in baggy zoot suits carried their musical instruments to the stage. Polly gasped when she noticed them. "What are they doing here already, and what in the hell are they wear'n?"

"Oh those baggy pants are the latest rage in California," Stella volunteered. "Saw them in *Vogue* a couple of months ago."

"How can you afford that ritzy magazine?" Eileen asked, forgetting Stella's background.

"We can't worry about fashions now. It's really late and we gotta get this place cleaned up so we can make ourselves look stunning," Polly tossed her hair with a la-de-da air. Eileen shook her head and began tossing crepe paper and tissue flowers into a box as others added to the collection.

"This wouldn't have taken so long if more people had helped. I know Cavanaugh had to work today, but where in the world are Deloris and Aggie?"

Eileen and Stella exchanged glances before Eileen said, "You haven't heard."

"Heard what?"

"Deloris won't be graduating with us," Stella said quietly.

"What? Why? Oh, Sister found out she's engaged."

"Even worse, she forgot to keep her knees together," one of the other girls nearby snickered.

"What? You're kidding!" Polly gasped.

"Polly, you can be so naïve. Why do you think she kept *forgetting* to take off her protective apron after rounds?"

"And didn't you notice her leave class a couple of times?" another young woman asked.

"Running to the bathroom during report when Sister Gregory was present sealed her fate," another chimed in.

"She would have made a great nurse, and she's finished all the work except finals. Couldn't she convince Gorgon that she was just sick—maybe appendicitis like Celie?"

Eileen answered, "I think Deloris was just so tired and sick she flew into a rage when Sister said no hussy would be part of her graduates." When everyone gasped, she continued. "Cavanaugh was in a bathroom stall and heard everything. Dee told Sister she was no hussy, and a hell-of-a-lot more Christian than she was who didn't know a thing about love. Then she told her that she and Robert had gotten married at Christmas when he was drafted."

"You're kidding! How did Gorgon react to that?" Polly gasped. Eileen could hardly answer amid all the exclamations. "Robert was drafted? No wonder she's been so depressed." "And she didn't tell any of us!" "I can't believe it!"

Eileen was finally able to answer, "Sister told Delores she was relieved of duties. She should call her parents, pack her things, and to please be out of the dorm by the end of the shift. Cavanaugh said she almost fell off the pot when Dee told her, 'I'm not calling my parents; I'm calling my husband who failed his physical. And then we will go celebrate that I don't have to put up with you anymore.' She told Sister that she really wanted to be a nurse, but she was so tired of pretending."

"When in the world did all this happen?" Polly sighed.

"Just last night," Eileen said. "You were on duty; and when someone went up to tell you, a patient had just coded, and, well, we all heard how crazy things on your floor were."

"So, we let you sleep til time to decorate. And, well, we didn't want to just burst out and tell you here with so many ears in and out."

"I just can't believe it. That makes me so sad." Polly flopped down in the middle of the floor.

Eileen pulled on her hand. "Come on, Polly. You can't be sad tonight. Like you said, you gotta shake a leg and get glamorous for the final dance."

Most of the girls headed for the door, chattering about the latest shocking news as Aggie entered through the same door. She was dressed in a brown tweed suit with coordinating hat, gloves, and heels. Polly said, "Hey, there you are. Why didn't you help decorate for our big shindig? And, why in the world are you dressed for a business meeting instead of the dance? Don't tell me you aren't coming to the dance either."

"Don't be silly," Aggie said while removing her gloves and pulling pins from the hat. "I may not be the sexiest gal in this place, but I do have a couple of racy things to sashay in. You ladies have the place looking real snazzy. Sorry I couldn't help."

"So what gives? Where've you been all day?" Eileen asked while picking up pieces of crepe paper.

"Well, you know how Polly teases about us getting drafted when we graduate next week?"

Hay nodded as Polly bristled, "Yah, but that was just a joke... I thought. Aggie?"

"Don't worry, Polly. It was a joke for you, but the government is begging for nurses. Today a couple of us took the bus to Ark City to complete the final recruitment steps. We'll be inducted into the Army as 2nd Lieutenants at graduation."

Clasping her hand to her mouth, Polly's "No!" was lost in the wail of the clarinet warming up. She brushed angry tears with her other hand as Hay gave Aggie a hug. The sudden crash of the drummer dropping his set mimicked Polly's heart.

"Oh, Garrity, don't be upset. We all have to do our part to help in this war, and everyone can't entertain the troops by shaking their tail feathers from the roof of the student nurses' dorm." Aggie laughed as she reached for Polly's hand.

Polly jerked backed. "How could you? I thought we were all going to be nurses here together!And then you and Cy were getting married. Now you're going off to some God-forsaken place and going to get killed, and... Oh shit! Oh damn! I'm so mad at you, Beat! Where did you get this stupid idea?" She stamped toward the door. Reaching for the handle, she abruptly turned. Tears streamed down her cheeks. Hay looked from one to the other, flustered. Polly finally walked back over, and all three friends hugged as Polly continued to cry. "This is your crazy freshman mentor's fault, isn't it! You always idolized that damned Mary McHugh. When she joined up, I should have known you would do the same thing."

"Polly, this has nothing to do with Mary. You're insinuating that I can't think for myself."

"I'm sorry, Aggie. I know if anyone has her own mind, it's you. Couldn't you have at least given me a hint you were doing this?" Looking at her friend she added, "What does Cy say?"

"Well, we've talked about it a lot, and he—oh my, he'll be here in less than an hour, and you'll finally get to meet my prince charming.

Need to get these dowdy duds off so I don't scare him away." Aggie winked at Polly and helped put decoration boxes behind the bandstand before they rushed out the door.

Charging up the stairs, Polly exclaimed, "Lordy, I wish I had a drink! This is just too much earth-shattering news for one afternoon!"

"All of this makes it seem real--- that we're graduating and leaving this place," Haysighed. "How will we survive without each other?"

"Darn it, Eileen, this is no time for nostalgia! I'm already a real mess after Deloris's and Aggie's bombs. It'll take me forever to look ravishing for the guys who show up."

"Think Johnny'll come in for the dance?" Aggie asked as they began stripping while barely in their room.

"Don't know. The few times I've seen him, he says it's so busy on the farm in the spring. It's been weeks since I saw him last and invited him to our big doinz! But, I'm gonna look gorgeous and ready to cut a rug with the guys who do come." Laughter, fragrant soap, and forbidden sensual perfume created a festive ambiance through air of the nurses' dorm.

Later in the evening, the allure of her gauzy yellow dress exuded romance as Polly danced in Johnny's arms. With the last notes of "Moonlight Serenade," most young women's heads rested on partners' shoulders. But, the dreamy atmosphere burst like an over-inflated balloon when the band changed tempo with "Boogie Woogie Bugle Boy of Company B." Polly gyrated to the jazzy rendition, shaking her hips as Johnny appreciated her enthusiasm and kept pace. When the song ended, he pulled her to him laughing, and they joined Aggie and Cy at a table along the wall.

"Boy these nuns sure don't know anything about atmosphere, do they?" Johnny said. "It's brighter in here than at my high school prom."

"Sure makes it hard to get a good drink," Cy added.

"What do you mean? These cokes look great; I'm dying of thirst. Thanks." Polly swallowed a big drink from the glass Johnny offered. Then she sputtered, "How did you?"

"Shshshshsh!" the group hissed as couples nearby glanced over.

"How did you guys get that stuff in here?" she whispered as they tried to conceal raucous laughter.

"Why do you suppose it used to be called bootleg? Getting it in was easy compared to getting it into the cokes with these eagle-eyed nuns." Cy glanced around. "I bet if they checked, 99% of the guys have a bottle. Right, Johnny?"

"Sure, and the nuns are dying for someone to drop one so they can have a nightcap."

Cy laughed. "Glad you showed up tonight, Johnny. If one of us gets kicked out, the other can keep the girls happy dancing." Everyone laughed as Cy glanced around the room. "I haven't seen Deloris and Robert. Thought they'd be here by now to enjoy one last dance before he ships out."

Polly and Aggie exchanged glances. "Speaking of getting kicked out," Polly whispered. "You haven't heard."

After Polly shared the news about Deloris, Johnny said, "None of that really surprises me, except I hadn't heard that he was finally told he didn't have to go. Sure hope the exemption was just for flat feet or something simple.

Aggie answered, "I think it is a heart murmur, and lots of people have those and never know it. If this war lasts much longer, they probably won't exempt guys for it."

"I can't believe Uncle Sam was going to snatch him up anyway, leaving his brother who had polio to run the farm alone," Cy added. "You know what that's like, Johnny."

"Sure do. Dad's too old to do all the work; it's hard enough with the two of us. But, Uncle Sam doesn't seem to realize that. I got called up a couple of weeks ago."

"What? Oh, Johnny!" Polly almost jumped out of her chair.

He pulled her down and wrapped a calming arm around her waist as Cy asked, "Ya think that was really Uncle Sam or that scheister, Bruenwortz? He only got to be head of the draft board for the local townships through some real underhanded shenanigans."

"But what about you being drafted?" Polly almost yelled impatiently.

"Calm down, Pauline. I'm not going anywhere; Dad couldn't make it without me. Bruenwortz didn't see it that way, though. That idiot insisted, even though my brother Alphonse is married and has a couple of little guys, that he could help Dad. Hell, Alph can hardly take care of his own place as crippled as his hands are."

"So what happened, Johnny?" Aggie asked snuggling closer to Cy.

"Dad had a fit when he saw the letter giving me 48 hours to report. We drove into Colwich right away and tried to call Charlie Williams, our legislator in Topeka. He wasn't in the office, so Dad sent a telegram and said we were going to drive to the capital on Thursday morning instead of me reporting for duty if we had to. Mom was jangling her rosary beads all day and was so nervous she could hardly fix supper. That night we were blowing out lamps, getting ready to go to bed when a car pulled into our yard -- scared us all---that time of night and three brothers serving. Dad put his arm around Mom's shoulder and nodded for me to answer the door. Instead of the awful news we were bracing for, Bill Osborne, the telegraph operator was smiling. He said he just got a call from Charlie who told him the telegram he was sending 'has to be delivered tonight.' Bill said, 'I was glad to drive out here with it. It's the only telegram in the last couple of years that's made anyone happy.' The message stated someone had made a mistake."

"Oh, thank God!" Polly sighed.

"That's wonderful!" Aggie agreed.

"Old Bruenwortz didn't think so. He was really pissed the next day when I walked in with the telegram ordering him to return my status to 3F and declaring there'd be an investigation into how it got changed."

"Oh, it makes me sick to think about you going. Why in the world did you say you kinda wanted to? I'd think you'd be happy to be safe here and get to dance with beautiful nurses." She giggled.

"There's lots of folks who are angry and make life miserable for guys like me and Cy. Can't understand why healthy guys like us are home when their son isn't. I can't really blame them, but they forget Mom and Dad already have three sons who are serving in the Pacific and Europe. Like I told you earlier, when we get a letter from Ben or Joe or Leo, I just feel like such a louse, especially with two of them younger than me facing the Nazis and Japs."

Statements of protest sounded from Aggie and Polly until the band moved into a new song that caught Polly's attention. "I think we've had enough serious talk." She mischievously pulled Johnny up. *"Is you is or is you ain't my baby?"* she sang with the band.

Johnny laughed and took another drink before following her seductive figure to the dance floor.

Returning to the table after the song, Polly asked, "Hey, did Cy tell you what Aggie did today?"

Cy smiled at his strawberry-blonde sweetheart. "I thought I'd let her share her patriotic news."

Johnny looked at Aggie as the music of "That Old Black Magic" enveloped them. She leaned across the table and described her day, ending with, "You are looking at future 2nd Lt. Agnes Beat. You may wait to salute." Cy squeezed her waist.

"Wow, that is some news. I guess, congratulations." Johnny was puzzled. "What do you think of this, Cy? Aren't you worried?"

"I'm quite proud of my darl'n."

"I'll probably be assigned here in the States to care for returning wounded. The VA hospitals are already overflowing, and some have been short staffed since a year ago when Roosevelt said the military had enough nurses and the Red Cross stopped recruiting. Guess he thought that the war was going to be over soon. Now there's a big shortage. And, if you'll excuse me, I have to go to the lady's room." She kissed Cy on the cheek as she left.

"I think I'll do the same, except the men's room," Cy excused himself.

Johnny watched them then turned to Polly. "Please, don't let this patriotic bug bite you," he whispered in her ear and pulled her close.

"Oh, you don't have to worry about me; I don't want to go to any warzone! I'm afraid of the sight of blood."

Rolling his eyes, Johnny shook his head. "I am serious, though," he said.

"And why should you care since you only see me every few months?" Her teasing was tinged with significance.

"Guess I'll have to work on that—if you'd like."

She squeezed his knee and nuzzled his ear in answer. Then moving away a little so she could see his face, Polly asked, "How are things with your brother, Ben? Have you heard from him lately?"

"What's the Church investigating?" Cy asked as he returned to the table.

"Oh, it's much too long of a story to tell again," Johnny said, as he stood up. "Besides, I want to dance." His hand caressed Polly's shoulder.

As Aggie returned to the table, the notes of "I'll be Seeing You" reverberated through the hall. "Darn, last dance already!" Aggie said.

"Guess we'll soon have to call that our song," Cy noted as he wrapped an arm around her shoulder. Moving toward the dance floor, he nudged Johnny. "Come on."

CHAPTER 13

"YOU TWO GOTTA HURRY! Don't want to miss your own graduation," called Cavanaugh as she left the dorm and Polly and Aggie dashed in.

"We know; can you come help us?" Polly begged.

Mildred asked, "Are you guys just getting off duty? Night shift ended over an hour ago."

"A lady I sat with all night waited til this morning to have her baby and begged me not to leave. Don't even have my good uniform ironed. I'd planned to get off early enough to do that." Polly took the stairs two at a time.

"Don't worry, I can iron while you get beautiful," Mildred reassured her.

"Lord, I need a bath, but I'll be lucky to wash my face and put on some make-up."

Keeping pace with her friends, Aggie added, "I'm so exhausted; I'd rather just sleep than go to the ceremony, but Dad and Mom would be so disappointed."

"To say nothing of Sister Gregory possibly holding your diploma if you didn't show up, Miss Class President. Were you working OB, too?"

"No, I was floating and having an easy night until about 5:00 AM. We had two emergency surgeries—some guys having a farewell party before reporting for duty. One of them didn't make it, and the other won't ever see action -- lucky if he ever walks again." The conversation mixed with other voices and laughter as young nurses left for graduation. Polly begged, "Mildred, I'll get my uniform ironed, but I hafta have some coffee and something to eat. Could you go to the canteen and sneak us up some donuts and huge cups of coffee?"

"Sure thing." She started back down the hall and bumped into two other nurses looking spit-shined and professional. "Hay, Polly and Aggie need help. Go to the canteen and get some coffee and donuts or something. If Roy gives you any grief, tell him it's an emergency and graduation day; it should be on the house. If he gets upset, bat your eyes and leave," she ordered. As Hay rushed off, Mildred grabbed Stella's hand and pushed her into Polly's room. "Start ironing their uniforms, and I'll help with their hair. I don't think those two can think well enough to know what they need."

Later, in the hospital chapel, the heels of the soon-to-be graduate nurses were heard clicking down the hall as they dashed into the foyer where they met Sister Gregory's icy glare. She handed Aggie the crosier to lead her classmates down the aisle. The others found their positions, and Hay squeezed Polly's hand and said, "Just think, last night was the last time any of us has to work without pay!Slavery ends now!"

During the ceremony, the new nurses were recognized for their achievement. Celie was remembered as a bright candle that was snuffed out before adding her light to the world. An empty place between two graduates marked the spot where she should have sat. Unfortunately, no spot was left for Deloris or the two other would-be graduates who had also been discovered married before their husbands shipped overseas. Diplomas would be mailed.

Father Schaffers thanked the young nurses of the class of '43 for making the sacrifice to forego a memory yearbook. "During this time of rationing, saving that paper and ink may seem insignificant, but each act helps our men and our government," stated the priest as the congregation nodded approval. Then he introduced the four young women, including Aggie, who would officially become 2nd Lieutenants at a ceremony later in the day. "Your patriotism is admirable and a testament to your generosity. We know that you will be with us a little while longer until Uncle Sam officially calls you into service. The anxiety of that wait is also a sacrifice, and we pray perhaps this conflict will end before that time. May God go with you and all of the graduates of St. Francis School of Nursing class of 1943."

Then all the young nurses rose to recite together, and Monsignor Schaeffers blessed the young women: "May the blessing of Our Lord Jesus Christ come upon you and remain with you forever."

"Amen." The graduates filed out of the large chapel wrapped in the inspiring notes of "Ave Maria."

White uniformed ladies and squeals of celebration filled a reception hall as congratulations were exchanged. "Oh, Polly, I'm so proud of you for not giving up," Cavanaugh crooned while hugging her classmate. Several of the new nurses within hearing agreed.

"You sound like you had doubts; that doesn't make me feel very good."

"Well, if you had packed your suitcase any more often that first year, it would have fallen apart," Hay chimed in.

"Oh, don't exaggerate! I was just a little homesick!" Laughing, Polly admitted, "I still almost puke every time I think about how miserable I was. The only reason I made it through that year was because someone was always unpacking that damned suitcase and hiding it." She tried to scowl at the circle of friends as each feigned mock innocence. Amidst laughter she added, "Besides, there just wasn't anything else for me to do. I'm too mouthy to make a good secretary." Then, glancing across the room, she said, "Oh there's my folks and my sister, Nonie, looking lost. I better get them some cake." She waved to a short lady and large gentleman who were obviously feeling out of place.

"Hi, Mom and Daddy. Hey, Nonie, you guys want some cake?" She put her arm through the crook in her mother's arm from which hung a large purse.

"That would be nice, Polly," her mother answered. "Do they have coffee, too?"

"Why don't you sit down with your folks. Nonie and I will get cake and drinks," said a familiar voice behind Polly. Her heart skipped a beat as she turned.

"You came," she sighed. "I didn't see you at the ceremony."

"It was pretty crowded," Johnny answered. "Hello, sir, I'm Johnny Wetta." He extended his hand to Polly's dad.

"These are my parents, Sara Pearl and Steve. I guess Johnny just told you his name." She was smiling like the Cheshire cat. "Let's sit over there with Hay and her aunt."

"We'll get some food. Right, Nonie," Johnny said, turning toward the refreshment table. Suddenly feeling the need for safety in numbers, Polly guided her parents toward Eileen and her aunt who were looking rather lonely.

After introductions, her father asked, "So, this Johnny fella must be kinda special to come to your graduation. How does he know Nonie?"

"Well, we met at a dance, and he's just a nice guy." Polly tried to be coy. "As far as Nonie, they—"

"Oh, Polly, nice guy my goat! He is super and you guys are head over heels!" Eileen interrupted. "No need pussy-foot'n around. Your parents aren't blind!" She winked at Steve as Johnny and Nonie returned with cake and drinks.

At the same time, Polly's sister, Helen, joined them. "Hi, Mom."

She kissed her mother and gave her father a loving hug. "Hi, Daddy. I sneaked away from work for a few minutes to congratulate my lil' sis." She gave Polly a hug and took a bite of her cake and was rewarded with a slap on her hand. "Hi, handsome, good to see you again," she greeted Johnny.

"Well, it seems everyone knows you, Johnny," Sara Pearl said, looking from him to Polly.

"Don't you just love these black stripes on our new nurses' caps?" said Cavanaugh, who had suddenly appeared with her parents. "You know what they are really? Dollar signs tightly woven together." In reply to questioning eyes she explained, "Now the nuns have to pay us for all the work we've been doing for nothing for the past couple of years." Everyone laughed. Then seeing Johnny, she said, "Well, hello, Johnny Wetta. I didn't know you were coming today."

"I didn't know myself until it started raining this morning. Can't cut wet alfalfa, so I got a few hours to watch all you lovely ladies become nurses." He winked at Pauline.

"Yeah, like there wasn't just one you really cared about seeing!" Helen scoffed. Then receiving a menacing look, she stole the rest of Polly's cake. "Thanks, lil Sis. That'll probably be my lunch; I gotta get back on the floor." She took a handful of peanuts from a bowl on the table and added, "Johnny, you'll be a sweetie and get her some more, won't you?" She gave him a peck on the cheek and told her parents goodbye.

Turning back to Polly, Helen added, "Oh, I almost forgot. I just saw Sister Gregory headed to the emergency room. She told me to tell you not to worry about moving out of the dorm today since you had to work the last couple of nights. I have tomorrow off, too, so I'll help you and Mildred move to your apartment. Maybe when my lease is up, we can find something together," Then she waved to everyone. "You all

have fun while I'm busy saving lives." Laughter and goodbyes followed
Helen as she hurried off, and Johnny returned from another trip to the
dessert table.

Polly took a couple of bites of cake then said, "I am starved for
some real food. It looks like the reception is toning down. Suppose
we can sneak off to Max's for some burgers? It's a little place across the
street." No one complained about that idea, but Eileen and her aunt
said they had other plans.

"I have to work tomorrow, Polly, but I'll help you move when I get
off if you can wait that long." Eileen said.

"I'm so tired, I might sleep til then. Thanks." Everyone shared fare-
wells, and the party moved to Max's.

Polly finished off the last of the fries and yawned. "Oh, I'm sorry I
should have asked if anyone else wanted the last of those."

Johnny laughed. "You weren't kidding about being hungry, were
you?" As he reached up with his napkin to wipe catsup from the corner
of her mouth, Steve and Pearl exchanged knowing glances. Then Johnny said, "This has been real nice, but that alfalfa will be dry by the time
I get back to the farm. I better be going."

Polly asked, "I know you say that your brother Leo isn't great at
farming, but can't he help your dad a while?"

"No, Dad needs more help." He replied in a strange, almost sad
tone before standing. Sara Pearl announced that they needed to head
to the depot to catch the bus back to Wellington. Steve and Max, the
café owner, were laughing over a fishing story when Johnny excused
himself and quietly paid the bill at the register. Then he left without a
real goodbye. Polly felt deflated. *It was nice of him to pay the bill, but he
didn't even say goodbye!*

Outside the café, Steve said, "I sure wish that young fellow would
have let me help pay for the food. Hope we get to meet him again,

Polly." He kissed his daughter on the cheek outside the restaurant. "He seems like a nice fella."

"Yes, but he sure was in a hurry to leave. Didn't say a proper good-bye," Sara Pearl noticed.

Before she finished speaking, a car pulled to the curb and Johnny came around to open the door. "I thought maybe you could use a ride to the bus station." The elder Garritys smiled, but Polly beamed.

After Steve and Sara Pearl got into the car, Johnny turned to Pauline. "Well, Nurse Garrity, congratulations, again." Her parents turned away from the windows as he gave her a quick kiss. "How are you ladies going to move your things tomorrow?"

"I don't have much, and we can stuff it in boxes and make a couple of trips if we need to. The apartment's not far." Polly stifled a yawn.

"You go get some rest. I'll see you sometime soon." Johnny's warm lips caressed hers with much more passion than earlier and left her breathless: then he sped off with Polly's parents.

CHAPTER 14

A FEW WEEKS LATER, Helen barely tapped the door before walking into Polly's small apartment. "Hey, Lil' Sis, wanna go to Max's for some hamburgers and cokes?" Removing the pins of her nurse's hat, she added, "Why are you staring at that chemistry book looking so glum? You've graduated!"

"Oh, Helen, I've wasted the last three years! I can't remember any of this stuff for State Boards. Just thinking of those two days of tests makes me feel like puking."

"For pete's sake! Stop the whining! You worried yourself sick all through school, now this! Polly, every nurse who ever lived was afraid of the boards, but they didn't drive everyone around them nuts!" Helen flopped onto a sofa, avoided a couple of springs, kicked off her white shoes, and massaged her feet. "Where's Mildred? Working?"

"Who cares as long as she's not here boozing."

"Having roommate trouble? Well, then you sure need a change of scene. Come on; brush your hair and put on some "stick lip" so we can get to Max's to celebrate payday." Helen walked into the bathroom to freshen up. "New graduates have to treat with their first paychecks."

Polly had been half listening, but "paychecks" snagged her attention. Helen jabbered while washing her face. "How did it feel to get your first real money?"

"Oh my gosh!"Polly rummaged through her purse. "I thought this was about breaking that syringe last week. I almost tore it up." Polly ripped open a white envelope. "Wow! 78 dollars! I'm rich!" She hugged Helen who shook her head.

"Well richer than yesterday. But, you drive me nuts, Pauline! That basset-hound face staring at a dumb chemistry book and worrying about that envelope all afternoon. You gotta start look'n for the parties in life, Pauline. Speakn' of, shake a leg so we don't miss any more fun."They met Mildred coming up the stairs. "Hey, Millie, ya wanna go to Max's with us?" Helen asked.

"Hell no, I already had something better. And it's Mildred not Millie." She pushed past Helen and Polly. "See ya later, Pols."

Excited chatter and noisy laughter greeted the sisters at Max's. White uniformed young women and others in jeans and tight knit tops were celebrating. A few young men in military uniforms or interns in whites were also jammed into booths, enjoying themselves. "Hey, Polly and Helen, over here," Hay called from a booth at the end of the room.

"What took you so long? We couldn't really party without the Garrity girls," Aggie added while scooting over in the booth.

"Oh, I had to drag Sour Puss Polly away from her books. She was studying!" Helen announced.

"Ya gotta be kidding!"

Someone had put nickels into a table juke box and "Straighten Up and Fly Right" surrounded them.

"I'm gonna buy that record and play it nonstop if she keeps worrying about State Boards," Helen announced as Polly glared and everyone laughed.

"One Coke and one root beer, right?" An elderly gentleman wearing a white apron sat the drinks on the linoleum table top.

"Thanks, Max; you're the best!" The sisters laughed. The group shared burgers and fries while regaling tales of the first weeks of being real nurses. "Nothing's really changed much," Cavanaugh said, "until today when I got $81 for doing the same work I've done for free the last year!"

"$81? I got $78!" Polly whined. "Hey, I just realized, we were told that we'd get at least $90 a month after taxes." Suddenly frustrated comparisons of discrepancies in pay replaced the festive atmosphere.

Finally, Helen stood on the seat and whistled shrilly. "Everybody calm down! Cost of anything you break is deducted from your pay until you pass the boards."

"Well, that's crappy!"

"We've been their slaves for three years; they owe us!"

Other complaints halted when Helen whistled again.

"Is this a party or a nag session? You were all happy until a couple minutes ago! Another round of Cokes, Max. This time on me!" The party atmosphere resumed as the juke box was fed, and everyone sangthe nonsense lyrics to "Mairzy Doats and Dozy Doats"composer in attributes at the end.

The following week, about 25 young women dressed in suits, hats, and gloves gathered in the train depot ready to board the 4:30 AM train to take the state boards to become registered nurses. The loudspeaker announced, "Central Chief arriving from Denver for Emporia, Kansas City, and points east." As passengers moved toward the platform, another young woman rushed into the depot and called, "Hey, wait for me!"

At least five voices chimed, "Deloris!" Suitcases banged one another as they welcomed her with hugs and questions. "What are you doing here?" "Can you take the boards without your diploma?" "It's so good to see you." Aggie patted her rounded belly.

They moved toward the train as Deloris explained that Sister Gregory had called her and their other expelled classmates told them that with the dire need for nurses, she would allow them to take final exams. If they passed, they could take the boards. "She even apologized for calling me a hussy," Deloris finished as the girls stowed luggage above seats. Gossip and laughing filled the car and distracted the young women from the tests that awaited.

Over the next two days they would have to prove their proficiency in psychiatric, surgical, obstetrical, pediatric, and general medical nursing -- and, of course, the dreaded pharmacology. The first evening, tears of relief and fear of failure replaced the friendly banter of the morning. At the end of the second day, most of the women were exhausted and slept on the train back to Wichita.

One afternoon in October, Mildred returned from work to find Polly staring at a manila envelope. "Well, how did you do?" she asked, noting Polly's pale face.

"I'm afraid to open it."

"For gosh sakes, Pauline!" Grabbing the envelope, Mildred tore off the seal, pulled the contents part way out, then smiled and handed it to Polly.

She pulled out the heavily embossed paper and flopped to the couch, "It's a miracle! I passed." A grin of disbelief spread across her face. "I really don't believe it!" Tears of relief welled in her eyes.

"Did I get any mail?" Mildred asked.

"Oh, I'm sorry; I forgot. Yes, you got a letter too from the Nursing Boards. It's on the table." The elation on Polly's face was replaced with apprehension as she realized Mildred received a business envelope, not manila. Her uneasiness was interrupted by noisy footsteps rushing up the stairs.

Aggie didn't bother knocking before barging in. She didn't have to ask when she saw Polly's face. They jumped up and down, hugging one another. "Let's go to Max's!" Polly squealed before looking across at her roommate. "Well?"

"Shit!" Mildred tossed aside her letter. "Don't wait for me. Think I'll head to the Brown Jug."

CHAPTER 15

ONE EVENING, Polly looked up from tending a young mother to see Sister Gregory observing. As Polly left the room, Sister said, "This is the first time I've had the opportunity to congratulate you on State Boards, Miss Garrity." Polly blushed as Sister continued, "You are young but quite capable. Would you be interested in being the head night nurse in the maternity ward? Of course, there will be a slight raise in pay." Polly's smile lit up the dim hallway.

Always stellar, Aggie was excited when Sister congratulated her and said, "We know you enjoy surgery, Miss Beat, but when things get hectic in emergency, you will be sent there. Your composure and quick thinking in stressful situations will be appreciated, and, as I told your mentor Miss McHugh when she was still here, it will be good prep for the military." Aggie thanked Sister who added, "You make us very proud, Miss Beat, for volunteering your talents during this awful war. By the way, do you ever hear from Miss McHugh?"

"I received a note at graduation; she'd just been accepted into the new flight school for nurses. She expects to be sent to England to care for the fliers who are wounded and lucky enough to make it back across the Channel. She asked for prayers in capital letters."

"God bless her, and you too. Maybe a miracle will occur and this debacle will be over before you have to report."

"Polly, how are things going with Mildred? She doing ok?" Aggie asked one day.

"I think so. I wish she didn't drink so much. She admitted that she had a bottle of vodka hidden in her suitcase when we took State boards. She drank the whole thing the first night to settle her nerves and had a ferocious headache the second day of tests."

"I can't imagine trying to take those tests with a hangover. At least she can work as a GN and take them again in the spring," Aggie said. "Hey, Cy's coming to town Saturday night, and we're going to the Blue Moon. Any chance Johnny'll be coming in?"

Polly shrugged but smiled wistfully. A farmer's free time was limited, especially with few young men to help older farmers. "Not sure, but I've already got another date."

"Really, Polly!"

"Yea, maybe we will see you and Cy at the Blue Moon. And maybe even Johnny."

Aggie started to comment but stopped herself. However, her raised eyebrows dimmed Polly's smile.

Polly had to work Thanksgiving Day, so she invited her younger siblings to the city to celebrate the following weekend. Nonie and Dorothy along with Buddy and Bob, came via Greyhound. Polly watched several young men in military uniform getting off the bus, and she laughed and shook her head when she spied her sister Dorothy's wild, red hair adorned with a soldier's cap. As she exited arm in arm with two young soldiers, Polly greeted her with, "You're lucky Daddy isn't here to see you." She gave her a slap on the rear and tossed the cap to one of the men.

"Ouch! Don't be jealous, Sis," Dorothy teased as she turned to tell the men goodbye.

Nonie, Buddy, and Bob followed. "Oh, it's so good to see you all!" Polly declared as her siblings appeared. Greeting them with hugs, she caught scrumptious aromas that even overpowered the diesel fumes in the bus bay. "Are those Thanksgiving leftovers?" she asked hopefully.

"And a special mince-meat pie Aunt Pete made just for her favorite niece!" Dorothy added. "You better thank me for not sharing it with the soldiers."

"She would have given them all the food if she thought she could get more attention!" Nonie gave her older sister a hug.

"It all smells delicious," Polly sighed, "definitely better than hospital Thanksgiving dinner." After collecting luggage, the Garritys trekked to the apartment.

"How far is your place?" Buddy asked.

"Only about ten blocks." Polly led the way, carrying one of the suitcases.

"Well, for heaven's sake, we should have asked some of those soldiers if they were going our way. They would have loved to carry our stuff," Dorothy declared. Her siblings rolled their eyes.

"What do we get to do here?" Bob asked, looking up at buildings taller than any he had ever seen.

"We'll talk about that and make plans over supper. Helen might get off in time to come over later."

"I know what I want to do," Dorothy exclaimed as she pointed for Nonie to look at the mannequins in store windows.

"Welcome to our humble abode. It's not much, but it's home," Polly announced while opening the apartment door.

"It's kinda small, isn't it!" Dorothy commented. "Where are we all gonna sleep?"

"Dibs on the sofa!" said Bob and Buddy as they started to flop on the sad piece of furniture with tattered brown upholstery. Uncharacteristically, Nonie had beat her brothers to the couch, so they tumbled on top of her.

"Be careful, it isn't very sturdy!" Polly warned as creaking wood complained, and the brothers slid off with help from Nonie's shoving.

"On second thought, the floor might be more comfortable," she said moving to one side to avoid a sagging center. "I think those springs are shot."

"I found my place," Dorothy called from the adjacent room where she sprawled across the bed. The boys were going to dive bomb her but halted when Mildred came out of the bathroom and stood with one hand on her hips.

"Not here five minutes and destroying our furniture! Who invited you guys anyway?" Then she laughed. "Our stuff is so ritzy, the roaches don't even like it! Hi guys, I'm Mildred and just so sorry I have to go out of town and miss you all."

Polly introduced her siblings before Mildred picked up a suitcase and laughed, "My sympathies, Roomy! Hope we still have an apartment when I get back Sunday."

After Mildred left, Polly playfully punched her brothers in the chest and stomach. "Great impression, guys. Don't be so juvenile! Pallets on the floor are better than our soldiers have!" Then turning toDorothy in the bed, she said, "If you value your life, out! Nonie and I will share the bed." As she stood in the doorway near the bathroom, a whiff of alcohol reached her nostrils and concerned her.

Dorothy brought Polly back to the scene when the young red-head sauntered past, patting her older sister's cheek with a sly smile. "The mattress isn't quite to my liking anyway. Rather lumpy!"

"Our furniture may not be the best, Lady Astor, but we are free and on our own!"

After the succulent, replayed Thanksgiving supper, Nonie suggested, "Maybe tomorrow you boys would like to go see the Boeing factory where I help build planes?" Animated questions flew from both, and Nonie finally said it would be easier to answer at the site the next day. "However, with all the security you can't actually get on the lots, but there are great observation decks. If we're lucky, you might get to see a plane coming off the assembly line."

"Well, I suppose I can tag along to see dumb planes if we get to go shopping first," Dorothy said. The boys groaned, and Polly promised something more interesting while her sisters window shopped and dreamed.

Riding the trolley to Boeing at the edge of the city, Nonie pointed out the area where she lived with some friends. "Too bad we couldn't live together," Polly said, "but that long trip across town all the time wouldn't make much sense, especially with winter coming."

At the factory, Dorothy pretended nonchalance as Nonie explained the assembly work in various buildings she pointed out and answered her brothers' questions about the huge facility. "This building closest to us is where the final assembly of the B-29s takes place," Nonie explained. "Every time a plane is finished, a huge bell rings and everyone cheers. It's pretty special and makes me feel like I'm helping our soldiers in a little way."

"How many planes are made here every month?" Bob asked.

"Right now, we finish three B-29s every day," Nonie answered with pride, "but the goal is at least four if the war doesn't end soon."

"Wow!" the boys exclaimed. "I hope it doesn't end until I get to shoot a few Japs," said Buddy. His older sisters attacked his romantic ideas with a quick lesson in the reality of war and made him wish he had kept this thought to himself.

Nonie continued, "Besides the big B-29s that I work on, other people in those structures farthest away build at least 275 trainers every month."

The boys were awestruck, and even Dorothy was impressed. "Really! That's almost ten a day! How many people work here?"

"The latest number I saw was over 25,000."[2]

Nonie explained a little about the assembly line. Then Bob asked, "Why do they build so many trainers?" but his words were lost in a loud noise and wild cheering as the enormous overhead door of the closest building opened. The rumbling roar of revving engines wiped out the cheering, and a gigantic plane nosed its way into view.

"Wow! She's a beaute!" Buddy exclaimed. "I can't believe how huge that thing is!"

"Yea, they're big but they fly super fast, and since they're pressurized, they can fly higher than other planes." Nonie couldn't hide her pride. The siblings stood in awe as history taxied in front of them and then out of sight.

"Sis, you should be really proud of your work," Polly remarked. "It can't be very easy."

"What do you do on 'em, anyway?" Bob asked.

"You've heard of Rosie the Riveter? That's me. Most of the time I crawl into tight spaces and rivet parts of the tail section of the fuselage. Sometimes I operate a grease gun—really very sophisticated work," she laughed.

"Yea, that's why you brought home those dirty, greasy coveralls to wash. Yuk!" Dorothy exclaimed. "What an icky job! I'd never do it!" she added adamantly.

"Well, it pays good, but I'm moving into the secretarial pool next week, so no more grease, and I'll still be part of the war effort. And that makes me proud. ."

"You should be, and you get paid a lot more than I do," Polly complimented her. Looking at Dorothy, she added, "I guess you'd rather be a nurse where you can dress in a nice white uniform?" she questioned. While her young sisterwas contemplating this, Polly added, "Then you can clean up puke and shit!"

Dorothy squealed, "Oh, never! Absolutely not! Never, never, never!"

"Thank God!" Nonie stated. "Pity the poor patients." All the Garritys laughed as Dorothyhmphed and put her hands on her hips.

"It must be time to catch the trolley back." She climbed down from the observation deck and stomped toward the stop.

That evening, the siblings sat on the living room floor bantering over Parcheesi when a knock on the door interrupted them. Polly's voice softened as she spoke to the visitor before he entered. Holding his hand, she said, "Everyone, this is Michael. We work together at the hospital sometimes. I told him that we might have an extra piece of mince-meat pie for him."

"What about our game?" Buddy sounded jealous.

"Bob and I were playing as partners, so you can continue without me."

"But we want you to play, too," Bob said.

"Maybe I should postpone that piece of pie for another time," Michael said.

Nonie rose from the floor, "No you won't. Hi, I'm Polly's sister, Nonie." Then she turned back to the floor. "And you boys are rude. Get up and introduce yourselves."

"It's ok." Michael moved toward the door.

"You are my guest, and these children are going to straighten up now," said Polly. "If they can't there will be no pie or molasses cookies for them."

"Hey, we aren't children," Buddy protested. "I'm a freshman in high school."

"And, I'm a junior," Dorothy added.

"Then I'd suggest you get up and start acting like it," Polly said. There was another knock at the door, but Helen didn't wait for anyone to answer. "Hi, all, I heard there was a Garrity party here." The younger Garritys happily gathered around their older sister. Then following Polly's eyes, the boys shook hands with Michael.

"Well hello, Dr. Burdett. I'm surprised to see you here." Helen couldn't restrain herself.

After the greetings, Nonie said, "Helen, you entertain Dr. Michael or Burdett. I'll help Polly get dessert," and pushed her to the tiny kitchen.

"Hey, whose house is this?"

"Who is this doctor fella? And what happened to Johnny Wetta. He seemed super!"

"He's also a farmer and never around. A girl has to be sensible. Michael is fun, and I get to see him more than once every couple of months, and he actually takes me to movies and things."

"Hey, you two are sure slow; we're hungry," Bob called from the living room.

"Coming," Polly answered, happy to escape Nonie's questions. She and Nonie served pie for all. "Here's a piece of the best mince-meat pie you'll ever taste." She sat down next to Michael and thought, *Oh Lord, am I doing the wrong thing?* She dreaded the grilling that would come from both Nonie and Helen later.

The following week, as Polly got off duty, Dr. Michael Burdett was walking down the hall. "Hi, Polly, I was just coming to see you."

"Well, you are a lucky man—five minutes, and I'd be out of here on my way home."

"I'm almost finished for the day too. Would you like to join me for a cup of coffee at Max's? I can come back and finish paperwork later."

As Polly relished a bite of cherry pie, Michael asked, "Have you heard that the Benny Goodman band will be in town in a couple of weeks for a special Christmas dance?"

"Who hasn't? Playing at the Silver Notes, right. That should be a wonderful dance. I love his music, especially 'Stompin' at the Savoy.'"

"How would you like to get romantic with me dancing to their music?"

"Oh, Michael, that would be so much fun and so exciting. But, I heard the tickets were gone before most people knew Benny was coming, and they must cost an arm and a leg."

"Don't worry about that. I have connections." Michael smiled as he touched the corner of her mouth then licked his finger. "Little cherry pie missed your mouth."

The bell above Max's door jingled and Polly's heart almost stopped when she saw Johnny Wetta looking at her and Michael. He turned, and as he left the world stopped with the clang of the bell.

"You know that fella?" Michael watched Johnny disappear and noted the transformation of Polly's face.

"Yea, met him at some dances out at Colwich. He's probably looking for Helen or Eileen. They cut a mean rug together." Her attempt at nonchalance was unsuccessful.

"Well, I need to get back to the hospital and finish some work before I forget what I did for which patient; otherwise, I'd walk you home. You ok, Polly?"

"Oh sure, long shift just catching up, and I need to get out of these shoes. Thanks again for the invitation to Benny. That will be so much fun."

Michael helped her into her coat. "This thing feels threadbare; you better ask Santa for a new one." Outside, a blustery wind wreaked havoc on Polly's hair. He gently pushed it from her face then kissed her on the forehead. "We can make plans for the dance later." When he kissed her again, his warm mouth met a numb reception.

Damn, damn, damn, Polly, stop feeling this way, she scolded herself while walking to her apartment. *Michael just invited you to a dance everyone is trying to find tickets to. What the hell is wrong with you? Like Johnny would ever take you to something like that!* She slapped herself. *That's not nice; he's a great guy, just doesn't have time to think much with—*

Her self-chiding halted as she turned the corner and saw a farm truck parked in front of her apartment house. As she neared, Johnny got out and she controlled herself not to run and throw her arms around his neck.

"Hi Johnny," she beamed.

"Hi yourself." He was not nearly as thrilled.

"What are you doing here?"

"Frankly, I don't know after what I saw at Max's. I started to just go home and then decided I needed to get something cleared up. So, I turned this damned, stinky truck around and came here." He seemed both embarrassed and annoyed.

"Let's go inside; it might smell better." Polly attempted a joke.

His face showed it had fallen flat, "You always entertain two fellas on the same afternoon? My old farm truck not good enough for you?"

She tried to take his hand, but he jerked away, which ignited her Irish. "Damn it, Johnny, your truck is just fine, but how am I ever supposed to know if you are even going to show up again. You call maybe once a month and expect me to be free to go to the Blue Moon or someplace at the drop of a hat."

"Well, excuse me for needing to work and not having a phone or …" Their eyes exchanged angry fire. Then his passionate lips met hers, receiving a passionate welcome. When they separated, both almost gasped for air. He said, "I think we better move away from this truck to talk."

"Wanna come up?" Polly asked as they reached the apartment house steps.

"No, I gotta get back to do chores. It'll be dark by the time I get home now. Hadn't planned to be in town this long."

"What are you doing here on a Thursday afternoon and in the truck?" She folded her arms around herself to ward off the cold wind.

He pulled her close. "I brought a load of hogs to the stock yards. Hoped to catch you at the hospital before you got off. Sister Mary Joseph told me you were already gone, but she thought you went to Max's with a friend. I think that doctor is more than a friend."

"How would you know?" Polly was defensive.

"The way he was looking at you. What's going on, Pauline. I thought we had something special."

"You are special, Johnny, but am I?" His face immediately flashed anger. "Don't go getting mad again, but I never know about you. Like I said, you don't call, and I never know when or if you're going to show up. I get damned tired of hoping you do, just to be disappointed so many weekends. I know that you're doing the work of three men with all your brothers gone now, and older farmers needing help. But you do know how to write a note, don't you?Or can't you call me from the town telephone office?"

"I guess I'm so tired at night, I forget. Guess I need some lessons in how to treat a special lady."Hesitating, he reached into his pocket. "Will this help to make up for leaving you on a lurch so often?" He handed her tickets to the Benny Goodman Christmas Dance. "These mightbegin to show how special you are."

"Oh no," she gasped with tears in her eyes.

"What's the matter? I thought you would be excited to get to dance to the biggest… That doctor already asked you."

Tears ran down her cheeks as she looked up at him.

"Guess I have quite the competition. Handsome, rich, and close by."

"Johnny, you are just as handsome, and the money doesn't matter, but the being close… I'd much rather go with you, but that wouldn't be right to Michael since I already… Maybe you can ask someone else, and we could sneak a couple of dances with each other."

"Hell no." At his words, Polly pulled away. "I'm not going anywhere I have to watch some other guy with the most special woman I've ever met. You go with Michael, but then we need to figure us out."

"Sure you can't come up for a minute and warm up so we can talk more now? What will you do with those tickets? I know they're awful expensive."

He pulled his hat on and kissed her gently. "Gotta get home before Dad kills himself with the chores. Don't worry about the tickets. Jim Meyer will probably buy them from me. You know that he and your sister Helen are becoming quite an item."

"Really! Helen failed to mention that when she gave me hell for dating Michael." An embarrassed smile met his eyes. "I'm so sorry, Johnny."

"We'll talk later." He walked to the truck and started the noisy engine then chugged off leaving a ghastly trail of the stench of hog manure in his wake.

Polly's head continued to rest on Michael's shoulder after the final notes of "I'll Be Seeing You" had faded. Benny Goodman thanked everyone for coming and wished all a Merry Christmas, but Polly still lingered in Michael's arms until she heard Helen's voice. "There you are. Been looking for you guys."

Polly jerked her head up and blushed when she saw Johnny's cousin, Jim Meyer. "Jim, this is Dr. Burdett." Helen introduced the men, who shook hands, but Jim didn't look overly friendly.

"Michael," the young doctor clarified.

"Hey, you guys want to go some place to eat? I'm starved after all that dancing." Helen was oblivious to Polly's discomfort.

She looked from her sister to Michael, who said, "I made reservations for us. Maybe we can do it some other time." Polly thought, *Thank God, last person I want to be around with Michael is Johnny's best friend, ruining a perfect evening and making me feel guilty.*

"Yea, thanks for the invite, Helen. Nice to see you, Jim," she lied, and the couples lost one another in the crowd.

"So where do we have reservations?" Polly asked as Michael helped her into his car.

"A surprise not far." Michael was mysterious. "So, who is this guy Helen's dating? He didn't seem real friendly."

"Oh, I think he's ok. Don't know much about him." Michael pulled her close as her black satin dress slid easily across the car seat, and she rested her head on his shoulder. She was thinking, *Where did the romantic, dreamy feeling go? Damn why'd we have to run into Jim and Helen?*

"Have I told you that you look ravishing tonight, Polly?" Michael nuzzled her hair and then turned her face toward his when the traffic light turned red. As their lips met, she relaxed in his embrace until his hand moved from her shoulder to under her faux fur wrap and gently caressed the side of her breast. A horn sounded behind them.

"I think you better drive, Michael, and yes you told me. Thanks," she said, but thought, Oh shit, now what? She shifted just enough to gently move his hand. "Wasn't the band fantastic? They sound even better in person than on their records."

"Yes, they were great. What was your favorite song or part of the evening?" His hand had dropped to her hip.

"Gosh I don't know—music or drinks?" she giggled. "I really loved the champagne; I've never had it before," she giggled again. "But for the music, 'My Sister and Me' makes me think of Helen or Nonie and me, but 'I Can't Give You Anything but Love,' is so romantic and so real with how broke I am. How about you?"

"Definitely 'I'm Glad There is You.'" Michael began to croon, "In this world of ordinary people, extraordinary people, I'm glad there is you. In this world of overrated pleasures and underrated treasures, I'm glad there is you."

"That's so sweet." Polly kissed his cheek. "You have a great voice."

"Years of glee club and church choir." He pulled over to the curb.

"This doesn't look like a restaurant." She stared up at what appeared to be an apartment house, *hopefully not a hotel!*

"Hope you don't mind. I thought we could listen to some more Goodman or Dorsey without the noise of waiters and other diners."

As he opened the car door she said, "Well, that would be nice, Michael, but like Helen, 'I'm starved after all that dancing.' I really need something to eat."

"Don't worry; Innes Tea Room prepared a nice assortment of food for us, and I had my maid come in and set it up. I tried to make reservations at a couple of places yesterday, and the maître' ds laughed like I was nuts. Said they'd been booked solid for tonight since people heard Benny would be in town." He took her hand and helped her from the car. Nuzzling her ear, he whispered, "The maid should also have more champagne chilling."

"Well, that definitely sounds good." Polly relaxed as Michael's arm around her shoulder guided her to the door.

As "Baby It's Cold Outside" played in the background, Michael poured the last of a bottle of bubbly. Polly said, "Ok, but this is definitely my last glass." She enjoyed the candlelight reflected in the clear, golden liquid before taking a sip. Relaxing in his arms, she relished another sip before he set her glass on the coffee table. Then Michael pulled her against him on the couch and licked champagne from her lips, caressing them with his tongue. Looking up into his eyes, she pulled back slightly. "Maybe I shouldn't have anymore; I might not make it up my stairs."

"You don't have to," he whispered into her ear as his hand reached under her dress and caressed her thigh and sneaked his handfingers toyed under the edge of her panties.

Polly put her hand firmly on the top of the skirt of her dress to halt Howard's. "What do you mean?"

"Baby it's cold outside; we could keep each other warm all night." He pulled her back against him and passionately kissed her neck as a finger stroked the edge of her breast before his hand slid inside her bra and gently cupped it.

Polly thought, *Oooh that feels nice; I know I should make him stop, but...* She sighed instead and enjoyed Michael's hands fondling unexplored areas, arousing sweet sensual pleasure hitherto unknown.

Her head rested on the back of the couch as his lips nuzzled her breast. When his hand began to pull down the elastic of her panties, a siren sounded in Polly's brain, and she opened her eyes. *What am I doing?*

Grasping his hand, Polly sat straight up. "Michael, this has been a perfect night, but I think you need to take me home."

"Ah, come on, Polly. There's just one thing missing from this being as you said perfect." He pulled her to him, and his hand was suddenly grappling with her panties."

"No, Michael." She jumped from the couch, "I don't do that!"

"Ah shit! You're kidding!"

"No, and I don't plan to until I have a wedding band on my finger."

"You mean, you never? I didn't take you for being so old-fashioned!"

Polly snatched her coat from the floor. "Are you driving me home, or do I need to walk?"

"Don't be stupid; it really is cold outside." He rose from the couch and picked up his overcoat.

"Oh, so now I'm stupid!" Polly jerked away as Michael attempted to help her into her coat.

"Don't ruin a great evening, Polly." Michael opened the door for her.

In the car, Polly broke the ice. "I'm sorry, Michael. The dance was really fantastic, and the champagne and… Even if we did… well you know. I just can't imagine working with you every day after. Besides, I really believe sex should be special, just for the person you marry."

"Hmmm," he sighed. "Polly you have no idea how many doctors and nurses 'play hospital' after hours." Feeling her chagrin, he added, "You're so innocent; I think maybe that's what makes me want to be with you. But, you're right, that's exactly why working together after would be hard, especially for you. But, it sure would have been fun to take the risk." His devious grin spoke volumes. And she had enough champagne to fondle the thought, wondering if she was a prude.

CHAPTER 16

WHEN POLLY'S BROTHERS came for Thanksgiving, they had brought along strange items that she had requested. However, she wouldn't divulge her plans. During the month of December, Mildred received the same mysterious shrug each time she questioned the long-johns and socks soaking in red or green dye in a couple of discarded buckets Polly had found at the hospital. Her roommate presumed these things had to be part of Polly's exuberant Christmas spirit. Shortly after Thanksgiving, her roommate began decorating their apartment until Mildred finally wondered, "What are you doing, competing with Bucks and Innes's?"

"No, silly. It's just the first time I've ever had any money to buy anything, and I want Christmas to be special. I'm so tired of people being sad because of this stupid war. Besides, have you seen the window displays at those stores? O my gosh, Mildred, one has a six-foot Santa that laughs and waves, and another has a train with steam that whistles as it rumbles on tracks under Christmas trees decorated with tiny flags. It's so much fun to live in the city and have a little money for a change."

"You might have money, but mine barely stretches between pay-checks," Mildred complained.

"It would probably go lots farther if you didn't have such selfish friends."

"What are you talking about? I don't have selfish friends."

"Old Charter and Jack Daniels are stealing you blind, Mildred. And not just your money but your zest for life. All you do is sleep when you aren't at work or at the bars."

"Well, Miss Goody Two Shoes, you enjoy your share of booze, so don't act so high and mighty!"

"I know I like to drink plenty, Mildred, but I'm worried about you. You've been throwing up and hungover so bad you barely make it to work. Nurses on your shift have asked about you."

"You're all a bunch of prissy bitches talking behind my back!" Grabbing her purse, she sneered, "Guess I'll give you something to really talk about," and the door slammed.

Polly shook her head. *Guess I really blew that. Dear Lord, let me know how to help her.*

The unmistakable sound of someone puking awoke Polly the next morning. Oh shit! she thought opening the bathroom door to be greeted by the rancid odor of vomit. "You ok?"

"Do I look ok?" Mildred gasped lifting her head from the commode. Bits of vomit clung to her stringy hair, and a swollen cheek wore a bluish-green bruise.

"What in the world happened to you?" Polly reached to the shelf above the stool for a washcloth and soaked it with cold water before attempting to place it on Mildred's forehead. But, the hungover roomie retched in the bowl again. After this bout subsided and Polly gave her the cool cloth, she glanced at her watch for the first time. "Mildred, you're already late for work. Let's get you cleaned up fast."

"Polly, there's no way I can work. Could you please"—She jerked back to the stool with dry heaves.

"Damn, Mildred, I have to work the night shift." But Polly threw on her uniform and was soon out the door sprinting toward the hospital, thinking, *Jeepers, Lord, when I asked you to help me with Mildred, this isn't what I meant!*

One Saturday not long after, Polly, Aggie, and Eileen Hay were downtown shopping. As they stood outside a store window admiring the patriotic display of Santa and his elves with US flags flying from their packs, Christmas Carols from a small choral group added to the atmosphere. That's when Polly noticed tears rolling down Eileen's cheeks. "Thinking about Bill?" she asked, handing her friend a handkerchief.

She nodded and brushed tears away. "I really hoped the boys would be home this year. Amazing how much I miss that pain-in-the-butt brother. I even miss his goofy friends and worry about all of them!"

"I know; we just gotta keep praying our troops can defeat Hitler and the Japs soon." Polly hugged her and looked at Aggie with special meaning.

"Speaking of pains-in-the-butt, how are things with Mildred?" Aggie asked.

"I think a little better. She's slowed down the boozing since the night she fell in the street and was so under the weather she couldn't get far from the john for an entire day."

"Lucky she had you to cover," Eileen said.

Polly changed the subject. "You know we need to plan something special at the hospital since we all have to work Christmas Day. I don't want to spend it depressed and down in the dumps with the poor freshmen. Remember how I cried so much Christmas day the year we had to stay and work. I think it was harder on me than the patients."

"Why do the nuns always make the freshmen stay here on Christmas? I think that was the worst day of all nurses training," Eileen remembered.

"Maybe they're trying to teach that seniority wins privileges," Aggie suggested. "Someone is always sick, so someone will always have to work, even on the most special days. Since we are low people on the totem pole again, we have to work. At least we're assigned day shift. So, what has your crazy mind already been dreaming up, Polly?" she asked.

"Let's have some hot chocolate and talk about it." They stepped into a small café where she shared the ideas that had been brewing since Thanksgiving, not only in her mind, but also in the buckets of dye. When they left the café, they bumped right into Dr. Michael Burdett.

"Hi, ladies, I'd offer to buy you a cup of coffee but looks like you just enjoyed some." He dabbed chocolate from the edge of Polly's lip and smiled suggestively as she blushed.

"Yea, we were just heading home," Eileen said with an air of diffidence.

"But Polly can stay and visit," Aggie added almost apologetically.

"No, I have things to do. Nice to see you, Michael."

"I'll stop by later." He touched her shoulder before watching them walk away.

"Thanks lots, Aggie. Like I need your permission to spend time with Michael."

Aggie was taken aback by Polly's outburst. But, Eileen ranted, "Well, maybe you need to think about what you're doing. Are you playing him or going to break Johnny's heart? Do you even know what's happening?"

Polly stopped and looked at her friends. "I'm sorry, Aggie. And no, Eileen, I'm not sure at all what I'm doing. I thought I really liked Michael, but after the night we went to Benny Goodman dance—well, things are kinda weird. But Johnny's so seldom around even now.

"So what happened at the sensational dance?" Aggie asked as they walked along.

"Nothing at the dance and nothing that Michael wanted afterward at his place."

Eileen asked, "What did he want at his place?"

But Aggie gasped, "Really! He tried to get in your pants?"

"What? He did what?" Shoppers streaming by bumped into them as Eileen halted, open mouthed.

"Shhhhh! For heaven's sake, Eileen! We're not talking about it."

Eileen and Aggie exchanged glances, and Eileen was emphatic, "Maybe not here, but we sure are talking about it when we get back to the apartment!"

If she had to work on Christmas, Polly was sure the maternity ward was the best place to be. Each infant seemed more miraculous than usual. Monsignor Schaeffers and the Sisters made visits to all the patients and gave each new mother and baby a small crèche. Before leaving, they told Polly and the student nurses to have a blessed holiday. Sister Gregory reminded her to call over to the convent if things became too hectic, but Christmas was usually quiet at the hospital. It was one of the only days the Sisters did not work unless absolutely necessary.

At noon, Polly told a couple of the students to pass the word that there was an emergency meeting at the main desk. As the puzzled young ladies gathered, Polly noted many puffy, red eyes and glum faces. But smiles transformed their faces as she took the pins from her nurse's cap and donned a Santa hat that she had made from red flannel, tinsel, and bells. She knew that her friends were doing the same on other floors. Because Polly, Aggie, and Eileen knew the student nurses might get in trouble with silly hats, they gave each an angel halo made of silver tinsel and pinned tinsel angel wings onto the pockets of their stiff white uniforms.

"Now try not to let that fall into a bedpan!" brought laughter from all. Then she said, "I remember my freshman Christmas; I think I cried with every bedpan I cleaned. I'm sure I even cried tears into some of the patients' bath water." This brought more laughter amidst some eye dabbing and nose blowing. Then Polly winked at the young women. "Let's make today special for the patients, and it will be a fun day for us."

Local school children supplied red and green holiday mats that replaced the standard white mats on the lunch trays. Polly told all the student nurses that since they had so few patients, they should deliver meals in small groups and sing Christmas carols. By the time their shift ended, the student nurses were almost reluctant to leave Polly, who was finishing her charting still wearing the silly Santa hat.

The threesome met after their long shifts ended at 7:00. They retrieved the contraband they had collected from several hospital linen closets or brought from home, and then they sneaked into the student nurses' dorm. Once in a restroom on the freshman hall, they locked the door. There, Eileen and Aggie squelched laughter as they tied three pillows around Polly. Someone knocked on the door, but Aggie shouted, "Go away! I need some privacy!"

"What?! This bathroom is for all of us. You can't lock the door!" She knocked louder.

"Go away!" Aggie put her face into one of the pillows to muffle her laughter.

"Well damn, hurry up." The voice outside sighed as she moved away.

After Polly's pillows were secure, Eileen and Aggie giggled while pulling on green-dyed long underwear, and Polly stretched a pair of huge red long johns over the pillows. Then she pulled on a beard fashioned from sanitary napkins, and donned the Santa hat that she had worn all day. She tossed similar green ones to her friends. By this time, Eileen was laughing so hard she could be heard outside.

"Ok, I want to take a shower. Open this door, now!"

"We look like rejected elves! Where in the world did you come up with this idea, Polly?" Aggie looked at her friends and then at herself in the mirror. She applied large circles of lipstick to her cheeks and tossed the tube to Eileen, who struggled from the floor where she had been attempting to pull on ugly green socks.

Another voice demanded, "I need to go to the bathroom. Let me in before I pee my pants."

"Well, elves, I don't think we can hold them off much longer!" Polly said. "It's show time! We better hurry." They tossed a conglomeration of decorative hair pins, combs, lotions, and other small gifts from brown paper bags into pillow cases they held open for each other.

As they slung the white sacks over their shoulders, keys rattled at the door, and a familiar voice demanded, "What are you doing locking this bathroom door. You know that—"

"Ho ho ho, Merry Christmas!" Aggie and Eileen jerked the door open, revealing Santa Claus and his elves. There were squeals of happy surprise and delight. Along the hall, doors opened and other students joined the parade moving with the visitors from the North Pole. Hannah, the ancient dorm mother, stood in shock. Eileen noticed and grabbed her hand.

"Now, Miss Hannah, you come along with Frederick to the lounge, and we'll see if Santa has something for you." Then she let forth her unforgettable, cackling laughter. Hearing Eileen's infectious giggling, an unfamiliar smile lit Hannah's face.

After all the girls and their house-mother had received gifts and Santa and her helpers were paid with many grateful hugs, the three spirits of Christmas headed to the restroom to change. Aggie took off her hat and looked in the mirror and smiled. "You know, none of us works in peeds so they missed our holiday celebration. Since we're still dressed in these holiday getups, let's go see the little kids."

"Aren't you afraid we might scare them?" Polly uncharacteristically questioned. "As you said, we do look pretty ridiculous."

"Oh, if their parents or the nurses on duty think the kids will be scared, we won't go into those rooms," advised Eileen.

The strangely outfitted trio visited several wards of St. Francis hospital on Christmas night in 1943. As word spread that Santa and her friends were in the building, requests for their appearance bounced from ward to ward. When the young women were finally walking back to the bathroom to retrieve their clothes, they were exhausted but still laughing with the fun.

"Gosh, I'm starved!" Polly realized. "We were so busy, I didn't have time to eat much all day. Just munched a few goodies patients' families brought."

"Same here," said Eileen.

"I don't know if I'm more tired or hungry," Aggie commented. "But I know if I go home without eating, I won't be able to sleep, and I gotta get my beauty sleep. In the morning, Cy's coming to take me home for the day."

"Ohhhhh!" her friends teased. "Well, the canteen's already closed. Where shall we go?" Eileen asked.

Polly said, "It's Christmas. Nothing will be open except—"

"Max's!" the friends finished together.

As she started to remove her costume, Polly looked at her friends with a huge smile. "Shall we?"

"What?" Eileen asked, confused.

"Visit Max's as Santa and her elves," explained Aggie.

"That'll be hilarious!" Eileen burst out laughing again.

The three entered Max's, and a tired looking waitress dropped a piece of pie and gawked. Then she smiled like a child on Christmas Eve. The four or five lonely customers applauded, and Max came from behind the counter to eye his visitors. Looking at each carefully and pulling down slightly on Santa's beard, Max said, "Well, Miss Elf Hay , Miss Elf Beat, and Santa Garrity, I bet you all had to work all day didn't you?" In reply to their nodding heads, he said, "Christmas supper is on me."

When they finished their burgers and fries, Max brought each a piece of cherry pie with ice cream. "Thanks, Max, you're the best," they chimed together.

"No, you ladies are!" he replied, shaking the little bell at the tip of Aggie's elf hat.

Polly said, "I'm so exhausted, I don't know if I can make it home."

"You could sleep at my place," Aggie offered. "Maggie's gone, and I'll be quiet when I get up. Cy isn't coming til after 10:00, and you know no matter how tired you are, you'd never sleep that late."

"Sounds great, your place is closer and I hate going home to a dark, cold apartment alone. What about you, Eileen? Is your aunt home?" She watched Eileen scraping the last crumbs of pie from the plate.

"Oh Lordy, Aunt Gretta is having some kind of dinner party for members of her bridge club who don't have family near, and she'll expect me to be sociable. That's the last thing I want to do! She's probably already having a cow because I'm not home now. She's wonderful and rent is the best, but sometimes…"

"You're welcome to come to my place too," Aggie offered.

"Nah, we have plans to do some girly stuff tomorrow," Eileen laughed. "I think I'll just enter the house as Elf Frederick, shock Auntie and friends, and have an excuse to take a long relaxing bubble bath."

Aggie and Polly joined her laughter as they put on their coats to leave. "Bye, Max and Mable," and "Thanks for Christmas supper," and "Merry Christmas, everyone," flowed from the happy ladies as they left the small diner.

"You know, because Helen going home I just knew I'd be homesick, but I think this has been one the best Christmas's ever."

"It has been great," Aggie agreed. "All because of you."

"Well, I just had a wild idea; without you two it couldn't have happened."

"How could Christmas be anything but fantastic when you're Santa or an elf?" Eileen's laughter echoed through the streets as they neared her aunt's house. "The only thing that would have made it better is if there really was peace on earth." The friends nodded and embraced Eileen, knowing her thoughts were with her brother and friends fighting in Europe.

She laughed in an almost embarrassed manner before asking, "How about if we say a little prayer for all our fighting men?" The three young nurses stood hugging one another and recited the Our Father in front of the brightly festooned house. Their minds were thousands of miles away. "You keep safe. Little Brother," Eileen whispered. She wiped away unwanted tears as the friends finished the prayer. "Ok, Eileen," she admonished herself, "don't be a sad Sally on Christmas!" She broke from Aggie and Polly's embraces and laughed as she plodded up the walk toward another holiday party.

CHAPTER 17

THE SOUND OF LOUD KNOCKING at her apartment door woke Aggie before 8:00 the next morning. "Oh, be quiet!" she growled, pulling a pillow over her head and snuggled under her blankets. "For goodness sake!" She jumped up, realizing what the sound was and shrieked as her feet touched the frigid floor. Pushing them into her slippers, she grabbed a bath robe and rushed across the living room and opened the door to her frumpish landlady.

"Some man is on the phone—wants to talk to you. Follow me." She turned toward the stairs.

"Hello?" Aggie picked up the heavy, black receiver.

"Hi Ag, this is Cy. Hey, any chance you can get in touch with Polly before I come to pick you up? I just saw Johnny Wetta yesterday, and when I told him that I was coming in to get you, he said he sure would like to see Polly and try to convince her to come out to meet his folks."

"Sure, I can tell Polly." Aggie's sleepy brain was now wide awake. "But what if she doesn't want to come, especially with me telling her instead of Johnny asking?" The landlady in the doorway pointed to the clock.

"You can convince her!" Cy laughed. "We'll see you gals in a while."

"Bye." Aggie smiled, replaced the receiver, and said, "Thanks, Mrs. Sturving," before taking the creaking stairs two at a time. Aggie bounded into the apartment, "Polly, Polly!" The aroma of fresh brewing coffee tickled her nostrils. "Oh my, that coffee smells wonderful. I'm so glad you're up."

"Why? What happened to sleeping as late as I want? We don't have to go to work, do we?" she asked while pouring cups of steaming coffee from the metal percolator.

"No." Aggie reached into the fridge for some milk. "That was Cy, and you won't believe what he wanted." Aggie explained about Johnny wanting to see Polly. "He'd really like you to come back home with him for the day to meet his parents."

Polly tried to stifle a huge grin. Then the chipped coffee cup trembled, and she had to set it down. "Oh dear, Aggie," Polly gasped, "that's almost like asking me to marry him." Her smile faded. "I don't know what to do. We just had a big fight about Johnny thinking that I'll jump at his bidding."

"You do really like him, don't you?But there's the matter of Michael, right?" Polly nodded and Aggie continued, "I know he's nice and he has money, but, well, Johnny just seems more like us."

"What, does that mean?" Polly scrunched her face.

"Oh, you know, comfortable, easy to be with, like you've know each other for ages even if you just met."

Polly rolled her eyes. "I just don't want Johnny to think I am sitting around waiting for him, that he can keep showing up without warning."

"That's really understandable," Aggie said. "Want me to try to call Cy back, even though Mrs. Sturving will have a fit."

"No, that'd be too complicated. I'll tell Johnny that I'm coming to keep him from being embarrassed because his parents are probably expecting me, but this better be the last time he makes plans that take me for granted."

Aggie smiled. "Perfect."

Polly gulped the last of her coffee, suddenly excited. "I gotta get home and get ready. I have no idea what to wear!" A devilish smirk spread across her face. "Maybe my Santa outfit? That would impress his folks!" Her ornery laugh echoed in the cold morning kitchen as she hugged Aggie before grabbing her coat.

The men stopped at Aggie's apartment first. She told Johnny that Polly wanted to talk to him alone and, "No, she isn't real happy about this."

As he climbed the stairs to Polly's apartment, a barrage of conversations sped through his mind. He met an icy glare, and Polly looked almost formidable in a black turtleneck sweater and grey slacks. However, the fragrance of Evening in Paris offered hope. "You look swell, Pauline. I'm sorry I didn't talk to you earlier about coming to the farm. The idea just popped up when I was talking to Cy last night."

"So, an idea just pops in your head, and you think I should jump!"

"Well, no, it's just that… Pauline, I really don't want to fight; I have a little gift for you." He took a small white package tied in a red ribbon from his pocket.

She frowned. "I don't have anything for you."

"That's ok. I just thought of your green eyes when I saw this."

Polly removed the ribbon and peeked into the box. "Oh, Johnny, it's awfully pretty, but now I want to change clothes. I'll just be a minute."

Johnny said, "Why? You look great; I never saw you in slacks before," but it was lost to a closed bedroom door.

Polly emerged a couple of minutes later wearing a dark green sweater that contrasted with a beige skirt that skimmed her knees. She fluffed her hair and turned her back to Johnny. "Will you help me fasten the chain? Don't you think this emerald stone looks especially pretty with this sweater?"

Johnny's large hands struggled with the clasp as he said, "I wish it were a real emerald, but I'm pretty sure it's not. I see why you changed your sweater, but why the slacks?"

Polly felt giddy with the aroma of his aftershave. When he succeeded with the necklace and his hands moved down her arms and gently turned her toward him, she said to herself, *Get a grip. Don't let him think he can waltz in after not seeing him for two weeks, and all is hunky dory.* As his lips gently brushed hers, she turned her head. "I think we better not keep Aggie and Cy waiting."

Polly was so quiet during the drive that both Johnny and Aggie tried to tease her into relaxing. Aggie even risked telling Johnny that he was lucky that she was around or Polly would not have come. "Don't you know that a gentleman gives a lady more warning and doesn't presume that she'll drop everything at your beck and call?"

"We discussed that," Polly stated. "He knows how to get in touch with me now, don't you?"

"I most definitely do," he laughed. Not long after, Cy pulled his car off the road where Johnny's Chevy waited.

The guys exchanged plans to meet later, and Aggie hugged Polly. "Relax and have fun; this is just a day in the country." Then she noticed the small green stone sparkling inside the top of Polly's coat. "Oh, Polly, that is so pretty. Was it a Christmas gift?" Polly put her finger to her lips and glanced toward Johnny. "I'm so glad that you agreed to come," she whispered as Polly got out of the car.

"Sorry ole Nelly is so cold," Johnny apologized as he backed the coup onto the road. "We both might warm up faster, if you moved a little closer."

Pauline glanced his way and then moved across the seat and cuddled up. "You know, Johnny Wetta, I'm only over here so I don't freeze to death."

"I'll remind you of that when the heater starts burning us out."

It wasn't long before Johnny said, "Here we are," and turned the car into a cedar-lined lane.

This is really nice." Pauline was enticed with all of the trees.

"When I was a kid, none of us thought they were pretty because we had to help plant them and constantly carry water to keep 'em alive." He slowed the car and pointed through a couple of cedars. "We also helped plant the pear, apricot, and cherry trees in that orchard, and of course, we had to keep them watered, too. Dad and Mother have always loved trees, and they do produce great fruit."

As soon as she saw the white, two-story, stucco house, Polly's heart jumped into overdrive. She took a deep breath to calm the tornado in her stomach.

"You ok?" As Johnny turned off the ignition, he was surprised to see she was pale. "Don't worry! They don't bite." He laughed, adding, "except for my sister Annie."

When the young couple walked through the kitchen door, succulent aromas of roast beef accompanied the unmistakable luxury of homemade bread. These tantalized Pauline's growling stomach, reminding her she hadn't eaten since the hamburgers at Max's the night before. A petite lady with silver hair neatly braided in a crown turned from the stove. She had been spooning butter into corn but wiped her hands on the flowery apron that protected the grey dress dusting her ankles. Reaching for Pauline's hands, she smiled. "It is so nice to meet you, Pauline. I'm Anna, but call me Grandma like everyone else. Makes it less confusing around here. We've told Johnny for ages to bring you to the farm." Her soft voice quivered with a hint of German accent.

"I work crazy hours and don't have much free time." Pauline covered for Johnny. "Your home looks so large, and it smells wonderful," she added as Johnny helped her from her coat and hat.

"It seems small when all the boys and Marie are home, but we don't have to worry about that right now." With a catch in her voice, Grandma turned back to the stove.

Johnny introduced his sister, who walked into the kitchen from an adjacent room. "Pauline this is my baby sister, Annie." Then he took the coats to hang up.

"I'm the baby because Mother and Dad saved the best til last," she joked and gave Pauline a friendly wave as she walked across the kitchen and took flatware from a drawer. "I like your skirt. Guess I need to get more fashionable and start showing off my legs too."

When Polly saw that Annie's skirt reached mid-calf, she thought, *Thank God I changed. They might have fainted if I had on slacks!* But, she asked, "Can I help?"

Annie handed the flatware to Pauline, picked up a large match, and lit it from a flame on the cook stove.

"Thanks." Annie motioned her toward the dining room. "It's so gloomy outside today; we need to get some light in here." As flames from several candles on the table and the sconces on the wall were lit, they reflected from the knives, forks, and spoons which Pauline set at each place. She puzzled about where Johnny had disappeared as Annie continued, "The porches on each side of the house are nice shade to help keep the house cooler during the summer, but they keep this room awful dark in the winter."

"The candlelight looks so pretty, and this tablecloth is gorgeous! You didn't have to go to so much trouble!" Pauline said as Johnny entered from a door that seemed to lead to a cellar. He was carrying a large jar of pickles and two bottles of red wine.

"Hey, Annie, where's Dad?"

"Well, Johnny, you bringing a young lady home is almost like the return of a prodigal son! Dad is probably still out killing the fatted calf!" Annie joked as her brother glared.

"You make me sound like a real loser. I just had to look awhile to find the best." Johnny winked at Pauline, whose blushing face confirmed Johnny's words. The kitchen door opened, and a taller, older copy of Johnny walked through the kitchen door amidst frigid cold air.

"Sorry I'm late. A couple of ewes are probably going to lamb this afternoon; I knew that damned buck jumped the fence long before we found him. Now we're having lambs in December instead of March!"

Grandma Anna turned from the stove with her finger to her lips and nodded toward the dining room.

"Anyway, I needed to get them fresh straw and bed them down good." He doffed his heavy cap and walked through a door on the opposite side of the kitchen. Above the sound of water being pumped he said, "Looking forward to meeting you, Pauline, but not til I wash off this sheep stink." Without a breath he added, "Sure smells great in here, Mother."

Johnny had already opened the wine and was pouring it into beautiful crystal glasses his mother held when his father came out of the washroom still combing his hair. "Dad, this is Pauline." Johnny handed both a glass of wine.

"Oh my, aren't you just a pretty little thing!" The elder Wetta smiled.

"Well, thank you, Mr. Wetta. It's nice to meet you." Her words were met with disapproval.

"We'll have none of that formal stuff. I'm Dad or Grandpa or even Leo, but Mr. Wetta is for strangers and scoundrels." He put his wine down and took Pauline's hand and kissed it gently.

Annie rolled her eyes and Johnny shook his head and said under his breath, "Speaking of scoundrels!" Playing along with the regal behavior, Pauline curtsied to the elder gentleman's amusement.

Placing her hand onto his arm, Johnny's father asked, "Will you accompany me to the table, my dear?"

"I think I should help bring in the food," Pauline hesitated.

"You go ahead, Pauline," Johnny said. "Dad doesn't often get the chance to demonstrate his French charm. We'll have the food on the table in two shakes of a lamb's tail."

As they visited, Pauline realized that Johnny's father was quite intelligent. They discussed geography and the governments of Europe and related them to the war. He said, "When this war is over, I hope our politicians have more sense with a peace treaty than they did the last time. You can't treat people the way we did the Germans at Versailles and not expect them to retaliate." At the same time, he was easy to talk to, and Pauline realized Johnny was much like his dad. In contrast, his mother seemed quiet, which Pauline felt masked a discreet wisdom.

When Pauline mentioned that she loved the house, Grandpa, told her, "It started as a homestead log cabin which is now the kitchen. "I helped my dad add this room, the parlor, and a bedroom a few years before Anna and I married. With the help of neighbors, we eventually added a couple of work rooms and the four bedrooms upstairs."

"You're obviously a good builder."

With pride Leo finished, "A few years ago, the boys and I built the two long porches and put the water pipes and pumps into the kitchen and bathroom."

Grandma Anna smiled. "Leo and the boys have made my kitchen so nice with the piped in water and new cabinets, and the porches keep the house cleaner and more comfortable."

Pauline rose and gazed through a window at the large lawn. A large area beyond it looked like it was probably a vegetable garden. She said, "This place has to be beautiful in the summer, but so much work." Even though the lawn was in its winter sleep, Pauline noticed several bushes and a large arbor that Anna told her was intertwined with grape vines during the summer.

When the dishes were cleared, Johnny suggested they join his parents in the living room. Instead, Pauline said, "Why don't you and I help Annie wash and dry the dishes first?"

Annie grinned mischievously and handed Johnny a tea towel. He looked at it as though it was an alien object. Pauline, on the other hand, said, "Someone spent a lot of time embroidering fruit designs on these towels."

"I've always enjoyed doing it, and these old flour sacks are rather dingy looking without some kind of decoration." After the dishes were clean, Annie said, "Pauline, you're supposed to be company; you've helped enough. I'll finish tidying the kitchen. Go visit the folks."

In the living room, Polly noticed a small side-table with pictures of three young men in military uniforms lovingly arranged in a semi-circle. As she examined the photos, Grandma Anna pointed out which was Joe, Ben, and Leo Jr. Then she pointed to a picture of a young nun nearby. "This is our daughter, Marie, or Sister Laeta. She's a nurse too," her pride sang out, "and she lives in Iowa with her order of nuns." A delicate lace doily rested under the photos, and a statue of the Sacred Heart of Jesus behind them. A votive candle was flickering at his feet, and a flag hung on the wall. Pauline thought, *I bet thousands of prayers have been said here in the past couple of years.*

The sound of shuffling cards broke her reverie. "Do you play canasta?" Leo asked as he dealt cards on a small table near a sofa.

Johnny pulled a couple of hassocks close. " I don't think we"ll have time for a full game, Dad. Maybe we can talk through the basics."

"My gosh, how many cards do we each get?" Johnny told Pauline that she could pick up her cards and look at them. Then he explained how the game was played. As the foursome discarded and drew more cards, Pauline commented, "I usually cuss these long fingers of mine, but they come in handy with all these cards."

"You have beautiful hands, dear," Grandma Annie said. "They are delicate like a piano player's, not like my short, stubby farm woman hands."

"Now, Mother, your hands are just fine." Leo patted one of the reddened workers.

Johnny interrupted, "Speaking of hands, this better be our last one. I want to check the sheep." As he spoke his sister came in with a bright red face and carrying the fragrance of winter cold. "Hey Annie, where've you been?"

"Went to get the mail," she set two military envelopes and one that appeared to be agreeting card on the little table with the photos and smiled at her mother. "Better than Christmas presents, from Ben, Joe and Marie." She gave her a peck on the cheek, then walked from the room.

Grandma rose and lovingly fingered the envelopes, saying, "I wish she had gotten one from Willie. I know she is worried sick." Leo came to stand beside her.

Johnny touched Pauline's arm and discreetly asked, "Would you like to walk around outside a little or would you rather stay in here where it's warm?"

"Oh, I'd love to see a little of the farm."

When they stepped into the kitchen, Annie said, "My work boots are over here still defrosting. You better put them on or your shoes will be ruined and smell like the barn lots. You might want to wear my coat too. It's not great, but will keep you warmer and then yours won't smell like the barns."

"Thanks, Annie. That's so nice. If you're sure."

Annie smiled, "Like I said they already smell, so hope you don't mind. Besides, I think I'll take a nap.

As Pauline sat on a work bench to pull on the boots, Johnny said, "I wish you had left your slacks on so you wouldn't get as cold as you will in that skirt."

"Do you have any idea how out of place I'd feel in slacks with your mother and Annie in long dresses? I'd feel like one of the hussies Sister Gregory always refers to." She wrapped the heavy woolen scarf around her head and asked, "Didn't you want to read the letters?"

"Mom and Dad say a couple of prayers before opening them, maybe even say a Rosary. Used to open them at meals and try to read them." Johnny finished buttoning his coat and continued. "Between mom's quivering voice and tears even—if the news was pleasant, meals were pretty much ruined. Now Annie and I read them after the folks, and we share our thoughts later." He pulled on his gloves adding, "I think I told you that Ben sends special letters to me through Jim, didn't I?" Polly nodded and squeezed his hand as she noted the concern in his eyes. "Maybe I'll let you read his latest when we go meet Cy and Aggie."

"I'd like that," Polly answered.

As the wind enveloped them when they stepped away from the house, she was happy to have the warmer coat and heavy scarf. On their way to check the sheep, they stopped at the large barn to toss some extra oats and hay to the horses. Johnny said, "The weather must be going to get bad. The cows don't usually come up until later in the afternoon. I better close the gate to make sure they stay near the barn for milking."

When they walked across the lane to another large lot, Pauline was grateful for the boots; there was no way to avoid all the sheep droppings. As Johnny slid back a large door, the putrid odor of sheep manure surrounded them, and Polly involuntarily lifted her arm across her mouth and nose. Johnny laughed. "Pretty rank at first."

"I thought with all the bedpans and shit I've cleaned up, odors wouldn't bother me, but this is… wow!" Her voice was muffled by the heavy sleeve and scarf she pulled across her mouth and nose

A ewe stood in a corner with two tiny babies. She was still cleaning one of the lambs while the other was trying to stand on wobbly new legs. "Looks like she gave us twins," Johnny whispered. The panting of the lambs joined with occasional baa's and a hum of sounds from across the feed bunks that divided the barn. Johnny told Pauline that the barn housed about 500 sheep.

No wonder it reeks, she thought.

After deciding the new mother and her lambs were ok, Johnny rolled the big door open wide enough that he and Polly could squeeze through. Once outside, Pauline took a deep breath of cold fresh air. As they walked past corn cribs and a machine shed on the way back to the house, she realized that this farm was definitely too large for the two men to operate alone. With three other sons off to war, the entire family put in long hours to keep up with everything. She felt a twinge of guilt for ever feeling neglected by Johnny.

When they returned to the house, he announced, "We have one set of twins on the ground. Gonna have to watch that ewe; make sure she feeds 'em both."

His father replied, "Maybe I better go check on her."

When Johnny reported he and Pauline had just done that and the ewe needed some time, his dad seemed disappointed. Johnny told him, "It's getting colder and the wind is picking up. Feels like snow comin'. If you want help with the milking, we better get to it pretty soon, even if it's early."

Grandma Ann said, "Before you go back out, we want to tell you about Ben's letter. Don't you think, Dad?"

Leo smiled, "Yes, we can take time. It is quite a newsy Christmas gift."

"Really?" Johnny said. "Ben get a big promotion?"

"Not that we know of," Grandma Ann said, "but he did get to meet a really special person."

Pauline and Johnny looked at each other and then at his parents wondering what in the world they were talking about.

His mother picked up a *Sacred Heart Messenger* magazine that the family received monthly. "Remember this article that we talked about a few month ago?" She held it to an open page with a picture of a rough looking monk. "This monk is Padre Pio, and he has the wounds of Christ in his hands and feet."

"I remember; it's called a stigmata," Johnny said. "We wondered if they were real and how bad they had to hurt how he could still walk around and say Mass every day."

"You wondered if it was real," Annie interrupted.

Pauline's medical training kicked in, and she asked, "Do they bleed? He wouldn't have any strength or live very long if they were bleeding like Jesus' wounds bled."

"Well what does this have to do with Ben?" Johnny wanted to know

Anna began, "Their crew had been grounded because of fog and snow, so after morning Mass one day the chaplain said he had been wanting to take them to a monastery up in the mountains where a saintly priest lived."

Leo wanted to also share the news. "Ben wrote that they got to go to aMass that Padre Pio was saying, and afterward, the crew got to meet him, and the guys could see the blood on the thick cloth wrapping this holy man's hands.

Anna added, "According to the article in the *Messenger*, this priest has been abused and tormented for being a hoax even by his fellow priests, But, the bleeding has lasted so long and has been investigated by so many doctors that the Church is now recognizing how saintly the man is."

"That is really something," Johnny said picking up Ben's letter. "I'd like to read this right now, but we better get to the milking, Dad, if you want some help.

Turning to Pauline, he added, "I think we need to leave for Wichita as soon as we're finished.. Bet Cy an Aggie will be at the stop early." The men put on their chore coats and work boots and went back out.

Grandma said, "I'll make some sandwiches to eat on the road. Johnny seems concerned about the weather moving in."

Annie sliced some bread and Pauline slathered on mustard as Grandma sliced leftover roast. Then she opened a jar of pickles and beautiful wine-colored beets.

Johnny walked back into the house. "Dad said to eat without him. He's going to feed the chickens and then watch the ewes for a while."

"Annie and I will wait for him. You and Pauline can eat or take the sandwiches with you if you think you need to go now."

"Let's eat here—less messy," Johnny said as he pumped water to wash up first. Even though they were in a hurry, a relaxed atmosphere permeated the cozy kitchen as they ate by a coal-oil lamp. In answer to Pauline's question of how they preserved the delicious, spicy beets, Grandma described some of the work of putting up food the previous summer. Large slices of chocolate cake followed the sandwiches.

Pauline said, "Oh, my goodness, that looks wonderful, but I can't eat another bite."

"Then we'll wrap it up for you," Annie said, pulling out a sheet of waxed paper.

Johnny was pulling on his coat, "Save me a piece for later, Annie. I'm going out to get the car warming up."

Pauline picked up her dishes to take to the counter, but Grandma and Annie insisted she was to get ready to leave so she and Johnny could beat the snow. On his return, Johnny already had flakes melting in his hair and on his shoulders. As she started to say goodbye, Grandma gave her son a box to carry for Pauline and said, "Child, you need more meat on your bones so you can stay healthy for your patients."When Johnny opened the car door for his sweetheart, she waved to the two women huddled on the porch and thought, *This afternoon was much better than I expected. I think I could really enjoy his family and this beautiful farm.*

They arrived at the meeting spot before their friends, so Pauline tentatively asked, "I understand if you changed your mind; would you like to share the letter you got from Ben?"

"Sure. It's really kinda funny and sounds much more like Ben. He's obviously adjusted to the job he has to do, but this war still won't be over a minute too soon. Don't mind some of his language." Johnny laughed and handed her the letter…

> *Hi Johnny,*
>
> *We are grounded due to fog today, so thick like being wrapped in cotton or wet curtains. Don't think I could sit in the pilot's seat for 5-10 hrs. anyway. Just got the worst ass chewing of my life, and lucky not in the brig waiting court-martial. Used some Yankee ingenuity on our last run and disobeyed orders. Big wigs get more riled than Dad ever did when we tried doing something our own way on the farm. I was just pissed that we were losing so many men and planes recently. The Krauts seemed to be waiting no matter the changes we made in routes. Since I was leadplane and feeling real itchy, my navigator and I had studied aerial pho-tos of places crews had been hit hard trying to figure things out . We saw shadows that seemed out of place but the clouds can do that. Anyway, all the crews were antsy getting in the air. The time to the drop was like waiting in a duck blind, only we were the ducks. Finally…*

I was about to head down for the bomb drop when I saw a strange shadow in the terrain below. One section of the forest just looked different, like the trees were flatter and the colors different. I thought that area was about the size and arrangement I had seen on maps we had studied of German artillery nests. This one seemed bigger; the nests had been so well camouflaged that there was no way we could detect them until we were being blasted. Breaking formation was prohibited and impossible once we went in for a bombing run. The bombardier and his instruments is actually in control of the plane during the bomb run. I quickly broke radio silence and told Fred, the bombardier to hold up in taking over, then got off the radio.I dipped my wings a couple of times to signal the others. (I told the Brass I just couldn't control theplane from floating to the left.) Gupta, the pilot on the right, looked over, and I signaled at the area that I had noticed. He dipped his wings and glided to the right giving the German nest a wide berth. The squadron behind followed suit as the Germans began blasting . Some of the planes were hit, but since we were not directly in the Krauts artillery path, the damage wasn't crucial and all planes stayed in the air to continue the bomb run. After we were well past the range of the Germans, our planes suddenly "overcame the crazy wind currents "and fell back into closer formation, and we finished our raid. For some reason the CO didn't appreciate the fact all planes returned that day—or maybe he did.

He cussed and yelled and I even learned a few new phrases Mom can never hear. Then he told me he was too busy to fill out all the crap for a court-martial and to get the hell out of his office. Then he ordered me to take a shower or he'd change his mind. Our showers are clear across the compound –longer than football field. The water's ice cold and there's seldom heat in the tent!

129

Well, when I told Sam, my co-pilot, about the CO's tirade and "punishment" he shouted "Halleluiah! We'd all decided you were banned from cards with us til you showered. How can you stand yourself, Wetta!?"I figured up and it had been 39 or 40 days since I had really soaked or soaped—sunny Italy is damned cold in the winter. Don't dare tell Mom about that; she'd have a hissy. . . .

Pauline giggled and said, "Ben must not have a good sense of smell!" and Johnny joined in the laughter. Cy had just pulled his car next to Johnny's so discussion of the letter would wait.

Aggie and Cy had enjoyed the afternoon playing cards with her sisters and parents. Before leaving, she told all of them that she had received notice to report for duty in two weeks. She swore Cy to secrecy until she found the right time to tell Polly. Before climbing into Cy's car, she promised her misty-eyed parents, "I'll be home before I report."

CHAPTER 18

"THIS IS SO PRETTY," Pauline remarked, "almost magical like today." She snuggled closer to Johnny, who wrapped his free hand around her, pulled her close, and kissed her cheek. In the back seat, Cy winked at Aggie, and they cuddled for warmth.

He whispered, "Told you so."

When the car shimmied a little, Johnny put both hands on the wheel. "This snow is really starting to come down," he said. "If it keeps up, we'll have a good cover on our wheat, Cy." A conversation about farming ensued, so Aggie leaned forward to chat with Polly.

Outside of Polly's apartment, Johnny wrapped one arm around her and lifter her face to his. "Thank you for coming today." He pulled her closer as she shivered.

Is it only the cold? she thought.

"I had fun and your parents are wonderful, though I probably gained five pounds."

Any other words were lost as his lips urgently found hers. His hand reached inside her coat, and she softly crooned. Laying her head on his chest, she sighed. "Cy and Aggie will wonder where you are."

"Hell, right now they don't even know we exist." His mouth smothered hers.

"We better get off the landing before Mrs. Jenkins hears." Polly unlocked the door.

He followed her inside and fumbled with her coat buttons. He stopped after succeeding with the first couple, and reached under her sweater. "Oh, Johnny," she crooned. Then she sighed and stepped out of the half-buttoned coat. "That feels so good." *Why don't I want to fight it like with Michael?* she wondered. "But, Johnny, you gotta go. Remember the snow, and Cy and…"

"Shhh," he said, "I told you that they… Oh, shit!" His eyes had focused and he could see out the window behind her. "That snow is getting heavy. Damn weather! You are saved for the night, my dear." He turned to the door but pulled her back for another prolonged kiss. Taking a breath, he pulled away and stepped outside. "We almost forgot to take this food in." He handed the box to her with another quick kiss before bounding down the stairs.

Pauline leaned against the door grinning and thinking, *Damn snow may have saved my virtue.*

Before midnight, a prairie blizzard was blowing through Wichita, piling at least twelve inches of snow by early morning. Large, white flakes were still blustering in gales when a large limb crashed on the roof and woke Polly. She looked out at the white scene dimly lit by a streetlight. The houses across the street were invisible. Polly realized that Mildred wasn't home. *She must have stayed at the hospital when the storm got bad. I sure hope the guys got home safely. How am I going to get to the hospital this afternoon if this storm keeps up?* The bedside clock said 4:20, but she was wide awake with concern.

Polly put on her robe and slippers and turned on the radio in the living room. Rolling the dial slowly, she finally heard music amidst static. She jiggled the dial and put her hand on the contraption for a better signal. Finally, clipped messages could be deciphered. "City shut down.

Do not venture out. Boeing shifts halted today. No schools open and hospital staffs do not attempt to come." Oh dear, the nurses will have already worked a double shift in a few hours, Polly thought. But looking at the blinding white flakes, she knew she could never make five blocks to the hospital. Well darn, here I am wide awake, and I can't even go to work.

While heating some hot chocolate, she remembered Grandma Anna's gift and brought the heavy box to the kitchen. Inside she found homemade bread and butter wrapped in waxed paper. Cookies were in another package, and then Pauline gasped. "Oh wow, boiled spice cookies! Grandma Annie, you are an angel." She relished the rich flavor as the soft treat brought back happy childhood memories. Uncovering jars of canned beef, tomatoes, corn, and peaches in the bottom of the box, she felt suddenly wealthy. There were also a couple of onions and a few potatoes. "Our cabinets will barely hold all of this wonderful food," Polly commented out loud as she walked to the window enjoying last bites of the succulent, spicy cookie melt in her mouth. Listening to the wind, she sipped hot chocolate.

After relishing the last crumbs of her second cookie, Polly became a flurry of energy. She put most of the food away, and with a sigh, began taking down Christmas decorations. Mildred with her Scrooge attitude would be happy to see the apartment stripped of all the "bah-humbug" Christmas stuff. After carefully wrapping the first ornaments she had ever purchased, Polly placed them in the box she had just emptied. Then she cleaned the apartment and rearranged the furniture before 7:00. When she glanced at the jars of food, she said aloud, "Chili!" while thinking thatthe heat of the stove would help warm the drafty apartment.

As the soup simmered, she glanced through some magazines from a stack she had just arranged. Munching on another cookie, Polly yawned, thinking, I think I'll crawl back in bed with this magazine to stay warm. The aroma of the simmering chili was relaxing. I better turn that old stove off in case I fall asleep she thought.

Snuggling under the covers, her eyes rested on a young couple enjoying a candlelight dinner in the magazine she was thumbing through. Her thoughts turned to Johnny and the previous day. She closed her eyes and recalled his strong arms pulling her close to stymy her shivering as they walked around the farm. The fragrance of Old Spice was both invigorating and comforting in the crisp winter air. The magazine dropped from her hand as she fell asleep remembering their good night kiss and the erotic pleasure of his hand inside her coat tenderly caressing her breast. Hours later, when another even larger limb broke from the weight of snow and slammed onto the roof, Polly awoke with a start.

"Oh my gosh!" Polly gasped jumping from bed. She glanced at her clock then looked at the window. *Wow, I really zonked out.* She could smell chili, but something else. *Did I turn off that burner?* The smell of natural gas was stronger as Polly scurried to the kitchen. "Thank you dear Lord that noise woke me!" she prayed turning the control of the extinguished burner to off. She rubbed frost from the window, and even though snow was still falling, she could see across the street thinking, I bet I can make it to the hospital. After setting a helping of the chili to re-heat, she went to the bathroom to ready herself for work.

After pulling slacks on under her uniform and her heaviest sweater over, Polly enjoyed a bowl of soup before tugging her rubber boots and donning her coat. Johnny's hand inside the thread bare wrap again frolicked across her mind as butterflies tickled her lower regions. "Damn it, Pauline, stop it. You'll end up like Deloris!" She yanked the blanket from her bed, folded it in half, and wrapped it around her.

Even so, the first blast of cold air burnt her lungs as icy flakes stung her face. After the first few steps her boots were filled with snow. She argued with herself, "Maybe this isn't a great idea. But think of everyone who has worked almost three shifts by now." Even bundled like a Sherpa, by the time she reached St. Francis, she looked like a lopsided snowman and her feet were close to frozen from breaking through drifts.

When Polly walked into the hospital, Sister Mary Joseph, head of nurses, gasped. "Polly, you are a sight; you could have frozen in this storm!" She helped her pull off the snow filled boots and icy, snow-packed gloves and began warming her hands. Then Sister helped the young nurse out of her now dripping outerwear and added it to a steaming pile near the clanking radiator. "Come into my office and stand by the register. We need to get you to the cafeteria for some hot coffee before you can go to work. I'll find some dry shoes while you warm up. Your friend Eileen is probably still there; she came in a few minutes ago, but she didn't look as frozen as you do... or you," she added, looking up at Aggie who stood at the office door also bundled like an Eskimo.

"You girls really should not have risked coming in, but the nurses who have been on duty since yesterday afternoon will appreciate it. They are exhausted and almost asleep on their feet. Of course, some patients are getting rather testy, especially those hoping to go home today."

"Ok, Sister, I'll give them some of my super-duper back rubs to calm their nerves. But, I better get my hands warm first; don't think anyone wants icicles massaging her body." Polly smiled as she rubbed her hands above the radiator.

"Perhaps you could give Sister Gregory one of those back rubs to calm her nerves, so she stops hounding the poor student nurses to work like veterans," Sister Mary Joseph whispered. Then she turned brighter red than Polly's cold face as she blessed herself and looked heavenward sighing, "Forgive me, Dear Lord, I must be suffering from lack of sleep, too! And, Miss Garrity and Miss Beat, you did not hear me say anything about Sister Gregory."

"Say what, Sister?" Polly smiled. "I think my ears are frozen; they aren't working yet." She winked at the short, pudgy nun who was everyone's favorite.

"We don't tell you girls often enough how wonderful you are."

"Oh, we're just doin' our duty, Sister." Aggie laughed as she gathered her wet clothes.

"Just leave those; I'll have cleaning staff hang them in the laundry. Go get some coffee while I find dry shoes and socks." She waved merrily to Polly and Aggie as they went in separate directions. Even though Eileen and Polly were unaware, Sister knew their days with Aggie were ending soon, so late in the evening, after the patients were comfortable for the night, she insisted they all take a dinner break together.

When Aggie walked into the canteen at 8:30, Eileen and Polly were already at a table. "We were hoping you'd make it," Polly called as she pushed a chair away from the table for her.

"We already ordered you a coke and an egg sandwich. Roy is kinda grumpy and doesn't have much food to offer," Eileen announced. "He did say the nuns told him all food is on the house for staff."

"Poor guy is probably dead on his feet," Aggie said. "Hey, Roy, have you been here since the storm began?"

"Yup," he answered brusquely. "I did get a few hours of sleep last night. Sister Mary Joseph said to fill the coffee pot and leave the canteen door open. Then she showed me an empty room to sleep in for a while. Sure wish this storm had waited til we got more supplies after Christmas."

Picking up her sandwich, Aggie said, "Well, we can't always plan things the way we want."

"I have a feeling you're thinking about something more than the storm. What's up, Aggie?"

"I didn't plan to spend my last week at St. Francis helping in psyche while surgery and emergency are so dead," she said, glancing sheepishly at her friends.

"You got your orders." Polly choked as a couple of hot tears escaped.

"What orders?" Eileen asked with a mouth full of french fries? Then she saw the letter with the official government insignia that Aggie had set on the table. She reached for Polly and Aggie's hands.

"A few days before Christmas," Aggie answered Polly's question. "I was trying to find the best time to tell you both and not upset you. I wanted to wait until after the holidays."

To her amazement, Polly smiled and saluted her. "Well, good luck, Lieutenant Beat. You better take damn good care of yourself, and you better write!" Then all three hugged with tears rolling down their cheeks. Roy looked over and shrugged his shoulders.

"Nurses!" he said and glanced at Sister Mary Joseph, who walked in looking like a ghost coming in from the blizzard.

"Thank goodness you girls are all here," the nun said. "I would hate to say this more than once."

"What's wrong, Sister?" Aggie asked.

"You look like you need to sit down." Polly pulled out a chair where the quivering nun almost fell. Aggie got up and retrieved her a cup of coffee.

"Thank you, dears." She glanced from one to the other. "The police just brought in three bodies they found frozen in snow banks in the area."

"Oh my, those poor bums who live in the park and the alleys! I didn't even think what they do in this weather," Eileen gasped.

"A couple were, as you say, Eileen, 'bums,' but one was one of our nurses."

They all gasped and waited as Sister looked at Polly.

"It's Mildred, isn't it?" Polly almost whispered.

Sister nodded. "We tried to keep her from going home last night, but she insisted she'd be fine. Said she'd stop at the Lil Brown Jug to warm up if she got too cold." Tears trickled down Sister's cheeks and dampened the wimple around her neck.

Aggie wrapped a trembling Polly in her comforting arms as the radiator hissed ironic warmth.

Chapter 19

THE BLIZZARD right after Christmas was a precursor to a winter that seemed to drag on and on. Adding to the misery for Polly, was the problem of stretching her paycheck to pay Mildred's portion of rent. Instead of celebrating with each pay check, and occasionally purchasing some pretty underpants, .she sat at the kitchen table budgeting down to the penny. "Lil Sis, we'll straighten it out when I move in with you in May when my lease is up," Helen replied when Polly asked about the extra cash she had found after her sister recently dropped by.

"I'll keep track of every cent. If we weren't going to be roomies soon, I wouldn't accept it." Polly's was adamant.

However, reaching into her coat pocket to discover a $5 bill a few days before rent was due in January sent Polly on a never solved quest until mid February. "What are you doing with my coat, Aggie?" she asked walking into the nurses' locker room.

"Just hanging it up. Someone must have knocked it off the hook. How many new babies did you all have in OB today?" Aggie changed the subject as she put on her own coat.

"We had four; about ran us ragged," Polly put a sweater on before donning her still thread bear coat, then reaching into the pocket for her gloves. "Aggie I should have known it was you," she held up a $5.00 bill and two ones. "I can't take this. And don't act stupid."

Aggie smiled. "You can take it, and you will. Those orders are the first official work of Lieutenant Beat." She hugged her best friend. "Polly, I finally report in two days, so the Army will be taking care of me. I really want to do this."

Tears stung Polly's eyes as she choked, "Eye eye Lieutenant. I hope the military is more organized in fighting this war than it's been with your paper work" She brushed hot tears away. "I'd tell em to 'stick it' at this point. The 18thof February is hardly the 5thof January like they told you at Christmas"

A couple of days later Aggie was officially inducted into the Womens' Army Corps as a second lieutenant. She reported to basic training near San Antonio, Texas.

March 1944

Hi Garrity and Hay,

Sorry you have to share a letter, but don't have much free time and this saves Uncle Sam paper. Well, I guess I'm really in the Army. Our mornings are spent learning military stuff, the rules and protocol. After a month, I've started to figure out who to salute & how, who not to smile at (hard for me), and don't feel quite so stupid all the time. You'd both be cackling if you saw me in these ugly dungarees; they are so stylish! Guess the Army is trying to prevent any fraternizing (Army lingo for kissy face) between men and women soldiers.

We work on the floor of the hospital in the afternoon. Some of the wounds these men have are so horrible. I thought I'd seen bad stuff working emergency, but it's unimaginable what poison gas, shells and shrapnel do to flesh and bones. By the time we see them state-side, they've been treated in field and ship hospitals. Almost sadder than the physical wounds are the psych problems. So many of the guys don't want to live with their mutilations. Just as horri-

ble are the guys who appear fine, until looking in their eyes; there is so little we can do for the many, many men who look just fine but have invisible injuries that make them totally incapacitated! Often, we just have to hold a guy's hand and sit with him. Nursing is so different in the Army, and you were right, Polly; Sister Gregory was good prep. Sometimes I hear her insisting in my ear, "Don't act like a ninny; use that brain God gave you."

I've applied to be part of the flight nurse program and hoping to hear soon. In the meantime, we get to hike w/ a 25lb. pack on our backs and bivouac (camp out) for a few days! Probably won't bother taking my stick lip!!Gotta get to work.

Love ya,
Aggie

✤

April 1944

Hi Aggie,

Gosh it was great to hear from you. Wow, flight school, how exciting, and maybe a little less dangerous since you'll be in those specially marked "medical" planes the enemy can't shoot at like the hospitals that accidentally get blasted by bombs. I know you'll make it!

Compared with your new life, mine is boring, but you might be proud to know that I'm trying to be more patriotic and support the troops in better ways than giving them a show from the roof of the nurses' home. (Even though they will remember that longer!) Hay and I are volunteering at the emergency medical station at the soldiers' canteen downtown once or twice a week. Working

141

there has sure opened my eyes that every guy in uniform isn't terrific. Some are real creeps! They line up for their penicillin shots to get rid of the clap and aren't even ashamed. They laugh and joke like it's noth'n. I know sometimes I may act a little wild, but I can't understand how anyone can jump into bed with someone they aren't at least planning to marry. Some of these stupid guys are screwing anything that wears a skirt and probably don't even know her name.

Then we're supposed to be so nice and treat them like heroes because they're headed off to war! I ram in that penicillin needle in as hard as I can and hope it hurts like hell! Maybe I should be nicer, but these guys make me sick! I guess this is the way some of them hide how scared they are, but risking syphilis and worse is so stupid! Why do some men think with their ding dongs instead of their brains?!

The maternity wards are busier and more crowded all the time. We no longer have a nurses' breakroom (never got to use it anyway) or a fathers' lounge. Both have been made into wards, and private rooms are non-existent unless someone's donated a wing to the hospital. In fact, hardly a week goes by that we don't have patients in the hall. OB is almost always such a happy, busy place to work.

"I'm so sorry you had to be out in the hall so long, Mrs. Spexarth." Polly apologized to the young mother as she and an orderly moved her bed into a room with another patient. "We've had so many new babies this week."

"Oh, don't worry about it. I know you're doing the best you can," Mrs. Spexarth said. "With three little ones at home, I'm used to trying to rest in the middle of a circus. I just wish the doctor would let me go home so someone else could have this room."

"Good heavens, Mrs. Spexarth," Polly gasped. "You just had your baby two days ago. You can't get out of bed except to sit in the chair for a week; otherwise, you could have terrible complications."

Mrs. Spexarth laughed, "Oh, Miss Garrity, I had my first three babies at home and was up and around the next day taking care of business. By the time the baby was a week old, I was doing laundry and cooking for field hands. If it wasn't for the new Stork bill and all the encouragement for mothers to live healthier, Little Johnny would probably have been born at home too."

Polly smiled. "I remember when my brothers were born. My mother did the same thing, but medicine has come a long way since then." She finished tucking in the bed sheets and fluffed the pillows as she talked. "We want you to relax and take care of yourself while you're here, so it's easier for you to care for your baby and those little ones when you get home."

"If I lay in bed for a week, I'll be too feeble to do anything! Besides, since you are so busy with new mothers, the sooner you dismiss some of us who are more experienced, the more room and time you'll have to care for those who really need you," Mrs. Spexarth noted.

"Well, I don't make the rules; I just try to follow them—sometimes," she laughed. "Now, let me help you back into bed, Mrs. Spexarth."

"Please call me Therese," she said, looking at Polly's name tag. "Garrity. That name sounds familiar."

As Polly helped Therese get comfortable, she said, "Are you from around Wellington? There's a whole bunch of us Garritys down there."

"No, we live outside of Colwich, a little town about twenty miles west of Wichita."

The young nurse was filling a glass of water which began to tremble. "I know a few people from that area," Polly said. She almost whispered, "I love the dances out there."

"They can be fun," Therese commented. "Who do you know?"

The sound of another patient's call button saved Polly from answering. "Sounds like someone else needs me now," she said as she picked up the bed linens. "Is there anything else I can do for you now?"

Theresa shook her head as she settled back on the fresh pillows. "I already feel like royalty. Perhaps we can talk more later."

Throughout her shift, Polly dispensed medicine, gave sponge baths, changed linens, and taught some new mothers how to change a diaper. By 2:00, she was thinking, *If nothing unforeseen happens, maybe I'll be off in time to talk to Patty and even Alice about moving in. Gotta find someone to help with the rent or I'll be out on the street.* Mildred's death had hit Polly hard emotionally, but it was now hitting her pocketbook.

The doors from the delivery area swung open, and orderlies pushed a gurney holding a young mother who had just delivered her first baby. "Sister said to let you know that this patient might need some extra TLC when the happy juice wears off," one orderly whispered to Polly. She took the chart and saw the words she always hated, "Husband in Military." A notation in Sister Margaret Mary's writing added "(Navy in Pacific)."

"Damn, I hate this war!" Polly mumbled.

The orderlies gently lifted the new mother to one of the beds lining the hall. "I thought you were going to get some open rooms today," one commented seeing another patient in a bed lining the corridor.

"We did, but we have already had two new babies on this shift. I had just found a room for my last hall patient late this morning in time for new arrivals. Lots of guys gave their wives farewell gifts before shipping out."

"Think of it this way, Garrity," the other orderly said, "you have plenty of job security." The men smiled and waved as they pushed the empty gurney toward the delivery bay.

Polly looked down at the young mother who was moaning quietly and said, "Hi, Mrs. Rubenstein. I see you have a brand new baby boy. That's so exciting!" Tears glistened on the cheeks of the patient who smiled weakly. "Would you like a drink of water?" Polly gently lifted the patient's head from the pillows to help her take a sip.

The hall was more active once afternoon visiting hours and the next shift of nurses arrived. *This is an awful place for a distressed new mother,* Polly thought. "What are you going to name your little boy, Mrs. Rubenstein?" She checked her vitals.

"Jacob, like his daddy." Just saying the name brought more tears to her cheeks. Polly wiped them with a tissue and placed a couple more in the patient's hand. "Jacob's in the Pacific somewhere. I sure hope our little guy isn't already walking by the time he gets to see him." She blew her nose and attempted a smile.

"Hey, Garrity," a young woman called from the nurses' station where several white uniformed women were gathered. "You're missing report. Need you up here."

Oh hell! How'd it get so late? Polly thought. "Be there in a minute." Smiling at the patient, she said, "Mrs. Rubenstein, will you be ok for a few minutes? The shift is changing, and I need to let the new nurses know how to best take care of of you this evening."

"That's fine, but please call me Mary Francis."

As Polly rushed to report. She glanced back saying out loud+++, "Why does this sweet patient fill me with dread instead of joy?"

"What did you ask?" one of the waiting nurses asked?

"Oh nothing. Just trying to remember something," she lied.

Chapter 20

REPORT WENT QUICKLY; the main topic was concern about the hall patients. During report, the main desk called to inform the nurses that another patient had been admitted for delivery. Polly kept glancing toward Mary Francis. "Lord, it's going to be a busy night," the head nurse commented. "Isn't that three already today? Let's hope none have complications. Garrity, how's your newest patient doing?"

Polly said "I think Mrs. Rubenstein will need some extra care. Her husband is on a ship in the Pacific, and naturally she's upset. She just delivered her first baby, and she's one of our lucky hall patients."

"Shit! That's no place for any new mother, much less one in that situation," another nurse said. "Who does she have with her?"

"No one, so far," Polly answered. "I was just going to find out about --"

The phone at the main desk rang again, and the head nurse answered then rolled her eyes. She nodded when a nurse mouthed, "Another one?" They dispersed to their patients as she waved them off.

"You're lucky to get out of here, Polly," her friend Connie said as they walked down the hall. "We probably won't sit down all evening and will have to work into next shift to do any charting."

"I think I'll stick around awhile, at least until someone comes to be with Mary Francis," Polly said as they neared the beds in the hall.

"Looks like an extra pair of hands might be helpful."

Connie gave her a friendly hug. "You're a real peach, Garrity. Thanks bunches. You know they won't pay you for overtime."

That would help with the rent. Darn, if I stay very late, I won't get to talk to anyone about moving in. I'm sorry I couldn't help you more with your boozing, Mildred, but you sure left me in a pickle.

"How ya doin', Mary Francis?" Polly asked as she gently touched the young mother's arm. She was facing the wall and shrugged her trembling shoulders dejectedly.

"Well, you're in luck. I don't have a thing to do at home, so I'm staying for a while to treat patients to backrubs with my fantastic fingers." A couple of her friends getting off duty stood down the hall and mouthed, "Are you coming?" She shook her head and waved goodbye to them.

"How does a backrub sound?" she asked, returning her attention to the new mother who shrugged her shoulders again. "I bet you need to use the bedpan first, don't you?" Mary Francis shook her head, but Polly knew that she should really try to relieve herself and urged her to do so.

"Out here?"

"Oh, I'm sorry. I forgot to get one of our privacy screens," Polly said and walked a few steps down the hall to retrieve it. She set the contraption up around Mrs. Rubenstein's bed, but realized that it didn't give much privacy, especially with sounds and odors. "You know, I'm not supposed to let you get out of bed for a couple of days, but I sure understand how you feel about trying to use a bedpan out here. They are bad enough in a room. How about if I get a wheelchair and take you down the hall to a bathroom?"

Mary Francis smiled at that suggestion.

Afterwards, the young mother's tense muscles relaxed under Polly's caring hands. She talked about her family in Illinois, also home for her husband's family. When Jacob received his orders to be stationed at the naval base west of Mt. Hope, Kansas, they thought it was a typing error. She smiled a little when she told Polly, "Isn't it the funniest thing that there's a naval base in Kansas, the farthest place in the US from water? Jacob has some cousins who live in Hutchinson, and they offered for me to stay with them. We decided it would be an adventure since I'd never been out of Chicago. I could stay with relatives, get a job in Hutchinson, and we could at least see each other on weekends."

Mary Francis sighed and said that living with the cousins didn't work out. "But, I found a job teaching at Mt. Hope, and we found a little room with some meals. Life wasn't too bad until Jacob was shipped overseas." She explained she didn't want to break her teaching contract, nor did they have enough money for her to go back to Illinois. After Jacob left, she discovered she was pregnant and knew she should be close to family, but that would have meant borrowing money to pay for the train. By the time she had saved enough for a ticket to Chicago, her doctor didn't want her to travel.

"How'd you get to the hospital?" Polly wondered, suddenly understanding that this young mother might be all alone.

Mary Francis blushed. "My doctor. A friend took me to my appointment this morning, and Dr. Lies said I needed to go to the hospital. We hadn't expected that, and Sally had brought her little girl along and needed to get home. The doctor said he could bring me in since he was driving in to make rounds anyway. Then he would be here to deliver the baby."

"Dr. Lies is very kind," Polly commented.

"Yes. He had me call my mother in Illinois from his office and tell her she needed to come. Hopefully she will get here tomorrow or the next day if she's lucky enough to squeeze onto a train with all the troops traveling."

"I'm sure she'll be here soon," Polly said as her heart ached for the new mother. She also recognized she wouldn't be finding a new roommate this evening. "I'm sure your mother is excited to see you and her new grandson."

New tears of homesickness were in Mary Francis's eyes. "I hope so. She and Dad were so angry when I married Jacob. They said, they'd never speak to me again. We're Catholic and he's Jewish. I had to tell them through the door that we were going to Kansas."

"Oh, Mary Francis, I'm so sorry. But your mother said she will come now?"

"Yea, I knew they didn't mean it; they're just afraid with all the rumors about the Jews in Europe." Then she laughed a little. "And coming to Kansas must have about killed them. It's kinda like going to the moon for people in Chicago who think it's still the Wild West. About a month after I wrote about expecting a baby, Mama sent me a pretty card. She said they were happy for me and wanted me to come home, but, as I said, money is short."

Polly thought, *You don't have to tell me about it!* "Believe me, I've heard some really crazy stories about what people think of Kansas," Polly said. She made her patient giggle as she shared a couple of silly ideas. "And, what do you think about living in Wild West Kansas?"

Mary Francis answered that she loved the gorgeous sunsets and open spaces, the people were so friendly, and the kids worked so hard in school. Soon she was yawning, and her voice drifted. Polly pulled the privacy curtain around the bed as she stepped away with the intention of going to the main desk and calling maintenance for more privacy screens.

However, she noticed three call buttons blinking and knew she had heard the buzzers sound earlier. The nurses were all so busy it was hard to keep up. Connie zipped out of one room, and Polly waved to her that she would answer the light closest. Both patients needed to use the bedpan, and both insisted it was stupid that they could not get up and go by themselves. Polly was beginning to think perhaps Mrs. Spexarth was correct about the totally bedridden rules. They were certainly going to drive the nurses crazy.

After she and Connie had answered all the call buttons, Polly checked on Mary Francis, who was still sleeping, then called maintenance. "It doesn't look like we are slowing down on deliveries, Harold," she told the man in charge who obviously did not see the need to find privacy screens in the store room. "These mothers need something, and you don't want me to go rummaging through your precious stuff do you? Oh, and, Harold, please make sure the screens don't have ten years' worth of dust on them before bringing them up." She hung up with an exasperated sigh and noticed Connie smiling broadly.

"For someone who says she doesn't want the responsibility, Garrity, you sound and act more like a head nurse of this ward than those being paid for it."

"Oh, pooh!" she answered. "I'm gonna give a few backrubs until Mary Francis wakes up. She has absolutely no one, and I don't want to just leave without saying goodbye."

When Polly stopped in the room that Theresa Spexarth now shared with another lady, Polly was shocked to see Theresa returning from the restroom with the help of a visitor. Pursing her lips, Polly said, "Mrs. Spexarth! You're not supposed to be out of bed! What am I going to do with you?"

"Darn it, Therese, I told you I didn't think I was supposed to help you to the bathroom!" The visitor was obviously embarrassed to be caught breaking rules.

"Now, Miss Garrity, didn't I ask you to call me Therese? And, I've already explained what I would be doing if I was home. Besides, I could hear all those buzzers of others needing help and was trying to save you some work."

Polly said, "Ok, Therese, let's get you back into bed." She winked at her visitor to allay any intimidation and added, "And if you can behave yourself while I give your roommate, Mrs. Jarowski, a backrub, you just might get one."

Later, as Polly was massaging Therese's back, the patient relaxed in the luxury. "Oooh, I don't think I've ever been treated like such a queen. This would feel so nice after a day of working in the garden and canning. When you said that you were giving backrubs, my sister said she just might have to have another baby so she could be treated like a princess."

"That's a pretty big price to pay for a backrub!" Polly laughed as she massaged Therese's arms. "You deserve a little pampering after all that hard work. In nursing school we were told that good nurses made time to give a backrub or to do something to make each patient feel special during every shift. Unfortunately, with so many mothers and babies, we hardly have time to attend to the medical needs."

"Well, even though I love the attention, I'm going to tell Dr. Lies I really want to go home tomorrow; you could have one less patient to worry about and one more bed for someone else." Suddenly remembering, Therese changed the topic. "Oh, you were going to tell me who you know in Colwich, but my sister told me that you know one person pretty well."

Polly had recognized the sister from wedding dances. She smiled and asked, "And who is that?"

"Johnny Wetta is pretty sweet on you. Isn't he? Everyone thought Johnny was a confirmed bachelor since he must be close to thirty years old; he's never been serious about anyone."

"I don't know that he's so serious," Polly retorted. "We're just enjoying dancing and having fun together."

"Oh, believe me; he's serious! His family lives right across the field from us, and his parents were wondering why he was driving all the way to Wichita to see someone. That is, until they met you. They're right, Polly, you are awfully nice, and just as cute as Leo said."

Polly's face flushed, but she thanked Therese. "Well, I'm going to leave after I check one patient. You try to behave yourself and stay in bed. Do you need anything else?"

"Nothing now, but I bet I'll see a lot more of you." Theresa laughed as she snuggled back into her pillows. Polly's heart thumped with joy, and she tried to subdue the smile that blossomed like a peony across her face as she walked out of the room.

She was on her way to check on Mary Francis when she bumped into Connie. "What are you still doing here, Garrity? I thought you answered one call light and then checked out. It's almost dinner time."

As though on cue, the elevator door opened, and the rattling of metal dinner trays interrupted the quiet of the ward. "I got kinda caught up with some patients," Polly answered. "It's so late now; I might as well help pass trays and sit with Mary Francis until visiting hours are over."

"Do you really enjoy working for nothing?" Connie asked nonchalantly. "You better not make this a habit, or you'll make us all look bad and we'll hate you!"

"Guess I didn't become a nurse for the big bucks!" Polly laughed. "Mary Francis just needs someone right now. Visiting hours will probably be rough when all the daddies come, and she's in the hall to see or at least hear them!" She lowered her voice because they had arrived at the screen around the new mother's bed. Pulling it back and seeing that the patient was awake, Polly said, "Hello, are you feeling any better after a little rest?"

Mary Francis nodded her head and attempted a smile through misty eyes. "When can I hold my baby again?" she asked.

"We're serving supper right now, and then the babies will come for a little while," Polly said. "Do you need to use the commode before supper?"

"I'm ok," the young mother said, adding, "I don't feel like eating anything."

As the clanging of trays and the clicking of heels continued outside the curtain, Polly retrieved a hairbrush, lipstick, and compact from the metal night stand at the foot of the bed. "Can I help brush your hair and maybe put it up a little so it's out of your way when you want to eat?" she offered, realizing that Mary Francis lovely, long hair had not been brushed since delivery. "Then after supper you might feel better with some makeup."

"No need. I'm not hungry, and no one's coming to see me, so why waste makeup trying to be pretty?" She almost choked.

"Now, that's not true. I happen to know a very handsome young man about five hours old is excited to see his beautiful mommy," Polly answered. Mary Francis sniffled through a little smile and took the brush. "Besides, sometimes don't we just get gussied up to make ourselves feel better? I'm going to help pass trays, then I'll be right back," Polly reassured her patient, pulling the privacy curtain around the bed as she left.

While she handed out trays from the large cart, Mrs. Knight, one of the older nurses, told Polly that she was an angel to have stayed so long. "I told Connie she had to call Sister to come help us or get some more nurses up here because twins are being delivered right now and you need to go home. I saw you're on again at 7:00 in the morning."

"Twins, how nice, but that mother will probably need lots of care. Unfortunately, Sister has already worked her legs off today keeping maternity and the nursery going with so many deliveries in one day." Polly smiled and asked which patients still needed food. When she returned, most of the trays had been delivered so she took one for Mary Francis and another for the additional patient in the hall. Polly delivered that patient's first, chatted a minute, and then went to the screened in cubicle.

"Don't you look nice!" she said as she pulled back the screen. "I bet you will even be able to eat a little. You want to be strong enough to hold your little guy." In answer to the shrugged shoulders, Polly set the tray on the night stand and pushed the screen out so she could move the stand next to the bed. She also pulled up a chair to visit while Mary Francis ate.

"I don't want to eat while you have no food," the young mother said.

Polly had just started to protest when Connie moved the screen. "We have an extra tray. Knowing you, Miss Garrity, you didn't have lunch during your shift. Eat this for us so we don't have to return it to the kitchen." Then she was gone as swiftly as she came.

"Oh, Miss Garrity, I forgot that you worked the earlier shift," Mary Francis said. "You shouldn't still be here taking care of me."

"Remember, it's Polly, and I'm not here just for you. We had lots of babies today, and I knew the nurses could use the extra help. If I was really working, I couldn't sit down and have supper with you, now could I?" Mary Francis looked at her skeptically, but Polly continued, "Try the homemade chicken and noodles; they are delicious. Some people gripe about hospital food, but I think it's pretty good, and it's nice to have someone else cook for me."

Mary Francis admitted that the noodles tasted good. Since Jacob left she hadn't cooked much or eaten as well as she probably should. Amid their conversation, hospital noises of beeping call lights, nurses scurrying to answer, and the rattle of empty trays continued around them. Connie came in to pick up their trays and announce that the babies would be brought any minute.

CHAPTER 21

MARY FRANCIS PERKED UP. "I hate to ask, but Polly would you stay for just a little bit? Then you can meet my baby? Unless you're too tired. I know you must be exhausted." Polly smiled and gave the patient a hug. When her baby arrived, Polly helped the new mother uncover the infant so she could admire the tiny toes and beautiful soft skin of this latest gift from God.

"I remember how excited I was when my mom had my baby brothers and children." She related stories of when her brothers were tiny and the silly questions she asked. "One time I asked my mom how he knew the baby was a boy or girl before they put it in a pink or blue blanket. When my mother asked me if I had a 'ding-dong,' I felt so stupid! I thought I'd die." She and Mary Francis giggled.

As the sounds of the daddies' voices filled the hall, Polly told stories of shenanigans she and her sisters used to pull on the farm before moving to town, any chatter to distract the young mother from thinking about her husband overseas. That was the worst part of working in maternity during this war. And, this patient was completely alone with no family to console her or to share the excitement. As she talked, Polly was sending a prayer heavenward that Mary Francis's mother was able to get on a train from Chicago.

Breaking regulations, Polly had allowed Mrs. Rubenstein to keep her baby during most of visiting hours. An obviously distraught student nurse timidly pulled back the curtain. "There he is! Mrs. Crinkston is about to skin me alive! I'm so sorry I forgot to pick up this little guy since he was hidden behind the curtain."

"No need to apologize," Polly said. "It's my fault for not reminding someone, but Jacob wanted to cuddle his mommy a little longer." Then she turned to the patient, "I think you're getting tired and ready to let Jacob go back aren't you, Mary Francis?" She nodded her head but snuggled the babe, relishing his innocence before handing him over.

"Mrs. Crinkston can't believe I lost a baby or left one with parents during visiting hours. She's having a conniption fit, Miss Garrity," the student explained.

Polly patted her shoulder and said, "You can bet it isn't the first time, Ruth. I'll go with you to return this little one." Looking back, she told Mary Francis, "I'll be back in a couple of minutes."

After visiting the nursery, Polly took a minute to stretch her aching shoulders and massage the back of her neck. I'll take Mary Francis to the bathroom again and then go home and fall in a heap, Polly thought. As she walked toward the screened cubicle, Monsignor Schaeffers, Sister Eugenia, the hospital administrator, and Dr. Morris walked through the double doors at the end of the hall. *What in the world are they doing in maternity this time of evening?* A heavy, ugly knot formed in her stomach, almost making her throw up. *Oh no. Please, Lord, no!* She walked toward them. "Good evening, Monsignor, Sister, Doctor. Can I help you with something?"

Very somberly, Sister asked where Mrs. Rubenstein's room was. Polly's eyes filled with tears, and instead of answering, she asked, "Is it her husband?" Sister nodded as she swallowed hard. Dr. Morris inquired how the patient was doing and who was with her. Polly grabbed her handkerchief from her pocket as hot tears rolled down her cheeks.

She motioned for them to move into an alcove near the doors. She certainly didn't want anyone to overhear this conversation. Then Polly pointed out Mary Francis' little cubicle in the hall and briefly told them her story.

"And that is why you are still here, my dear? I was certain I saw you come in before 6:30 this morning." Sister smiled gravely and patted Polly's arm. Everyone agreed the room situation had to be remedied before they told Mrs. Rubenstein that her husband's ship had gone down in the Pacific.

"Are you sure there are no empty rooms you can move her into?" the doctor asked.

Polly had to control herself not to say, "Well, we have a couple, but we like to keep them available for our naps and in case we want to screw a doctor!" Instead, she answered, "There are absolutely none. We're just going to have to ask a patient to move out in the hall."

"No one will do that without a ruckus," the doctor commented.

"There's a wonderful patient who probably will if I tell her what happened. I'll see if Connie or Knight can help me move her so we can get Mrs. Rubenstein into a room before you visit with her."

"Is it a private room?" Dr. Morris asked. He quickly learned those no longer existed with the bevy of babies born recently.

Sister accompanied Polly to visit Mrs. Spexarth, whose husband was just getting ready to leave. When she saw Polly, she said, "Lawrence, this is the young nurse I was telling you about. Wish I was rich enough to take you home for a daily backrub, Miss Garrity." She laughed as her husband shook hands with Polly and greeted the nun. "I thought you were going home hours ago," Therese remembered, giving Polly an opening to explain what she needed.

"Oh my goodness, the poor little thing!" Therese gasped as tears filled her eyes. "Of course, I'll give her my part of this room. If you let me go home with Lawrence, it would be much easier."

"Well, we can't do that tonight, Therese," Sister Eugenia answered. She obviously knew the Spexarths. "But, I will talk to Dr. Lies in the morning to see if he will dismiss you early for good behavior." Turning to Polly, the nun continued, "You'd better go check on Mrs. Rubenstein. With visiting hours ending, the hall will get noisy, and she might be wondering where you are. Make up some excuse that you were trying to finagle a room for her." As Polly left, Sister told Therese, "Let's get you packed up for a quick move so Monsignor and Dr. Morris don't have to wait much longer."

Therese asked Lawrence to take home her cards, especially the sweet, homemade creations from her their small children. He gathered these and a couple of other things, kissed Therese goodnight, and said he would get out of the way and plan to come back the next day to take her and little Johnny home.

Over the intercom, a pleasant voice said, "Visiting hours are now over. Please respect all our patients' need for rest. Visiting hours are now over."

Polly had stepped behind the screen just prior to the announcement, and Mary Francis was obviously happy to see her. "I was afraid that you might have gone home without saying goodnight," she said. "You do need to go, Polly; you must be exhausted."

"Oh, I'm okay, I'm used to double duty. I'm sorry I was gone so long, but I was looking at new twins in the nursery. In fact, because of those twins, Dr. Armstrong was late making rounds. But, he dismissed a couple of patients so we will have a room for you as soon as housekeeping can get it ready."

Soon the halls were fairly quiet, so she said, "I'm going to check to see if your room is clean so we can get you moved. I'll be right back." When Polly stepped from behind the screen, two nurses were placingTherese's bed, along with another one down the hall. Connie waspreparing to enclose them with the screens that had finally arrived. The strong aroma of antiseptic greeted Polly when she entered the now vacant room to see Sister Eugenia wheedling a mop. "Sister, what are you doing? Where is housekeeping?"

"This time of night, it would take forever to get anyone. Figured it's easier to just do it myself."

"I'll get the nightstand and windowsills," Polly offered picking up a rag and spray bottle. "Where is Mrs. Jarowski?"

Sister explained that she had overheard the conversation with Therese and offered to move to the hall also, saying, "I think this young mother will need all the privacy she can get."

"Oh, how kind of her."

Sister smiled as she patted Polly on the cheek and bundled up the linens "I wouldn't be a nun if I didn't believe that most people are truly kind and caring. Well, I guess we're ready. I'll drop these off and tell the men to come. Then I'll help you move Mrs. Rubenstein."

Polly returned to Mary Francis. "Well, let's get you into a room and ready for bed?" She tried to sound pleasant. Moving the screen to block a view of other hall patients, she released the brakes on the wheels of the bed.

The amiable voice again came over the intercom, "We invite all to join us in night prayers. Heavenly Father…"

Polly thought, *Oh, Lord, please help this young mother to endure this awful news and the months ahead.*

"Could you use some help, Miss Garrity?" Sister Eugenia appeared and took the end of the bed, guiding it toward the empty room as she introduced herself. Monsignor and Doctor Morris walked toward them. Once in the room, Polly took the patient chart from the end of the bed and handed it to Dr. Morris, who was still in the hall. Then she helped Sister make sure the young mother was settled and comfortable. When the cleric and doctor entered the room, Polly moved back to the corner. She felt like she was in a trance as Monsignor introduced himself and gently told Mary Francis the horrible news.

The new mother gasped, and an almost animal-like keen escaped her as she put the edge of the bed sheet in her mouth and rocked back and forth. Sister looked at the exhausted young nurse and gently said, "Polly." She snapped out of her stupor and stepped forward to support the patient who was rocking harder and trying to smother her keening with her pillow. Suddenly, she gasped, "Sick!" Polly grabbed an emesis basin from the nightstand and placed it front of Mary Francis just in time to catch most of the vomit.

After throwing up, the young mother sobbed as Polly held her, and Sister produced a cool cloth to clean her face. Then the nun scrubbed up what missed the emesis.

"Is there anything I can do for you, my child?" Monsignor gently asked.

"What happened?" She hiccupped between sobs.

"Your husband's ship was destroyed during an air raid on their convoy," the elderly priest said. "I will leave the telegram with Miss Garrity for you to look at later." Mary Francis nodded as she continued to sob. Then he delicately asked, "Forgive me for being so abrupt, Mrs. Rubenstein, but with your name I was wondering if you would like for me to contact a rabbi for you?"

The weeping patient shook her head, but choked out, "We, he wasn't very faithful, and after I moved to Kansas, it was so hard for me to get to Mass." Sobbing even harder she wailed, "Oh, God! Is this my punishment? If so, I hate you, God! I hate you!" She threw herself back against the pillows. Rolling over, she began beating them.

"Oh, my dear child," Monsignor sighed, "God doesn't work that way. He knows your heart, and also that there are few synagogues in Kansas and no Catholic churches in Mt. Hope. God loves you just the way you love your new baby. He aches for you and will help you."

Her body was shaking as she cried in desperation.

The young doctor stepped forward. "Mrs. Rubenstein, I'm Dr. Morris. I'm on duty tonight, and since your physician isn't in the hospital, I'm going to give you a little sedative to help you through this crisis."

"No, I don't want any drugs like that! I don't want to become an addict," she moaned hopelessly.

"Mary Francis, you won't become an addict, and you aren't being weak. You've had a really difficult day delivering a baby, not having a room, and now this horrible news." Polly coaxed her, "A sedative will just help you rest a little so you can care for little Jacob. Won't you let the doctor give you something?"

The young mother grabbed the hand that was caressing her hair and nodded as if totally defeated. "Can I hold my baby?" She almost choked through her sobbing.

"Let's get you something to make you feel a little stronger first," Sister said. "Some juice and a snack before Polly brings little Jacob in will help."

The doctor gave Mary Francis a quick shot and said, "That will help you relax, Mrs. Rubenstein, so you can rest tonight. I'll check on you in the morning." He signaled Sister Eugenia to follow him into the hall, so the nun handed Polly the drink.

She helped the young woman manage the liquid. Later, after the distraught patient ate a couple of crackers and cheese that Sister had magically produced, Polly helped her in using the commode. Then she brought her a warm washcloth to clean her hands and another to cool her face.

Connie knocked lightly on the door and asked how her patient was doing. Polly shrugged her shoulders and said, "I bet you need to take vitals and give meds."

"If this is a good time," Connie whispered. "With the mother of twins needing special care and another who decided to become a bleeder this evening, we never would have made it without you in here, Polly. But, I better get acquainted with this patient so you can go home. It's after 9:00." Then turning to Mary Francis, she introduced herself and explained she needed to take her blood pressure and temperature. After that, she gave her the adjusted medications prescribed by Dr. Morris.

"I'll stay for just a little longer," Polly said, seeing Mary Francis start to cry again when she heard Connie quietly mention her needing to go home.

"When are you going to bring little Jacob?" The young widow yawned.

Connie's eyebrows rose sharply, saying, *Are you crazy?* She looked at Polly, who said to her patient, "Miss Martin and I need to talk a minute; then she will stay with you while I see about little Jacob." She patted Mary Francis's hand and went into the hall with the head nurse.

"Do you know who is in charge of the nursery tonight?"

"Yes, Old Crankshaft herself who acts like every baby is her property and each was born on a schedule that will be followed to a T while in this hospital." Polly answered as they walked toward the nurses' station in the dimly lit hall.

Connie added, "You know if a mother has a problem and can't see her baby at scheduled time, Crankshaft won't bring the baby later. She even gives babies of nursing mothers a bottle instead of breaking her rules, and the poor mother can be miserable until next scheduled feeding time!"

"Oh, to hell with Crankshaft and her damn rules!" Polly exclaimed. "I'm already in her doghouse tonight. I'm going to get Mary Francis her baby." She started down the hall. Then she asked, "Is there any decent coffee or a coke at the station? I'm dying and need fuel to fight that old dragon!"

"You need some rest, Polly," Connie told her. "The bottom of the pot is all we have, and it would be awful. But, I do have some good news to give you firepower to get the baby. Sister Eugenia called up right before I went to check Mary Francis' vitals. She had just talked to Mrs. Rubenstein's father in Illinois. Her mother got on a train late this afternoon, so she should be here tomorrow morning if she doesn't get bumped by some troops. Monsignor is planning to meet her train."

"Thank God!" Polly sighed. "That's the best medicine she could have right now."

Mrs. Knight had walked up in time to hear part of the conversation and asked, "What do you prefer to drink, Polly, a coke or coffee? I'll go to the canteen while you fight the dragon lady."

Polly laughed and told Mrs. Knight she would be happy with anything she could find this time of evening. Then brandishing an invisible sword, she slapped her (horse's) hip and quietly galloped toward the nursery. Less than ten minutes later, Polly returned, grinning from ear to ear with a tiny blue bundle.

Looking up from her paperwork, Connie gasped, "How did you do that so quickly!"

"Long story. I'll tell you later," Polly smiled. "But, I did learn that Dragon Lady evolved from a broken heart out of the flames of WWI," she said before walking into the young mother's room.

Mary Francis was crying softly when Polly brought in her tiny son. She immediately put her aching arms out and caressed him with kisses and tears. Polly could only imagine the young woman's thoughts as she tried to hum to her baby through sobs. Polly sipped on the cup of hot chocolate Mrs. Knight brought her as she watched the sweet scene. When the young mother was obviously too tired to hold her baby any longer, Polly took him back to the nursery with a promise to return.

Polly adjusted Mary Francis' blankets and turned out the lights before sitting down on a lounge chair from the former fathers' waiting room. *Leave it to Connie or Knight to find this; bet it was in some janitor closet,* was the last thought she remembered until Sister Mary Joseph was gently shaking her shoulder.

"Polly, dear, you have to go get some decent rest."

"Mmm, what?" Polly awoke confused, but she soon remembered the sad room she was in.

"Your fellow nurses and Sister Eugenia are concerned about you," Sister said gently. "You need to get some rest."

Polly stretched and whispered, "What time is it?"

"It's after midnight. Sister Gregory said for you to go to the student nurses' dorm. She has a room for you, and I bet she even found a new toothbrush," Sister Mary Joseph told her.

Polly yawned and asked, "How many new babies and mommies did we end up with today?"

"Six babies and five mommies. All doing well tonight, thank Our Blessed Savior and His Holy Mother too. If this keeps up, we'll pass last year's baby record by November."

As they walked into the hall, Polly whispered, "How many did we deliver last year?"

"2,224 babies here at St. Francis," Sister said with pride. "Can you imagine all the schools we will need in a few years?"

"I can't imagine how many more babies there will be when all the soldiers return from the war!" Polly laughed. "Oh, I'm sorry, Sister," she blushed.

"That's fine, Polly. Just because I have been called to a different vocation doesn't mean that I don't appreciate that sex is a natural, beautiful gift from God. That's why I love working in maternity, even when we sometimes have nighttime emergencies." She lovingly looked at Mary Francis, who was sound asleep, and made the sign of the cross over her. "I think she will sleep the rest of the night with the medicine Dr. Morris gave her. Poor little dear. I hope her mother arrives safely," Sister said as they walked into the hall. "It won't be the same as her husband, but at least it will be family. Polly, your halo is shining tonight. You are one of the most caring and talented nurses I have ever worked with."

Polly whispered, "Thank you, Sister."

The nun patted her shoulder and told her, "I wish I could tell you that you didn't have to come in so early, but you know how busy we are. So, you have sweet dreams for a little while, Dear."

"You too, Sister. See you in a few hours."

They parted in different directions while Polly wondered which student nurse she could borrow some clean underclothes from.

As soon as she arrived back on the maternity ward the next morning, Polly checked on Mary Francis, who was still asleep. *Guess the sedative really did the trick.* After report, she tended the new mother and told her she would be back as she had time during the day.

"Mrs. Spexarth, you take care of yourself and don't go overworking when you get home," Polly instructed as she signed off on the papers that Dr. Lies handed her before leaving.

"Oh posh, and none of that Mrs. Spexarth stuff. We'll probably be neighbors before long!" Polly turned to hide her blushing as the patient continued. "I've had so much rest here; I feel like a new woman and can't wait to get home to the kids. Seeing and cuddling them will be better medicine than any hospital has."

Polly smiled. "I'm happy you get to go home. Giving up your room last night was so kind." She turned to the man walking into the room. "Hello."

"Hey, Lawrence," Mrs. Spexarth said. "This is Polly, Johnny Wetta's heartthrob."

"Seems like the rumor-mill still works well in Colwich. You're just as cute as everyone says." Polly blushed and shook hands.

"It's really nice to meet you. But around Johnny, I'm Pauline. He thinks Polly is a parrot's name."

"Johnny has always been a smart fella," Lawrence replied. "Nice to finally meet you."

As Polly left the room, she saw Monsignor Schaeffers accompanying a woman attired for travel coming down the hall. Polly thought, *Thank you, Lord;* then she ordered another tray for lunch. When midday meals arrived, Polly and a student nurse delivered the trays to Mrs. Rubenstein's room.

"Oh, Mom, this is Polly, the nurse I told you about. I could never have survived yesterday and last night without her."

"Just part of our duties." She patted the woman's shoulder.

"This is my mother, Patricia Reagan."

"From what Mary Francis told me, you have done much more than your duty."

"Have you seen your new grandson?" Polly took her patient's vitals as they talked.

"Only through the nursery window." I can't wait to hold him—just hope I don't fall asleep before then." Patricia could not hold back a telling yawn.

"I'm sure you're exhausted from traveling all night. Maybe the coffee on your tray will help." After visiting a little more, Polly started to excuse herself and said, "We'll bring the babies after lunch. Normally, no visitors are allowed on the floor at that time." Both mother and daughter looked like they had been slapped. "Maybe I can find a gown and mask to hide you, Mrs. Reagan." The sun shone again in the small room.

The afternoon went quickly; Polly was trying to finish some charting during a quiet moment when she saw Monsignor Schaeffers and Sister Eugenia approaching. They visited briefly about Mary Francis and baby Jacob's health. Sister asked, "Polly, have you met Mrs. Reagan?"

"Yes, she seems very nice, just exhausted. Are you here to take her to a hotel, Monsignor?"

"Why, yes I am, for tonight. But we are thinking that might present a problem after a while." He looked at Sister Eugenia.

"Polly, you've already done so much, and I hate to be intrusive; but I've heard that our young nurse who died in the blizzard was your roommate, and it has left you in somewhat of a bind. Mary Francis will be here for at least a week or maybe two. The cost of a hotel room will become…"

As she listened to the kind nun, Polly did not attempt to hide her smile as she thought, "Thank you again, Jesus. That might save me until Helen's lease is up and she can move in."

Chapter 22

Hi Polly,

Well, I made it—by an inch almost too tall! Planes will be cramped, and tall nurses would be miserable. Over weight nurses don't exist here.. They keep us running and working so hard any extra weight fell off long ago.

You wouldn't believe all the studying to earn our wings— nothing like regular nursing. I pray I never have to use: ocean survival and religious procedures in an emergency. We spent time in an altitude chamber so we can recognize injured patients having problems. With no idea where we'll be stationed, proficiency in tropical, arctic, and desert survival are essential. We took care of lots of different wounded in a frigid chamber with inches of snow one week. Dressed in heavy parkas with gloves and lots of blankets made moving so cumbersome and forced us to learn to make adjustments. The next week we sweltered in chambers dripping with humidity and heat trying to imitate conditions on the Pacific Islands. So life is never dull because between these extremes we've learned to jump out of a plane with a parachute. Really quite thrilling Polly. I could just imagine you whooping through the air the first couple of times. The 234 hours of in-

struction with so much new information to learn in addition to all simulations will make the nine weeks fly by. Not much time for partying. We're all looking forward to the last couple of weeks; we'll be flying with graduate flight nurses.

Last week we practiced over and over loading-litters. It was amazing to...

"This plane is obviously on the ground already." Lieutenant Patterson spoke to more than sixty sets of eyes. "Techs, until patients arrive, you will be responsible for helping unload the supplies. Remember, it could be live ammunition, food, medicine, or even animals." He moved his focus to the women. "Nurses, many times, when you land you've been flying for 9 hours without a break. Upon arrival at destinations, you will rush to the nearest site to relieve nature—and hope something's available. We'll forego that during this drill. Instead, stand ready for the arrival of patients. If no one has appeared to help re-configure the plane, you will pull up floors and pull down bunks until help arrives." The nurses looked around and were happy to see a ground crew. "Any questions? Looks like, Lieutenant Beat, you are our lucky first nurse, and Corporal Zemco, you are the surgical tech on this flight."

Both stepped forward and saluted Lieutenant Patterson who said, "By the way, you're being timed and the clock is running."

The tech quickly climbed on board and opened the cargo deck to hand supplies out to the ground crew at the same time several other men came running from nearby underbrush. Aggie sprinted to the open passenger door and jumped up twice before pulling herself inside to lower the stairs.

"Good morning, Captain." She saluted the soldier with a medical insignia on his helmet. His dirty, blood-stained camo was not the medical attire she had naively expected.

"Don't have time for that damned stuff," he barked. "Start listening and taking notes so we can get these men aboard."

Aggie wrote furiously, using short comments and abbreviations. Barely glancing at the first ten or more men being carried by on litters, she realized it was essential to match names with the medic's orders and to make the patients comfortable. Some had never flown and would be scared to death. *Can't you please slow down a little!* her mind screamed at Patterson. But instead, she smiled at one of the patients. *Use the brain God gave you, Miss Beat! Just Listen.*

Aggie reached down and touched each man on the remaining litters carried up the stairs. With the last man, she turned to thank the doctor and clarify a couple of things, but he was already running for cover. *Get into the plane, you idiot!* She dashed up the stairs, pulled them in with her, and secured the door.

She was taken aback at the plane's transformation. What had been a fuselage half-full of crates, was now crowded with patients in triple bunks lining both sides of the plane. She also noticed that the other nurses and techs had gathered at the cargo door and opened the one she had just closed so they could observe inside.

Aggie moved to the nearest bunks. "Hello, Martin." She spied the name on his fatigues as she secured the straps of the soldier in the top bunk. Looking at the one below, she said, "Wilson, you must be one special guy." The soldier looked puzzled. "You're here in the middle, like the frosting in an Oreo cookie." His smile relaxed Aggie as she knelt to secure straps on the lowest bunk, and she recalled the orders about his injuries.

After straining on straps and adjusting a couple of loose bunks, she finally met her surgical tech close to the center of the plane. "I think I have everyone from here back, Lieutenant." He smiled.

"Thank God." She exhaled heavily.

"You about finished in there? Time's still running," Lieutenant Patterson yelled, and the other personnel moved from the doors.

"Oh, shit!" Aggie said and slapped her hand over her mouth. But, she smiled, thinking of Polly. She and Zemco bounded for the door, and Aggie yelled out, "Ready for takeoff, sir."

The nurses and techs on the ground shouted approval and applauded as Aggie and her surgical tech saluted.

"Attention!" Patterson yelled. "No one should celebrate. You're all dead!" Aggie could feel the heat rising to her face. "You two get down here with your team." While they joined the nurses and techs, the ground crew emptied the plane. The instructor continued, "You spent 18 ½ minutes on the ground. If you were in a combat zone, the enemy could have killed every one of you and your patients by now. Before anyone graduates, you will all be able to perform this in less than 10 minutes!"

"Good Lord," Aggie sighed, feeling exhausted from trying to remember the doctor's orders in addition to the physical stress.

"You might want to blame the ground crew, but they operate as fast as they see the flight nurse process the injured. That will be the end of field training today. Fall in; return to the classroom for debriefing and figure out how to cut the time for loading litters in half."

Everyone formed up and marched across the tarmac toward the base buildings, Aggie—drowning in a sea of shame.

That evening, as she and her friend Fey walked toward their barracks after mess, a couple of nurses approached from across the compound. "Hey, you want to join us at the officers' club?" one asked.

"No, I just want to take a long shower and wash my hair," Aggie answered. But she thought, *After today, I've probably lost officer privileges.*

Aggie recognized a voice behind them. "Oh no you don't, Lieutenant Beat. No moping for flight nurses." In the waning light, Aggie recognized a couple of instructors approach and saluted.

"You were just Patterson's guinea pig today cause he knew you could take it," one of the nurses said. "And don't worry about the saluting. Tonight we're just Wanda and Edna, not your instructors. Florence is probably already at the club."

Florence waved them over at the same time a waiter set down mugs and a pitcher of beer. He also served a couple of tall drinks with pieces of pineapple decorating the edge of the glass. "Hi, ladies, hope you don't mind me getting this party rolling. I knew you'd want a piña colada, Edna, and I presume you'll want beer as usual, Wanda."

"Right you are." The ladies found seats around the table.

"Hope beer is ok, lieutenants," Florence continued. "I also ordered an extra pina, in case one of you wanted one. If not, I'll drink anything."

Aggie and Fay clarified they were not lieutenants that evening and admitted to never having had a pina colada. After chitchat, Aggie said, "I'm so glad we finally have a chance to visit. Since the first day of class I've wondered where you have served. Each of you teaches like you have first-hand experience. Dr. Chomin even defers to you sometimes when he's lecturing." Agnes leaned forward, lowering her voice, "Which is a miracle for any doctor."

Everyone burst into laughter before Fay said, "And that's putting it mildly! Most were first in line when the Lord handed out arrogance!"

Wanda confessed, "Well, we kinda have an advantage over him and the doctors." Answering Aggie and Fay's puzzled expressions, she continued, "We've been flight nurses since before the war began and been on lots of rescue flights in the Pacific."

"Really? How did you do that? The Army just approved this division and started these classes last year?" Fay was skeptical.

"We were lucky enough to live in California and to be a part of Aerial Nurse Corps of America there," Wanda explained.

"We wanted adventures, so we hopped on a ship for Hawaii," Florence chimed in.

"You weren't in the Army, right?" Aggie asked. "I've never heard of the Aerial Nurse Corps."

"The Corps isn't part of the Army, even though the founder, Lauretta Schimmoler, was trying to convince the military of the need long before the war. But that's another story." Edna sipped her fruity drink before continuing. "We were actually in Honolulu working for an air show when we saw the ad for nurses needed, and we thought we'd be crazy to leave paradise. After Pearl was attacked, we were just sort of swallowed by the Army."

"So, were you at Pearl during the attack?" Aggie and Fay were awed.

Edna nodded her head and quietly said, "Paradise suddenly turned to hell, and we were treating patients who somehow lived through its fires. Wanda and Florence were just getting off duty at the Aeia Plantation Hospital. I had the day off, but we all went back to the hospital after the first wave of the attack. Because that hospital had some connection to the military, many causalities were brought there along with military medical personnel. None of us could have imagined what we treated. Unbelievable a human body could be shattered to such grotesque distortions, but the person inside was still alive. Triage was easy for many of the poor guys."

"With all the chaos, no one knew we weren't military until days later," Wanda picked up the story. "Suddenly we were working between Aeia and the base hospital, transporting patients and accompanying orderlies on supply runs. Aeia wasn't equipped for so many badly burnt patients, but the base hospital sent supplies. The doctors and supervising nurses just kept giving us orders. I don't think anyone slept for the first couple of days. Everyone just worked." Wanda sipped her beer.

Florence continued, "A few days later, Wanda was in what was left of the canteen when she heard a rescue flight was being sent to other islands that had been attacked. We told our supervisors we were part of the Aerial Corps and would like to help if possible. We grabbed a bag, filled it with bandages, towels, aspirin and things like that , and were on a flight before we had a chance to worry about the danger."

"And too exhausted to think! We all fell sound asleep as soon as we were airborne and didn't blink until we were setting down a couple of hours later."

"Talk about training under fire! You gals probably have seen and done more than any of us ever will," Aggie complimented. "No wonder you're so great at teaching these classes."

"I'm surprised that the Army brought you back state-side when nurses are needed so badly in the Pacific," Fay said.

All three of the experts laughed before Florence said, "Well, this makes a lot more sense than when we had to come back last year to take the course. At least now we're officially recognized to teach what we've lived."

"You had to take this course last year?" Aggie was shocked. "You probably could have written it."

"Well, you know Army protocol. Everything has to be by the book. After we went on occasional flights and worked for a couple of months with the Army, someone realized we weren't even in the military. The Brass liked what we were doing and wanted us to continue, so we were officially inducted. But there wasn't time for any military training. When the Medical Ariel Evacuation School was opened at Bowman, the big wigs decided we needed to attend to be official," Florence said. "So, they started rotating through all of the ANCOA flight nurses in the first few classes."

"You're kidding! After already serving almost two years? Why didn't you refuse?" Fay was outraged.

"Then we'd lose our wings and couldn't fly anymore," explained Wanda.

"How could you stand being in classes with all us ninnies and being taught by guys who knew zip compared to you?" Agnes asked.

"Oh, no one was a ninny, and most of the instructors knew who we were, and sometimes they asked us to verify and clarify info. Besides, we got a nice rest that we desperately needed by that time. Flying is really hard work, and seeing all the horribly wounded soldiers takes its toll. Besides, this is lots safer than Hawaii," Edna explained.

"We're sure lucky to have you instructing. Are all the classes now taught by you pioneers?"

"Most. As I said, we rotate state-side, teaching, advising and getting a little rest."

Florence explained, "Unlike nine weeks, the first classes were only four and missed important training the nurses needed. They had to figure out so much on their feet, like we did before any training. But each class has been better with more experiences."

Wanda added, "Of course, in the beginning, there was such a need to get flight nurses to the war zones. If the military had just listened to Lauretta, they could have had this all in place. But you know the big shots were not about to take advice from a woman."

Aggie laughed, "If my friend Polly was here, she'd be having a hissy fit about such idiocy! She hated stupid rules and found so many ways around them." The conversation evolved into stories of attempting to land under fire and then into the more mundane topic of the beauty of the islands…

…there's much more I'd like to write, but you know- paper shortage. Have fun with the new babies, and try not to jab the guys at the USO too hard. Behave yourself; have a drink for me

at the Blue Moon, and tell the old crowd I miss them, but I'm truly happy and proud to be here.

As always,

Aggie

CHAPTER 23

Hi Beat,

Darn! I so hoped that this Thanksgiving we could be thanking God that the war is finally over, and you and all the soldiers would be home or at least on their way. Gosh, it was so terrific to get your letter. I can't imagine you, the most stylish among us, in ugly Army dungarees! Sure hope the guys you are helping appreciate what a special nurse they have.

I guess the war is heating up even more, if that's possible. Johnny insists if it isn't over by Christmas, young nurses will be "highly encouraged" to enlist. I love America, but I sure don't want to be in the Army. Can you imagine me following some yelling sergeant after I finally got away from Gorgon? I can't believe all the BS about those flight nurses who had to go back to school to keep their wings. The Army would probably kick me out the first week, or worse yet, throw me in the brig.

The weather here is cold again, and my feet freeze walking to the hospital in these cheap cardboard shoes. Gotta save up for some heeled rubber boots. Sure hope we don't have any blizzards like the one at Christmas last year.

I get off Thanksgiving Day, but hafta work that night. John-

ny and I went to the Blue Moon last weekend, and I was complaining that even with the day off, I can't go home for a big turkey dinner. He offered to drive me home to Wellington or out to the farm to have Thanksgiving with his family. He promised to have me back in time for night shift. Wow! My folks met him at graduation, and my sisters loved him, but taking him home or going to the farm for Thanksgiving would be another big step. Know what I mean?

By the way, Johnny said that he saw Cy out at Mt. Vernon at a turkey shoot a few weeks ago. He tried to convince him to come out to the Blue Moon with us, but you know Cy! Johnny said he's fine, but I bet he misses you; I sure do.

Well, I gotta wash my hose and iron my uniform for tomorrow. With new regulations for military letters, this will be too heavy to mail if I write much more.2

Miss your smile, Aggie. Praying the war ends soon. I sure don't want you sent any place close to the fighting if Johnny is right! And, I sure as hell don't want to be a WAC or WAVE! Damned War!

Garrity

❧

Marianna, Florida
Early December 1944

Hi Polly,

Since completing flight training, I've been winging my way all over the country, accompanying wounded soldiers after they are checked out at the hospital here. We take the guys to the mili-

tary hospital closest to their homes for more treatment. That way
their family has a better chance to see them and encourage them
to get well. Some are in such awful shape. The psyche cases are the
saddest because the guys look ok, but their eyes are hollow. Some
big wigs think they're faking, but the panic and fear of these patients is frighteningly real. No one could fake the terror in their
voices screaming about being overrun and yelling at everyone
while trying to escape or use anything within reach as a weapon.
Some get pretty dangerous and will do anything to escape. Keeping them medicated is all we can do, War is so awful!

Well, this has to be short—lots going on. Just want to say
Merry Christmas, and so happy about your Thanksgiving with
Johnny. Bet it was a great day. You probably read about those
spies the cops nabbed in Maine. The government seems to think
things are heating up in Europe, so I'll probably be deployed there
soon, meaning no more letters for a while.

So much for the season of Peace on Earth. Be sure to find
some elves to help entertain the student nurses on Christmas.
That was such fun. Love to you and Johnny.

Miss you all,
Aggie

❧

Christmas Card
1944

Merry Christmas Aggie,
Hope this card catches up with you in time for Christmas. I
don't want to think about you going to the warzone, especially

this time of year. Guess we have to keep praying. Johnny's brother Leo (they call him Spud) surprised the family when he walked in the day before Thanksgiving. He had been in a hospital in California for weeks with a terrible staph infection and almost lost his hand. Not a great way to get out of the Navy, but Mrs. Wetta is sure happy to have at least one of her sons home.

Hay met a guy from KC when she was on vacation. She came back with stars in her eyes, and is ditsier than ever. I hate it, but I wasn't surprised that she applied and was hired at Childrens' Research Hospital in KC. Now she can be closer to Eddie and find out if "he's her baby." She's sure keen on him, but I miss her so much! St. Francis isn't nearly as much fun with you both gone. Anyway, Santa has no elves. Not sure if she is up to training a new pair, and I'd look even more weird than last year all by myself.

I sure hope Santa blesses you with lots of guardian angels to keep you safe, Aggie.

Merry Christmas,
Polly

Chapter 24

January 15, 1945

Dear Aggie,

Gosh, I wish you were around so we could talk and talk and talk. So much has happened in the past few weeks; it'll take way to much paper to tell you. Christmas seemed pretty dull after last year. No Santa and elves. We seasoned staff helped the student nurses and patients by doing some singing and elf stuff like last year but it wasn't as silly and fun as last year. I actually volunteered to work because one of the newer nurses who was scheduled has two little ones. I figured she needed to be home more than I did. Johnny came to get me the next day to celebrate a late Christmas with his family. Sound familiar? We sure missed not sharing the fun time with you and Cy like last year. At least Johnny remembered to ask ahead of time.

Oh yea, I almost forgot...

Polly was on the floor building a lopsided house with Johnny's nephew. "Ok Leroy, we're almost finished. Do you wanna put this red block on the roof like a chimney?" The chubby two-year-old clapped his hands and reached for the wooden block.

"Yea, yea, yea. Red," he said before smashing it onto the forlorn creation. Noisy clattering and clunking of falling pieces of wood colliding woke Leroy's infant brother who was nestled in Grandma Anna's arms. The crash of the toy house and sudden crying of little Larry got the attention of the men playing cards in the next room. Leroy clapped his hands again then scattered blocks in all directions with his feet. "Boom, boom, boom," he laughed until a block flew into Pauline's face.

"Leroy, stop!" his mother grabbed him saying, "Oh Pauline, I'm so sorry. Are you ok?" Leroy started wailing when he saw blood on his new friend's forehead.

"I'm fine. The corner of the block just hit me in a bad spot." Johnny was in the living room now and handed her his handkerchief. "Oh Leroy, don't cry. I'm ok."

"I think someone is overly tired," his dad, Alphonse, said. "Think it's time we get these boys home."

"You're just afraid I'm going to win my money back if we play anymore, Alph," Johnny laughed as he helped Polly from the floor. "But, I owed you a game or two I guess. Sure appreciate you coming over to help Dad with the chores this morning so I could go get Pauline."

With the babies bundled and calmed down, Alph and Veronica wished all Merry Christmas. After they departed, Johnny's sister Annie brought a wet cloth for the cut above Polly's eye. "I think you may need more than this, Pauline, but it's a start. Johnny's handkerchief looks pretty bloody."

"I thought it felt that way but sure didn't want to frighten poor little Leroy. Head wounds can spurt blood and look so much worse than they really are." Polly removed the handkerchief and looked at her hand with bright sticky goo seeping between her fingers. "Oops,

I think I need a bandage." The ladies headed to the bathroom to take care of the wound while the men gathered up the cards before heading out to do chores early.

Later on the drive to Wichita, Johnny asked Pauline, "It was nice of you to play with Leroy so Vronie could take a little nap. Too bad he got a little wild." He touched a finger to the bandage on her forehead.

"He was just excited. I'm fine, and I had fun today." Pauline rested her head on Johnny's shoulder.

"It's a lot easier driving back this Christmas than last. Remember?"

"I sure do. That turned into quite a storm." Pauline changed the focus, "It was also a lot nicer to be prepared for going to the farm and not have to scramble at the last moment." She smiled at him slyly,

"I know I was really presumptuous last year. Hope I've learned a little since then," they both laughed.

"Yes, you have, but I still had to change clothes again and put on my favorite sweater." Playing with a small sparkling green bracelet on her wrist, she continued, "I can't believe you found this gorgeous bracelet that matches the necklace you gave me last year. They look like a matched set, purchased together." She jerked upright and stared at him with sudden realization, "Did you buy them together last year, Johnny?"

"Don't rightly recall at the moment," earned him a punch in the shoulder followed by a skeptical face and pursed lips which he leaned down and kissed.

"Johnny, pay attention to your driving!"

He laughed, "You know I keep wondering if you're ashamed of being seen with me?"

"What in the world are you talking about?"

"Well, I've invited you for Thanksgiving and Christmas twice. The only time you invited me to Wellington to see your family was when you wanted to go fishing last Fourth of July. Hey, I just remembered, that was at the spur of the moment too."

Polly's mouth flew wide open, and she sputtered for and excuse.

Laughing, Johnny said, "Calm down. Calm down. How about we go see your folks for a combination of Christmas and New Year's next Friday or Saturday? You must get off a few extra days in payment for volunteering for Christmas."

"That would be real nice Johnny. I was planning to take the bus home on Thursday after work to say Merry Christmas and be back in time for our early New Year's Eve date. Gee, I'm sure the folk's would love to see you, and it'd save me bus fare."By the time they arrived at Pauline's apartment, plans for the weekend outing were made.

"Do you think that this awful war will be over by New Year's Eve next year?" Polly asked the following Saturday evening as Johnny drove to the Blue Moon.

"Hell, I sure hope so. I thought it'd be over by now as hard as we've been hitting the Germans. But, Hitler seems only more determined and doesn't care what it costs in the lives of his people or country. Reports of the fighting going on right now in horrible winter weather are unbelievable. Hope you're ready to be drafted, Pauline, because I bet it happens soon."

"It won't happen.! People have been talking about that for the last couple of years. Gee, I wish I hadn't let my thoughts sneak out loud. We're going out to celebrate New Year's so no more war talk! Now let's talk about something happy like you and Dad going fishing the last of December. Didn't you guys about freeze your butts off?"

The popular dance hall was packed with all their friends like Pauline's sister Helen and Jim Meyer and Stella and her husband Dr. Jackson all wanting to forget the war and hoping for a better year ahead. Lots of feminine squeals broke above sounds of the already noisy ballroom when Eileen Hayes and Eddie arrived. Glasses clinking to many toasts and raucous laughter filled the air the few times the band took a break. Whether their energetic renditions of songs like "Chattanooga Choo Choo" or romantic strains of "Star Dust", the merrymakers filled the dance floor. "Don't Sit Under the Apple Tree" and "Pennsylvania 6 5000" among other lively tunes brought animated singing and spirited dancing.

Much too soon, the strains of "Auld Lang Syne," filled the hall transforming the revelers into a somber group. When the band leader added an extra verse, kinda like a prayer that this would be the last time singing that song with our troops still fighting, Pauline tried to hide her tears, but Johnny handed her his handkerchief. "Talk about throwing cold water on a party," she sniffled laying her head on his shoulder until the count-down interrupted followed by lots of noise makers, hugs and kisses. Everyone seemed to kiss and hug everyone else expressing hope for the future.

When the notes of "I'll Be Seeing You," finally interrupted the celebrating, Johnny and Pauline had to look for one another and break away from other partiers to share the last dance. Near the end of the song, Johnny whispered in her ear, "You know, I'm getting awful tired of looking at the moon or sunset and thinking of you." Pauline looked puzzled until he broke their close dancing embrace and took her left hand from his neck. "How about we stop dreaming we see each other?" As the final notes played, Johnny slipped a ring onto her finger, and Pauline looked totally flabbergasted, and finally threw her arms back around his neck. "Oh yes, yes, yes," she whispered.

Eagle eyed Eileen was hugging Pauline, jumping up and down before the music died away bringing everyone's attention to them. Instead of the New Years Eve party ending, the newly engaged couple had provided incentive to continue celebrating at Pauline and Helen's apartment until the landlord threatened eviction.

Chapter 25

A week later, Pauline was sitting on the floor with near the big Philco radio playing checkers with Leo sr. Johnny brought in an arm load of wood and added a couple of large pieces to the pot-bellied stove. "Ha, ha," Pauline said laughing as she triple jumped three of her opponent's kings.

"Well, I'll be damned!" Johnny's dad was dismayed but pleasingly surprised at the skill of his future daughter-in-law. "Is that any way to treat your future father-in-law?"

"Speaking of in-laws, have you two picked a date yet?" Annie, who was sitting across the room asked.

"We've decided why wait around any longer, so we want to get married before Lent." Johnny answered." After that, we'll be so busy with farm work, planting oats and haying, then wheat harvest."

"Of course, We need to check a calendar to see when Lent begins, and talk with my folks," Pauline said.

Leo called to the kitchen, "Mother, let that stuff go til morning and come join us. Bring the calendar along too."

"Why do you need the calendar?" Grandma Anna sat down next to her husband on the sofa.

Holding Pauline's hand Johnny answered, "We want to know when Lent begins so we can start planning this wedding. Since the Church doesn't allow weddings during Lent, and farm life is so busy after, especially helping with farming for guys who are gone overseas, we want to get married before."

"Oh my. Lent is really early this year. It begins February 14th," she handed the calendar to the young couple.

"Wow can people even get married that fast?" Annie asked.

"They just need to have the Bands of Matrimony announced in the bride and groom's churches for three weeks beforehand," Leo, who had served on the church council for years answered.

Pauline and Johnny looked at each other knowing they had a lot to discuss and an important decision to make fast. "I guess we need to talk to my parents," Pauline said. Then she blushed brightly before laughing, "Mom's first question will be, 'Are you pregnant?'"

"O my, I hadn't thought of that. Everyone will be gossiping," Annie said. "I was just thinking it will be fun to plan a wedding fast instead of dragging it all out."

"We know how tongues like to wag no matter what," Johnny growled. Pulling Pauline to him, he added, "We'll just have to work on that so the busy-bodies have to double check their calendars before the end of the year," and laughed.

Pauline blushed, "Johnny!"

What do you think Father?" Grandma looked up at Leo Sr.

"I think it's up to this young couple to decide. You two have a lot to consider in a short time. But for now, Johnny you better switch on that contraption or we might miss the President's talk.. The cylinders whirred to life and warmed enough for the static on the radio to clear as Johnny sat down in the overstuffed chair behind Pauline. The sounds of the National Anthem filled the living room followed by introductions and announcements including the latest news about the unrelenting German offensive that had begun in the Ardennes Mountains of Europe before Christmas.

When President Franklin D. Roosevelt began his State of the Union Address, the attention in the room was electric. Pauline gently massaged Johnny's leg and observed Mr. and Mrs. Wetta tightly holding hands. The President's description of the fighting and costs in lives and wounded were sad statistics. However when he said that the Army Nurse Corps needed at least 18,000 more nurses to fulfill requirements of 60,000 crucial for decent care; therefore had become essential, Grandma Anna gasped and put her hand to her mouth.

Johnny held Pauline's shoulders while Leo said, "What the hell does he mean?" Johnny dared to shush his father as Roosevelt continued. "The care and treatment given to our wounded and sick soldiers have been the best known to medical science. Those standards must be maintained at all costs," he said. "We cannot tolerate a lowering of them by failure to provide adequate nursing for the brave men who stand desperately in need of it."

When the State of the Union Addresswas over, Pauline stood with Johnny's help and looked at him, "You were right. You said all along this was going to happen

"Oh, my Dear, they surely won't really draft nurses will they?" Grandma walked over and hugged Pauline.

"They can't really draft women, can they?" Annie asked looking at her brother

Leo was adamant, "Never heard of such a thing, and the US better not do it. Congress won't vote to approve it if any of them want re-elected."

"Well, Mr.Wetta," Pauline began, "The reports are really bad, and can you imagine some poor soldiers wounded and waiting in a bed for care because there aren'tenough nurses?" As she finished she realized her future in-laws were all staring at the pictures of Joe, Ben and Leo Jr. on the small table with Rosaries lying beside them. "Oh, I'm sorry. I didn't mean…"

"Let's have some coffee and pie," Grandma Anna said. "Happy I saved dessert." She moved to the kitchen followed by the family. Johnny had his arm protectively around Pauline, and was deep in thought.

She started to help serve, but Annie told her she was a guest. "After all tonight is actually supposed to be celebrating your engagement."

Leo said, "When you asked Pauline to marry you, I thought, 'Finally.' I was afraid you were going to let her get away," he smiled at Pauline. "Never thought it might be Uncle Sam who'd try to steal you."

"Well, like I've heard you often say, Grandma, We'lljust put it in Our Lord's hands." Johnny's face expressed obvious surprise at his fiance'swords. "Guess I'll start making lists of what we need to do and find out if we can get a wedding organized in a month. First thing is talking to my parents, though. Do you have enough gas stamps to go to Wellington on Wednesday? That's my next day off," she asked Johnny.

"Don't worry about gas stamps. I have connections."

 Pauline took a bite of apple pie smothered in sweet cream. "You make the most scrumptious pies in the world," she complimented her future mother-in-law, then said, "Goodness, Johnny you need to get me to the depot or I'll miss the train back to Wichita., and you'llhave to take me. Sure don't need to use more gas stamps then necessary."

He was helping her into her coat when Grandma said, "You all need to hurry, but be sure to tell your parents that we will help any way we can," Grandma hugged her. "In fact I will write her a note first thing in the morning. Johnny be sure to get the address before Pauline gets on the train."

As Johnny opened the door, a gust of cold air swept into the kitchen. "Thanks so much. Feel free to send any ideas you have, I know

Mom and I will appreciate it. My two older sisters basically eloped, so this is all new to us. Bye all."

After work the next couple of afternoons, Helen and Pauline did lots preliminary planning and list making. Most importantly, the bride-to-be made an appointment for her and Johnny to meet with the rector of the Cathedral down the street early Wednesday before they went to Wellingt

CHAPTER 26

ONE SATURDAY MORNING in late January, Johnny picked Polly up as soon as she got off night duty. They were going to Wellington again so Pauline could talk with her mother about wedding plans and the men could go fishing since the weather had been unseasonably warm. She teased her fiancé. "I don't think my sisters would even ask where I was if you showed up without me."

When Pauline handed Johnny her suitcase and she put a large package in the car, the aroma of fresh bread was so overpowering, she felt like she had stepped into a bakery. "What is that wonderful aroma?" Polly asked, glancing into the back seat. "What is all of this?" Knowing good food was especially difficult to find for townsfolk, Grandma Anna and Leo had insisted that Johnny take along a couple of baskets of canned goods from the cellar and some homemade bread.

Not waiting for an answer other than Johnny's smile, Polly rummaged through the packages; her nose led her to four loaves still slightly warm. Polly tore off a huge chunk and began munching. "Your mom must have hardly slept!" she garbled with her mouth full.

Johnny laughed and said, "Starving? There's butter in there someplace."

"This is heavenly just the way it is." She bit another chunk of what she said was the most wonderful bread she had ever tasted. "Mom makes bread, but nothing like this — especially since she's always trying to save by cheating on ingredients like eggs & milk. What's all this food for anyway?"

"Mother said she knew it was hard for your family to get a lot of things with the war, and your mom had mentioned something about making sandwiches for the troop trains going through Wellington. She just wanted to help out a little." Johnny talked as Polly snuggled close. He wrapped his right arm around her; soon her head rested on his shoulder. Before they were out of Wichita, the drone of the tires and the aroma of wonderful food had lulled her sound asleep.

"Wake up, Sleeping Beauty. We're here." Pauline stretched and yawned as Bob and Buddy, who were in the yard getting fishing gear ready, came over to the car. Enticed by the aroma of the food, they didn't have to be asked to take the baskets into the house. Almost before setting them down in the kitchen, the boys tore into the bread. "That's enough for now, you two," Polly's mother, Sara Pearl, ordered, taking what was left of a loaf of bread from them. "How are ya, Polly? You look tired," she observed, giving her fourth daughter a peck on the cheek.

"I had to work last night and just woke up. I must have fallen asleep before we got ten blocks from the hospital. Hope I didn't snore." She gave her fiancée a quizzical look.

"Not any louder than my brothers." He laughed as her complexion turned bright pink. "How are you, Pearl?" He greeted Polly's mother with the name most of the men used to tease her.

"Hello, Johnny, glad you could come again, but you know that you don't have to bring food every time." She patted his arm, still a little uncomfortable in how to welcome this new young man. Dorothy wandered into the kitchen, sleepy-eyed and still in her PJs.

"Hi, Red," Johnny teased. His dark, handsome features had always sent Polly's red-haired teen-aged sister Dorothy swooning. Now she squealed and ran back upstairs. Motivated by the aroma of homemade bread, she was soon dressed and back in the kitchen.

Sara Pearl poured Pauline and Johnny cups of coffee and set a plate of the bread and butter in front of them. Dorothy got a mug for coffee and helped herself to the bread, and asked, "What's in the big box?" She started to open it when Pauline slapped her hand.

"That's Jo's bride's maid dress. And you don't need to snoop even before she tries it on. Especially with buttery fingers. Dorothy stuck her tongue out at her older sister.

"I wonder where your father is," Sara said, looking out the window to the side yard. Then she glanced at the clock. "Look at the time! We need to get busy making sandwiches or we won't get them to the station by the time the troop train arrives."

Pauline retrieved a large, cast iron skillet from a cabinet and heated it for frying eggs. Her mom tossed her an apron and sliced more bread. For a change, Dorothy helped without complaining and buttered the slices. Of course, she would occasionally sneak a small piece of bread or egg that just happened to break off.

"Hey, there's my favorite, most beautiful nurse in the whole world!" boomed Pauline's dad, Steve, from the doorway. "Give me some apples." He smiled at his daughter. She wiped her hands on the apron and reached up to wrap her arms around the neck of the large man. "Hi, Daddy." She kissed his cheek and added, "And, if Helen was here, she would be the most beautiful nurse in the whole world," to which her father laughed. Then seeing Nonie, Polly said, "Hey, Sis, where you guys been?"

Polly released her dad so he could shake hands with Johnny. Nonie said, "Oh, we had to go check a few meters this morning, and then Dad said he wanted a newspaper at the drugstore. You know he isn't about to buy one, so we had to wait around until some guy finished reading his and left it at the counter."

"Dad, since when are you so interested in the newspaper. I thought you just listened to the radio to find out what is going on in the world," Polly commented.

"Well, since I might be going to work at that big airplane factory in Wichita, I gotta know more about the world. Besides, the newspaper's great for wrapping sandwiches," he answered. "Be sure to save the funny page. I need a good laugh as much as any soldier."

"I didn't know you're going to work at Boeing!" Polly was surprised. "How are you going to get up to Wichita? Are you moving in with Nonie?"

Her younger sister was adamant, "No way!"

"A bunch of us have applied. Charles has a car, and we'll all pitch in for the gas. We can sure use some extra money around here with those brothers of yours always starving. Right, Pearl?"She nodded as she assembled sandwiches. "I'll do that if you want to get the baskets," Steve said, and he took over the process.

Her father had never helped in the kitchen when she was still living at home, so Polly was surprised with the new behavior. He set the paper on the counter and motioned Johnny over to wrap the sandwiches while they discussed fishing plans. They were going to meet up with Uncle Charlie, who had a worm farm that Johnny liked to check on.

The women chatted about wedding plans, and the men were happy that the really cold winter weather still hadn't arrived so they could fish in January. Even though Polly had to fight unwelcome yawns, working with her family again was special.

Abruptly shrill factory whistles cancelled their conversations. "Good lord, what is that?" Polly asked, looking out the window as every dog in town added to the racket.

"Oh, that's the new town whistles. It means we gotta hurry!" Sara Pearl explained, wiping her hands on her apron and hanging it on a nail by the door. "Train's comin' in 15 minutes." The ladies quickly washed their hands and fingered their hair into place while laughing and shoving each other for room in front of the small mirror over the sink.

"Anyone have some lipstick handy?" Dorothy asked.

"Girls, you don't have time for that; let's go," their mother admonished.

"Now calm down, Pearl," Johnny said with an ornery grin. "We'll drop you all at the train station before we pick up Charlie. Right Steve?" he asked as Polly's dad was coming in from the back porch with their fishing gear. "Of course, I may have to stick around awhile to make sure none of those hungry soldiers tries to steal my girl," he added, giving Pauline a hug.

"Steve, why are you dragging all that stinky stuff through the house? Go around!" Sara yelled at her husband. Bob and Buddy were starting through the back door with their gear but decided a trip around the house might be wise. Johnny joined the guys in the longer walk to the car. "We'll never all fit in your car," Sara protested after him.

"Bet we'll find room somewhere," Dorothy grinned as they all rushed out, carrying baskets of newspaper-wrapped sandwiches and cookies.

Pauline squeezed in front between her dad and Johnny, and her mom and Nonie piled in back. "What do ya think you're doing?" Johnny hollered at Dorothy as she plopped herself on the hood of the car.

"Dorothy Garrity get your butt in this car!" Sara demanded.

"Oh, leave her there, Mom. It'll take too long to make her get back here," Polly wisely advised. "Let her play princess so we can get moving."

"I'm directing," she sang in typical Dorothy fashion. "Onward, James," she ordered, glancing back at Johnny.

197

"Yes, madam." He obeyed and threw the car into gear as Bob and Buddy jumped onto the running boards, swinging one arm through the open window frames and grappling the fishing gear with the other.

"Oh, heaven help us all!" Sara shook her head and put her hands over her face. "Can you even see the street, Johnny?"

Driving across town, the group in the overloaded car looked like a bunch of Okies on Hwy 66.

As they neared the station, the thundering train approached. Shrill screams filled the air as Johnny sped up to beat the engine across the tracks. The car bounced roughly only a few feet in front of the train.

"Johnny!" everyone screamed.

Pauline punched his arm. "That was stupid! We could've all been killed!" Buddy and Bob both lost their grip around the windows and tumbled to the ground as the car slid to a stop, barely missing other people carrying packages.

"What is the matter with you?" Pauline complained as she grabbed a basket and started to rush off toward the tables set up along the loading dock. The steam from the train's brakes enveloped the group as Johnny grabbed her arm.

"Not so fast, sweetie." He planted a big kiss on her mouth in front of God and everyone.

"Johnny, when did you have a snort of whiskey?" she gasped, tasting him.

"Your cagey dad had more than newspapers under his arm when he came in." Johnny laughed. "You have fun with your mom and sisters, but don't get too friendly with all these GIs." He smiled and hugged her again before she scooted away.

"You watch your drinking with my crazy father and uncle," she warned before hurrying to the serving tables. He whistled shrilly at her back view, prompting Polly to sashay more provocatively.

The atmosphere on the platform was festive with lots of people and lots of food. The soldiers wasted no time getting off the train, and the smiles and full mouths demonstrated their appreciation for the food. Like many small towns along the troop train routes, the people of Wellington joined together to express gratitude to the soldiers for their sacrifice. Of course, Dorothy and Nonie spent more time flirting than dispensing food. Looking at them, Polly thought, *You'd think they'd never seen a guy before! But, I must say that some of these boys do look mighty handsome in a uniform. (Too bad I know some are real sleaze balls!)* She recalled men she had treated at the soldiers canteen. Polly tried to put them from her mind and not judge all the military by those few. She knew most were scared and homesick even before leaving the States.

As Polly handed out sandwiches and cookies, joking with the soldiers, she realized that some had to have forged papers to get in the service. They looked as young as Buddy and Bob. Many had Southern accents that were musical and fun to hear. One blonde-haired, blue-eyed boy in uniform who Dorothy was entertaining said, "I ain't et an egg sandich since I left Kentuck, and thisn's bread's most a good as my mama's."

It seemed like only a couple of minutes before, "All aboard," was shouted up and down the line. Any food still on the tables was grabbed or shoved into greedy hands, and a few men were sent off with kisses from appreciative Wellington girls. The quiet that replaced the revelry created a somber mood as those left behind thought about where the young soldiers were headed and remembered why there were so few eligible men around town.

The town worked to wipe down and put away the boards and sawhorses that were used to create the tables. Some could be seen dabbing tears as thoughts turned to sons or brothers. Polly watched the distance swallow the train and wondered if Aggie was on a similar transport headed to some port to be sent overseas, and she sighed thinking, *God bless them all! I sure do hate war.* Then she smiled ironically, realizing how spoiled she and the rest of the people in the US are compared to those in Europe and the Pacific. The inconvenience of rationing was nothing compared to bombs dropping on your cities and foreign soldiers trampling across the land. *I hate war, God, but thank you for all the blessings you have given us Americans!*

As the crowd thinned, unwelcome exhaustion seeped into Polly's mind and body. She didn't want the wonderful atmosphere of the train station to end, so she called to Nonie, Dorothy , and her mother, "Hey, let's walk home up Main Street so we can window shop. We can stop at Walt's and have a root beer float or chocolate soda—my treat." One of Sara Pearl's friends had asked her over for coffee, and Dorothy was joining some high school girls to chase senior boys. So, Nonie and Polly took one of the empty baskets and started up the street to enjoy themselves.

The long marble counter at Walt's was as shiny as the mirror, which reflected spotless soda glasses and the stainless steel malt maker. Polly and Nonie climbed onto a couple of stools, and Polly spun around like a five year old. Nonie shook her head at the immature behavior. "Can I help you ladies?" the young soda jerk asked?

"I think I'm too tired to even decide. What do you recommend?"

The teen boy said, I like vanilla-cherry, but root-beer is always good."

"Why don't you decide for us, Nonie," Polly suggested

She said, "Let's be risqué and try the cherry-vanilla soda and the root-beer. We can share and enjoy both."

A man came from the back room, drying his hands. "I thought I recognized some voices I've missed. How are the Garrity Girls?"

"Hi Walt," they chimed.

"What are you doing back in town? Are you moving home to work at the hospital, Polly?"

"No, I'm actually home to finish plans for my wedding next month. Nonie's taking a break from typing secret orders at Boeing."

"Don't be silly Polly," Nonie blushed.

"Well, whatever you do there, Nonie, I'm sure it's important," Walt said. "Congratulations, Polly. Do I know the lucky fella?" He handed the girls a couple of napkins when the waiter failed to do so, and tore up their ticket.

"Thanks, Walt," both girls said. "I didn't realize how hungry and thirsty I was," Nonie added after her first long sip. "Thanks for the suggestion Polly."

Polly nodded as she took a long sip before answering Walt's question about her fiance'. He assured her that she deserved the best before moving to another customer.

"Even though these were on the house, it is so nice to be able to buy something fun once in a while, isn't it, Nonie? Remember the years we had to stand in food lines for supper. I was so embarrassed; I thought I'd die, especially when someone I knew walked by. I never dreamed I'd have the money to buy a pretty wedding gown."

"What's it like? Does it have lots of lace and frilly stuff?"

"Really, Nonie? Can you even imagine me in something like that? It's a simple Princess Style according to the store clerk, made from a light-weight brocade with a subtle pattern. Best of all, I got it and the bride's maid dresses really cheap because they were left from left-over autumn stock. Not the colors I really would have picked, but spring styles aren't in yet, so have to take what I can get. Come over some evening after work to see."

"I think I would rather be surprised at the wedding. No matter what, you'll look so gorgeous."

Pauline answered, "Well, thank you, but you know my nurse friends all say I look just like you, so guess you're complimenting yourself," she laughed.

"Oh, you're nuts. But, I'm stuffed now," Nonie said as she finished all but the last few drops of her float.

"Me, too." Polly smiled before slurping the last miniscule drops of liquid up her straw, making an awful noise. Then she again spun around on the stool, laughing.

"When are you going to grow up?"Nonie sighed as other customers who knew Polly enjoyed her antics.

"Hopefully, never." Polly waved goodbye to all the customers as she and Nonie left the small store.

"You know you probably ought to think about acting a little more mature," Nonie told her. "You're getting married in three weeks."

"Don't be so serious, Nonie, it'll give you ulcers," Polly warned. "You would probably die if you were getting married and your honeymoon cottage was going to be a chicken house," she added nonchalantly as they walked down the street.

Nonie stopped in the middle of the sidewalk, her mouth agape. "What in the world are you talking about? You are not living in a chicken house, are you?"

"Well kinda," Polly answered. "It used to be anyway; but when I saw it last week lots of hay was the only thing inside. Nonie, close your mouth; it will be fine. Johnny's parents promise it will be spic and span before the wedding, and I know his mother would not think of us living in a shack. Really, the little house looks like it will be so cute after we get it cleaned up and painted."

"But why did you say it was a chicken house?" Nonie wondered.

"No one was living in it, and Johnny's brother and his wife needed a warm dry place for their chickens. So they used a little house on the corner of their property for their hens," Polly explained matter-of-fact-ly. "Hey, here's Mr. Farley's hardware store; let's go in and see how he's doing." She opened the door and was halfway through before Nonie could protest.

"Hi, Mr. Farley, how ya doin?" Polly called as soon as she saw him shelving buckets.

"Polly Garrity, how are you?" he exclaimed, climbing down from the ladder. "I hear you're a real nurse now. You must be the best the hospital has seen." He wanted to hug her but did not want to become emotional. He politely skipped to a new topic. "Hi, Miss Nonie, how are you?"

"I'm fine. Gosh you have so many different types of things in here than you used to. The store really looks great, Mr. Farley. Mind if I look around?"

"That's what we're here for," he answered. "As it's become more dif-ficult to get hardware items with the war, I've had to, as the salesmen say, 'diversify.' Look as much as you want and maybe you'll find some-thing you can't live without."

Polly asked about his children and was shocked to learn that Pete was in high school and realized that was why the teen who waited on them at Walt's seemed so familiar. Angela was already in sixth grade. "That's amazing. I move away, and kids grow up instead of staying little like I remember them. I didn't even recognize Pete when he served us sodas!." She gave Mr. Farley a chance to talk about the joys in his life.

He finished with, "Polly, there's no way I can ever thank you for helping so much, especially being so good to Mary at the end. The kids and I couldn't have made it if you hadn't been here for Mary." He swal-lowed hard and added, "For all of us. The months around her death are still a fog. If you hadn't stopped in so often the year after, we would probably have starved."

203

"I loved helping and taking care of Mary and also my Aunt Bridgie so Uncle Charlie could work with his worms and sometimes go fishing. Mary and Aunt Bridgie are why I became a nurse." Then, she announced, "Well, I have some news, Mr. Farley. I'm getting married in a couple of weeks."

"Polly, I'm so happy for you!" He smiled and earnestly added, "I sure hope he is a great guy who deserves you."

"Oh, he's better than she deserves!" Nonie teased from behind a shelf of kitchen items.

A broad smile lit his face, "Well, if you're getting married, come back to the storeroom and see if you can take something off my hands. I'm tired of it taking up space and gathering dust. You come too," he told Nonie. The girls followed the middle-aged man through a door into the back room. Amid boxes of supplies was a large shape covered with a tarp. He pulled off the canvas to reveal a beautiful, brand new, white gas stove!

"Where in the world did you get that?" Polly gasped. She knew anything made of metal was impossible to buy. "The maintenance guys can't even get parts to fix the heaters at the hospital!" She and Nonie ran their hands lovingly over the appliance as though it was the Holy Grail.

"I think it was a gift from God. It came one day about a year ago by mistake. I kept informing the company, but they kept saying they didn't know anything about it. After never getting a bill I got tired of arguing with them. Then I got the idea that God sent it to me for you, Polly," he explained.

"Oh, Mr. Farley, I can't take that. You could sell it for a lot of money." Nonie looked at both in awe.

"Polly, I would probably be laying in a gutter someplace, and who knows where my kids would be, if it wasn't for you helping us for almost two years with no pay. This is for you. Besides, my store would be torn apart with women rioting if I put this out on the floor to sell. Then the G men would be investigating me in less than a day to find out how I got my hands on it. You'd really be doing me a favor to just take it off my hands."

"Just say thank you, dummy," Nonie smiled.

"Oh, thank you, thank you, thank you!" Polly hugged him. "Come on Nonie, we gotta go tell Johnny and the folks."

"But no one else!" Mr. Farley warned. Polly signed "lips sealed" before dashing out of the store and ran most of the six blocks home while Nonie yelled at her to slow down. Sara Pearl wouldn't believe the story until Nonie confirmed it. Polly never did get her nap that afternoon because she paced the floor like an expectant father as she waited for the guys to return from fishing.

When she told Johnny, he said he had to see this stove to believe it. Even when Mr. Farley again removed the tarp, he felt he was seeing a mirage. Smiling from ear to ear, Johnny said, "Well, Pauline, we might not have a great house to live in, but you've got a dandy stove to cook on!" He squeezed his soon-to be-bride around her waist.

Mr. Farley insisted the tarp went with the stove, "Otherwise, it will be stolen before you get it to Colwich."

CHAPTER 27

LETTERS FROM FRIENDS

March 1945

Hi Garrity,

Congratulations!!! I am so excited to hear your wonderful news. You and Johnny were made for each other. By the time you get this, you will probably already be the farmer's wife with a new little Wetta planted—ha ha!

You may have heard from Cy that my orders were changed. Our hospitals are now being flooded with casualties coming home from the Battle of the Ardennes. It must have been pure hell. Taking care of the wounded has made me feel stupid thinking we were cold and made any kind of sacrifice for coming to work during that blizzard last year. (Gosh it seems a century ago!) We have treated so many men who lost fingers, toes, and much more from the freezing storm, in addition to battle wounds. The worst injuries haven't even arrived state-side because men are not stable enough to make the long trip from Europe.

Even so, we are transporting many with missing limbs and other critical injuries; it's a miracle they survived. There must be some pretty great medics on the battlefield to have kept so many from bleeding to death. That was the only good thing about the frigid cold. I have to pray to control my emotions when caring for the guys who've lost part of their face and others who are horribly disfigured from fires. I know it's not professional, and Sister Gregory would be disappointed in me even thinking this, but some of these guys are in such awful shape, it probably would be better if they hadn't made it! Gosh, what am I thinking? That I'm God!Sorry, I've just had too many flights all over the country with brave young men who are horribly maimed.

These mini-hospitals are pretty crowded with 25 or 30 badly wounded patients, basic supplies, meds, and some food. Many of the guys have oxygen or drips and lots of other tubes that like to get tangled anytime we hit turbulence.

We transport soldiers up the east coast, to DC or New Jersey, sometimes add patients from bases there, then head to Chicago and on to the West coast. Sometimes we head back to Florida empty. That's when I get a little sleep or possibly read one of the ASE books one of the guys dropped. Those are a God-send.

So you won't have a hissy fit if you hear rumors, I was in Wichita for a little while last week bringing patients to the VA hospital. I let my folks know, so they could meet me and someone special. I did ask them not to tell Cy that I was flying in which really threw them for a loop. They were even more "thrown to meet a wonderful, caring pilot that I've flown with lots.

Polly I now understand so much better your confusion over Michael. Dad was not too happy that I was "cheating" on Cy and with someone "not like us". This really upset me, but I tried not to ruin our short time. When I thought about it later, I realized that I probably sounded a little like Dad when I advised you that Johnny was better for you than Michael. Capt. Marshall is great, ---handsome, and funny and HERE. But he sure didn't make my dad happy.

Anyway military life has kept me so busy that I didn't realize how homesick I was. Really tough saying "goodbye." Probably will sneak in and out of Wichita if it's on our flight plan in future.

Oh, almost forgot. You remember Mary McHugh who was the first SF nurse to join Army? She sent congrats for me joining military—saw it in "The Stethoscope." She sure needs our prayers—also a flight nurse, but evacuating in areas of heavy fighting. Besides that, she's so devastated. Her brother John was killed—plane exploded during bomb run. So sad!

Well, gotta get some shut-eye so I look glamorous for the guys! You know that's the real reason the army took me! Ha ha!

Love ya,

Aggie

April 28, 1945

Dear Aggie,

I can't believe we've been married for over a month! I have just been too busy to write, and who knows if you will even get this, guess it can just be a diary to myself if it comes back. Johnny and I were so lucky to have wonderful, warm weather in February for our wedding. We were married at the cathedral in Wichita. Maybe it's terrible vanity, but I felt like a queen walking down the aisle of the cathedral with Daddy by my side. Johnny looked so handsome, but his brother Spud, our best-man, was making goofy faces, and I almost burst out laughing. He told me that I looked too serious for a pretty bride. What a card! I'll admit I was more nervous than I expected.

After Mass, we had to go to the photographer for pictures

before we could even enjoy our own wedding. Of course, the guys brought some whiskey to celebrate while taking them, so we were all having a great time and no one was feeling any pain by the time we got to the party at the farm. I was starving and really needed to eat. Thank God, dinner was ready. Johnny's mother and aunts and friends had hams and sausage and roast and so many mashed potatoes and salads. They must have been cooking for days, besides half the night before. Guess I better stop about the food since you're probably dying for some home cooked meals.

The band was so smooth at the dance; I almost hated to leave, but when we saw our chance we sneaked out. We wanted to get away from Johnny's crazy friends who would bother us all night if they had any idea where we were going. He said he had the perfect place they would never think to look.

Beat, I couldn't believe where Johnny took me for our wedding night. We stayed at his old maid Aunt Mary's house—right here in Colwich! Isn't that just awful! What was even worse, she was there! Can you imagine? Johnny said she was half-deaf, but I was concerned about the other half. Obviously, our big night was not the romantic rendezvous I always dreamed. Oh well, things have improved now that we have our own place -- even if it is a converted chicken house, ha ha!!!

A lot of elbow grease and a little paint and home-made curtains have turned it into our cute little love nest. It'll do until Johnny's folks retire from the farm in a few years, and then we'll move into their big, beautiful house. We spend almost every day there anyway. Johnny is so busy with fieldwork. If not there, he's trying to keep machinery running when it's impossible to get parts if something breaks. Grandma, Johnny's sister Annie, and I have started to plant the huge garden, and peas, lettuce, radishes, and onions are already peeking out of the ground.

Well, I better close and fix some food to take to the guys. I had forgotten that keeping farmers fed means fixing food constantly!

Almost like feeding a baby but lots more food.

Haven't had time to miss working at the hospital, but miss you lots Aggie.

By the way, yes, Miss Smarty Pants.; you're right. A new little Wetta is expected in December!

~~Garrity~~ *Mrs. John A. Wetta*

PS: May 8th: *Happy I didn't get this in the mail earlier. Yes, Miss Smarty Pants.; you're right. A new little Wetta is expected in December!*

That's almost as exciting as…

Even though it was a Tuesday, the Wetta family had gone to 6:00 AM Mass as usual. It had been quite a while since Ben had written, and though no one spoke about it, everyone was concerned. After Mass, the family ate a quick breakfast, then the men headed to the machine shed to make sure the haying equipment was ready to start cutting the new alfalfa crop. Grandma Anna and Annie wanted to finish planting green beans before the sun was too hot. Polly got to stay in the house to clean and iron.

She switched on the radio for some music (even though the Wettas thought it should only be on at night). She was setting up the ironing board when suddenly an announcer interrupted "Sentimental Journal" and said that the President would address the nation in five minutes. Polly ran out the south door and hollered for Johnny until he looked out of the shed. "Come quick. Bring your dad and Spud. The President is going to make an announcement on the radio." Johnny waved his hand and disappeared into the shed. Polly ran around the house and told Grandma and Annie to come quick.

When they came into the kitchen they were still shaking dirt from their aprons and wiping soil from their hands. They entered the kitchen at the same time the men came in from the opposite porch, just in time to hear Truman's voice. Johnny's mother turned pale as she heard, "This is a glorious hour." Spud pulled out a chair and patted his mom's shoulder. When the President said that Germany had surrendered, the mother of two soldiers, who had tried to be so strong for too long, broke into tears. It seemed that a dam of worry and heartache burst. Johnny's dad pulled out his handkerchief and went out onto the porch. Polly hugged her mother-in-law and gave her a tea towel to replace the small handkerchief already soaked with tears.

Then Pauline plastered Johnny with a big kiss and even kissed Spud. She jumped up and down with Annie, who was cheering and crying, too. Spud and Johnny pounded each other on the back and wondered when Ben and Joe would be home. Annie sat down rested her head on her mother's shoulder. Much of the President's speech was lost in the celebration.

As things in the house quieted down, Leo senior walked back into the kitchen, stuffed his handkerchief into his pocket. He pulled a chair next to Grandma and took her hand in his, which elicited more tears from them both. As she brushed tears from her cheeks, Polly got the cups she had just washed and poured coffee. Spud adjusted the radio volume to better hear the rest of Truman's words.

"Much remains to be done. The victory won in the West must now be won in the East. I want that emphasized time after time, that we are only half through. The whole world must be cleansed of the evil from which half the world has been freed. United, the peace-loving nations have demonstrated in the West that their arms are stronger by far than the might of dictators or the tyranny of military cliques that once called us soft and weak. I would like to know what the Germans think about that now."

"Yeah, I guess we showed that mad man who was weak," Spud laughed. Annie was crying. "Don't worry, Sis. The Japs'll give up soon, and Willie will be home too, and Mother'll be fretting about another wedding." Then he hugged his mother, "Don't worry about Joe, Mother. You know he's so ornery, he's gonna be fine. Remember he wrote that most of the fighting is over wherever he is. Worst thing is trying to keep peace among all the units wanting jeeps and fuel and stuff they think he can create out of thin air."

Grandma Anna, dabbed her eyes before nodding her head and smiling weakly. Then as always thinking of others, she said, "We need to go make sure Margie has heard."

"She's at work at Boeing," Annie reminded her. "And you can bet everyone's really celebrating there."

"Even if she was home, she'd know," Johnny called from the porch where he had gone for a moment by himself. "Come listen to this!" Even though Colwich was two miles away, the family could hear the church bells ringing and car horns honking. In fact, it sounded like a parade of cars were coming from town headed by Frenchy, the cop with his siren leading the way.

Leo Sr. surprised the entire group by announcing, "We're all going to town to celebrate with our friends and neighbors." In Colwich, there were lots of short snorts shared, lots of tears, and lots of singing until the noon Angelus sounded and people passed the word that Father was going to have Benediction in thanksgiving, and to pray that Japan will soon surrender, and all the boys in the Pacific fighting would also be home soon.

CHAPTER 28

HAWAII

Late August 1945

Hi Polly,

Congratulations both on being Mrs. Johnny Wetta and being pregnant! Wow has life changed since I last wrote. You're no longer a nurse but a farmer's pregnant wife. And, the terrible, awful war is finally over…

Aggie sat in a nook she had discovered on the deck of the ship to enjoy a bit of privacy and the beautiful Pacific morning. As she wrote to Polly, her words were interrupted with a sharp whistle and, "Now hear this. Now hear this," blasting over the loud speaker. She jumped up and pulled on her nearby life-jacket as everyone nearby scrambled to do the same. Everyone scanned the seas and sky for an attack. The speakers continued, "At 1900 hours EWT [Eastern War Time], August 14, President Truman announced that Japan has surrendered—" No one heard the end of the announcement. The ship burst into celebration!

"Oh, thank you Jesus and Blessed Mother Mary," Aggie yelled and jumped into the air. She ran to find her nurse friends when a young sailor grabbed her and swung her into the air. She squealed with delight and enjoyed his kiss. People banged on pipes and anything else to make noise. Aggie spied the nurses rushing on deck and she flew into their midst. Tears flowed down her cheeks as she hugged her new friend, Rose, and danced a jig.

A couple of sailors grabbed each of the girls and joined the dancing on the crowded deck. The ship seemed to float higher in the water as the relentless, terrible danger soared from the ship amidst the ecstatic voices.

Knowing the war was over made the sight of Hawaii a week later even more wonderful. The palm trees were tall and majestic; the ocean was clear and beautifully blue, and the air wasn't humid like Florida. It really was an island paradise, except for the remnants of the December 7 attack still visible in many places. The sunken ships in the harbor were especially awful to see.

The relieved nurses had wild stories about landing on rescue missions under radio silence. They didn't know if friendly troops or Japs would greet them because some of the islands changed control so quickly.

There were still several islands to be evacuated to make sure all the soldiers, especially the poor prisoners of war, were safe.

I have no idea when I'll be home, but my military contract states that I must "serve at least four months after fighting ceases and longer if deemed necessary by the War Department." Even though I miss Cy and everyone, I love what I'm doing and feel like it's really important. I also enjoy all the beautiful places I'm getting to see. Mostly, I thank God every day that the war is over, and we don't live under that constant cloud of awful danger. Seems impossible, but one of the nurses said they just never thought about it. She just did her work like they were any other place.

I do miss you, and can't wait to see your big belly. My love to you and Johnny.

Aggie

Sitting in a seat near the door of the plane, Aggie folded the letter and placed it in her satchel with the pen. *Can't believe I had time to relax a little while today. But, I better go check on my patients, especially the psyche guys.* As she got up Aggie thought, *It'll take years, and they may still never recover from all they've been through.*

"Hi Greg, how ya doin?" She gently took one of the soldier's hands.

"I'm ok, but sure wish you'd take these straps off my arms and legs. I won't try to get out that door any more. I'm sorry. Just got kinda confused when we took off. Couldn't quite remember where I was."

"That's ok, Greg, you've been through a lot. But, I think we better leave the straps on. Captain said we are headed into some turbulence, and they will just keep you safer in that bunk. I heard that you're originally from Arizona. Did you live in the desert area?"

"Yea, pretty dry with big cacti. Lots different than all the green on those islands."

"Bet that desert will look pretty good when you get home." Aggie had quickly learned that friendly talk was the best medicine for most of the men.

"I really need to pee, Lieutenant, but can you have the corpsman help me?"

"Sure thing, Greg. If you need me later, let me know." Aggie moved away and called Corpsman Ashton to help.

She talked with another patient about his younger brother who pitched on a little league team. The soldier told Aggie how excited he was to watch a game, but a loud burst interrupted them. Then an unnatural growling replaced the monotonous droning of the plane as it banked sharply and shook. Aggie said a quick prayer in her heart, grasped the Miraculous Medal hanging around her neck, and flew into action.

Trying to recall info from the Ditching & Crash Procedures class at Bowman, she worked in auto-pilot mode. The young flight nurse and the corpsmen on board secured oxygen canisters while reassuring patients and double checking straps and litters, tucking in all the extra blankets and clothing as padding . They were tying down everything that was sliding and bouncing down the aisle when Captain Clemens announced, "Sorry, everyone. We lost an engine and our second is sputtering, so we may be going swimming. I'll try my best to reach one of the atolls that should be close by."

The night was deep cave dark, and most of the atolls had been deserted since the war ended. No lights shone in the endless miles of the Pacific to guide the pilot. Greg moaned loudly, but Aggie took his face in her hands. "Sargent Schmidt—Schmidt, look at me. Look at me." The soldier knew it was an order. "Our Father, who art in heaven…" She began and commanded in his ear, "Say it so all can hear." She seized her Miraculous Medal again, for a mili-second before moving to secure other patients. The corpsmen and Aggie scrambled from soldier to soldier amidst sounds of the groaning plane, clanking bottles, and clanging metal clasps. The words of the Lord's Prayer wove through the chaotic noises. When she and Corporal Ashton met in the aisle, she said, "Go up with Schmidt and the other psyche patients and do your best. I think they might need some strong arms."

"Right, LT." He maneuvered toward the front of the descending plane. As Aggie worked her way between triple tier bunks, she smiled and spoke reassuring words, while praying, *Blessed Mother Mary, please beg your Son. These guys have already been through so much. Don't let them die when they're so close to going home.*

The Lord was with the flight; the captain brought it down with a bumpy landing. Trying to secure the last of the safety straps, Aggie lost her balance and was thrown to the floor and tossed down the aisle. The silence in the cabin erupted into cheering when they came to an abrupt halt.

"You ok, LT?" asked a young sailor who looked from his low bunk to Aggie on the floor.

Looking up, she smiled and said, "Just peachy, now!"

"Lieutenant Beat, you ok?" Corporal Jeffreys, one of the corpsmen, asked while offering Aggie a hand up.

She attempted to scramble to her feet, but stumbled in pain trying to regain her footing. "I'm fine," she said. She hoped it was true and grabbed the flashlight from her belt. "We better check the captain." She started toward the cockpit, but Captain Clemens met her at the hatch.

"Oh, thank God, you're ok," she said.

"Everyone ok back here?" he yelled. Cheers and whistles answered him.

"We'll check each patient, sir." Aggie saw that Corporal Ashton still had Greg in his arms. The distraught patient trembled and wept silently. She could hear Ashton softly talking about a big dog he couldn't wait to get home to see. She patted the technician's shoulder and said, "Jeffreys, work your way to the back from here and I'll work from aft forward."- Flashlight in hand, she joked with the soldiers and inspected each one to confirm their enthusiasm wasn't veiling more injuries from the landing. When she heard, "Great fly'n Capn'" and "Glad you were at the controls, Captain Clemens," she realized that he had followed her.

He greeted the men, accepting their thanks and encouraging them. "Aggie, after you check the guys, I need you forward to help Harry. He walloped his head pretty good," he whispered.

"You sure? I can go now."

"How about I visit with the guys back here a little, LT," he said loudly enough for the men nearby to hear. "Lieutenant McGhee is on the radio trying to contact HQ. Bet he could use a drink of water."Aggie's heart leapt, but she said, "Sure thing, Captain; can I bring you anything?"

"Naw, just want to check the guys; I'll be in the cockpit soon."

"Hey, I wanted you to take care of me; he ain't nearly as purty as you LT," the next patient complained.

"Hey, Lt. Beat, were you telling the angels to 'beat' their wings under the plane?" one of the men joked as she passed.

Pausing to laugh and loosen his straps, Aggie teased, "I left the praying to you, Marx. I was too busy making sure my 'babies' were all tucked in." Aggie worked toward the cockpit as fast as possible trying not to arouse undo attention. Stepping into the makeshift galley, Aggie almost tripped over the thermoses and food containers that had been knocked from their hinges. *We're lucky everything's still sealed; we'll need this stuff if we're here awhile,* she thought as she poured a tin mug of water.

The metallic odor of blood greeted Aggie as she stepped into the cockpit and casually asked, "I heard a fly boy hero up here is thirsty? How ya feel'n, Harry?" The odor was confirmed when the flashlight beam revealed his face with red liquid still heavily seeping through the captain's handkerchief and other makeshift bandages. She expected some injuries, but not this carnage. As soon as Aggie loosened the belt that Captain had used to apply pressure to the head of his badly injured co-pilot, blood spurted from the jagged wound. Shards of broken glass from the shattered windshield were imbedded in his face and shoulder, and a thick tree branch had rammed through the fuselage and rested across the soldier's lap. "Can you hear me, Harry?" the flight nurse asked, pulling a suture needle and thread from the pack at her waist.

"He's pretty bad, isn't he?" Captain Clemens asked as he squeezed back into the tiny area.

"It doesn't look good. Can you direct the beam here?" Aggie asked and handed the flashlight over. "And, put your other hand here to slow the bleeding so I can see to stitch." Then she added, "Sorry, please, Captain."

"Hell, don't worry about protocol, Aggie, just try to save Harry." The blood flow meantthe co-pilot was still alive, but it made sewing the wound a challenge. Captain Clemens did as directed.

They were making progress when the radio crackled. "Have your location charted, Captain. A rescue plane's on the run way now. How's McGhee doin? Over."

"Guess they'll have to wait a second." Clemens looked at Aggie.

"Working as fast as I can."

"Come in, sir, this is Hickam Field. Come in." The radio was quiet for a second and repeated, "Come in, sir, this is Hickam Field. Come in."

"Just a little bit more," Aggie pleaded.

"Flight 372, this is Hickam Field. Come in." There was a moment of silence. "Hey Chuck, where the hell are you? What's happening out there?"

Aggie nodded to Captain Clemens that he could move his hand.

He flicked the radio switch. "Flight 372, here. Sorry. Kinda had my hands full."

"Well, good to hear you now. How's Harry?"

"He's in better hands now that Lt. Beat's in the cockpit, but he lost a lot of blood. Tell the air jocky that's fly'n the rescue plane Harry says, 'Give that big horse the whip.' Over and out." McGhee moved slightly in reaction to Captain's words and the pain of the needle as Aggie stitched the long gash across his forehead and closed the wound in his cheek. Then she moved to the shoulder, carefully removing shards of glass before beginning to stich that area.

"With all the blood he's lost," Aggie said, "he will become dehydrated without fluids. When I get this stopped, I'll need to start an IV." The pilot's ashen face concerned Aggie. *He's suffering from shock.* "Captain, why don't you drink this water I brought for Harry. He can't drink it now anyway, and you have to be thirsty." When he took the bloody tin mug, she saw that his hands were shaking. "It had to be a whole lot worse crashing from up here than in the back. You guys are both lucky to be alive," she commented as she finished stitching, and the bleeding seemed to have halted. After wrapping gauze around Lieutenant McGhee's head and making a bandage pad for his shoulder, Aggie took the mug from the pilot and surveyed the destroyed cockpit. "Can I get anything else for you, Captain?"

"Maybe coffee if we have any left—when you have time." The adrenaline rush from saving the plane filled with wounded was obviously wearing off. "Can't believe I crashed this old girl. She's been my baby, getting us through so many tough spots the past three years."

"Well, she must need a rest. I'll check about the coffee," Aggie said, and she stepped from the cockpit.

"Thanks, Aggie, you're an angel," Captain said.

"Just doin' my duty, sir," she replied. "And you're a darn good pilot. It sure wasn't your fault the engines blew. I'm grateful you were at the controls. Most guys couldn't have found this island and landed the way you did, in the dark. Not a patient was hurt; that's almost a miracle."

"It may be," Clemens yawned. "Oh, if the guys ask, pass the word that it will be after daylight when the rescue flight gets here. Everyone needs to try to get some shut-eye."

She returned to the cabin with the flashlight dimmed and washed up in a makeshift basin. Corporal Jeffreys approached. "Everything ok up there?" he whispered. He picked up the flashlight to focus on the basin so Aggie could wash. Seeing the red water and her stained fatigues, he added, "You ok, LT?"

"Lt. McGhee's pretty bad," she replied. "We were so lucky. The cockpit's in shambles and part of a tree's lying on Harry's lap. How's everything back here?"

"Ship-shape—as much as can be. After everything these guys have been through and the places they've slept in the past few years, most feel pretty lucky and comfortable in their bunks. Oh, Ashton asked for you to check Anderson and Golby. I think they are due for some more morphine. We gave Schmidt some aspirin, and he finally settled down. Hope that's ok. We knew something must be wrong for you to have been gone so long," he finished.

"I had to put in lots of stitches, and now I need to get an IV started for McGhee so he doesn't get more dehydrated, but I'll check the guys first. Thanks for taking care of things. Can you take the captain some coffee?"

"Sure thing, ma'am."

"Check to see that he is looking ok. He's showing signs of shock, taking the crash personally. Also check McGhee's vitals; let me know if I need to get that IV started before I finish with Anderson and Golby."

After Aggie checked on the special cases and a couple of other guys needing to talk, she and Jeffreys worked together on the IV. Then they joined Ashton who was looking out at the night from the open cargo door. "Thanks for all your help, guys. We make a good team," Aggie said.

"That's what we're here for, LT," Ashton replied.

She smiled. "Well, I still appreciate you, but now we all need to try to rest too before it starts gett'n light and the guys are hungry. You wanna take the aft section?"

"Yes, ma'am," he answered and walked to the back of the cabin.

Corporal Ashton had opened the forward and cargo doors for ventilation, and a warm tropical breeze drifted through the plane. Aggie made one last check on Anderson, who had been struggling with pain and gave him a small dose of morphine. He was still awake and wondered if she would read to him from The Immortal Wife. "Do you like books?" she asked

"Never used to before the army," he whispered. "But it sure helps kill time, and it took my mind off of the Japs out in the jungle and what was going to happen." When the medication began to work, she slipped away.

Even though she was exhausted, Aggie was too keyed up to sleep and poured herself a tin mug of cold coffee and went to the forward door. The tropical night was warm and beautiful; the overcast sky cleared to reveal a nearly full moon. Now waning toward the west, it highlighted the fronds of nearby palm trees. The sounds of a few night birds calling to mates could be heard amid the lapping of the Pacific. *What a romantic scene!* Aggie thought as an exhausted tear trailed down her cheek and dripped off her chin. She suddenly realized how badly she missed Cy.

The only self-indulgent reverie Aggie had allowed herself was brought to a halt when she glanced down and saw that the moon highlighted their precarious landing spot at the very edge of the atoll. *Sure glad I looked before jumping down to find a place to go visit Mother Nature! Otherwise I'd be in the water with nasty gashes from those rocks.*

Glancing around with the flashlight, she wondered how close the rescue plane would be able to get to this big lady. *I sure hope they sent a full crew to help move all the wounded. It will take forever if it's just five of us, and I am starting to ache all over.* Aggie took a minute to collect her thoughts and realized her tumble down the aisle wasn't funny. *Guess I'm lucky nothing seems broken—not sure about these ribs though.* After easing herself down from the plane, she held her aching side while searching for a place to relieve herself. In the moonlight, she could see that her entire leg and hip were turning a dark color.

No wonder, I feel sore. My whole body may be purple. Returning to the door, she lookedup at the plane, wondering how she was going to pull herself back in with her bruised muscles.

"Need some help?" Captain Clemens reached down a strong hand and pulled her up.

"Thanks, Captain. And thanks again for the safe landing," she said.

He laughed. "Cut it a little close, didn't I." He jumped down from the plane while she shook her head.

Aggie went to the cockpit to check on the co-pilot. He was asleep but breathing steadily. She removed the empty IV and checked Lt. McGhee's stitches, which still held, then returned to her seat and pulled a Rosary from her pocket. Thanking God for blessing the flight, Aggie-joined the men in soft snoring.

The plane was bathed in dim morning light when she awoke to a nearby patient calling, "LT, LT, I hate to wake you, but I really gotta go bad." Jumping at the sound of his voice, Aggie had to stifle a gasp. She gritted her teeth as every nerve and muscle screamed in protest. Offering a quick prayer to keep moving, Aggie told herself this pain was nothing compared to what many of her patients were suffering. She dove into the work of the day, trying to protect her ribs as much as possible. She was sure a couple were broken. The corpsmen also sprang into action when they heard men waking. Corporal Ashton assessed the food and water situation and asked Aggie if she had any idea how long they would be stranded so he could plan rations.

"I'll go ask Captain if he's heard anything from our rescuers," she replied. After filling a couple of tin mugs with water, Aggie stepped into the cabin. "Mornin', Cap'n. Sorry it's not coffee," she cheerfully whispered. "How's Harry doing?"

"Thanks, Aggie. At least we have water." Then answering her question, he said, "He groans every once in a while, and he sure looks bad doesn't he?"

"Well, considering how the plane looks, he appears to be very lucky, as are you. By the way, you have a real shiner and swollen right cheek. Must have hit the instrument panel or something," she said gently touching his face. "You want a compress for that?"

"Naw, I'm fine," he said as the radio began to crackle. Aggie looked surprised but turned to Harry to check his pulse and feel his face for a fever. He groaned and opened his eyes slightly as a scratchy voice came over the radio.

"Morning. You still there, Captain Clemens? Over."

"You just caught me in time. We're all thinking of going to some swanky restaurant for breakfast. Over," he answered and winked at Lt. Beat, who shook her head and smiled as she helped the co-pilot drink some water.

"Well, try to sit tight for a little longer. Captain Stone just reported that he should be landing on Eniwetok in less than an hour. How's everyone holding up? Over."

"Still here. Over," Clemens replied. Seeing Aggie motioning for him to ask a question, he added, "Wait, any supplies on that rescue plane and a crew to help move all these wounded men? Over."

"Five guys on board besides Stone. Water and some C rations and emergency medical supplies. Over."

"Thanks, private. Over and out," Clemens said before the operator signaled off.

"Well, that's good news," Aggie said. "I'll go help make sure the others are at least getting some water this morning."

"Sure thing; and pass the word to the men that we should be out of here before too long."

Aggie moved among the men, dispensing basic meds and checking bandages. Then she helped Jeffreys and Ashton make sure all the men had some water and used the urinals. They loosened the safety straps on those confined to bunks. When they heard the low drone of a descending plane, excited yelling broke the morning air. Aggie wrapped her fingers around her Miraculous Medal and smiled with relief.

Even though he had landed on a dark night, Captain Clemens sense of direction was right on target. His baby had stopped less than 30 yards from the landing strip with only part of it in water. The rescue plane came to a halt just a short distance from the wreck. The crew on board jogged to the stranded B-54 and flew to work.

Less than an hour after the second plane had landed, all of the wounded were safely transferred, including Lieutenant McGhee. Captain Clemens made a last check of his plane, taking the picture of his wife and little boy and his guardian angel pin from above the pilot's windshield. He patted a wing before jogging to the waiting B-24.

CHAPTER 29

MORE LETTERS

October 1945

Hi Aggie,

We saw Cy at the Mt. Vernon turkey shoot and he filled us in on some of your adventures. It sounds like life is really busy. Hope you have a camera and time to take some pictures of beautiful Hawaii between saving soldiers.

At least you don't have to worry about being shot down while on your missions of mercy. I'm so glad that you didn't have to go into any battle areas under fire, Aggie. I'm really proud of you and how patriotic you are. I know I acted pretty mean when you told me you had enlisted, but I was so worried and I guess I was kinda mad that you were so brave when I was too chicken to even think of it. Besides, I would be too dumb to make the right decisions as fast as you have to with so many patients in such bad shape. Your days in emergency were good training for being a flight nurse. So sorry to hear about Mary's brother. Been praying for her safety.

Oh, I forgot to tell you that Johnny ripped off part of his thumb while harvesting corn! It's sure lots easier taking care of patients you don't know than someone you love! When I saw jag-

ged bone protruding from the flesh of his thumb, I almost fainted. I thought about you and all the horrible things you must have seen. After Johnny was hurt, I told him, "Now I don't even have as much to love as I married!" That was a pretty stupid and selfish thing to say with so many poor women who will never see their husbands again or are receiving them back missing arms and legs. I should be ashamed of being so silly over Johnny's missing finger. I am trying to be more mature, Aggie.

Have so much more to tell you, but better close or this will weigh too much.

Wetta

October 1945

Hi Garrity,

Since we have no patients until we arrive on Luzon in a few hours, I have time to write a little about our crazy life. You won't believe it, but I have just spent two days in Japan—don't faint. The parts that haven't been bombed are truly beautiful. We are now picking up wounded on far outlying islands, Guam, Kwajelein, Leyte, Luzon, and more. I'm getting a real geography lesson of Pacific islands. We aren't supposed to be on flight duty for more than 18 hours, so we had a layover in the land of the rising sun before we could pick up patients for the flight back to Hickman. Of course, we weren't anywhere near Hiroshima or Nagasaki.

All of the Japanese people we saw were so humble and polite, constantly bowing to us but never looking us in the eyes. If someone wanted to paint a picture called "Defeat," they could paint a picture of any of the surviving Japanese people. Seeing them makes me so sad and confirms that wars are made by politicians who really don't see the face of their decisions. The people of Japan were all puppets with strings pulled by corrupt politicians. They lost not only their pride but their roots and everything they believed was important. Sorry to rant!

Rosie and I treated ourselves to a rickshaw ride around the city, and we were amazed at the charm amid a failed system. That ride was quite an experience. We knew we were helping the man pulling it by giving him business, but I still felt it was cruel to sit in a cart being pulled by a person hooked up like an animal. Such a different culture.

Better close. Nearing the islands where we pick up our patients and go to work. Some of these guys from the last days of the war are so skinny. Even if they weren't wounded, they would be sick.

Love to both you and Johnny. Hope to see you by Christmas.

Aggie

November 1945

Hi Aggie,

I must have too much time on my hands with the cooler weather and the fall butchering done, so I'm going to write my friend I miss so much. You remember Aileen Kessler who was a class behind us? You probably know that she joined the Navy after graduation. Well, she got home a few weeks ago, and she and Spud are dating. We keep hoping that Cy stops by and tells us that you are on your way home.

Oh, Aggie, you'll never believe what I did the other night. First of all, I was exhausted from helping butcher all day (another story). But, Johnny really wanted to go to a wedding dance, and I knew I would have fun once we got there. Anyway, I was in a hurry to heat water for our baths and fix a nice supper of fresh pork. As soon as we got home, Johnny went right to the barn to milk our cow.

When he returned, I was still sitting in the middle of the kitchen floor, trying to pump up the gas for the lights. "Damn light! What is wrong with you?"

"Pauline, what are you doing?"

"What the hell does it look like I'm doing?" I burst into tears. "I don't even have supper started cause I can't get the lights to work!"

He listened to me yelling for a while; then he reached over and flipped a switch. Just like magic, the room filled with wonderful light. That's when I burst out crying. (I do that a lot lately.) But, Johnny hugged me, and I had to start laughing and said, "You smart ass!" He stood there grinning. I forgot that we had gotten electricity hooked up the day before. It's so wonderful—when I remember to use it.

Besides learning to flick a switch and turn on lights, I learned much more on butchering day. The men had slaughtered four hogs before the sun was up while the hogs were still asleep. I never knew that if animals get upset, the taste of the meat can be ruined. Johnny came for me after killing the pigs. Believe me when I say that I almost fainted when we drove into his folks' yard. Four white, gutted hogs hanging from trees seemed like something from a nightmare!

Later, when we were wrapping the meat in butcher paper, Grandma made me feel good. She said, "You are really good at wrapping and so fast."

I told her, "It's kinda like changing a slippery, little baby's diaper. The faster you do it, the easier it is." Oh my, Aggie, remember the hundreds of diapers we changed every day working in the nursery. All those babies!

Well, the really exciting news here is that our little bundle of joy is due in about six weeks. Grammy (my mom) and Grandma Anna have been helping me make little gowns and diapers galore. We've received some blankets and all the other things babies need—there's so much stuff! Grandma can't understand why I don't want to nurse instead of spending money on bottles that will have to be cleaned and sterilized. She just doesn't understand that nursing is so old fashioned. Only low class, poor people do it anymore. You never know if the baby gets enough, and I just know with my dinky little boobs I would starve the baby. Grandma has been such an angel and so helpful otherwise. I just gotta let her talk.

I'm a little scared of delivery. Hope I don't get some mean old nurse like Swafford, but that I'm lucky enough to get some sweetheart like Beat or Garrity! Ha ha. Really, hope I can be brave and not scream and yell my head off like some of those crazy women we would make fun of. We really were pretty awful at times when we imitated them back in the dorm. I know, you're thinking that I was the awful one. You always were such a saint, Aggie. Guess that's why you were brave enough to join the army.

Gotta end this. I know I'll have to send it in at least two envelopes or it will never get to you. Hope you are home by Christmas.

Polly

A couple of days after sealing the letter, life provided more material for a newsy letter. Pauline had spent the day helping Grandma Anna finish canning the meat while Johnny and his dad worked in the corn field. Because the men wanted to finish the harvest before rain turned the fields into a mud pit, supper was late. Grandma insisted, "Johnny and Pauline stay to eat. We have plenty fixed, and you don't need to go home and cook something this late, Pauline."

She replied, "But, our cow needs milked."

"That cow can wait for a little longer," Johnny called from the washroom. Later, as they enjoyed scrumptious apple pie, Grandpa Leo said, "Mother, you want to tell these two the news?"

Johnny looked puzzled, but Pauline was totally unprepared when Grandma Anna said, "We are moving to Wichita right after Thanksgiving." Her young daughter-in-law dropped her fork and seemed oblivious that her mouth was wide open and still half-full of apple pie.

"Where will you live?" Pauline finally asked. "I didn't think you were planning to move for years."

"Some friends are selling their house and moving to Arizona for health. It has a nice big yard for the grandkids to play in and a really nice garden spot," Leo said. "It's time for us to move out so you two can get settled before that new baby arrives."

Tears glistened on Pauline's cheeks as she got up to hug Grandma. "Oh, that is so nice of you, but are you sure you're ready to leave the farm?"

Grandma smiled and patted her hand. "We're getting too tired to keep up this place. After the boys return, they'll be getting jobs in Wichita anyway, so it will help them too if our house is there."

Johnny shook hands with his dad and said, "Well, I knew you were looking at places, but sure didn't expect this to happen so fast."

"Hope you don't mind, but Spud wants to keep living here and help with the farming until his GI bill is approved and he can begin college. But with the big house and Spud out raising hell most nights, you won't see him much," Leo said. "Hope you don't mind, Polly."

She smiled and shook her head, *How can I complain when I will have an entire house instead of two tiny rooms for three people? The chicken house was a cozy starter, but it will be wonderful to have a real house!*

Anna got up from the table to clear the dishes, and Pauline began to help. "No, no, you and your little one are all tuckered out from butchering. Johnny, you need to take your wife home," Anna said. As she looked at him, she noticed someone coming onto the south porch. "Goodness, who could be here, this time of night?" A tall young man in an Air Corps uniform stood in the doorway with a pretty young lady whose face glowed with happiness.

"Any food in this house for a hungry soldier?" he asked.

Grandma Anna dropped the plates she had picked up. She whispered, "Ben," as pent-up joyous tears trickled down her cheeks.

Chapter 30

"You'd think a war had ended or something," a first lieutenant Air Corpsman said to the young woman at his side. Her Army dress uniform had the insignia of an Air Corps Captain. They stepped off the train amid a circus of humanity in drab army green, navy blue, and spiffy dress white military clothes. "Looks like most of Chicago is in uniform."

"Yes, and I am tired of wearing it! Tomorrow I'm going shopping!" the young woman stated emphatically

"Mary, I thought you were so proud of being an Army Air Corps flight nurse," the lieutenant commented.

"I am, dear brother, but you have to admit, this dingy color has gotten boring and does nothing to enhance my beauty." She laughed, tossing her long dark curls. "Besides, I'm ready to celebrate and party, and these aren't exactly party clothes."

"Oh, do I have a wild woman to take care of in the wicked city? You aren't going to become one of those painted women under the gas lamps luring the farm boys, are you?" he teased as they joined the crowd moving into Union Station.

"First of all, John McHugh, don't think you need to take care of me. After surviving this war in Europe for the past three years, I think I'm perfectly capable of handling myself even with "husky, brawling men with big shoulders." She quoted Sandburg's popular poem and winked at her brother. "However, I will let you be gallant and guide me through this mess and get us a cab."

They looked around the famous station, admiring the high chandeliers and taking in Union's landmark clock before climbing the marble steps of the grand staircase.

There they were greeted by a cacophony of sounds. News boys shouted headlines. Car horns honked, sounding like a flock of geese. Cabs looking for fares were the noisiest. The sidewalk was crowded with military personnel bound by the glue of blood and memories that would visit in nightmares for years. They waited for taxis lining Adams Street, two abreast, ready to speed commuters to their Chicago destinations. The cabs vied for parking space and inched out after picking up passengers. Mary and John found a spot among the crowd jostling for a ride. Someone bent to pick up a suitcase and accidentally pushed Mary into the woman next to her. "I'm so sorry," she said, looking at Aggie, then smiled, adding, "Lieutenant Beat!"

"That's ok, Captain," Aggie said at first not really looking at the other officer but, out of habit she began to salute. She had noticed the double bars and gold wings with a superimposed N on Mary's uniform. Then a smile spread across her face. "Mary McHugh?"

"I sure am!" Mary dropped her duffle bag and the two old friends wrapped one another in warm hugs. "What a small world!" Noticing Aggie's wings with the N, she added, "St. Francis can be proud turning out good, patriotic nurses. Where did you serve, Aggie?"

"We were Stateside until the war in Europe ended;then we were sent to the Pacific, but didn't arrive in Hawaii until after VJ Day. We had it easy compared to all of you who served during the fighting."

Rosie could not stand being left out of the excitement. "When I heard some of the stories of the nurses we relieved, I wondered if I could have made it under the conditions they faced during combat. Hi, I'm Rosie Kennedy. Where did you serve, Captain?"

"In Europe, and no more of this 'Captain' stuff. We all did our part in different ways. I'm Mary McHugh," she added.

"I'm sorry. I forgot you didn't know each other," Aggie said. "Rosie Mary McHugh. was my mentor in nursing school. Rosie and I served together out of Hickam." The women smiled greetings. Then Aggie looked at John who was obviously with Mary. "And you are?"

"Hi, ladies, I'm John McHugh, Mary's brother. Pleased to meet you both. I'd shake hands, but…" He glanced at the suitcases in each of his.

"That's ok," Aggie replied. She smiled as the sun reflected off the shiny Miraculous Medal dangling from the handles of each duffle bag. Then remembering, she gasped, "I thought your plane exploded and you were killed!"

Mary put her arm through John's and began, "We all did—it's really along…

At the same time, Rosie interrupted, "Did you serve together?"

Mary answered, "We both served in Europe -- at first flying mostly out of England. But, with different units and seldom saw each other even early in the war." She smiled at John and added. "After D Day, I was in Italy and then finally France from where we were evacuating prison camps in Germany."

"That's interesting, but back to John's plane exploding, and you supposed to be dead. That's what I want to know about," Aggie said.

"That's a really long story, and it's so noisy here," John said. "Let's try to get a cab now," and he waved eagerly to one pulling up."

The driver honked and squeezed his car near the curb before jumping out. He limped around the sedan to help with luggage.

"Good afternoon, officers. I bet you're all headed out to Fort Sheridan, aren't you?" Obviously, he had picked up more than one GI excited to be officially discharged.

"We'll be going out there first thing tomorrow," John said, motioning to Mary. "Right now we need a hotel, but one so we can get to the base easily," John said.

"And hopefully reasonably priced and close to good shopping," Mary added.

John looked at Aggie and Rosie, "Are you ladies headed out to Sheridan too?" When they nodded their heads, he suggested, "Maybe we could all share the cab and search for a hotel together."

"Sounds great," Rosie answered.

"Well, you heard the lady: hotel and shopping near Fort Sheridan, if possible," he told the cabbie. Doffing his military cap in a chauffeur-like motion, John said, "Hop right in ladies."

Amid laughter, Mary scooted across the back seat, making room for new acquaintances. "I just told John that shopping is number one on my agenda after I get discharged tomorrow. I'm so tired of military clothes."

"That's exactly what we want to do," Aggie said. "Before going home to Kansas and Oklahoma, we want to buy some nice clothes and enjoy a few sights of the big city."

"Really, you're from Oklahoma?" she asked, looking at Rosie who nodded. "You probably don't remember, Aggie, but that's where I'm from. Shawnee." Then she added, "Oh, shopping'll be lots more fun with friends!"

"First thing we need to do is find you a hotel," the cabbie said.. "Don't know how many discharge centers Uncle Sam has, but it seems half of all the people who fought in this war are coming through Chicago. Don't get me wrong, it's great for business, but the crowds! Must be kinda frustrating, especially after what you've all been through."

"Oh, it's rather exciting seeing so many happy people sharing the same feelings, and it's terrific seeing all the beautiful, big buildings and… and… Well, it's just exciting!" Rosie replied.

"It won't be when you try to get a room. Everything's packed. I'll take you down to the Lakeview area. It's not the closest to Sheridan, but there's lots of hotels, and most of the GIs stay in the area since some hotels were military-only during the war." He slammed on his brakes as a group of sailors in white middies stepped into the street, instigating other squealing brakes, honking horns, and angry remarks that interrupted his monologue. "HeyBuddies,ya made it back to the States;you don't wanna get killed before you even get home!" the cabbie added to the clamor. "Sorry about that, ladies," he apologized to the young women who had been thrown against the front seat with the abrupt stop.

"It may only be mid-afternoon, but I think those guys have been celebrating for a while," Mary observed. "Glad your brakes work."

"Yea, gotta be ready for the GIs and the crazies non-stop celebrating," he observed. "As I started to say, The Drake is close to good shopping and all the best sights of Chicago. It'll be easy to get out to Ft. Sheridan 'cause the military runs buses from there. It used to be awful pricey, but since the Army commandeered it during the war, the prices are still pretty good for service men and women. You're lucky it's only about 2:00. In a couple of hours finding a room will be impossible!"

As the cabbie chattered and maneuvered through traffic, his passengers stretched their necks out the windows to see the sights and point to Chicago landmarks and attractions.

When the cab pulled up in front of a luxury hotel, he hopped out to help with the luggage. Then he advised, "The Drake is a great place with decent prices, not as high as some along here. If you can't get rooms inside, try the Crescent across the street and the Lakeside down the way. All the hotels in the area are good and safe — some just aren't as patriotic as others with prices for our returning heroes."

"We aren't heroes," Aggie said, taking her suitcases. "Just did our duty."

"You're all heroes to me. I couldn't fight, and I sure appreciate you that did. I'd hate to think about speaking Kraut or Jap."

"Thanks, sir," John said as he placed a couple of bills in the cabbie's hand.

"Oh, Lieutenant, that's way too much; one is more than plenty," he said and put a bill in John's pocket. "I'm grateful for your service to our country so much; I'd give rides for free but gotta feed the kids. Lots of luck to you all," he called as he jumped behind the wheel and honked. He gave a final friendly wave over the hood of the cab.

His passengers all returned the wave, and then Rosie said, "Hey, John, we want to pay our part for the ride."

"Naw, let me be a gentleman. Now that we're almost civilians, it'll be nice to treat women like ladies and not check for bars and stripes."

"Well, that's right chivalrous of you, far be it from us to keep you from being a gentleman. Thanks a lot." Aggie and Rosie laughed.

The four officers grabbed their luggage and pushed through the gilded doors of the hotel. "Holy Toledo! Look at this place!" Aggie gasped. "That cabbie has to be nuts; it'll probably cost a month's pay to stay here a couple of nights."

Mary and Rosie stood gaping at the walls and ceilings ornately decorated in Italian Renaissance style. John said, "Well, there's only one way to find out," and he walked toward the front desk. "Come on, ladies, stop gawking."

"Good afternoon, Lieutenant," the desk clerk greeted him. Glancing at the women, he continued, "And Captains and Lieutenants. I hope you all aren't needing a room. We only have one left. It's $25 a night, but there are two beds and, of course, a private bath."

John turned to the women and saw three soldiers coming through the door. "Well, I guess $25 isn't bad for Chicago and this swanky place," he said. "Mary and I can try some other place, and you ladies can have this one," he suggested.

"What if you can't find another one?" Rosie asked, noticing a couple more Army nurses walking toward the desk. "It's getting later by the minute."

"Sir, I don't want to rush you, but others are waiting," the professional concierge interjected, nodding to soldiers now forming a line. "Will you be taking the room?"

"Yes," Aggie answered him. "We'll take it."

"But, who is taking it? This is a reputable hotel with standards. I'm sure you understand," he said with a haughty sniff.

"Yes, we understand, and we are highly reputable officers of the United States Army-Air Corps. We haven't had much privacy for the past few years, and I'm sure we won't mind being a little crowded. We certainly don't have any indiscreet activities in mind to ruin your reputation."

The concierge's mouth dropped open; he was taken aback by the pretty lieutenant's feisty words. He looked beyond her and the rest of the group and announced, "I'm sorry, fellas and ladies, we don't have any more rooms." He added under his breath, "Good luck finding one around here this time of day." To the four friends he said, "Ok, someone sign in, and pay me before the manager shows up and starts yelling about too many people in a room, especially a guy with three lovely ladies!."

Aggie stepped back and looked to John to sign, allowing him to be the gentleman again. Looking at Rosie, she said, "I'm sorry, I didn't even ask if this was ok. I just figured Mary and John had as much right as we do to that room."

Rosie looked up at the ceiling before answering. "Well, I don't know if this is quite up to my standards!" Then she added, "Are you kidding? This place looks like a palace!And, like you said, it'll be a whole lot more privacy than we've had in the past few years. The more the merrier!"

After the concierge gave John the room key, the four headed for the elevator. While they were waiting, Aggie said to Mary and John, "If you don't want to share the room, we won't be offended. I just figured with the line forming we better make a decision."

"I'm glad you're so smart, Aggie. We're probably all lucky to have a room." Mary nodded to another group of soldiers coming through the hotel doors.

"You ladies sure are trusting." John expressed brotherly concern about Agnes' naiveté. "Guess you must figure if you handled all the war threw at you, you could handle an Oklahoma farm boy if he got out of line."

"You bet we can, buster." Aggie and Rosie both glared at him, and Aggie held a clenched fist aimed at John's eyes before bursting into laughter. "Besides, I figure anyone who has a Miraculous Medal on his duffel bag and his watch must be a decent fellow." John looked surprised that Aggie was so observant and fingered the medal on his watch. "I noticed those before we even got in the cab with you."

"Well, these are pretty special medals." John fingered the one on his bag. "The military can keep any medals the Air Corps has promised before I'd give these up! I credit the Blessed Mother talking to her Son with the fact I'm back in the US safe and sound."

Before Aggie or Rosie could ask questions, the elevator noisily announced its arrival and its iron filigree door opened. An elderly black operator, smartly clad in standard elevator operator attire, folded back the grate. "Good evening, ladies and gentleman," he said cheerily as he reached for luggage. "Sorry 'bout all the noise. This ole girl has almost been through the war herself with all the soldiers, sailors, and brass through here the past few years," he laughed. "Yes, sir, we seen our share of soldiers. Going up!" His voice shifted for a second as he closed the rattling doors. Then he continued his spiel. "Sure is nice to see some pretty ladies now. Come in all stiff and proper in uniforms then go out shoppn' and turn into Cinderellies. Mmmm." His incessant chatter had not allowed anyone to give a floor number, but he stopped at 17. "Well, I believe here we is. Since no one wait'n, I can help you ladies with your luggage."

John looked at the room number on the key. "How did you know what floor we need?"

"Only room left open, last trip I made up, so I figured had to be," he explained as he reached for a suitcase.

"Oh, we can make it," Rosie said. "We're used to lugging these around. Thanks for the entertaining ride—ah, what was your name?"

"Why you're very welcome, Miss Lieutenant. Been my pleasure to help some of our prettiest returning heroes. I'm Clifford," he said. "But I might as well help you right down the hall here since I'd just be stand'n here wait'n for you, Lieutenant Sir."

"Well…" John began rather sheepishly.

"He's stay'n with us, and we're gonna have a wonderful time!" Mary crooned as she reached out and tussled her brother's hair. The ladies giggled like school girls.

"No, really, I'm—" John started to explain.

"Come on, Johnny, the night's young, and we got lots to do." Aggie put her arm into the crook at his elbow and started down the hall. John shook his head, smiling at defeat in the hands of three wild women.

"See you later, Clifford," Rosie called.

The elderly operator shook his head. "Mm! Those ladies are three silly nurses. Bet they kept their patients laughing all the time. That poor guy with them has his hands full." Then he pulled the door shut for the trip down.

CHAPTER 31

AFTER ORGANIZING their luggage against the wall, the officers pushed the beds closer together to give John room to sleep on the floor. Then they took turns freshening up from their long trips. Leaving the bathroom, Rosie said, "Even though you can tell the towels aren't new these are some of the thickest I've ever felt."

"These beds are mighty comfortable too," Mary answered from where she was resting.

"This place is beautiful now, even after being occupied by the military during the war. Can you imagine what it looked like before that?"

"I'm sure it was ritzy," said John. "But instead of admiring our fancy barracks, I want a big steak!" He was emphatic.

On the way out for the evening, Clifford entertained them with information about where to find the best food and what sights they shouldn't miss. He even had suggestions where to go for dancing and celebrating.

Mary said, "Clifford, just to clear up any ideas that we are up to indecent and immoral behavior, John here is my brother."

Clifford nodded his head and laughed heartily. "I knows you ladies were too nice to be any hussies. I done seen enough of 'em being sneaked in here over the years. Seen all types of peoples in this job, some like you all, gold! But, some were, well… Mm mm mm!"

"Oh, aren't you sweet," Rosie said as Clifford called out, "Main floor! Watch your step."

"You all have a nice even'n, now." He tipped his hat to the ladies as they smiled goodbye.

The lights of Chicago were just coming on as they left the hotel, and the fuchsia and lavender tinted sky announced the sun was setting. "Oh, John, can you wait just a little longer for your steak? I'd love to see the sun set over the lake." John shrugged and motioned for his sister to lead the way. "Hurry before it's completely gone," Mary urged, walking briskly in the direction she must have sensed was the way to the water. The group followed and soon realized they could smell the great lake.

"She's always had an amazing sense of direction and finding places," John explained as he motioned for Aggie and Rosie to follow.

"Don't you think it will be awful cold on the beach?" Rosie asked, wrapping her coat around herself.

"We can handle it to see a pretty sunset," Aggie called while adjusting her scarf. The wind picked up as they walked from the protection of the buildings. Less than a hundred yards ahead of them was endless water, sparkling like a kaleidoscope as the sun dipped closer to the horizon.

The four reached the shore, and Lake Michigan appeared on fire with light and color. Gulls called overhead and waves slapped the sands performing an endless symphony. "Great suggestion, Mary," Aggie whispered. She closed her eyes for a moment.

"Well, it's not a romantic tropical sunset like you ladies are used to, but it is pretty anyway," she answered.

"And best of all, it's in the States and almost home," Rosie added. All four wrapped arms across one another's shoulders and looked out, each enveloped in private memories and appreciating their blessings.

Even though it was warm for November, the wind chilled after the sun went down, and Aggie and Rosie shivered. "We're definitely not in Hawaii anymore, are we?" Rosie cuddled closer as they walked along.

"It's going to take some getting used to real weather after living in paradise. Isn't it?" Aggie agreed.

"Guess that's one benefit of living through one of the worst winters of my life," John commented. "Is Hawaii really as beautiful as everyone says?"

Aggie nodded her head, but Rosie just shivered, so they turned their backs on the darkening water

Returning to the front of the hotel, the group disputed Clifford's directions as they searched for a great, priced-right place to eat. Walking a few blocks in the direction Mary insisted was what the elevator operator recommended, John was the first to spy a weather-beaten, wooden storefront with a sign painted on the small window.

"Well, Clifford's right about this place not looking special on the outside; unless we're wanting a dump!" Aggie commented as they stood under the tattered awning.

"This looks kinda shady. I'll check it out first," John said. He disappeared into the sounds of mellow jazz and the tantalizing aroma of grilled beef. While taking in the scene, someone called, "Hey, John McHugh, is that you?" Two Air Force pilots approached, and the speaker put out his hand. "I'm Captain Ben Wetta. Flew with Mary a couple of times after the war. We met briefly at—"

"Sure, I remember." John shook hands. "Great to see you again; sorry I didn't recognize you at first. Things were a little crazy last time we met."

"Hey that's fine. There was lots of excitement and other things on your mind. Just glad to see you again. Doing ok, I guess?"

"Yea, yea." Mary's right outside; I'll go get her," He noticed the pilots removing their caps. Turning, he bumped into his sister and their new friends.

"When you opened that door, it smelled so good we weren't waiting for your opinion," she explained. Turning to the tall, dark-haired captain, she continued. "Hi, Ben, great to see ya. Wow, I guess I should have saluted. When did you get the second bar?"

"Oh, it's a little something from Uncle Sam for my thirty-four. Good to see you too. You remember Frank?"

"Of course I do, and congrats to you also, Frank," she said, noticing his captain's insignia. "I know you both deserve those."

"Thanks, Mary." He wrapped his arm around her waist, pulling her to him in a more-than-friendly hug. "And your noses have led you to a great place. Food's the best I've had in four years," he said. "Right, Ben?" he added, looking at his companion.

"Never tell my mom, but it's as good as what I ate during my short visit home," Ben answered. Aggie thought he looked and sounded familiar but couldn't think of how she knew him.

"Are you gentlemen finished with your table?" asked a waiter who approached the pilots.

"These folks can have it," Frank replied.

"Well, that party is next," he said, glancing at another group of soldiers a few feet away. "But, I'll have one ready for you in a few minutes." He smiled at Mary, Rosie, and Aggie, and was gone to clean the table.

"Oh, Frank Dillon and Ben Wetta, these are new friends that we just met. They were flight nurses in the Pacific. This is Agnes Beat and Rosie Trowbridge." Then Mary explained to them, "As the war wound down and after, we flew together out of Italy."

"Happy to meet you, Lieutenants." The men shook hands with the nurses.

"Ben Wetta!" Aggie exclaimed. "You're from Colwich, Kansas, and have a brother Johnny and a wife -- ah, ah --"

"Margie," Ben finished. "How do you know that?"

"I was best friends in nurses' training with Polly, Johnny's wife."

"Really, what a small world," Ben exclaimed.

"Gosh, I don't believe this. It's wonderful to meet you, Ben. Suddenly, it seems real that we're almost home."

The waiter returned. "Sir and Ladies, we have a table for you. Please follow me."

"Hey, let's get together later," Frank suggested.

"Yes, let's, do," Aggie and Mary agreed. "Where?"

They quickly made plans and agreed on a USO nearby. The ladies and John followed the waiter as the pilots headed for the door. "See you later, ladies and Lieutenant Miracle," Frank laughed and waved to John as they left.

"Will this be ok?" the greeter asked as he pulled out chairs for the ladies. The table was in the middle of the room and seemed surrounded by a convention of military personnel.

"That cab driver wasn't kidding about this area being a gathering place for soldiers and sailors," Mary commented as she sat down.

"You're right about that," Rosie agreed, glancing around the room.

"Your menus, ladies and sir," the waiter said. He passed what looked like half a sheet of old newspaper to each. "Course, you might want to just order the special everyone seems to like. The best 12 oz T-bone steak in Chicago with all the fix'ns." He looked around the table questioningly.

"That's what I'm hav'n—and the coldest beer in the house," John answered.

"Sounds wonderful," Aggie said. "But I can't eat a steak that big. Ya wanna share?" she asked Rosie.

"You, bet."

"No, both of you order your own. I'll eat what you don't," John advised.

"Well, I can't eat that much either," Mary commented. "But, I bet I know someone who won't let it go to waste." She glanced at John who nodded.

"Sure wouldn't have picked this place on the décor, but it's been a long time since I've been near food that smelled so good." John was glancing at the open beam ceilings, tattered wallpaper, and bare wood, all of which gave the place a destitute appearance. But the smooth jazz softened the atmosphere. Perhaps the relaxed ambiance made everyone who had lived through the hardship of war feel more comfortable than the glamour of a fancy restaurant.

"And what would you ladies like to drink?"

"Cold beer." They answered in unison and then broke into laughter.

"How about I just bring a big pitcher and some mugs?" he suggested.

"Sounds great."

While they waited for their meals, the officers talked about their luck meeting each other outside of Union Station and getting the last room for a decent price at a wonderful hotel. The good fortune of their driver bringing them to what seemed to be the hub of Chicago activity was appreciated. They also quipped about the fluke of already running into friends amid the thousands of service people in the city.

"I don't think any of it is luck; I think we have all been blessed by God," John quietly interjected. Aggie and Rosie looked at him appreciatively. "I wouldn't feel comfortable saying this to everyone," he continued, "but since you appreciate the Miraculous Medal, Aggie, I presume you must be Catholic—or at least respect faith."

"Absolutely, on both counts," Aggie replied. She started to say more but the waiter appeared with frosty mugs and a large pitcher of beer with beaded moisture glistening down the sides.

"Here you go, Captain and Lieutenants," he announced, setting the welcome brew in front of John. "If I get too busy to bring more when you need, just holler, 'Hey, Tony.' Oh, your steaks are next on the grill." He left to welcome more customers into an already crowded place.

John poured everyone a mug of the cold suds, and after all were filled, Mary lifted hers. "To peace and being back in the USA." Satisfied sighs followed the clinking of the mugs.

Aggie noticed John's eyes were closed as he truly savored his beer. Or, perhaps he was giving thanks for it. She was sensing something special about this young man. Looking from him to Mary, Aggie said, "Now, I really would like to hear this 'long story' that you mentioned earlier about meeting up in Germany. And why did Frank call you Lieutenant Miracle?"

John and Mary exchanged glances and smiled. "You want to tell the story?"

"Well, I will tell you what I know, and then you can fill in the details." Looking from Aggie to Rosie, she took another sip of beer and began. "John was part of a bomber squadron of twelve planes that flew out of England until after D Day. When we talked, we would always tease who had the more dangerous missions. Even though John is my baby brother, he assigned himself my protector long ago and always insisted being a flight nurse was more dangerous."

"You didn't really think that, did you, John?" Aggie asked dumbfounded.

"Well, yes, those medical flights were dangerous. Because the planes carried military supplies, sometimes including ammunition, on the flights to pick up wounded, the red cross or medical insignia wasn't painted on your planes. Right?"Aggie and Rosie nodded. "Even when accompanied with fighters in the area, I thought those medical planes looked like big lost geese flying alone."

"Yes, but the Germans weren't much interested in a lone plane.

They really wanted to destroy your bomber squadrons that were playing havoc on their factories and supply depots," Mary explained.

"So, you two got to see each other occasionally?" Rosie asked.

"Once in a while at first, until D Day. Once some runways in France and Italy were in our hands, the bombers were flying into Germany from closer range. John and I were in different parts of France and I also flew out of Italy. I tried to keep up on his squadron through the military grapevine. But, I'll never forget the day in late September when we were unloading the last patients from our most recent flight into Italy. One of the ground crew officers said my CO wanted me to report to her office.

"I wondered what she wanted, but as soon as I saw her face I thought, *Please, not John! Please, please let John be ok!*" Aggie reached for Mary's hand as tears of remembered stabbing grief welled up in her eyes.

"My CO told me that his plane was blown up in midair; all twelve crew members were killed. She said some other things, but my mind, trained to react to crises, was a total mushy fog. I remember arguing surely some of the soldiers parachuted to safety. They couldn't all be killed!I think I must have almost been in shock because I don't remember the rest of that night at all."

Rosie brushed sympathetic tears off her cheeks, and John refilled her beer. "Hey, this is supposed to be a celebration," he said. "Maybe we need to change the subject. God obviously answered Mary's and everyone else's prayers." He gave his sister a gentle hug, knowing how she had suffered.

"Lord, no! You can't change the subject now!" Aggie insisted, looking at John. "This is an extra special celebration. You can't stop telling the story now just because some nurses are showing emotions we hid throughout the war. Besides, our steaks aren't here yet." Turning to Mary, she asked, "So how long did you think John had been killed?"

"Until after the end of the war."

"How awful!" Rosie answered. "Oh my gosh, you were a POW, John; you weren't helping evacuate camps! Mary I'm such a ninny!"

"It's ok the cab came up when you were asking. After I got the news about John, I was able to get a couple days bereavement leave and went to his base. The guys in his squadron were really nice and sympathetic. Some of them were taking the loss of the flight almost as hard as me. One told me that he'd like to give me some hope, but he saw the plane explode. If they ever even found dog tags, it'd be a miracle. Even so, since a couple of parachutes were seen before the explosion, for awhile I checked names posted of those recently confirmed dead.

A couple of guys in the squadron had said that yes, there were some parachutes, but the airmen attached were obviously dead. "No one could have lived with all the shrapnel and artillery the Krauts were throwing at us." He was never identified among them, but everyone was declared dead because other guys in the squadron saw the plane explode. I just kept praying for a miracle until the day two of the guys in his squadron brought me all of John's belongings.

"The day I received a cable from my parents was almost as bad as receiving the news from my CO. They were so devastated, and, of course, now they were even more worried about me. It about killed me not being able to be home for them. But, the fighting was so heavy; there was no way to take any leave. Even when I was on an evac flight, I never had more than a few hours at the most in the US, so there was no chance to go see them. I called them from Florida a couple of times and DC another when I came in with the medical flights, but, even the calls were awful; they were so sad. They had lost all the staunch, we-can-do-this attitude that I had witnessed growing up on the farm. After talking to them, those long flights back to Europe with no patients to take care of seemed to last forever. I tried to pray and not think of Mom and Dad, or John and the terribly wounded men I had helped, but it was hard not to get depressed."

"Those flights did get long, didn't they?" Aggie knew from experience. "How many did you make?"

"By the time the war finally ended, I had made ten. That's why I was assigned to shorter flights airlifting POWs from various camps to the hospital in England and then Italy."

"What was it like helping evacuate the camps?" Rosie wondered. "Were the men all in terrible shape?"

Mary nodded. "I prayed constantly, so I wouldn't fall apart. I tried to joke with them. Some were so malnourished and in such horrible condition. Once in a while, I searched the face of a patient with awful facial wounds wondering if he could be John, and then I'd tell myself I had to stop that and accept God's will."

"Why did you even think he had survived with the explosion and accounts of the horrible battle?" Aggie asked,

"I just kept thinking that we were so close, I'd feel it if John had been killed."

The waiter appeared with a huge serving tray loaded with sizzling steaks, mashed potatoes, baked beans, and coleslaw. "Here you go, folks. You want another pitcher of beer, too." He said this more as a statement than a question, and he set down a pitcher of water and was off before anyone had a chance to reply.

"Guess he figures he can read minds," Rosie laughed, looking at the mouthwatering food.

John had bowed his head and was making the sign of the cross. Mary quietly began, "Bless us, Oh Lord, and these Thy gifts..." Aggie joined her while Rosie bowed her head. "I never would have done that before the war," Mary confessed. "After finding John, I promised God I would never be embarrassed to pray."

"Mary," Aggie said, "if you want to finish the story later, we'll understand."

"It's ok now that I've started." Mary took a drink of beer and then a bit of steak before continuing. "By April, I had been transferred to Rheims, and we thought we had evacuated just about all the camps and were making plans in hopes of being sent home. In early May, Army headquarters got word from the Russians that they had found over 9,000 American POWs at a camp near Barth, Germany on the Baltic Sea. Since this was in their territory, the Russians wanted to liberate them to Odessa, but the 'mulish, obstinate' Americans refused to be liberated by them."

John interrupted. "Can you imagine? American GIs refusing to obey orders from those Red Commies and not wanting to go to Russia."

They all laughed, and while John explained, Mary ate. "Taking us all the way down to Odessa made no sense. The Russians tried to convince us that we deserved to relax at their wonderful seaside resorts, and then we could be taken by ship to England. We were afraid that we would probably never see home if the Russians 'liberated' us. Besides considering the poorly equipped group that first showed up at Stulag Luft #1, we figured we'd be walking or, at best, riding old grey mares all the way across Europe."

They all laughed again, and Rosie asked, "Were the Russians really that poorly equipped? Was there a big battle to liberate the camp from the Germans?"

"Answering your first question, yes, the Russians had pretty old stuff. And, no, the Germans didn't put up a fight. They had marched out of the camp three nights earlier leaving our officers in charge. Of course, there was no food or supplies. The Germans had wanted us to march west with them, but we refused. We knew if allied pilots saw almost 10,000 men marching along a road, they might think we were Germans and attack. Our CO, Colonel Zemke, was also smart enough to know if any halfway healthy looking guys started wandering around outside of camp, they'd probably be shot or beat up. He ordered everyone to stay in camp. Of course, some guys didn't, and most ended up killed as Zemke had expected.

"After the Germans were gone, Zemke organized a small group of guys who spoke Russian to head in the direction of the artillery barrages we had been hearing for days. They went out at night in an old charcoal-burning truck trying to find help. The third night, they met some Russian soldiers in a similar truck, and they all returned to Stulag Luft #1 so the Russians could check out the story of a camp of 10,000 prisoners, mostly American and British but a bignumber from other countries. That was on May 3, a day I will always celebrate.

"Several hours later, the first steps of liberation began when about half a dozen heavily-armed Russians showed up on horseback. The next day, a big contingent of horses and wagons pulled into camp. The wagons were filled with expensive loot the Russians had been confiscating along the way." John took a drink of beer and another bite of steak as the ladies sat in awe..

"So, when were you two reunited?" Aggie asked, remembering they still had not heard the answer to their main question.

"It took a week of red tape and haggling between those damned Russians and the Americans and Brits—some captured back in '40— poor bastards! Excuse me." John blushed and smiled. "Like I said, the commies wanted to transport us all the way across Europe to the Black Sea. The entire continent was torn up from bombs; getting to south of Russia would have taken months. And we would be in the hands of Russians!Anyway, the big wigs finally reached an agreement to allow our planes to fly into the Russian zone."

"You said the Germans left the camp with no food or supplies," Aggie interjected. "If it took that long to evacuate the camp, what did you all do for food? The Russians surely got you some, didn't they?"

"They must have confiscated animals from a huge pig farm nearby because we suddenly had all kinds of pork plus lot of potatoes. Best food we had in that prison. The Russians soldiers were really friendly and good guys. They're just caught up in the corrupt system of the big wigs, just like most of the German guards were.

"After being in camp for a while, we actually felt sorry for some of those poor guys. They were obviously beaten and the guards at Stulag Luft #1 were either old men or kids. Anyway, it wasn't until May 12 that our rescue officially began." John took a bite of steak.

"When did you find out that John was alive?" Aggie asked Mary as John was stillchewing his steak. He motioned for his sister to continue.

"The first day, the plan was to evacuate at least six thousand, the most malnourished and ill. Even if we weren't nurses on the flights, we were on duty processing men as they arrived in Rheims. You can imagine how crazy it was receiving that many patients in one day. We ended up receiving about five thousand as some flights went directly to England for the British POWs. Those we received who were in the best shape were treated out in the open, under trees in a park until enough tents could be set up

"I was assigned to the last of evac flights on the 13th. We knew we were bringing home about 3,000 more POWs, and we hoped the men would be in better shape than the previous day. Of course, we knew there would be a few stubborn, commanding officers who were determined to wait til the lower ranking men were liberated.

"Theresa, my best friend from home who had enlisted with me, was assigned to the same flight. The atmosphere was so different than all the others during the war. Everyone was celebrating, knowing we were honored to be evacuating what we hoped were the last of American military prisoners in Europe. The pilot told us no one was supposed to move away from the plane because he would fly in and not even turn off the engine. The soldiers would be lined up along the air strip, jump in and we'd take off. Remember the Russians had a ticking clock, hoping -to be able to keep some Americans.

As we neared Barth, the captain announced that we would have a couple of litter patients, so a nurse and corpsman would check on them while another nurse should stay at the door to try to check men in. Theresa and I decided she'd go with the med-tech. Then she said, 'Let's say a Hail Mary for all the men before we go to work.' "

John interrupted. "You want me to help you eat that steak? It's getting cold. Maybe you should take a break from the story." He could see recalling the narrative was difficult for Mary.

She took a drink of her beer. "I only want a bite or two more. This meat is so tender; I can't believe I've eaten this much. Help yourself to the rest, John."

He finished chewing his last bite of steak then said, "Well, you were telling such an interesting story, I wanted to hear how it ended."

"What?" Rosie asked, appearing dumbfounded.

"You idiot, John!"Mary said, punching his arm. "You finish the story!"

"Ok, ok," he quipped in his Oklahoma drawl, rubbing his arm in faked injury.

"Believe me, the morning of May 13, we were ready and waiting to put Barth behind us forever. You never heard such hooting and hollering when we heard the planes approach. Colonel Zemke had organized the men in groups of 25 or 30 along the air strip so we could load quickly. Most of the pilots didn't even cut their engines. They just slid to a stop, and the guys started jumping in. Because I had been a prisoner so much shorter time than many, I was assigned the second to last flight of officers. I was also healthier than many guys, so I could help load the high-ranking men who were in bad shape. Like Mary said, they refused to leave before everyone else was evacuated.

"Colonel Zemke had communicated we had some needing medical help to the pilots. Another guy and I were just lifting Major Brand onto a stretcher when a flight nurse in kakis approached. She sounded like a Southern angel. 'Hi, fellas, ya'll ready to go home?' I thought, I know that voice! Looking up, I couldn't believe my eyes. There, with the late afternoon sunshine glowing behind her, was Theresa Guffey, Mary's best friend from back home. I felt like I was seeing a vision."

"Theresa, it sure is good to see you,' I said. "She looked at me and seemed in a daze and just stared with her mouth wide open. Then she squealed then hugged me to all get out. Theresa was crying and laughing so much I got kinda emotional too. When she was finally calm enough to talk, she said, 'Oh, John, you won't believe it, Mary is here. She's helping load the men.' Glancing at the plane, I could see her stooped down, talking to Colonel Anderson as he was being lifted aboard. Theresa told the orderly with her to take my end of the litter Major Brand was on and grabbed my hand, pulling me along. I think I was almost in shock. Then she yelled, 'Mary, Mary, he's here! John's here!'

"Mary glanced up, though I'm sure she couldn't really hear Theresa with the noise of the engines. And then she noticed me. Her hand went to her mouth, and tears started rolling down her cheeks. I don't think you could even move for a few seconds, could you?" John asked, looking at his sister who nodded. Her eyes, like those of the other two nurses at the table, were welled with tears. Some streamed down their cheeks as the memory of the reunion roused deep emotion.

John continued. "A couple of the orderlies helped Mary down from the plane, and she ran toward me. We just looked at each other like we were seeing ghosts. Then we hugged and could hardly stop. I think we were both thanking God for a miracle. I know Mary has said that she was worried about me, but like I said, I was always concerned about her. When I let go of Mary, I took hold of my Miraculous Medal, and thanked Jesus and His Blessed Mother for their protection. After that, I became aware of all the noise around us. Before Mary and I could even talk, everyone was yelling and clapping and whistling. Theresa had wasted no time telling the crew who she had found. Oh, I almost forgot, Ben and Frank, who you just met, were the pilots. That's how they knew me."

"What a story!" Rosie said as she dabbed her eyes. "No wonder Frank called you Lieutenant Miracle."

"And, no wonder those Miraculous Medals on your bags are so special to you," Aggie observed. She was filled with unanswered questions about how John survived, but realized Mary was already pretty emotionally drained from the recollections.

CHAPTER 32

"YOUR STORY makes me feel that we lived a life of leisure and had a vacation in a tropical paradise," Aggie said.

"Well I know that's far from the truth," Mary said. "Too many of my friends served in the Pacific. But, tell us about bout the palm trees and the flowers. Were the Hawaiian Islands the tropical paradise we've heard?"

"Oh, they're ok, I guess," Aggie nonchalantly answered. "You know, ya see one palm tree, you've seen 'em all."

"What! Aggie, you know that's not true," Rosie exclaimed. "They are all so different, and swaying in a breeze at sunrise or sunset, they do look so romantic, just like picture postcards. I can almost hear the ocean against the sand just thinking about it. Aggie, I can't believe you didn't think.." she began. But a quick glance at her friend revealed that Aggie was joking. They all burst into laughter.

Then Aggie said, "Rosie's right. The tropical islands are unbelievably beautiful, even with all the destruction from the war. Everything is so lush and green, and the colors of the flowers and their fragrances are enchanting—almost feels like a fairy land. Sometimes after a rain, the flowers seem to pop up right in front of your eyes; there are so many different kinds everywhere, and they're huge. Some of them are rather strange looking and unusual compared to the flowers we're used to seeing."

"Like sunflowers," Rosie said dully.

"Being from Kansas, I happen to love sunflowers," Aggie laughed. "At least they're tough and can survive the prairie summer."

"Tough like all of us." John smiled. Nodding to the crowd at the door, he added, "But if we're finished, we better hear about paradise somewhere else and let others have the table."

John reached for the bill the waiter had left earlier, but Aggie and Rosie snatched it from him. "We're not going to let you be a gentleman this time, John. We are paying for our own dinners," Rosie said as Aggie nodded in agreement and they moved to the cash register.

Night had completely fallen, but bright lights led the way to evening action of the city. As they walked, the four soldiers laughed and enjoyed themselves, pointing out different highlights. The bond of shared wartime experiences created a special camaraderie and familiarity.

When they made their way to the USO, Ben and Frank were already there enjoying a first drink. "Hey, now the party can begin," Frank declared. "The most beautiful ladies in the military have arrived." The pilots rose and saluted in unison, as though a general had appeared.

"Can it, fellas," Mary ordered as they made room around the table for the newcomers. "We're all here to have fun and forget the military stuff." She noticed some women attired in stylish clothes. "I just wish we had some stylish dancing duds."

As she sat in the chair Ben held out for her, Aggie added, "You know, I'm real proud of serving in the military, but it'll be nice to wear pretty clothes and feel like a real lady again."

"You all are so gorgeous, you don't need fancy clothes," Frank said as the former flight nurses made comments about his line of malarkey. A waitress was walking by, and he grabbed her hand, "Hey, honey, not so fast. Our friends have arrived and need some drinks."

"Well, Major, I'm gett'n drinks for the officers over there, and then I'll be back. And the name's Violet, not Honey," she said and hurried off.

John said, "If we have to wait to drink, let's dance. This band's pretty good." He looked at Rosie, stood, helped her push her chair back, and said, "Let's cut a rug, *Honey.*" All the officers laughed.

"I'm ready to dance too, Mary. How about it?" Frank offered his hand.

As she rose, Mary looked at Ben and Agnes. "You two coming? Great music!"

"In a minute," Aggie answered. "We want to talk awhile." She gave a little wave as Frank and Mary moved toward the floor, already in rhythm of "Don't Sit Under the Apple Tree."

"So, I guess you're heading up to Sheridan for discharge tomorrow too and then home to Margie?" Aggie said looking at Ben.

"Actually, I was just home for a month. I left at 4:00 this morning, and I'm heading to report to Wright Patterson in Ohio."

"Really?"

"While I was home Marge and I spent a lot of time with Johnny and your friend Pauline. It sure took Johnny long enough to find a bride. We thought he'd never get married, but Pauline's a keeper. Such a feisty, lively, little thing; she'll be able to keep my brother in line, and she isn't hard to look at either."

"Polly is definitely spunky! You never have to wonder what she thinks about you." Aggie laughed then asked Ben, "So if you aren't being discharged, what are you doing in Chicago?"

"It's a good place for Frank and me to meet. He has a car, so we're driving up to Wright."

"You must love the Air Corps if you're stayin' in. What does Marge think of this? When will she get to join you?"

"Oh, I didn't re-up. As a trained pilot, I have to give Uncle Sam another year. Marge will be staying in Kansas, living with my folks. Duties at Wright will mean twelve or more hours six days a week, so we wouldn't get to see much of each other anyway."

"I just presumed when everyone who served overseas returned stateside, they would be discharged," Aggie said. "But, that was dumb! Someone's gotta keep protecting the country. Do you have any idea what your duties will be?"

"I'll be an instructor for some of the new pilots with focus on best ways to handle the B-17s. It would be nice to think we're really at peace, but the talk is that we'll be fighting the Russians if we don't keep up our defenses so they know they can't get by with anything."

"Some of the guys I served with had nothing good to say about the Russians," Aggie said. "In fact, some thought we made a mistake signing the peace treaty in Europe."

"Funny you should say that. We may have saved Europe from the Nazis, but the Commies are ready to come in the back door and spread their nasty ideas," Ben explained. "In fact, his cousin, who just returned from duty in the Pacific, also mentioned peace shouldn't have been signed in Europe the way it was. The US should have demanded that the Russians drop the communist shit, or we'd fight them til they were destroyed. Guess that caused a huge blowup. My dad pretty much threw my cousin out of the house."

"Really?"

"Ya, Dad and I had some pretty heated discussions too while I was home. It would have been risky to turn on the Russians since they helped us defeat Hitler, but they're weak now and their military is in bad shape. But, they sure as hell can't be trusted. Believe me, I'm sick and tired of war too, but the Russian leaders are vicious."

The others were returning. Before Frank sat down, he motioned to the waitress to bring refills for everyone then joined the conversation. "You two are way too serious! This is a celebration isn't it even if Ben and I have to stay in the military a little while longer keeping you all safe. You'd think Uncle Sam would make an exception with heroes like Ben since he flew 34 dangerous missions. I say give this man his discharge and let him be with his sweet wife, wouldn't you?"

"Oh hell, Frank, don't start that crap again." Ben sounded annoyed.

Aggie looked from one to the other puzzled. "Must be a heroic story there somewhere. Wanna share Ben?"

"Not really," he answered. "Frank's got a big imagination."

"Oh hell, don't be so modest, Ben. Obviously, I'm going to have to tell these ladies about your heroics if you won't." Ben took a sip of beer and looked at his friend.

"Ben would tell you that it was just a bombing run, like we always did. He was assigned as lead pilot. The Krauts had been tearing us to bits on recent runs, and we were losing so many planes and guys that we all figured every run we came back from was pure luck. Do you agree Ben?"

"I did have kind of a fatalistic attitude that day. Then I looked at Marge's picture abovemy windshield, and I thought about the last thing she said before I flew out of Lincoln: 'I know you'll come back to me, so we can have lots of little Wettas.' That day, I tried more than usual to say a few prayers as we flew toward Vienna area. I remember telling God He'd better take care of business for me if He wanted me to keep Marge happy." Aggie patted his hand before Ben related the event that had almost cost him his hearing. After the squadron he was leading was "blown off course" he got the worst ass chewing of his life from his CO. He described the event he had written about to Johnny almost a year earlier.

"And every plane returned home that day, and we bombed the hell out of Gerry," Frank said.

"You must have fantastic eyesight." Aggie smiled.

"Well, I did what needed to be done — no more heroic than what everyone else was doing."

"Sounds pretty great to me," Aggie commented.

Rosie said, "You people are way too humble. Aggie would never tell you that one of her evac flights went down at night in the Pacific, and she kept all her patients safe until they could be rescued. Even saved the co-pilot who was in bad shape from the crash landing."

"Really!And you think I did something special," Ben said. "This sounds much more heroic. Come on, Aggie. What's the story?"

With prodding she related the events of the harrowing night and the crash landing, downplaying her valiant actions.

Afterwards, John said, "Some people would say we are all lucky, but I think we are very blessed to have survived the war and even more blessed to be together this evening."

"I'll drink to that!" As usual, Frank lightened the atmosphere.

"Wonder what God has in mind for all of us in the future?" Mary commented as she raised her glass.

Then, trying to stifle a yawn, Ben added, "I don't know about the future, but this guy needs to get some sleep. It's been a really long day, so I'm going to head back to the hotel."

The group groaned with protests, but he waved off their comments.

"However, before I leave I do want to have one dance with the prettiest girl from Kansas in the Air Corps." He looked at Aggie and put his hand over hers. She laughed, and they headed to the dance floor as the notes of "Comin' in on a Wing and a Prayer," floated through the air.

"I hate to say it, but Ben does have a good idea," Mary said. "I'm exhausted too."

"One last dance?" Frank offered as he stood. She rose and put her hand into his.

John also stood and looked at Rosie. "We can't let this music go to waste. Let's join the others."

After the song ended, they exited into an atmosphere that was just as jovial and even livelier than inside the club. The evening had enough chill to help them feel the approaching holiday season. Streets teemed with celebrating GIs and lots of pretty girls enjoying the company of healthy young men again. "Do you suppose Chicago ever stops partying?" John asked no one in particular.

Frank answered, "Coming from Union Station, the cabbie told me this town has been one big party since VE day and only got bigger after VJ. With Sheridan being such a big discharge center, there's no end to the partying."Uniformed young men stood in groups, laughing and celebrating, many with their arms around the waists of young ladies. Some groups were singing, but all were obviously enjoying the evening and the reprieve from the anxiety of war. A few casually saluted or hollered respectful greetings to the officers as they strolled along. The aroma of hot dogs, pretzels, and popcorn wafted through the brisk air as vendors turned a profit while providing inexpensive food for the GIs.

"You know, this is kind of a safe zone isn't it?" Aggie observed. A couple of the friends looked at her puzzled, so she explained. "Don't get me wrong, I'm excited to go home, and I can't wait to see my folks, and Cy, and everyone else, but it's gonna be hard for a while adjusting to normal life, not feeling like you have to always be on alert and ready to react or someone might lose his life."

"She sure is right," Frank interjected.

"We've shared just a few events this evening, but everyone here has probably seen horrible things no one should ever have to see. Most all of us have had to make split second decisions that made the difference in life or death for not only us but lots of people." She looked at Ben. "Those things will be with us forever, and no one will really understand except this big, safe family

If I need to be by myself or I just don't feel happy sometimes, even though I'm safe at home, all of you and these people would understand."

"Aggie that is just what I've been feeling but didn't understand why I'm also feeling a little deflated to be going home," John said, putting an arm around her. "I'll be leaving behind a huge part of me. You know, you're a really brilliant lady," he added and hugged her. "And I'm luckier than most; I have Mary who understands," he finished and glanced at his sister.

Ben added, "While home, I would feel really out of sorts and grumpy at times, and it made me mad at myself. I couldn't understand why I wasn't more excited and happy. I know it bothered Marge and my mom especially. I wish I was as smart as you, Aggie. It would have been easier if I could have told Marge what was bothering me, but I really didn't know what it was."

Nearby, a young sailor with a voice to rival Bing Crosby's was crooning "The White Cliffs of Dover" to a group gathered round. As he softly sang, the final words, appreciative, respectful applause sounded. John said, "Let's pray it is peace ever after."

"Amen," Ben stated emphatically. "Now I gotta get a letter off to Marge and then get some shut-eye. Down there's our hotel, Frank. It's been great meeting you all and enjoying a night in the big city." He and Frank shook hands with John and gave friendly hugs and salutes to the ladies. "Aggie, we'll have to get together when I finish up in a few months. I'm sure I've met Cy." They exchanged their final goodbyes and went their separate ways.

Back at the Drake, the ladies let John use the bathroom first since he was going to sleep on the floor. Besides, they were making plans for the next day of shopping after their trip to Sheridan. "You know, this seems almost like a teen slumber party," Rosie laughed. Can you believe less than a week ago we were clear across the oceans! Life just is moving so fast!"

"Oh, I have a feeling it will seem to be moving rather slow when we get back to Oklahoma, Rosie. I can't imagine anything moving very fast in Shawnee," Mary laughed.

"I betchay'all are right!" Rosie said. "But we love it, don't we!" Then seeing the bathroom door begin to open, she jumped up and grabbed her toiletries. "My turn." She almost knocked John over as he exited. "I never shared quarters with a gentleman soldier before." Then she noisily locked the door while the others shook their heads at her antics.

"Even if she didn't know a thing about being a nurse, Rosie would have been great medicine for the soldiers," Mary observed pleasantly.

"Well, believe it or not, she is also a great nurse," Aggie said. "In fact, she was a terrific morale boost for me at times. From the first time we met en route to Hawaii, Rosie reminded me of a combination of a couple of good friends I had during nurses' training."

"And you all graduated?" John commented. "So, I take it Rosie's type does know when to be serious."

"All business and efficiency when called for," Aggie complimented her friend.

Clifford had brought extra pillows and blankets while they had been out, so John made up a comfortable pallet between the wall and Mary's bed while she and Aggie continued to chat. He lay down then said, "When our cab stopped at a light nearby, I saw a Catholic church. According to a sign, there's a 7:00 Mass every morning; anyone want to join me in thanking God that we're back safe and sound?"

"Sure," Aggie answered. "I would love to."

Mary grumbled, "Oh, I might as well! You are so noisy, John, you will have me wide awake!" Then she laughed. "Of course, I want to go and thank God, especially that we're going home together."

"You guys have an amazing story; it's almost like a miracle," Aggie said. "I know we're all exhausted tonight, but tomorrow I'd sure like to hear more about what the prison camp was like. That's if you don't mind talking about it, John."

"We can share more at breakfast and on the bus out to Sheridan," John answered. "And thanks, Aggie, for your thoughts tonight about going home being kinda hard. That really hit me. You're one special lady. We've got to stay in touch; that is if Cy won't mind."

"Cy would love to meet my new friends," she answered. "Thanks for the compliment. That's me, always sensitive and gentle." With a sly wink, she walked to the bathroom door. Pounding loudly, she yelled, "Hey, soldier, you've had more than your five! Who do you think you are, Mrs. Astor?" 1

The door yanked open, and Rosie tossed half a glass of water into Aggie's face. She squealed in shock as water dripped from her blonde hair. Rosie sashayed past and said, "Oh, excuse me, Lieutenant, I tripped."

John put a pillow over his head, thanking God for the softness and the happy laughter.

CHAPTER 33

THE NEXT MORNING, as John, Mary, and Aggie tried to quietly dress for Mass, Rosiegrumbled, "I guess attending a Catholic Mass won't kill me." All four soldiers left the hotel early. After the services, they stopped at a small mom and pop diner. The clanking of the tin bell above the door greeted them, as did a wiry-haired waitress. "Good morning, officers. You're out bright and early. I bet you're headed to Sheridan for discharge." Her crisp, light-blue uniform belied the shabby exterior of the small diner.

"You get lots of soldiers in here before going up to the Fort?" Mary asked.

"Only those who find the café when they go to Mass first." She brought mugs to the tables and poured hot, aromatic joe into their cups as they nodded their heads while she chatted. "Getting mighty frosty out there today, isn't it! I think you may be some of the last discharges to make it through our fair city before winter hits. We've been lucky this year with the warm weather. Now what'll it be? We have a special for soldiers we call the All-American Breakfast."

Smiling with the respite and to avoid another spiel from the chattering voice, they each ordered the special without questioning what was on it. "Stan'll get those going fast for ya," the waitress assured them, and she pushed through the metal swinging door.

While awaiting their food, John said, "It was nice to go to Mass and have the gospel read in English again; it's amazing how the words were so fitting for all of us after being brought through the war."

"Well, it was nice to understand the gospel and at least a few prayers. How do you guys understand anything praying in Latin?" Rosie commented.

Mary answered, "I'm sorry; I should have given you my prayer book. It has Latin on one side and English on the other."

"I could have shared with you too," Aggie added. "Being brought up in the Church, it is easy to forget how confusing Mass in Latin must be if you aren't Catholic. Next time, I'll help you more."

"What makes you think there'll be a next time?!" Rosie questioned rather icily. Then she laughed. "Just kidding. It was actually interesting, and the church sure smelled holy."

John explained, "That's remnants of incense from special celebrations. I really love when priests use it—makes me appreciate so much more how close God is and His power and love."

In short time, the waitress set four white plates in front of the soldiers, who looked from one another puzzled that the plates were empty. Before they could ask Belle, the waitress, she came back with platters of pancakes, eggs, ham and biscuits. "Hope this ok; I realized I forgot to tell you we serve groups family-style. Does it look any better than Army chow?" she asked as she refilled their coffee cups and picked up the creamer to refill.

"Oh my, it looks fantastic and like enough to feed the Army," Mary answered.

"Well, holler if you need anything," Belle told them and moved to wait on other customers who had come in.

When she left, the friends asked God's blessing on the food. John added salt and pepper to his eggs and took a big bite, followed by a generous slice of ham he cut off. "Hungry, John?" Mary said.

"As a matter of fact, yes I am," he answered. Then he washed the food down with a big gulp. They ate breakfast quickly with little chit-chat other than sharing a few silly ideas of what they were going to do when they got rich with their discharge pay.

John finally said, "Another cup of this real coffee would be nice before we head out," They talked about their anticipated discharges, wondering if the lines would be long and if it would entail more than just signing a paper and yelling, "Halleluiah!"

Glancing at her watch, Mary suggested, "We probably ought'a get a move on it if we want to make the early bus up to Sheridan."

"Well, good luck out at the fort. Hope your discharges go without a hitch," Belle said as they paid at the cash register near the door. They thanked her, and as they headed out, she called, "Thanks again for helping save the world for us."

Light sleet greeted them as they stepped out of the diner. "Oh! That waitress was right. Winter's arriving in Chicago, and this light-weight coat is not nearly warm enough," Aggie said. "Let's hurry."

Even, with the windy cold, the ladies couldn't help noticing window displays of new styles and fabrics along the way. "I sure hope this weather doesn't get worse before this afternoon and ruin our shopping," Rosie called as they hurried along. "I can't wait to shimmy into something exciting and colorful instead of drab Army-Air Corps uniforms." By the time they reached the hotel, only a few seats were left on the big Army bus.

When the female officers climbed on board, loud whistles interrupted noisy conversation. Soldiers were quick to offer a seat, and some even pushed buddies into the aisle. Someone called, "This day just keeps getting better by the minute!" John waved to the ladies as they were swept away in the jubilant atmosphere. He found a seat with a bunch of GIs who wanted introductions to his harem and wondered how one man could be so lucky.

The driver, a burly sergeant, bellowed, "Ok, all you ladies, find a seat, now!" Knowing better than to challenge that voice, several young enlisted men scrambled for a place. Some ended up piled together like a bunch of puppies. "I know a lot of you out rank me," he thundered and casually saluted toward some of the officers. "But, this is my bus and the Army has regulations for this free ride you're gettn'. Listen up or get off." He barked out a few orders and stressed that riders were not allowed to have food or move about while the bus was moving. The sergeant finished his tirade with, "Of course, if you are gett'n out in an hour, what's Uncle Sam gonna do if you disobey these orders?"

Everyone burst into raucous laughter, and the party atmosphere resumed as the driver threw the bus into gear. The trip to Sheridan went quickly as the soldiers shared war stories. Most of them were so farfetched that listeners booed the comedians who created tall tales to replace the awful truths. When the base came into view, the conversation surprisingly stopped as the soldiers realized they were about to conclude an unimaginable experience that had changed them and the world forever. The sergeant gave directions for where each branch should go as the bus joined others, forming a line in front of the large administration building. He also gave information about the return trip into the city, but few seemed to be listening. The air of the bus was electrified with the excitement, as so many had anticipated and prayed for this day almost constantly. The sergeant stepped down from the bus and saluted each passenger as he or she came down the stairs.

"Well, this is it," John said as he and the ladies headed toward the Army-Air Corps building.

"Hope it doesn't take too long," Rosie said. "I'm ready to go shopping." The discharge process was more tedious than long. There was a multitude of papers to sign, but they hoped the hassle would be worth the eligibility for benefits later. Aggie, Rosie, and Mary discussed the advisability of the soldiers signing the form declaring the government not be liable for any problems or illness that occurred later. "Who knows what might happen to them in a few years with some of the stuff they were exposed to!" Mary observed.

When John was given the paperwork for his earned promotion to captain, he declined it. "I just want out; don't need a higher rank." When asked if he wanted to sign up for the reserves, he adamantly answered, "No way!"

They were each given free-to-ride railroad passes and a prepared check. Each was saluted by a major who shook their hands and said, "Your government thanks you for your sacrifice and your service." Walking out into the cool brisk November day, John picked up Mary and swung her around in a circle, laughing. Then he threw his flight cap high into the air, put his head back, and yelled, "Thank you, Lord." They all ran, whooping and laughing like school children on the final day of the school year toward the ugly green buses waiting across the compound. The ride back to the hotel was, if possible, even more celebratory than the coming out to the base..

John left the ladies when they reached the hotel so he could meet friends. "So sorry I can't accompany you girls shopping this afternoon, but I will offer the sacrifice as penance for all my sins!"

Mary swung her purse and laughed. "Good riddance." After a lunch of hearty soup and fresh bread to warm up from the cold, the girls were ready to reward themselves with a lavish shopping trip unlike any of these young ladies from the prairie states had ever enjoyed. They all had unexpected extra pay for hazard duty and were ready to celebrate.

Chapter 34

Aggie held the door as the former soldiers entered the ritzy shops, where sparkling chandeliers, colorful fabrics, and aromatic perfumes overwhelmed their war-werie senses. The friendly clerks saw dollar signs and were delighted to help Army nurses still in uniform. The friends laughed, teased, encouraged and were brutally honest in criticism if an outfit didn't do justice for whoever was trying it on. When Aggie spied her comrade in a dull brown dress that was also too long, she commented, "You might as well keep wearing your uniform, Rosie, if you buy that dowdy thing!"

Sometimes, while no clerks were in the dressing rooms, they imitated them. "Oh, Lieutenant Mary, that outfit is just divine on you. It brings out the blue in your eyes and makes your dark hair radiant!" This would be followed by stifled laughter. They spied selections a friend might not have seen and encouraged one another to consider new styles. "Oh, Aggie, you have to try this on; it will be perfect with your blond hair."

They each purchased a nice dress suit to wear to professional interviews and a casual outfit, but they had the most fun searching for big-city dresses for doing the town. Though they were purchasing many outfits, their down-home values and stylish but sensible selections frustrated more than one clerk. They felt compelled to entice the ladies to purchase more couture styles which they often thrust at them. It was obvious that these stores had been frequented by many newly discharged ladies when the clerks made arrangements for the items to be delivered to their hotel.

Relaxing over a cup of coffee after their shopping spree, Aggie shocked her friends when she announced, "There's one other thing I really want to buy, even though it may be totally ridiculous and an obscene extravagance." Mary and Rosie both looked at her, wondering what obscene item Aggie was intent on. "I want a fur coat."

"Oh, Aggie, that would be so elegant!" Rosie sighed. "We deserve it, and we'll probably never be able to afford one again."

"What do you mean?" Mary asked with a pretentious wave of her hand. "I plan for my husband to buy me jewels and furs all the time." Then laughing, she said, "I hear real fur never wears out; it can be re-styled as fashions change."

Aggie was surprised. "You don't think I'm crazy? You both want to shop for furs?"

"I don't expect to find a big selection in Kansas and Oklahoma," Mary said.

Rosie chimed in. "We'll be having officer reunions with balls and fancy dinners. And the way you describe Cy's initiative, Aggie, he'll probably be a state officer in some ag organization soon. You'll be going to all kinds of conventions and stuff."

"I think we should go look at furs," Mary said decidedly.

"Actually, I've been kinda looking at them all afternoon as I checked out coats," Aggie confessed. "Hamptons had the best prices and nicest styles on the mannequins. And, the clerks weren't so pretentious there."

"Well, let's get back to Hamptons before they close," Rosie said, draining her coffee cup.

Grabbing the small packages they carried, Mary giggled. "Oh this is so exciting! I always thought the ladies wearing furs in the movies were terribly elegant! Thank you for suggesting it, Aggie."

The wind off Lake Michigan once again carried sharp ice crystals that whipped against them. "Oh yes, a sign from God, we definitely need fur!" Aggie laughed as they scurried down the sidewalk toward the most extravagant purchases they had ever made.

Later, as they almost skipped back to the hotel, they felt luxurious wrapped in the warmth of muskrat, chinchilla, and fox. Many heads turned, and plenty of whistles followed the young women who beamed with happiness as they began their new lives wrapped in promise.

While they were trying on their furs, Aggie told the others that she would like to stay at the hotel that evening to try to call Cy again. She had spoken briefly to her mother when she reached San Francisco and told her that she had to go to Chicago for discharge. At that time, she had no idea how long travel nor getting through military red tape would take. Mary and Rosie said that they were exhausted, so perhaps they should pick up something to take back to the room to eat.

The icy wind confirmed their decision to stay in. So, they stopped in a small deli on the way back to the hotel to purchase food for a picnic in their room. The rotund proprietor's eyes almost popped wide open when the three beauties bounded through his door in beautiful fur coats. His Italian accent prompted lively conversation as Mary mentioned different places she had been in his home country. While he sliced bread, cheese, and pastrami, Mary practiced the little Italian she had picked up, and Aggie and Rosie selected a couple of bottles of wine. The deli owner, so delighted to visit in his native language with a lovely ex-soldier, said, "No charge, no charge. You saved my home from the terrible fascist and Nazis! I owe you! Ciao, ciao!" He wrapped Mary in a hug and kissed her on both cheeks with typical Italian enthusiasm. Amid the enjoyable exchange, the former lieutenants slipped cash beside the register before waving cheerfully and stepping back into the frigid evening.

"That was fun!" Mary commented as they walked toward the hotel.

"Yea, I think you made his day, Mary," Rosie agreed.

Chapter 35

CLIFFORD DIDN'T ATTEMPT TO disguise his approval when he pulled back the rattling grate of the elevator. "Hmm, hmm! Yes, siree, it's truly a joy to see you young officers return from a shopping trip. A real treat for these old eyes! And, I been traipsin' fancy boxes into your room for hours on end."

"Thanks, Clifford. Had to get something to fight off this Chicago cold!"

He told them that Lieutenant McHugh had returned less than an hour earlier. They exited the elevator with a friendly wave. Mary tapped lightly on the door, and then used her key, calling, "Are you decent, John?"

"Yeah, I'm decent, but almost asleep," he said groggily from behind the bed. His head slowly appeared, and then a wolfish whistle filled the room. "Holy Toledo, ladies! Was the Queen of Sheba standing on a corner giving away money? Those are some fancy coats!"

The ladies sashayed around the room, modeling their furs, which was difficult amid the packages and luggage. They affected aristocratic mannerisms, and their upturned noses and extended hands were comical as they avoided tripping over the stacks of boxes.

"When you got it, you have to flaunt it!" Aggie pronounced, and they all broke into laughter.

"Well, you look like movie stars! You weren't kidding about shopping. I could hardly make my way to the shower with all these packages, but those coats top everything! Woohee! And two bottles of wine! You all must be ready to party!"

"No, we're just too tired to go back out to eat," Mary explained and set down the paper bag that was emanating wonderful aromas in the heat of the room.

"Besides, it's too cold and windy, even with these luscious furs," Rosie added, setting the wine beside the food.

Aggie chimed in, "Besides, some of us have phone calls to try to make." She added her bottle of wine to the quickly assembled buffet.

"Don't I just look ravishing, darling?" Rosie sighed, turning in another circle with the coat open to let the light shimmer off the opulence.

Mary said, "I'll tell you one thing; this gets hot fast inside!" She took off the coat, carefully hung it in the closet and reached for Aggie's and Rosie's to hang them up. Then the friends set out the improvised picnic and shared stories of their afternoon. John admitted to doing a little shopping of his own, and, after much prodding, he showed the ladies the shirts and slacks he had purchased.

"I hope you don't mind us not going out for dinner," Rosie said as she removed the deli wrappings and revealed scrumptious-smelling cheeses, pastrami, ham, and mouthwatering bread, still slightly warm.

John was pouring wine for everyone into glasses from the bathroom. "Are you kidding? This is much better! I would have given my left leg at times in the past year to have had just a little of this food, and I was one of the lucky guys."

"That's right, we haven't heard how you survived after being captured," Aggie recalled enthusiastically. So, over dinner they heard about the seven weeks spent near the Baltic Sea as the world was falling apart for the Germans.

"You know, I couldn't help but feel sorry for those guys. They were either haggard men, too old to be soldiers or skinny homesicks." John stated. "Most of them didn't want to serve Hitler. They were like us in a do or die situation, but they had a mad man in charge of their country."

"That's an awfully generous way to feel about your captors," Rosie observed.

"Those guys didn't have much to eat as we did when guys got care packages they always shared. At the end, when the Red Cross entered the camp before all the Krauts were marched out, I think everyone was sharing candy or cigarettes from our boxes with them. It was pretty sad when you think of it. No one really wins a war," he finished philosophically.

"And you know what?" Mary said as she tossed wrappings into the trash. "We forgot to bless this food before we ate."

"Well, we can thank Him now," Aggie said. "We give Thee thanks, Almighty God, for all the gifts we have received…" The friends mentioned food, warmth, being almost home, peace, and no more wars. Aggie finished the prayer, "Through Our Lord Jesus Christ."

"Amen," they all said emphatically.

Then Aggie said, "Now, if you'll excuse me, I have a phone call to try to make." She looked at her clothes and wondered, "Gee, guess I should change before going down to the lobby. I'm really not in the military anymore."

"Oh, you can wear that for a while," Mary reminded her. "Remember we have to wear our uniforms traveling home if we want Uncle Sam to pay. Oh, speaking of, see if you can steal a train schedule from the concierge, please."

"Will do. Say a prayer the lines for the phones aren't too long."

Aggie exchanged small talk with the evening elevator operator and missed Clifford already. Listening to the creaking sounds of the contraption and the rattling of the gates as they opened and closed at various floors, Aggie thought how in just a day, these were all a part of her. She thought, I sure hope Clifford works tomorrow so we can tell him goodbye. He almost seemed like their designated welcome home ambassador. Amazing how important some, seemingly insignificant, jobs are. It all depends on the pride the person takes in their work. The lavish chandeliers and sumptuous statuary stirred Aggie from her reverie, and she headed to the phone booths.

She stepped into the dark area and pulled the small bi-fold door shut behind her. Aggie was startled when an automatic light illuminated the area. Dropping her nickel into the slot, she thought, What will they think of next?

"Operator."

"I need to make a call to Pretty Prairie, Kansas, to the home of Ralph Pauley," she said, surprised that her hands were shaking.

"One moment please while I try to connect you." The operator's voice was nasally robotic. After setting the process in motion, the robot became human. "Pretty Prairie, that's sure a nice sounding place. Is that your home?"

"Yes, it is," Aggie answered, and a lump formed in her throat. Hearing the word "home" sent an unexpected wave of homesickness over her. It's amazing how a person can lock away all her special feelings and memories so she can do her duty when needed.

"Are you returning from the war?" the operator asked.

Must be a slow night, Aggie thought. I've never heard such a cheerful, talkative operator in the big cities before. "Yes, I am. I served in the Pacific," she answered, happy for something to break the lump before being connected.

"Well, welcome home, and thank you so much for your service." Then the robot returned. "That number is ringing." When a man's

281

voice answered, she stated, "That will be fifty cents for the first three minutes." Aggie dropped the quarters into the silver slot and heard the rattle and short ding as the phone tallied each. "You are connected."

"Hello."

"Hello, Cy, it's Aggie," she announced as hot tears trickled down her face.

"Oh, Aggie, it's so good to hear you. Your mom told me you called over a week ago. Where are you? When will you be home? Are you in Wichita already!"

She was happy for his stream of words, so she could get her emotions under control. Aggie finally laughed. "No, I'm in Chicago, Cy, but I will be leaving here tomorrow morning if there's room on the train. There seems to be all kinds of military people wanting to travel for some reason. Wonder what's going on?" She laughed and her natural teasing assured Cy that, though she had traveled the world and witnessed awful things, the person on the phone was still his sweet Aggie.

"Tomorrow! Wow! So, will you get to Wichita Friday morning?"

"I wish that were true, but I need to stop in Kansas City to see Aunt Margaret. She wrote me every week and sent so many packages of special goodies; I really owe it to her. I'll spend a day with her, and then I'm coming home." This time, "home" closed that silly lump in her throat.

"Oh Aggie, I can't wait to see you. I've missed you more than I ever thought possible," Cy answered.

"I missed you too, Cy, and I wish I could just come straight home, but—"

"15 Seconds," the nasally voice interrupted.

"No, you're right. You need to see Aunt Margaret. She's a special lady."

"If all goes as planned, I'll arrive in Wichita on the 3:00 train on Saturday. Cy, please tell my folks," Aggie added quickly.

"Time is up," the operator interrupted.

"I can't wait to see you!" Cy said quickly. "I love you, Aggie." Then the operator cut them off.

A huge grin spread across Aggie's face as tears streaked her makeup. She rummaged in her purse for a handkerchief and dried her tears before blowing her nose. Aggie stood in the phone booth to collect her emotions. She seemed to have lost control of her face and couldn't stop smiling—like the Cheshire cat, she thought. But Cy's words filled her mind. I love you, Aggie!

She blew her nose again, opened the door, and walked toward the elevator. But, she remembered the train schedule and turned toward the front desk. Luckily, the concierge was not busy. Aggie asked, "Do you have a train schedule for destinations south?" He rummaged through the desk before locating the correct one then gave her a pen and paper to write down information. "Thanks so much," Aggie told him. She returned the schedule and walked across the lobby to the elevators.

When Aggie returned to their hotel room, Mary looked up from packing and said, "We certainly don't have to ask if you got in touch with Cy! Love is written all over your face, Lieutenant!"

John glanced up from a book he was reading and gave Aggie an approving wink. Rosie strolled out of the bathroom, rubbing her freshly washed hair with a towel. "I wonder if Aggie got… Yea, she got in touch with Cy," Rosie hugged her friend.

"Said he'll pick me up in Wichita on Saturday," she answered nonchalantly. "Anyway, I think he did." She suddenly looked puzzled and tried to remember. "Oh yes, he said he loves me!"

"Woo hoo! Major declaration!" Rosie squealed.

"When are you planning to leave Chicago if you aren't getting to Wichita until Saturday?" Mary asked puzzled.

Aggie explained her plans to visit with her aunt in KC. "I wrote down the train schedule for points south." She handed it to Mary, who shared the notes with John. Aggie looked at Rosie. "I thought I would like to try for the 10:00 train in the morning. It gets into KC at 8:30 tomorrow night. There's a train leaving for Tulsa and OK City at 10:00 PM. You'd be home early the next morning, Rosie. What do you think?"

"Sounds great," Rosie agreed, brushing her long, brunette hair. She obviously was pleased someone else could read schedules and make plans while she relaxed in their expertise.

"If you don't mind us continuing to tag along, we'll be taking the same train," Mary said. "I think we've seen all of this 'hog butcher' that we can handle for one trip." She smiled at John while Rosie frowned in confusion. "Besides, I miss my mama!" she half-jokingly declared, but her misty eyes confirmed the truth of her words.

Rosie said, "I'm glad we don't have to say goodbye tomorrow, and I'll have company all the way to OK City. But what in the world do you mean 'hog butcher'? We haven't even seen the stockyards. Thank God!"

Mary and John laughed as Aggie smiled, recognizing their reference. John explained the Carl Sandburg poem. "I don't think a student ever graduated from Shawnee High School who couldn't recite that poem and several others. Mrs. Sharpsteen was a stickler on memorization and recitation. Wasn't she Mary?"

Mary nodded then rolled her eyes "I hated reciting poetry in front of everyone! But, you know, I think that poetry helped keep me sane sometimes during the past few years. Reciting those old poems in my head was a diversion on those long flights. Also these little books were a life saver." She held up a pocket size copy of A Tree Grows in Brooklyn. One of the guys left this on my final flight to the US."

"Oh, that's too bad," Aggie said. "Not for you," she clarified. "But the guy who lost it. Those books were like pieces of gold that the men hated to have to give up. And A Tree Grows in Brooklyn was almost as popular as the Westerns and sports books. I read parts of that book so often to comfort guys, I can recite them like your poetry."

"We'll have to find out who to thank for these little life savers," John added holding up his treasured copy of Lou Gehring. Somehow the Krauts missed a couple of them when they captured some guys. Besides the Mass our chaplain said when he could, I think those books saved our sanity. The Education of H*Y*M*A*N K*A*P*L*A*N made us all laugh our fool heads off and hope for good times again."

Then rising from the chair, he added "I have all my stuff ready; I'll go down to the concierge and arrange for a cab in the morning." Glancing around the room, John repaired the statement. "I think we'll need two with the extra boxes you ladies accumulated."

"You suppose we ought to leave around 7:30?" Aggie asked.

"For a 10:00 train? I was thinking 9:00," Rosie said.

"Well, you would be riding on a pump car a few miles behind the train," Mary said. "Remember the traffic when we arrived a couple of days ago."

"I'll ask for cabs a little after 6:00, especially with this ice. That way we'll have a better chance of getting seats and not end up standing all day. The train from DC was packed, and I bet they'll be the same going south."

"Oh my, when will I catch up on my beauty sleep?" Rosie sighed as John closed the door.

"You can sleep all day on the train," Aggie reminded her.

As they left the hotel the next day in the pre-dawn greying darkness, a wicked wind tugged at their clothes and belongings. Through the icy, swirling snow, Captain Ben Wetta came running up the street. "Hey, Aggie! Aggie!" he called as she was getting into the cab. "Wow! That is some coat! I wouldn't have recognized you if it wasn't for your blonde curls and Air Corps cap."

"Hi Ben. It's too cold for you run up here just to tell us goodbye."

"I have a little gift for Marge. Would you mind taking it to her? I figure you'll be going to see Pauline as soon as you can, and she can give it to Marge."

"Sure, I'll be glad to." The cab driver said something about the meter running, so Aggie touched Ben's hand and said, "Take care of yourself. You and Marge look me up when you get home." She climbed in, and he closed the door and waved goodbye.

The travelers were happy they had left early as hundreds of headlights from cabs turned the sleet to falling diamonds, and the car often skidded or seemed to slide erratically. Arriving at Union Station, they were again swept up in crowds of military uniforms and wondered if they had allowed enough time. But, the professionals behind the windows dispensed tickets with the speedy efficiency of Santa's elves and even exchanged pleasantries with the soldiers.

The day passed quickly as they visited with soldiers they met on the train and played cards. Rosie fell asleep before lunch and drowsed much of the day. Aggie said she was too excited and couldn't think of sleep. However, late in the afternoon, after a couple of hours delay in St. Louis, the rhythm of the train and the steady clacking of the wheels lulled most everyone into a deserved beauty sleep.

When porters came through with sandwiches at 6:00, the friends were amazed at the hour. They decided to splurge one last time to-gether and have a nice meal in the dining car. While they were eating, several people stopped by their table to thank them for their service. When they asked the porter for their bills, he informed the friends that it had been taken care of. Aggie remarked, "Gee, I think I'm going to miss all this nice attention," and the others smiled.

John said, "You know, there are so many people who didn't serve in the military but made lots of sacrifices for us. As they say, these people 'kept the home-fires burning,' and they don't get any recognition. This kinda makes me feel a little guilty." The ladies nodded agreement.

Aggie said, "I'm going to the ladies room to try to make myself beautiful, so Aunt Margaret won't think the war stole my looks."

"Will she pick you up at the station?" Mary asked.

"Heavens no. She doesn't drive. But, I won't be able to freshen up in the cab." By the time she returned, the glittering lights flying by the windows told the passengers they were in the outskirts of the city. Soon the train was slowing, and they knew the station would bring an end to this adventure. "Oh, before we forget and it's too late, we need to exchange addresses," Aggie said as a heavy feeling filled her chest.

"You already have mine, Aggie," Rosie reminded her. Aggie rolled her eyes and smiled as Mary wrote John's and her information on a sheet of paper from her journal.

The trained rolled to a stop, but Aggie's heart picked up speed. Why am I so shaky? she questioned herself as she stood and started gathering luggage. Guess I really hate to make this break and tell mili-tary friends goodbye. I wish I could just get on home and see Cy, and, of course, Mom and Dad.

"Let me help you with that," John said as she tried to pull down her large suitcase from the overhead rack. He had already helped Mary, and a sailor was helping Rosie.

"Thanks John. It's nice to have help and not have to tackle these extra bags alone." They moved with the crowd toward the door where porters helped the ladies down the steps, and others helped with luggage and directions for transfers. Between the noise of the train and the excited crowd, the air outside the train was deafening. John motioned to the station entrance where they could tell Aggie goodbye before she collected the rest of her luggage and the others boarded their train for the last leg. Travelers were shouting and squealing in delight as they recognized loved ones who were awaiting their arrival. Amid the noise, Aggie thought she heard her name, but told herself she must be dreaming. She tried to follow John through the horde of travelers. Then she heard a familiar voice next to her.

"Hey Beautiful, that's some fancy coat." Suddenly, someone took ahold of her large duffle and put an arm around her. Aggie's mouth popped open, and releasing her grip on her suitcase, her arms flew around Cy's neck. You're here! You're really here! Aggie's heart sang as tears flowed onto his heavy tweed jacket. His strong arms and the familiar clean aroma of Old Spice and lye soap confirmed Cy was real and not a dream.

Glancing back to make sure Aggie was still with them, Mary spied her beautiful coat being hugged by a strong, young man. She smiled and tugged on John's arm to stop him and Rosie. They waited until Aggie looked up. She lifted her hand slightly from Cy's back and waved to them through tears. They all smiled and waved before proceeding to their connecting train.

EPILOGUE

(A WEEK LATER)

"GOLLY, MR WETTA, we must really be old married folks," Pauline said as she rinsed a plate and handed it to Johnny to dry. In answer to his puzzled look, she continued, "It's Saturday night and we aren't going out dancing or even playing cards. Thank Heavens!"

"You're right, we're hardly ever home on Saturday night. But I really agree with the thank heavens. I'm exhausted after a week of moving Mom and Dad to Wichita, and then moving our things in here." He finished drying the last pot and patted her protruding belly. "Can't imagine how tired you must be with the work of moving while carrying that extra bundle around."

"Well, we are lucky that we don't own much yet so packing our place was easy. And you know your mom wouldn't let me lift any of their things that weighed more than a feather," Pauline laughed as the young couple walked into the adjacent room, and she stretched out on the couch the older Wettas had left behind. She kicked off her shoes as Johnny stoked the fire in the pot-belly stove and continued. "But it was real nice that Ben was home for a few weeks before your parent's big move. He and Marge were such help packing up the house. Besides, they are a fun couple. I wish he was out of the service so we could spend lots of time together. Have you heard from him since he left for Ohio?"

Johnny lifted Pauline's feet into his lap as he sat on the couch and began massaging them. "You are kidding right. The way his work load sounds, Margie will be lucky to get a letter every week" Changing topics, he said, "It's about time for Fibber McGhee and Molly isn't it?" He switched on the big radio next to the couch, and the cells began humming to life as the contraption warmed up.

"What in the world is that?" Pauline jumped as a crashing sound on the porch interrupted the peaceful whir of the radio. This was followed by other crashes like someone beating on a bucket, and then a continuous cacophony of noise of banging of pans and lids and whistles mixed with hooting and hollering.

"What the hell!" Johnny exclaimed, then a broad grin spread across his face as the kitchen door burst open, and their home began to fill with friends laughing and singing. Pauline stood aghast until he hollered to her above the din, "It's an old-fashioned schiverie!"

"Oh my goodness!" Pauline smiled as friends carrying all types of packages paraded around them and wound back to the kitchen to deposit assorted bundles.."

"I'll put this beef out on the porch to stay frozen," one friend called.

"Pauline you are so lucky. Look at all this counter space and wonderful cabinets for storage," came from a female voice as she deposited a couple of sacks of groceries.

"Open one of those cabinets and find us some glasses for drinks," Jim Meyer called.

"We need some plates too," came from Pauline's sister Helen as she and other ladies began unpacking sandwiches, pickles, cakes and other food and spreading it on the table.

Johnny asked Jim, "Since when do you need a glass for a drink?"

"Oh he's pretending to be refined," Nonie, Pauline's sister teasingly shoved him.

"Happy Schiverie!" called Leo Wetta as he handed a bottle of whiskey to Johnny who took a big swig. Aileen Kessler, Leo's date handed Johnny a bottle of RC Cola, then gave Pauline a hug before Johnny handed his wife the bottle of whiskey.

"Here we thought we were going to have a quiet night like an old married couple," Pauline laughed after taking a gulp of RC.

The Wetta farm-house suddenly felt like home with the noisy friends filling the rooms and an endless variety of food was shared. In the kitchen the new home owners opened gifts from well-wishers; everything from bags of sugar, no longer rationed, to a vegetable peeler and nice steel mixing bowl and other metal objects that were impossible to find at the time of Pauline and Johnny's wedding.

"What I want to know is what kind of illegal connections you two have?" Leo asked. "How in the hell did you get a stove like this?" This prompted many guests with the same questions and teasing accusations.

"Did someone sell his soul to the devil to get this thing?" Jim asked.

"Oh Jim, you know better than that!" Pauline said. "But it is a big national secret that we can't divulge," brought lots of grumbling and booing as the kitchen door opened.

"Well, I know we're late, but that's an awful welcome," Cy Pauley said as he filled the kitchen doorway.

The crowd laughed and multiple voices jumbled together to explain the booing and tease him about being late. Someone finally asked, "So who's with you? You said 'We're late.'"

When Cy stepped aside and pulled Aggie in front of him, Pauline squealed like a child receiving a long-dreamed-for pony. "For goodness sake, when did you get home, Aggie?" She almost flew across the kitchen and wrapped her arms around her friend. "I don't want to hurt anyone's feelings," Pauline said, looking around. at, "I love all your gifts, but this is the best of all!" She looked at everyone and gave Aggie a big hug.

"You look absolutely darling!" Aggie gushed, patting Polly's protruding belly. "I'm glad I got home in time to see you pregnant."

Someone interrupted with a toast., "To Johnny and Pauline's home!" Pauline took a "short snort" and gave Johnny a long kiss.

Then she added, "And to Aggie's safe return!" while tears ran down both she and Aggies cheeks as they hugged again, with the little watermelon belly in the way.

The Main Characters

AGGIE (AGNES) BEAT [PAULEY]

She and Cy Pauley were married in September of 1946. They lived on a dairy farm in central Kansas. Cy did become a board member of the Kansas Dairy Association, so Aggie wore her fur to several national events. After some time, she had it made into a stole with a matching hat and two tiny matching stoles for their twin daughters. After waiting years for God to send them children, Aggie and Cy decided to adopt a baby in 1958. When the baby was born, she brought along a twin sister, so Aggie and Cy were doubly blessed. They adopted a son a few years later. Cy died of a heart attack before their 25th wedding anniversary.

After the children were raised, Aggie returned to her career as a nurse until she was over seventy years old. She has always loved to travel and enjoyed staying in touch with her nursing school friends and fellow flight nurses who's number dwindles each year. Agnes became precious part of my life when my husband and I moved to Hutchinson, and Aggie attended the same church we joined. She was one of the first people to make us feel welcome, and at the time I didn't realize how closely connected we already were.

In spring of 2018, Aggie celebrated her 97th birthday. This fun-loving, gracious lady has stayed busy playing cards, enjoying family members, eating out, and participating in many church activities, always laughing and entertaining those around her. She has moved to Arizona to spend her last years with her daughter. I miss her and our weekly card games immensely.

POLLY (PAULINE) GARRITY

After marrying Johnny Wetta, Polly adjusted to farm life and loved to drive the tractor and help in the fields while a local young woman cared for the children. However, after the first few years of married life, she seldom had time for that. She delivered a baby girl shortly after the story ended. That baby is the author of this mostly true, historical novel. When I was two and having a toddler fit, my grandfather Leo Wetta declared I was being spoiled and needed a younger sibling. So, my parents had ten more children in the next 18 years, and I was never spoiled again. (My siblings would argue about that!) Mom and Dad followed Grandpa Leo's suggestion and kept the old farm house happy. Filled with Irish pride and spirit, Mom always demanded the best of all of her kids and was determined our clothing and attitudes never reflect the economic struggles we had. She was creative in "making do" and never lost her ornery spirit that loved to party whenever she got the chance. When Mom was nine months pregnant with her twelfth child, she died large underwear bright red and went to a costume party. Whe said, "I can either sit at home feeling sorry for myself, or I can go out and "whoop it and kick it." Mom loved babies, and she and Dad were equally delighted when each of their 39 grandchildren and 16 great-grandchildren (at the time of their deaths) were born.

After we kids were older, Mom returned to her first career. However, instead of babies, she was a compassionate nurse for elderly. She and Dad celebrated 63 years together before he passed away. Mom followed a couple of years later. The sharp pang Dad felt in his heart for staying home while his brothers served in the military during WW II never went away.

BEN AND MARGIE (BECKER) WETTA

The dates of Ben's service were changed for the story. Ben returned

to normal civilian life after finishing his obligations to Uncle Sam. While he was still serving in Ohio, Aunt Margie had a baby boy, Bob, who was four months old the first time Ben saw him. Like many military brides of the time, my aunt Margie lived with Ben's parents and Joe and Spud when they were in town. The young men liked to tease Marge and make her believe that baby Bob kept them awake all night when in reality they never heard him. My aunt and uncle lived in Colwich for several years, and most of their entertainment involved activities with Johnny and Pauline's family and, eventually, with Spud's. Ben and Margie had seven children, and Spud and Aileen had ten.

In the fifties, Ben and Margie moved to Colorado, where relatives loved to visit. They finally settled in Nebraska. For much of his life, Ben was a private pilot for an agricultural company owned by his brother Joe. During their retirement years, they renewed the friendship with Aggie. They all became "snow-birds" in Arizona during the winter. Margie was killed in an auto accident shortly before their 50th wedding anniversary, and Ben succumbed to cancer several years later.

ANNIE (WETTA) AND WILLIE BERGKAMP

Willie was in the Merchant Marines and served from the US to the South Pacific, refueling armored vessels and transporting supplies while facing danger from Japanese air strikes. The months between the end of the war in Europe and Japan finally surrendering seemed an eternity to Annie. After Willie finally returned home safely, he and Anna were wed and eventually added nine more cousins to the Wetta tribe.

JOHN MCHUGH

During World War II, John increasingly felt a call to serve God in a special way. Shortly after returning to Oklahoma, he entered seminary and was ordained a Catholic priest for the Oklahoma City diocese in 1955. After several years as a parish priest, Father John helped form a missionary order, The Society of Our Lady of the Most Holy Trinity.

He served the poor in many areas, including thirty years in Belize and later in the United States. He finally retired at the age of 90 but continued to inspire younger priests with his humble spirit and entertain visitors with his jovial stories. The miraculous reunion of Lieutenant

McHugh with his flight nurse sister Mary was recorded by a military photographer. It can be seen in the first couple of minutes of this video. https://www.youtube.com/watch?v=PGFDlMhfwgs&t=75s

MARY MCHUGH

Mary was a happy young wife and mother. Unfortunately, the day after Father John's ordination to the priesthood, her husband and son were killed in an auto accident. A couple of years later she again joined her brother, serving as his housekeeper and cook while he was a parish priest.

A Letter Home from Ben

Jan 3 -45

Dear folks,

We have some weather here now that reminds me of Kansas again. It's been snowing at intervals for the first two days, but doesn't stay over 12 hrs as it thaws pretty fast. It gave me an opportunity tho, along with eight other boys, to take a drive into the nearby mountains. The chaplain had told us he would take us to visit a famous monk, the first chance we had, so this was it. Padre Pio (or Pious) is a capuchin monk that was stigmatized with the wounds of Christ about 25 years ago. They appeared one morning after mass and he has had them ever since, they bleed at periodic intervals, and he goes thru the sufferings of Christ also, accompanied by a high fever. Many doctors have tried to heal his wounds, but it only irritates them, although he never gets infection in them. Many miracles have been worked by his intercession, in fact there are two blind boys there now. I would judge him to be 55 or 60 years old, about 5'8" tall, and is rather stout.

We drove up in the evening and slept in a small hotel in the village close by the monastery. We got up early in the morning (5:30) and went to Padre Pio's mass. He left all the American boys kneel in the sanctuary on the altar steps and our chaplain served mass for him, we also all went to Communion. After mass we went to the sacristy and saw and kissed his wounds, and received a medal from him. He was very friendly about it all, didn't seem like a probable saint. We then went back to the hotel and ate breakfast, four eggs, potatoes, bread and coffee. Next we drove to a nearby town to see a grotto where the angel Michael appeared. The grotto was started sometime in the 10th century and he appeared a couple centuries later, it is now a shrine, I bought several souvenirs at the chapel for you and Margie. We went back to the hotel for dinner, it was darn good too for Italy, we had soup spaghetti, chicken, asparagus, potatoes and wine. The room and two meals cost us $7.00 a piece, which wasn't bad for over here.

Well folks I'll say good nite, hope you're all as well as we are over here.

Love to all

Ben

PS Received "Time" today.

The Flight Nurses Creed

I will summon every resource to prevent the triumph of death over life.

I will stand guard over the medicines and equipment entrusted to my care and ensure their proper use.

I will be untiring in the performances of my duties and I will remember that, upon my disposition and spirit, will in large measure depend the morale of my patients.

I will be faithful to my training and to the wisdom handed down to me by those who have gone before me.

I have taken a nurse's oath, reverent in man's mind because of the spirit and work of its creator, Florence Nightingale. She, I remember, was called the "Lady with the Lamp."

It is now my privilege to lift this lamp of hope and faith and courage in my profession to heights not known by her in her time. Together with the help of flight surgeons and surgical technicians, I can set the very skies ablaze with life and promise for the sick, injured, and wounded who are my sacred charges.

...This I will do. I will not falter in war or in peace.

The Flight Nurse's Creed first appeared in a speech given by Maj. Gen. David N. W. Hay, the Air Surgeon of the U.S. Army Air Corps, on Nov. 26, 1943, to the seventh graduating class of flight nurses of the Army Air Corps School of Air Evacuation at Bowman Field, KY.

The Nightingale's Pledge

I solemnly pledge myself before God and in the presence of this assembly:

To pass my life in purity and to practice my profession faithfully.

I will abstain from whatever is deleterious and mischievous and will not take or knowingly administer any harmful drug.

I will do all in my power to maintain and elevate the standard of my profession and will hold in confidence all personal matters committed to my keeping and all family affairs coming to my knowledge in the practice of my profession.

With loyalty will I endeavor to aid the physician in his work and devote myself to the welfare of those committed to my care.

NOTES

Throughout the book, readers will come across the term a Miraculous Medal. This is a medallion such as pictured above that many Catholics wear to remind them of the love of the Blessed Mother of Jesus for each of us, her children.

The Association of the Miraculous Medal in Perryville, Missouri, notes that there is no superstition or magic connected with the Miraculous Medal, nor is it "a good luck charm." Rather, it is "a testimony to faith and the power of trusting prayer. Its greatest miracles are those of patience, forgiveness, repentance, and faith."

More information and explanation can be found at: https://www.thedivinemercy.org/library/article.php?NID=2942

CITATIONS

Angels." USAAF Flight Nurses in WWII :. February 7, 2011. Accessed August 28, 2011. http://www.nationalmuseum.af.mil/fact-sheets/factsheet.asp?id=15457

"The Army Nurse Corps in World War II." Army Nurse Corps. October 3, 2003. Accessed August 28, 2011. https://history.army.mil/books/wwii/72-14/72-14.HTM.

Barger, Judith. Beyond The Call of Duty. Kent, Ohio: Kent State University Press, 2013.

Crain, Aileen, ed. "Lauretta M. Schmmoler." ANCOA FLASHES.

Eisenhower, Dwight D. Address before the Canadian Club 1/10/46, Ottawa, Canada, January 10, 1946. Accessed August 26, 2018, https://www.eisenhower.archives.gov/all_about_ike/quotes.html

Eisenhower, Dwight D. ""The Chance for Peace" , 4/16/53." Address, "The Chance for Peace", Washington DC, April 16, 1953. Accessed August 26, 2018. https://www.eisenhower.archives.gov/all_about_ike/quotes.html.

"Flight Nurse's Creed." National Museum of the US Air Force™. May 01, 2015. Accessed August 17, 2016

Manning, Molly Guptill. When Books Went to War: The Stories That Helped Us Win World War II.

Mullins, William S., Col., ed. Medical Training in World War II, 1974. Office of the Surgeon General/ Washington DC

"The Nightingale Pledge." Stethoscope (Wichita), May 1943, Vol. IV ed., No. 7 sec

Richmond, Luther H., Maj. Gen with Marc L. Hamel. " The Coming of the Russians." .) World War II - Prisoners of War - Stalag Luft I. Accessed August 1, 2011. http://www.merkki.com/russians.htm.

Roosevelt, Franklin D., Pre. USA. "The President's News Conference on V-E Day." American Presidency Project:. Accessed August 28, 2011. :www.presidency.ucsb.eduhttp://www.presidency.ucsb.edu/ws/index.php?pid=12248#ixzz1WjG9WUcQwww.presidency.ucsb.eduhttp://www.presidency.ucsb.edu/ws/index.php?pid=12248#ixzz-1WjEXp6vu

"Winged Angels." USAAF Flight Nurses in WWII :. February 7, 2011. Accessed August 28, 2011. http://www.nationalmuseum.af.mil/factsheets/factsheet.asp?id=15457

In Special Appreciation

To Paul, my wonderful husband, who was my dedicated writing coach, never giving up on this project.whose incessant mantra has been, "What did you write today?"

My daughter, Kristine Hilger, who spent hours editing from earliest manuscript to final line edits. Her honest critiques tempered by encouraging suggestions have helped my book become a work of pride.

The rest of my family, who celebrated each milestone, no matter how small; especially Sara Bevins, Emily Wiggins and Robin and Jeremiah Hilger who organized a "Publisher Party" when I received my first offer.

Many cousins who sent emails, pictures and invaluable information. Duane Bergkamp, Bob Wetta, Karen Wetta and Marilyn Pullen Wetta provided unknown tidbits that added enlightening details for the book or blog.

Alexa Bigwarfe, my publisher, who had faith in this project and guided it to reality. She and her virtual assistant, Nancy Cavillones, taught me so much about the mechanics of blogging and cyber marketing.

Michelle Fairbanks, for her beautiful artistic design on the cover and promo materials.

Members of the 2000 Kansas Writing Project (part of the National Writing Project) who gave me confidence to believe in and develop my talents.

Candace King: for helping me find video and pictures of John and Mary McHugh plus many other interesting sources.

The Holy Spirit who planted the seeds of inspiration and nourished them into a book to honor God and His humble servants.

I conducted many hours of interviews to write this book. Some of these were conducted over a number of visits at various times

Bergkamp, Duane --- phone, cyber

Pauley, Agnes---multiple personal interviews

McHugh, John; ----- multiple phone, postal mail, personal

Wetta, Bob--- phone, postal mail, cyber

Wetta, Marilyn Pullen---cyber, phone

ABOUT THE AUTHOR

Gerri has been a life-long resident of Kansas where she was raised on a farm with lots of chores. She loved to sneak away to the barn loft to write terrible poetry and awful stories while dreaming about traveling the world. She received her Bachelor's degree in English from Pittsburg State University at the end of the raucous '60s. This was followed by years of teaching, raising four children with her farmer husband, and helping on their land. While pursuing her Master's degree in Education, she began to follow her dream of writing. After more than 35 years teaching thousands of high school students, Gerri now enjoys retirement, writing and traveling with her husband to visit their children and 15 grandchildren in four different states and to enjoy sites of the world.

Visit her website at http://gerriwettahilger.com.